KATE GREEN

SHOOTING STAR

HarperPaperbacks
A Division of HarperCollinsPublishers

This book contains an excerpt from the upcoming hardcover edition of *Black Dreams* by Kate Green. This excerpt has been set for this edition only and may not reflect the final content of the hardcover edition.

HarperPaperbacks *A Division of* HarperCollins*Publishers*
10 East 53rd Street, New York, N.Y. 10022

A hardcover edition of this book was published in 1992 by HarperCollins*Publishers*

Cover photography by Herman Estevez

First HarperPaperbacks printing: August 1993

Printed in the United States of America

HarperPaperbacks and colophon are trademarks of HarperCollins*Publishers*

◆ 10 9 8 7 6 5 4 3 2 1

PRAISE FOR KATE GREEN AND
SHOOTING STAR:
☆   ☆   ☆

"Green's writing is brilliant and flashy and will keep you turning the pages."
—*Cleveland Plain Dealer*

"Superior . . . Green definitely has a way with words. Her writing is smooth and clear and helps to heighten the suspense."
—*Boston Herald*

"A carefully constructed work, an ambitious, multilayered crime novel drawing from the psycho-thriller style."
—*Star Tribune* (Minneapolis)

"Green takes tinseltown clichés and beats a series of deeper meanings out of them . . . The reader is sucked into the vortex of the novel's power."
—*Booklist*

"The fun of reading Green lies in sitting back and being entertained by a story that combines the best of literature and suspense. . . . A satisfying read for mystery fans or anyone who just likes a good read."
—*Greeley Tribune* (Colorado)

"Green's writing is electric, drills holes in your mind. Her characters have depth; they dive into the reader and live with you after you close the book. She handles fiction jiu-jitsu with the precise clarity of a samurai swordswoman."
—Nathalie Goldberg, author of *Writing Down the Bones* and *Wild Mind*

"Well written . . Green's Nyia Wyatt belongs to that new breed of tough and independent women sleuths who are helping to remake the face of modern mystery fiction."
—*Denver Post*

Also by Kate Green

Black Dreams

Coming soon in hardcover from
HarperCollins*Publishers*

For *THE SUSPENDERS:*

Stephen Cohen, Mary Logue, and R. D. Zimmerman

The author wishes to thank the following people for their contributions in research and development: Mary Bendtsen, Ray Di Prima, Bob Feldman, Jane Green, Ken and Anne Green, Paul Green, Juan Gonzalez, Eddie Lewis and Mary Fiedt, Nancy Hardin, and Vickie Palmquist of *Wordsmith: Words by Design*. Also a special thanks to Jonathon and Wendy Lazear, Lazear Agency.

YOU ARE WALKING ACROSS THE PLAZA IN SANTA FE
*and, just out of sight, edge of your eyes, someone is following,
sound of steps exactly paced with yours as you pass the center of
the square. The Indians in the shelter of the Palace of the
Governors are selling their silver and turquoise. You turn slowly, almost nonchalantly because you know you'll spot him this
time. You stop and focus on the outline of something, wing of a
crow or a black arched doorway. He's right there behind you,
maybe fifty feet. He's the one pretending to be looking at a
tourist map, or gazing up at the mountains. He's the one reading a paperback on the bench right there. But you're not sure.
You can never be sure. He has to let you know you're being
watched. But he can't give it away.*

No.

*It can't be something that obvious, like following close
behind you on a street. All you'd have to do is just turn
around and look at his face, it would be too risky. Same for*

cars. Trailing you around town in a rented car, maybe. A different one every day. Still, all you'd have to do is look up in the rearview mirror at a stop sign, there he'd be, plain as day. It wouldn't work.

Besides, what I'm aiming for is this: you know damn well you're being watched, you have proof of it, even, proof you can take to the police if you want to. But you never see the person, you couldn't identify him in a lineup. You become hypervigilant, looking over your shoulder. Scanning in all directions, even at a party, a crowded room. Street corners. And when you're working, especially when you're working.

So you're on the set, last touches on your makeup, you step in front of the camera, final directions on how to play the scene, you get out there in front of the lights and you know. You know he's there, watching. But which one? Because they're all watching. Because finally that's your job, to be watched.

So be more specific. How will he let you know? So you're never sure if you're just paranoid, if you're making it up, but always feel this brittle edge that could break at any time.

My idea is this: he lets you know in some very concrete way that you've been seen. In some private moment. He could photograph you, telescopic lens, blow it up, send it to you. Or a letter, describe the moment exactly, so exactly you know he saw everything. Maybe that's the best then. Just tell you.

But when you turn to look, you see no one.

So there's always that fear, that not-knowing. And you can feed off that. Because that's when you're at your best.

ONE

JUST BEFORE SHE HEARD THE SHOT, SHE WAS afraid. Maybe it was just the darkness of the road, the utter emptiness of that landscape, the blue-black liquid night with the thin glow of Santa Fe in the sky ahead. A pickup truck passed her and she braked for a blind curve.

It was not a premonition so much as a physical sensation. She'd felt it for three days before leaving L.A., then settling in at the ranch: a catch in the heart, something hidden at the periphery. When she told Leonard about it, he said, "Good. It's the story coming alive in you. It's a good sign."

She did not think it was a good sign.

So when that feeling came over her, she glanced in the rearview mirror at the black of the Sandia Mountains against the black of the sky, turned off the tape player, took a deep breath, and said her name out loud, "Nyia." A kind of scolding, the way you'd talk to a kid. *There, there. Come now.* What her mother might have said had she been there: *You're always imagining things.*

The shot seemed to crack out of the hillside, a high-pitched sound more echo than noise. At first she thought her car had backfired. The second shot came: air-split, splinter, the windshield blown into a web of glass. Everything went into slow motion the way it does when you're dying, when your animal brain thinks you are. The car rammed sideways against the banked curve of the canyon road, scream of tires, and out the side window she glimpsed a yellow light, a house out there somewhere, little square of domestic safety before the car jolted over, a toy thrown on gravel in anger. It rolled and came to rest back on the tires, rocking a minute, headlights beaming across the rocks.

The road was not well traveled. Most people took the freeway between Santa Fe and Albuquerque, not the Turquoise Trail, the old scenic highway that wound up close to the Sandias, mountains called watermelon color because their sand looked pink at sunset. It took a few seconds, maybe longer—it was hard to judge because she wasn't *in time*—before someone stopped on the road above, a second car sliding to a halt directly behind it.

A man ran down to her, yanked open the car door, yelling, "She's okay, she's alive." There were two of them then, unsnapping the seatbelt, lifting her out, careful with her, she might be broken.

"You okay?" asked one of the men.

"No," she said. Then, "I guess so. I guess I'm okay."

Each took an arm, led her to the dry arroyo hillside, the cool pine smell, late June night. Her face was close to theirs, but they seemed far off. One man called loudly to the younger, "Go on up to Cerrillos and call the state patrol, will you?" The younger obeyed, scurrying up through twisted piñon to the road above. Nyia tasted blood in her mouth, her nose was bleeding. She tilted her neck back and stars came down at her like tiny spotlights. After a minute she stopped being dizzy.

The older man examined the windshield, talking to her the whole time, while she sat shaking. She thought again she'd be sick and when he opened the back door of the car she almost cried out but it was too late. Pages of the script scattered out of the open briefcase. An updraft through the canyon sent them zipping across the dirt. He slammed the door shut. "Sorry," he called back, chasing the white rectangles as they flapped against clumps of sage.

He returned to the car, bent into the front seat. "Look at that," he yelled. "That's what it was, all right. Bullet lodged right behind the seat, went clear through the upholstery. Nice car too. Mercedes." He was still yelling. "My sister has an El Dorado just about this same color. Cream. She can't keep it clean for shit. Yours don't have no mud on it though. You from Santa Fe?"

"It's rented," she said. "It's not even mine."

The police arrived, two state highway patrols and a squad car. A small man with neat black hair and round wire-frame glasses stood over her. She pointed. "That way, I guess, I'm not sure of the direction. Two shots, I think." It seemed that he asked her the same questions several times.

The policeman and the highway patrolmen mumbled between themselves, shining bright flashlights up over the piñon, sage, the bright green of the plants oddly illuminated at night against the sand.

"Probably some drunk," said the cop.

"Kids, I bet. Drugs, not booze," said another.

"Or poachers. They sit out here at night waiting for deer and rabbits."

"Some crazy person. Didn't Ortiz say something like

this happened back in March? Somebody filed a complaint about being shot at, like a sniper up in the hills, but I don't think he ever actually hit anybody. We got to talk to Ortiz."

Only then did they ask her, "Miss, nobody would have a reason to be shooting at you, would they?"

She said no. "Of course not. Why would anybody be shooting at me?" She said something stupid like, "I'm from Los Angeles," as if that explained everything.

They examined the car some more, regarding Nyia in her black leather skirt, jeans jacket, dark red lipstick. The Hispanic cop introduced himself as Officer Americo Quintana and handed her a piece of gas station paper towel and offered to drive her the twenty minutes back to Santa Fe. They'd already called for a tow truck. Quintana dug the bullet out of the floor behind the front seat.

"Looks like a thirty-aught-six," he said.

"Would've had to have been a high-powered rifle. Must have been straight up there. If he'd been off to the side like she said, the bullet would've glanced off the glass."

"Could have been a three-oh-eight or a three hundred Magnum," offered one of the patrolmen.

"Probably not, though," said Quintana.

"Probably not."

Nyia waited in the squad car until the tow truck came out and hauled her car up out of the ditch. She looked in the side mirror, pulling her blond hair back in her fist. With her hair back, her dark eyes looked round and scared. *I look bad,* she thought. The rush of adrenaline had left a metallic taste of shock on her tongue, and her skin was very white. Leonard was always saying that she looked like a cross between a deer and a shark; only he could see the shark, he said. She stared at herself in the mirror until she saw she was there again. There it was, that way of disappearing inside herself. *Actress.* The quality was trained and inherited. She became other people, blurred her edges into them. Transmuted. Sometimes when she was under stress, when she was scared or unhappy, she realized she was not really in there at all. *Just no one. Blank screen.* She was cold as she watched the men in the harsh beams from the headlights, their long shadows jerky and sudden.

Above the car on the black rocks, something moved. Nyia sat up slowly, letting her eyes focus on the movement of night against the sand hills. Slowly she rolled down the squad-car window as the winch yanked the Mercedes up the arroyo. Scanning the darkness, nothing there. Imagining things. Maybe a coyote, the wind.

It was like the scene she would play in a few days, only in the film it would be railroad tracks, an unmarked crossing, but the rest would be the same: car rolling into a ditch. Leaping from the open door at the last minute.

But she did not have time to leap tonight. It was the same, the story and the world. She did not like it, the events of the film repeating in small ways and then large, until the images in the movie began to fuse with the random events of her life. But that was the beauty of it, her director said. The parallel, the seeming coincidence, the larger pattern. Fine when it was a matter of seeing a pigeon landing on a bridge railing or hearing a song on the radio that was background in scene thirty-seven, take one. But when it was her car diving off a road against the rocks: no. When it was her life that was parallel to a script and when that life almost ended: no. It made her want to lock the pages of the screenplay into that briefcase. *Stay there. Just a few more days. Until the filming is over. Stay in the frame of the film.*

"Stay where you belong," she said.

"What did you say?" asked Quintana, leaning in the car window.

"Oh, I'm staying in Tesuque," Nyia said. "Out Bishop's Lodge Road."

"About ready to go then?"

"It's actually a little quicker to go through town. It's only about fifteen minutes from the plaza."

Quintana got in and they rode quietly toward the city lights, then through Santa Fe, that movie-set of a town with its maze of close streets hovering around the square plaza, the rosy adobes with aqua woodwork around doors and the churchlike windows, stripped-log *vegas* extending from rooftops and the smoke curlicuing from chimneys, that smell that knocked her out every time she was back here, sweet smoke of the piñon.

She had come out to New Mexico to shoot a film. It was the first time she had ever come here to work. Always before it was to rest, to hide out at the ranch, sit by the pool and look at the close humps of the hills and the horizon of the Sangre de Cristo Mountains in three shades of blue. The quiet. She had come for the quiet.

She caught Americo Quintana staring at her in the rearview mirror. "You really are Nyia Wyatt, aren't you?" he said. "Damn! Here I write your name down on all these forms and just now it hits me. I saw you in *Pursuit*. That was so great when that knife comes through the door right when you think the guy is wasted. Damn. I knew it was you. You look just like her. I mean, you, you look just like you." He laughed, hand to his mustache.

They circled through town and out the road to Tesuque. At the entrance to the ranch, Quintana stepped out to unlatch the blue wooden gate. Leonard Jacobs's property was really just a few acres set down in a low-hilled canyon. From the road it looked like a small farm, unassuming—a long adobe house, some outbuildings, a windmill. New Mexico natives gave Leonard a hard time about calling it a ranch. Told him he needed at least a hundred acres to call it that. Once in the compound you could see it was another Leonard Jacobs production: New Mexico ranch as New Mexico ranch, a created thing complete with *vegas,* latillas, tiled floors, dried chili peppers dangling by the long porch, even Christmas lights shaped like red plastic chili peppers strung along the porch roof, lit tonight.

As they pulled up to the house, Nyia saw Mirina, Leonard's wife, peer out the front window. A floodlight snapped on outside the door, lighting her face. Mirina yanked her braid from under a serape, coming out into the yard as Nyia stepped from the squad car.

"Is there some problem, officer?" Mirina asked. "Nyia, is Tess with you? What—have you gotten yourself arrested or something? Leonard!" Mirina called back to the house.

"It's not that at all, ma'am," said Quintana.

As she got out of the car, Nyia heard the screech of a peacock in the willow overhead.

"Are you all right?" Leonard ran past Mirina to Nyia, put both hands to her cheeks. "What happened? Where's the car?"

"I rolled the Mercedes." Nyia spoke quietly through her teeth. "Some fool shot at me and I lost control." Their eyes locked in, that dark intelligence of his penetrating. "Sound familiar?" she asked.

"Mirina said you went to the airport."

"I met Tess's plane, but she never got off. She missed the flight. She missed almost getting herself killed too."

He doesn't get it, she thought. He doesn't see it's the same. Nyia turned to Quintana and introduced him to Leonard. "The director," she added.

"Yeah, there's a lot of movie people live out this way," said Quintana. "Santa Fe is a Los Angeles suburb now. I met Redford when he was filming up in Truchas. My cousin had a bit part in that movie of his." Quintana offered his hand, explaining, "Seems like something like this happened once before, a couple of months ago. Some crazy out by Madrid shooting at traffic. I'll check into the records tomorrow. There's some weirdos live out that way. Hippie Anglos, burnouts who never noticed the sixties ended. The trouble is, there's no frontier left," said Americo Quintana. "No territories to head out for. The outlaws get claustrophobic. You ought to do a movie about it. I could tell you some stories."

"I bet you could," said Leonard. Mirina stood beside him. She wrapped her hand around his waist, leaning into his arm.

"Well, Mr. and Mrs. Jacobs, Ms. Wyatt," said Quintana, "in spite of the circumstances, this really is an honor. You know, we have a film festival here in Santa Fe. They showed all your movies a few years back. They were great, even the ones with subtitles. Well," he said, rubbing his chin and nodding as though he approved of meeting them all.

"So, that's it?" Mirina asked, her accent lyrical: Prague via Paris, New York, L.A. "No arrest? She's not hurt? Just the car?"

"That's correct, ma'am. We're pretty sure it's just a random thing. We'll look into it tomorrow. Go out there and search the area for tracks, empty cases that might have been ejected out of a rifle. See what we can find."

Nyia watched as the squad car drove out the dirt driveway toward the gate, the peacock quiet now above her in the willow. Until Quintana left, she hadn't realized she'd felt safer with him there. Don't go, she thought. Red signal light blinking and then he was gone. *A random thing.* She felt a little dizzy again at the thought of it. That's all death was then, a random thing. Drive out, scout the site tomorrow.

Mirina broke from Leonard's side and folded Nyia into her arms. "You need a drink, don't you? Are you feeling all right, Nyia?"

They walked back to the house and Nyia was relieved as the door shut behind her. A low fire burned in the big adobe fireplace, the room welcome in its elegance and austerity: black leather couch, rough wood table, paintings by local artists. A silver candelabra was lit on the mantel. Mirina walked to the kitchen, pulling the serape off over her head. Leonard held Nyia then, smoothing her hair down her back, stroking her leather skirt. For a moment, she leaned against him, put her cheek against his chest.

"Are you sure you're okay?" he asked. "You don't need to see a doctor or anything?"

Nyia drew away, settled on the couch, her knees pulled up, and he sat down next to her, his bearded face in his hands.

"I think I'm all right. Honestly," she said. "Just a little sore here, from the seat belt." She touched her throat. Maybe it hurt more than she thought. She wished he wouldn't hold her like that or sit so close. It was too much like before. Sometimes it was hard to hold back. His hair was silver, long on the back of his neck. He stared at the fire. He was so beautiful. Stop it, she thought. It's only because you're feeling vulnerable and scared. Don't get into it.

"So you waited and Tess just never got off the plane?"

"There was a message. I was paged. She's coming in tomorrow, late afternoon."

"It can't be happening again," he said. "It's just like last time, the synchronicity of it. But it went too far that time, the whole thing went too far. You know, when I first read that scene in the screenplay where the car rolls down the cliff, I thought, 'I've got to come at this some new way because it's been done.'"

"Well, now it *has* been done," Nyia said. "Leonard, you didn't have anything to do with this, did you? I mean, one of your techniques to inspire creative tension on the goddamn set?"

"What, am I an idiot? I'd never put you in danger, Nyia. Never. Even more so ever since Robin."

Since Robin. He always called it that. Never *since Robin's death.* Not *ever since Robin was killed.* Just *ever since Robin.* He always left it hanging like that. Unfinished.

"The whole technique is about psychology, not physical danger. Anyway, you heard the cop—they've had complaints, it's happened before. Some crackpot. It used to be, though, when that doubling of images began, I thought it was such a good sign. I used to get excited when it started up, when things I imagined or created started occurring in reality. I'd know the story was vibrating in the world. I'd know I was tapping something."

"Some part of you is actually pleased," Nyia said. "I mean, it's all very dramatic and intense for you—I get shot at like some cowboy movie."

Leonard rubbed his gray-flecked beard, almost talking to himself. "I can't have anyone or anything sabotaging this film. I can't let anything ruin it."

"What about me, Leonard? The film wasn't shot at, I was. Don't you get it? I don't want there to be synchronicity with this story. People are killed in this story. I want to be really clear about this. There's our work, there's this film, and there are our lives, our very separate lives. We've got to have some separation this time."

Nyia stood, wrapped her arms around herself, still cold though the piñon blazed in the fireplace. "Robin's dead, Leonard. It wasn't a plot point. An actual thing occurred in actual time."

Nyia held her palms to the fire, warming her hands. During the last film they had made together, one of the other actresses had been killed. Shot in an alley on location in a small town in Mexico. There had been signs then, too, of the script-story paralleling events in all of their lives. It had been a gag, though, until Robin died. Some sort of cosmic joke among the cast. They'd laughed secretly at Leonard's mirror-view of life and art that had become a terrible funhouse mirror, distorted and frightening. *Ever since Robin.* She'd been killed exactly like one of the characters in the film.

"It's the same thing all over again, Leonard. The script but no camera. No 'action.' No film rolling. No 'cut,' no 'it's a wrap.' It all really happened just like it's all really happening now. Like the story has a life of its own. And I want it to stop. I really want it to stop."

Leonard crossed the room and pulled Nyia toward him. "All right," he said loudly, to quiet her. "All right. What am I supposed to do about it? I've got a film to finish."

"You promised that if anything like this ever happened again you'd hire someone to be with me on the set. Someone to investigate."

"It won't disturb your work on the film to have someone watching like that?"

Nyia was silent. Someone watching? They were all voyeurs on a film set, there was no one who wasn't watching. "Please, you know what I want."

He tried to kiss her and she turned her face away, stepped back from him as Mirina returned, boots knocking on the tiled floor.

"Drinks," Mirina announced. "And then we all get a good night's sleep, all right? If such a thing is possible."

Leonard took the tray from his wife. "Nyia wants a private investigator to look into this."

Mirina sipped from a tall glass of wine. "I think that is a good thing. Just to be utterly sure."

"But the police are looking into it," he said. "Don't we have enough to concern ourselves with here?"

"You promised," said Nyia. She was careful not to beg. She was the lead actress in the film and she wanted this. She was demanding it. "I don't care if it seems random. You know there were so-called random things that happened last time. You ignored them. We all did."

Mirina and Leonard exchanged looks, one of their instantaneous telepathic glances from which Nyia always felt excluded.

"But Nyia is absolutely right," said Mirina.

"All right," Leonard said. "She's right, you're right."

Mirina was quiet for a moment, then said, "We'll hire someone in the morning. I'll take care of it." She handed Nyia a glass of wine. "Perhaps we're going to need some kind of security on the set as well."

"We're not going to let anyone hurt you," Leonard assured Nyia. "You know that, don't you?"

Outside the compound of the main house were several small adobe buildings set under a stand of cottonwoods near a corral. Nyia walked alone back to her cabin, stopping by the *vega* fence to watch the horses. It was strange to be staying out here in one of the small cabins. Not with Leonard in the big house. Not Leonard's lover. Three years since they had been together, really together, though they'd made love now and then, always sadly as if the whole thing were a memory.

Nyia opened the door of the cabin and fumbled in the darkness for the light switch, then pushed the large windows closed. She undressed and crawled, naked, under the heavy quilt. The mountain summer night was cold. For a long time she lay awake, thinking of the images in the portions of the script they had already filmed up near Canada and in Manhattan: a drowned man, a silent tango in an artist's loft, a truck bearing down on a woman fallen in a street, a tent in the rain. Then she reviewed what she knew of the upcoming script, a car stalled on train tracks, a fire in a motel bedroom, the lovemaking, the wedding.

She pulled the phone over next to her on the pillow and dialed her manager's number in L.A., waiting while the answering service paged her. Within minutes the phone jangled and Nyia grabbed the receiver.

"Nyia?" breathed Suzanne, voice thick with that Southern *ah.* She pronounced "Nyia" as if it were *Nah.* Most people said her name wrong and she'd have to tell them, "It's Nyia with a long *i*, like 'hi-ya.'" Suzanne's voice was open-throated and warm. "They said it was urgent. Everything all right out there?"

Nyia stuttered out the details, the dark arroyo, the shattered windshield.

"And you say Leonard definitely is hiring a private investigator?" asked Suzanne. In the background, a man cleared his throat, then a whisper. She pictured Suzanne in jade-green silk, studying the edge of a curved nail against the lamplight, her long, chestnut hair spread out over damask sheets.

"First thing in the morning," said Nyia.

"I'll speak to Leonard first thing in the morning as well, then. He does have a legal obligation to provide protection for you. I would say don't worry about a thing, but it wouldn't be the truth. You know what I think about the man," Suzanne added. "And Nyia? Try not to be alone, would you? I'm talking about alone with Leonard."

After she hung up, Nyia snapped off the light and in the black stillness she could hear horses moving around in the nearby corral.

She must have slept, for when she heard the sound of scraping on wood she started, sat up, and pushed her back to the wall. The figure sat directly across from her in a straight-backed chair, his head in shadow, arms at his sides.

"Leonard?" she whispered. She moved her hand to the nightstand, snapped the light on. The black-leather jacket draped on the chair across from her was empty. A frame above the chair held a Stieglitz print of Georgia O'Keeffe as a young woman.

She realized she was holding her breath. Her chest hurt. The wind in the cottonwoods overhead soothed her, but only for a second. She got up and shoved the jacket into the closet, pulled the white curtains across the window and checked to make sure the cabin door was locked.

After she turned the lights off a second time, she got up and checked again.

THE FIRST TIME HE KILLED HER IT WAS IN HIS *imagination. He pictured it. Waiting for her in the dark house in Laurel Canyon. He would be waiting in her room for her and while he waited he went through her clothing, the robes on a hook in her closet. He pressed the silk against his face, her smell close to his mouth. The cool texture against his fingers.*

No. Go back. He had the leather gloves on in the room, he couldn't even feel the silk. But he waited, just sitting on her bed, hearing her car in the driveway, the clank of the black wrought-iron gate, key in the lock, coming up the stairs now, turning on the light.

No. He had changed that. He'd been waiting in the hallway, he had his face covered. A ski mask. Once it had been a Halloween mask, the rubber kind that slips over your whole head, fleshy and cold. She'd passed the bathroom and he had simply reached out to her, stuffed the washcloth in her mouth, taped it, carried her into her bedroom.

So that's how it had been. That first time, in his imagination. He had run it through many times, planning it. He didn't know if he was planning it or savoring it. Maybe it was just part of the preparation.

It took a long time, maybe a year, before I could say my *imagination. I killed her in* my *imagination. In fact, it had to be pointed out to me repeatedly that I said* he *instead of* I. *I see that I still do that in my notes.*

She asked me, the therapist, why I said he *instead of* I.

Because that is how I see the picture. Outside of me, separate.

She had said, "That's called dissociation."

I said, "That's fiction."

She had said, "In real life, that's sick."

No, she didn't say that. But that's what she was thinking. Anyway.

I suppose, then, that it is a matter of my increasing health that I can now say, in writing, that I killed her repeatedly in my *imagination. Claim my fantasies as mine and find the proper channel for them. But it wasn't enough, the visions. I wanted to go* into *the visions, at least to enter them, if only briefly.*

"One sign of health," said my therapist, "is knowing the difference between pretend and real."

"But my success depends on forgetting that," I told her.

I suppose that is why I persist in this. It is a kind of quest. I am exploring the line between my imagination and reality. Between what is separate from me and what I can create.

However.

Reviewing my notes, I see that what is missing is the element of control. The unexpected turns in the road, your white car in front of me, the fact that you took the old highway. Sometimes I think that merely having you in sight is enough; it is when I try to enter the event itself that things become troublesome. If I stay just outside the action, and try to affect things mentally....

But tonight I entered and while there was some beauty in that I also felt cheated. I watched as your car sailed off the road but then the road curved sharply and I couldn't see or even hear the outcome. So that leaves me not knowing the end of the scene. It all felt so unfinished.

Furthermore, there is that terribly mixed feeling I have. Several factors: first, that I cannot bring myself finally to be done with it. It is as if I am constantly rehearsing, waiting for the exact moment when it will be imperative to follow through. The other is that these sorts of things, the car, the empty road, are so without any witness, that there is a sense of dissatisfaction. I feel that there must be some record, some way to see it all again. Review the footage. These notes are one way. But there is another dimension that I would like to add.

I was not accurate in my aim tonight and I know now that that was purposeful. I'm not ready to end it yet. I want to play it out for a while and refine my story. If I have things too fixed in my mind, there is no creativity.

Take two.

TWO

WHEN HE FOLLOWED PEOPLE, HE TRIED TO BE
respectful. Even though he understood that it was legal,
that it was his profession, it still felt invasive, filming
them like this, the poor woman out back with the man,
kissing his neck over morning coffee. He had them in
the video viewfinder now, the woman slipping her hand
down the front of the guy's bathrobe. The man lowered
the paper, kissed her mouth. The husband, his client,
was out of town, paying him eighty-five dollars an hour
to get his wife on camera with his business partner.
Harm Bohland wondered if the guy brought his own
bathrobe to wear or was it his client's? That would be
pretty cold, sleep with the guy's wife, wear his robe.

Now she sat down and passed him a bowl of strawberries. It made Harm feel like a real lowlife, filming
these little scenes of domestic bliss to be used against
people, screw up their lives. Then he remembered their

lives were already screwed up, he was only providing documentation.

He pulled in the lens to close-up as the guy changed his mind about the strawberries, took the woman's hand and led her back into the house. Okay, so it was a business. Let's see if he could get around to the side of the house and get a shot through the window.

Back at the office, still early, just after nine, Harm Bohland stuck the video in the VCR. Good. Very, very good. Ought to be a bonus in it for that close-up, he'd almost fallen off the adobe wall, balancing with the video camera, getting the shot in through that crack in the floral curtains. Harm clicked off the VCR and television, and poured himself a cup of coffee, staring out into morning traffic along Cerrillos. He even found himself smiling. A year ago, he never would have predicted that he would be sitting with a smile on his face at the start of a good day's work. Now that beat the hell out of a pension plan.

There were three reasons Harmon E. Bohland, Jr., had left the Los Angeles Division of the Federal Bureau of Investigation and gone into business as an accountant and private investigator. He was sick of wearing black shoes, he had turned forty, and he'd almost been killed in a shoot-out by some two-bit tax evader in a Tempe motel.

He reminded himself of these facts as he examined the worn toe of his cowboy boot propped on the wooden desk in his office next door to Ninety-nine-cent Movies. As he leaned back in the secondhand swivel chair, he pushed his straight blond hair, thinning, receding, up on his forehead. Nice boots, he thought. Brown cowhide with a strip of authentic snakeskin up the outside, those leather loops to hold onto when he pulled them on. And good to wear old jeans, worn-out white cotton shirt, finish up some details on a few tax returns. He could open the mail slowly, drink coffee from this cracked cup, the only remnant of his former employment. He thought about getting Nickie for a week-long visitation in July, going fishing up in the Sangre de Cristo Mountains, pulling in those sweet little rainbow trout and putting new strings on his twenty-year-old Gibson, which he only played when his son was around, begging to hear "Me and Bobbie McGee" just one more time before bed.

All that was good and it was reason enough even if the money was a little slow. Hell, he'd only been in business out here six months. Give it some time. It beat being shot at and getting nothing more than a cheap laminated wood nameplate with Harmon E. Bohland, Jr. engraved in brass to show for it.

Chance Number Two. That's how he thought of his life, even if Chance Number One, in the form of his ex-wife, Sandy, lived only a few miles away and they passed Nickie back and forth between them like a little ball. Well, he was doing what he could with the wreckage. Looking around him at the cluttered office, he thought life wasn't so bad after all, and when the phone rang he put his boots down on the floor and picked up the receiver. "Bohland & Associates, Accounting & Investigations. Bohland, speaking."

"Mr. Bohland," the woman said, "I'm in need of some discreet work on behalf of a rather important person."

"Who's the VIP?" he asked.

"An actress. My name is Mirina Jacobs, my husband is Leonard Jacobs, the director. Our production company, Visionfilm, is based in L.A., but we own a home out here, by Tesuque. We're wrapping on a film this week and next and our lead actress is being harassed. Her car was shot at last night on the highway back from Albuquerque. Old fourteen, just north of Madrid. The police think it might have been a random incident, some drunk crackpot, but we have reason to believe that some other factors might be involved."

Harm jotted quickly on a yellow notepad as she spoke. "When can you come in? I'd like to get the details in person, if you don't mind."

"Can you come here, to us? We're right on the heels of starting production tomorrow and all three of us would like to meet with you. You'll be remunerated for your time even if you don't agree to take on the project. Is that fair?"

He thought about it. Fifteen-minute drive out to Tesuque. Coffee, tea and bullshit at eighty-five dollars an hour. Morning shot, but what the hell. It was a pretty drive out there and she sounded important enough.

"Who's the actress?" he thought to ask.

"Confidentiality applies in your line of work, does it not?"

"Absolutely."

"Nyia Wyatt."

Harm Bohland took the phone away from his face and mouthed the name in air: *Nyia Wyatt.* Oh sure, sure, he thought. We make housecalls.

"Yeah, I could probably make it out there. Let me see what the calendar looks like this morning. Yeah," he said. "Nyia Wyatt. Around eleven?"

Harm Bohland took St. Francis Drive out of Santa Fe, heading north toward the Tesuque exit. A sign along the highway read, ENTERING TESUQUE INDIAN RESERVATION, but the only evidence of native culture from the road was a high wooden kiva ladder propped against a white trailer. Bohland's brown Jeep was dusty and full of gum wrappers and crushed Coke cans he'd been meaning to clean out of there for weeks.

He turned back up Bishop's Lodge Road, slowing as he passed black horses in a small corral, one horse lying on its side in the sunlight. Big houses, estates, fenced in by barbed wire, small metal signs announcing PROTECTED BY NATIONAL GUARDIAN, alternated with small adobe houses and old barns tucked down in the piñon-dotted hills. He slowed by a waist-high stone wall, heard the yelp of a guard dog standing behind a metal gate that blocked a dirt road. WARNING: NO TRESPASSING, announced a small red sign. Fitting that the Jacobses would live out here.

Mirina and Leonard Jacobs. Visionfilm. She'd run it all together as if it were one word. Maybe he should be embarrassed he'd never really heard of them. She sounded European, Austrian or something, he couldn't place it. Maybe they were those kind of people famous in Paris but you've never heard of them in Denver. He'd heard of Nyia Wyatt, though. Hadn't she won an Academy Award for Best Supporting Actress for that movie shot down in South America? Yeah, he'd seen the clip on "Arsenio Hall," but never saw the movie. But he'd seen her cop movies and the horror one with the special effects where she changed into a purple hologram and merged into other people, their features joining until they formed some third thing, some mutant twin.

Here it was. He stopped in the driveway to pull open the wooden gate. A peacock strolled through pasture grass beside the road. No dogs, though. He drove in the circular drive and parked next to a rustic wagon wheel propped by a bench in front of the adobe compound wall. Over near the end of the wall a red vintage '49 Ford half-ton pickup was parked under a cottonwood and Harm had the strangest feeling, looking at it, that it was a prop.

He wished he'd taken time to go to the library to do

a little background reading so he wouldn't make a fool of himself, but it was okay. Ask a question or two and most people ran at the mouth enough so you could wing it. He knocked at the arched door and it opened almost immediately.

"Mirina Jacobs. I saw you pull in," the woman said, extending her hand with a curt smile, businesslike but warm. She was one of those women who was aging with beauty. Had to be in her fifties; small, sharp features; crow's-feet; but good skin, clear and rosy. No tan. Probably didn't smoke. Her smooth hair was pulled back into a black braid, touch of bluish-red, henna maybe. Some kind of coloring. A contrast, that black hair, pale skin, still young-looking face. Her eyes were intense, hazel-gold, and she wore a black silk shirt and jeans and looked good in them. Money could keep you young, he thought. Or maybe she just did a lot of yoga and didn't eat Chee-tos.

"Thank you for taking the time to come out this morning on such short notice. My husband is waiting for us in his office and Miss Wyatt will join us in a moment." She turned, huaraches squeaking as she led Harm down a hall tiled in terra-cotta. "This way." One glass wall faced a courtyard where hollyhocks and orange poppies backed an aqua pool. The windows of the glass hallway were open and Harm heard the snort of a horse not far off.

"Mr. Bohland." Jacobs stood as they walked in. For some reason Harm had pictured him as older, a John Huston type, big with a protruding belly, bags under his eyes. Leonard Jacobs was fairly tall, a little over six feet, well-built and lean, looked like he worked out some or ran. His hair was white, salt and pepper beard, but he was much younger than Harm had imagined, early forties, maybe. The gray was premature. Harm saw he'd been so handsome as a young man, he'd probably been called pretty, and he saw why they were together, Leonard and Mirina Jacobs. They looked a little god-like, not like normal plain-looking folks. And they were rich, too, he thought. And Nyia Wyatt works for them. He reminded himself not to be too impressed by that and sat down in a cowhide chair opposite Leonard Jacobs.

Jacobs slid a file folder across his desk toward Harm and put on tortoise-shell glasses, expressed appreciation at Harm's coming all the way out to Tesuque, and asked him to look briefly through the file.

"To save time—there are some complexities here— I've had my assistant prepare some material for you, background information."

Harm opened the file, fingered the pages. The top sheet was a simple typed report of last night's shooting. Included were the license number of the car, name and location of the leasing company and body shop, name and number of the attending officer who had transported Nyia Wyatt back to the ranch after the accident. Efficient. All business. Beneath the typed report were a number of Xerox copies of newspaper articles about the murder of some woman named Robin Reese. Harm glanced through the clippings quickly, eyeing the headlines, then looked up at Jacobs.

The director leaned back in his office chair, fingertips pressed together. "Mr. Bohland, I'll get to the point. I need someone to look into the possibility that someone is trying to sabotage my films by killing off my actresses." He gave a short laugh that sounded more like a hiss, but it had the sound of a sob in it, way, way down under the voice. The man is on edge, thought Harm. Trying to keep it under control, but way down there, scared. He felt himself relax at the thought that Jacobs was human, not just some Hollywood cutout. "That sounds paranoid, doesn't it?" asked Jacobs. "Mirina thinks maybe I'm just a little paranoid."

Mirina had eased down in the chair next to Harm. "I think it's unwise to jump to conclusions, but I am totally in support of having someone look into it.

Professionally." She stressed that last word. "At least the possibility of some sort of harassment or threat," she added.

"Mr. Bohland, if you'll turn to the first of the news clippings in the file you'll see that this isn't the first time this has happened. Actually, there have been two incidents. Approximately eighteen months ago we were completing work on a film down in Manzanillo, Mexico, called *Dead Heat*. One of our actresses, a young woman named Robin Reese, was killed. She'd been out late dancing, drinking at a local club. The next morning she was found by a man who sold fruit out of a wagon pulled by a donkey. And bread, he sold big round loaves of bread. She'd been shot once in the head. Lying in the dust next to the back entrance of a little market."

Leonard Jacobs paused there and Harm Bohland had the odd sensation that Jacobs was picturing the scene in his mind, cinematically: melons, bread, bananas, a dead woman facedown on a street behind an adobe *mercado*.

Jacobs continued. "There was a brief investigation by the local police. A copy of the report is in the file you have there. I had someone translate it for me. They theorized her death could have been drug-related—a soured deal maybe—or a simple mugging. There were no arrests, they had no idea who did it. No witnesses. The gun was a Winchester .30-30 lever-action rifle, that's the only evidence they put together. Beautiful and talented young woman, Robin. Her whole life . . . well, you know."

Mirina Jacobs crossed her legs and picked up the story where her husband had left off. "Robin Reese's family attempted to sue Visionfilm for negligence," she said. "They had absolutely no case, but our lawyers advised us to settle out of court. Keep it out of the papers, keep the court costs down. Said a negligence trial could clean us out and make it almost impossible to get financing or liability insurance again. . . . But we felt very strongly that there was no case. We were not at fault. The murder was a terrible tragedy—but it did not happen during filming, it was off the set and off the premises of the condominiums where most of the staff and crew were staying and which did have paid security. At any rate, we refused to settle and the Reese family eventually dropped the case." She stopped there and looked to Leonard.

It was odd, thought Harm, the way they passed the telling back and forth between them. They must have been together for years. Long-married people did that.

Leonard went on. "Incident number two. A year ago, late spring. Miss Wyatt's house in Laurel Canyon, in Los Angeles, was broken into. She happened to be home at the time and surprised the burglar. The man assaulted her, there was a struggle, and he fled. This incident occurred during the grand jury investigation regarding Robin Reese's death. There was quite a bit of coverage in the *L.A. Times,* you'll find copies of most of the articles in the file there."

Harm leaned back in the cowhide chair; he'd look at the clipping later. Right now he watched Jacobs. Guy was tight, talking like a businessman at an audit, supplying information, but something under it all. Not a lot of eye contact. As he stood by the wall, he tossed a gold coin back and forth from palm to palm, a nervous habit. Hurried. Better things to do, get this out of the way. Like a woman's murder and a burglary and an assault were incidents—he used that word—that stood in his way.

Jacobs let out a deep breath. "They were unable to recover any prints in the house. The man wore gloves. Nothing was stolen. But the police discovered something that was strange. Six unused live cartridges were found in the driveway outside the house. .38-special cartridges. The man had emptied the revolver at some point, probably prior to entering the house.

"There was no apparent connection between these incidents. The weapons used were entirely different. But in any case, Robin Reese was a personal friend of Nyia's, not just a colleague, and the break-in was very traumatic for her. It elicited a great deal of grief in Miss Wyatt, not to mention fear. A kind of post-traumatic stress disorder. She was afraid, after that, to sleep alone in the house. In fact, she hasn't really stayed at the house much at all in the last year. Let's just say she was distraught after that."

"We all were," said Mirina. "You don't just shrug things like that off."

Jacobs turned to his wife. "Now we come to our current film—*Trial and Error*. We've been filming in Manhattan, then up near Canada, and now we're set to film the final sequence. We hope to wrap in several days, then return to L.A. to edit."

Leonard came out from behind his desk and leaned against a wall. "What I would like, Bohland, is someone on the set in these final days of filming. Talk to people. Observe. But it can't be an obvious thing. You know, 'detective on set of film.'" He fingered the air, supplying invisible quotation marks around his words. "It wouldn't work, wouldn't work. What I'd like is some kind of undercover thing. Let's say you're doing research on our filmmaking process, you're a writer, an academic. You're doing a study on post-modern technique, I've invited you here for a few days. Maybe you're from some university, you're free-lance, I don't know. So there's a front, a persona. Otherwise everyone will be nervous, it will destroy the whole dynamic. People will be unduly upset. Then, once the filming is done, we'll go to L.A. There, I'll have you talk with my accountant, look into my books, my backing. See if there is something I've missed, why anyone would want to do this to Visionfilm. Why would someone try to destroy all that I have tried to make?" He held out his open hand as if Harm might have an answer in that instant.

Harm took out his legal tablet and wrote some things down. "Do you have any ideas who might?" he asked.

Jacobs shrugged. "My former partner did time for securities fraud. I testified against him in the trial."

"John Sand," said Mirina. "He was in a minimum-security prison in San Diego for about a year and a half."

"And I've wondered about Robin Reese's family," Leonard went on. "Even though they dropped the suit, they were very bitter. They still hold us accountable." Jacobs held up his palm as if stopping traffic. "I wanted so much to leave Manzanillo behind me. *Trial and Error* was supposed to be a clean start. I just can't afford to have anything else happen." Then he added, as if an afterthought, "To Nyia."

Mirina touched Harm's elbow as she spoke. "The other thing is that you'd be a presence on the set for Miss Wyatt. Actually, she is the one who requested some form of investigation. And she would be the only one, aside from Leonard and myself, who would be aware that you are a detective, not a writer. We want her to have some peace of mind."

"When she's working she's like a sponge, that's her genius, but . . ." Leonard made a fist, then slowly relaxed the fingers, expanding to surround a round space like a camera lens. "She opens up to everything. She takes in impressions, amplifies them. She personalizes things that happen outside of her and uses them in her acting, but sometimes it can just be . . . it can go too far."

Harm felt that Jacobs was choosing his words carefully. "Are you saying that she could be taking last night's shooting too seriously?" Harm asked. "Connecting it with a previous trauma when it's really, as the police say, just a random incident?" Now he was saying the word too.

Leonard sighed. "I think we'd all like to believe it was random. But even if that is the case, what we need right now is a feeling of security on the set. Total safety for Miss Wyatt and for us."

"She's high-strung enough as it is," said Mirina. "She has a creative tension that sometimes does not adequately perceive the real—"

"From the imagined. Exactly, Mirina. Exactly." Jacobs complimented his wife as if the thought had been hers. "Look, I would do anything to make Nyia feel comfortable. When I'm directing, I can't offer a lot of emotional support to her. In fact, it's the opposite, I have to push her. The way I work with my actors, I create tension, not ease it. Artistic tension," he emphasized. "If a third party were looking into all of this, it would take a hell of a load off of me. I could go on to concentrate on the film. There'd be a feeling of protection. So in addition to investigating, what I would like is that you spend time with Miss Wyatt. Stick close to her, hang out with her, talk with her, take her out for breakfast. . . ."

There was a silence except for a crow's loud caw in the cottonwoods. Harm Bohland looked down at his notes. So the job was boiling down to this: Hang around a movie star as an undercover bodyguard in the guise of a nosy ivory-tower film critic. This definitely beat filing for extensions for late tax returns, but one thing bothered him. "Do you take the investigative aspect of all this seriously?" he asked. "You're not primarily seeking protection for Miss Wyatt, are you?"

"We absolutely take the investigative aspect seriously," said Jacobs. "Obviously there's a great deal at stake here. Nyia Wyatt's state of mind is her performance and her performance is my investment. She is my film."

"Our film," corrected Mirina.

Leonard Jacobs smiled at his wife. Harm noticed they talked about Nyia Wyatt as if she were a property. "Why not think of your role with us as an integral part of the alchemic collaborative process of the film?" said Jacobs.

This time Harm smiled. "Do I get a credit?"

"You bet."

Then, on cue, her call came from down the veranda. "Leonard? Is Mirina with you?"

"Down here," called Mirina.

Leonard stepped out of the office to greet her as she came in. He put his hand on her back and drew her into the room.

Suddenly Harm felt like a schoolboy, an autograph seeker. How strange to see a face like that in person, almost as if the face itself were a disguise. She was not tall in bare feet, but physically magnificent—bare shoulders, her arms just muscular enough, like she pumped a little steel with a personal trainer to stay trim. V-thin waist, slim hips. She wore, just before lunch on a weekday, a strapless violet leather dress up to her thighs, her breasts pushed up into curves by the fitted bodice. Her hair was wet, combed back from her face, and even without a smudge of makeup she was easily the most astounding-looking woman—man, human— that Harm had ever seen. It wasn't just beauty. He'd seen cover-girl pretty, he'd seen ravishing, in that plastic-surgeon kind of way not uncommon in Los Angeles, land of a thousand and one starlets.

In fact, there was something odd and disjointed about her face; her slightly crooked nose; large mouth; wide eyes set slightly apart; thin, almost invisible, highly arched brows. Her eyes were open in some kind of permanent amazement, both sultry and childlike. She palmed her wet hair.

"Excuse me," she said. "I didn't know you were here. Mirina, this is the dress I . . . Are you the detective?"

"Nyia, this is Harmon Bohland. He was with the FBI for a number of years and now he's a private investigator here in Santa Fe."

He stood and shook her hand.

Nyia eased into the chair behind Leonard's desk, crossing her long legs. Harm thought it a little odd, her sitting there. She was very used to being in this room, he noted. He tried not to act dumbstruck.

"We've been filling Mr. Bohland in on all the details, all the way back to Mexico," said Jacobs. "He's agreed that the undercover thing is the way to go."

Have I? thought Harm, and then he spoke up. The last time he'd been undercover had not been such a terrifically satisfying experience. "I have to admit I'm concerned about that part of it, Mr. Jacobs. There are ways to investigate discreetly. I'm not an actor."

"If the fee is a problem, if the undercover work is worth more of your time, that can be arranged. What about just until we're done filming here in Santa Fe? Once we get back to L.A., proceed as you normally would." Jacobs took a deep breath. "The thing is, I want to keep it quiet. There will be a lot of press here this late week. *Vanity Fair* is coming in a day or two, *The Village Voice* is sending someone. A photographer from *Rolling Stone*. And the other actors, Jack Drieser, Tess Juran. Why should they have to know about any of this? Especially if it turns out it is just some local weirdo up in the foothills. Will you think about it?"

Harm looked down again at the file. "I could give it a crack," he said. "Yeah, it might even be a little easier that way." Harm pulled out a contract from a folder he'd brought with him, penned in a higher hourly fee for the undercover time, and handed the paper to Leonard. Leonard signed quickly and went to his desk to write out a check for the retainer, bending close to Nyia Wyatt as he signed his name. She was awfully quiet.

"Good," said Mirina. "We start filming the day after tomorrow. I think it would be best if you two had a chance to visit before that. Perhaps tomorrow morning, here, ten o'clock?"

Nyia nodded. "That's fine with me." She looked toward Harm.

Mirina continued. "I'll have our production assistant call you with directions to the set location and he can answer any questions you may have. And I'm giving a dinner party tomorrow night, cocktails at seven. I'd like you to join us for that as well. In your undercover status."

Mirina stood and shook hands with Harm, and so did Jacobs. Nyia stayed seated behind the big desk.

Harm didn't see her until after he'd started the jeep. She appeared at the driver's side like an apparition in violet leather standing in the dirt road. Harm turned off the ignition.

"Mr. Bohland?"

"Just call me Harm."

"Harm?"

"Harmon. It was my mother's fault. She named me after her big brother."

"Can we talk alone? I mean, not here, not in Leonard's office tomorrow morning at ten o'clock." Her bare arm brushed his and she seemed totally unaware, in some ingenuous way, of her physical presence. She was so stunning he was almost embarrassed, but she seemed relaxed, scratching her neck. She could have been wearing a sweat suit. She leaned against the Jeep door, peering in at the garbage next to him.

Car wash, he thought. *Time for a little cleaning job, yes sir, Mr.-Bohland-just-call-me-Harm.*

"There's more to it. A lot more," Nyia Wyatt said. Her hair was drying now, the sun on it golden, strands blowing across her mouth. "Things they just don't know about. Things nobody knows. But you need to know."

She suggested dusk tonight, a drink, a walk up Canyon Road. It wouldn't be good to be seen at his office, she said. Why were all the attractive women he had met since his divorce either clients or involved with someone else or free when he was involved, if you could call the mishaps he'd had involvements? Then he smiled to himself. *Oh yeah. Nyia Wyatt is really interested in a former FBI accountant just starting out business as a private investigator with current cash flow equal to that of a paperboy. Asshole.*

He grabbed his legal tablet and scribbled *Pink Adobe, seven-thirty.* He glanced twice at Nyia Wyatt in the rearview mirror as he pulled away from the ranch. She was growing smaller, a speck of purple in the shadows.

POSSIBLE IDEA FOR SCENE:

He is watching her from a distance with another man. Sitting in a car by the side of the road, partly hidden by willows, he gets out, sits on the stone fence. Panorama: foothills behind the house, perfect New Mexico shot, low sand hills, piñon.

Close-up of him crouched there with binoculars. Shot through the double lenses as if trying to find her location. There: he finds the cabin with the big French windows, always open, curtains always pulled apart so he can see in, day or night. Sometimes at night she draws them closed, but not always.

But it is day now. Through the binoculars he watches her in the cabin with her lover, moving around the small space. Her lover is married to someone else. The idea comes that he will begin to film her on video, to document these clandestine moments for the man's wife. So that there is a purpose behind merely watching her with him.

He is going to film them making love and he is going to save the footage for the right moment.

Another possibility: Later, back where he is staying, he watches the video on the TV, the picture slightly out of focus and shaky as the lens zooms in. The anger builds in him. He is always in this position, far from the center, observing. Suddenly he smashes the TV with a broom handle. Scene of her making love on the screen as the TV is smashed against a wall. Him finally understanding that he's tired of just watching. He can no longer stay separate from the scene. He leaves the glass and metal scattered on the floor, gets back in his car, returns to the ranch, to the roadside where he hid that afternoon, her cabin in view.

THREE

"AM I KILLED?"

"Can't tell you that."

"I think it's only fair if I know," she said.

Nyia put the white veil on her head, headband tight on her temples, rhinestones and silk flowers slightly crunched. She looked at Leonard through the lace. He wouldn't tell her the outcome of the film. It spoiled the improvisation, he claimed.

"I'm afraid." She turned to him. *"I don't think I can go through with it."*

"No. She wouldn't be that open," said Leonard. "She's got to give him some sort of excuse." Leonard sat in a wicker chair in the corner of Nyia's room. The window was partially open, cobalt trim against the red adobe. The cabin made Nyia think of a little dollhouse.

"Come here," he said.

She shook her head. "Just tell me. Tell me what you want me to do."

"I want to show you."

"Just tell me."

She held out her hand. "Look what else I got." On her left ring finger, an engagement ring. "It's silver-plated with real diamond chips. Tacky, isn't it?" she asked. "It's to help me get into character. A trigger point. You know, I might actually keep wearing this. I got it at a pawn shop off La Cienega for fifty bucks. Somebody's grandmother's, I bet. It's engraved on the inside. 'Rita and Sam.' Isn't that romantic?"

"Nyia. Look at me. No. Look at me, don't look away. Go into character. Don't be Nyia now. Go away and come back Christine."

Nyia closed her eyes. *Rita Christine Nyia. Christine.* She took a deep breath and smelled dirt. Christine's afraid, but wouldn't say that. Then what? Some excuse, maybe. Pick a fight. Distance him that way. She pictured Hank's black leather jacket, motorcycle revving in the parking lot just outside the motel room door. Hank, straddling the bike, waiting for her to go.

Leonard looked down at the script, read the lines, "'Are you ready then?'"

Nyia turned to him slowly, holding the ring out in front of her. Adjusted the veil. "'You aren't going to wear that goddamn leather jacket to our wedding are you?'" Eyes lowered, she stumbled slightly toward the edge of the door.

"'You're drunk, aren't you?'" read Leonard.

"'Is it a sin to have one margarita on your wedding day? We're not even going to have a reception. We're not even having champagne. The least I could have is one margarita.'"

Leonard stood and took her by the shoulders.

"'We're going to be happy, or else,'" he read. "'We won't be like all those others. Or even like ourselves.'"

"'I can't do it. I'm scared. I can't go through with it.'"

"'You're drunk, that's all.'"

"'We'll wreck each other again, I know it. I think we just ought to leave it right here, exactly on this day, and it'll be perfect. No dinnertime, no kids, no bills, no jobs, no you driving off into the dust and me hollering in the kitchen. We could just stop here. Just stop.'"

"'I want to marry you,'" said Leonard.

He got up from the chair and put down the script. Nyia fingered the ring, turning it around and around. Leonard stepped toward her and the wind was warm and smelled of horses. He came close to her and Nyia felt her body in alarm, warm and dizzy beside him. *No: He's in character. He's playing Hank. Not Leonard.* This is the scene the way they would shoot tomorrow with Jack Drieser, who was playing the part of Hank. He was flying in today from New York. *Just running it through with Leonard, not real, just stay in character, it means nothing, nothing.*

Leonard bent to kiss her bare neck. He put his fingers on the buttons of her black shirt, delicately, almost not even touching. She looked away, his breath against her neck. *No, not right. Scene. Stay with the scene.* "'Stop,'" she breathed. "'Just say we died right here . . .'"

Leonard opened her shirt, kissed her chest. He pushed his face against her breasts, first one then another.

She backed away from him, one step. "'Don't you think so, baby?'" she asked. *Christine asked.* "'That if we never went any further into it, it would stay perfect forever?'"

"I want you," Leonard whispered. "Let me."

She shook her head.

He came toward her again, hand against her

back, under her shirt. She kept her eyes open. White roses on the wood table by the window. Kerosene lamp. He felt her stomach and her legs, moaned quietly. Pulled her shirt over her head, the veil falling with it, falling down onto the unmade bed. "Leonard. This isn't in the scene." He pressed against her through cloth.

"He loves you. He wants to marry you."

"Reality check, Leonard. You're not Hank."

He pushed his hands under her clothes, silver hair warm against her face. When she turned her head to the side, her neck was still sore from where she'd jolted against the seatbelt. Across the corral, through the flowers, Mirina would be sleeping; afternoon, heat and light, white day. *I want that man here,* she thought. *Harm. What kind of name is that for a man to save you?* Her body hurt in that place wanting to be hurt. "Leonard, please. I can't love you anymore. You're invading me."

"You're letting me," he whispered.

"I know, but I can't."

"You want it."

"So what? It doesn't matter anymore what I want, what either of us want. It's sick."

She pulled away, stumbled to standing, and crossed the room; pulling the veil on over her hair again, smoothing her hair down, naked from the waist, tight jeans, out of breath. Yes, she still wanted him. But what difference did it make? It was only this way, in a cabin in back of a corral, in a hotel room in Paris, on a boat in the Aegean. Stupid, ever to have wanted it out front, straight ahead, without the complication, the fraught drama of it all, covert and secretive so he could be illicit.

"We're just too old for this, Leonard. I've had too much therapy, for chrissake. You've paid for most of it. Okay?"

He laughed, out of breath.

"It's just work between us. I thought we agreed." Nyia turned to the window, sunlight catching the diamond chips. The diamonds were probably fake. Simulated. Rita and Sam. They were fake too.

"I miss you in my life, Nyia. I can't just cut you out. We were together twelve years."

"How long have you been married to Mirina?"

"Twenty-two years."

"Proverbial case closed, dear."

"She doesn't mind. You know that."

"I know, but I do. I mind." She shook her head. "Let's not rehash this."

"You still love me."

"Of course I do. I happen to love me too. Maybe for the first time."

"Is that the profound culmination of your analysis?" he asked.

She turned her naked back to him. "Exactly when is that Harm Bohland starting?"

"He can start whenever you want. Have him start right now if it'll make you feel better. I want you to feel safe here." Leonard stood at the window looking out across the pasture. He was quiet for a while, then asked, "Are you sure?"

Nyia slipped on her shirt and began to button it. She didn't mean to lie, but it was better that way. Safe. What a joke. It was his love that felt like danger. This would be their last film, she knew, because he'd never be able to stop. He just didn't get it.

"I'm sure," she said, and there was a way that she was happy about it and there was a way that she was sad.

It always took several minutes after Leonard left for a room to feel empty. He took up that much space. Or she let him. Yes, she knew that was part of it. She searched in the back of the closet for her old briefcase, and sat on the bed with it, holding it on her lap. It was an old-fashioned brown leather briefcase that had belonged to her father. He'd died of a stroke when she was seven. She still kept a brochure from the construction company he had worked for in one of the briefcase compartments. "Westward Ho: Neighborhood of Tomorrow."

She clicked the latch open and peered into the accordion pockets, lifted out a packet of photographs, thumbed through them. Now, here was a good one: Leonard at thirty. The year she'd met him she was fifteen. Her mother should have had him arrested, but she'd actually promoted the relationship, pushed them together. Sent them away on trips together to the Loire Valley. Here were early promotional stills. Nyia at seventeen in Rome beside the Spanish Steps, Nyia in a bikini, Côte d'Azur.

Looking at the pictures she realized how far she'd come since she'd left him. But there was always that power of his, seduction, charisma. That sensation of entering a story with him again, the story in and around the making of a film, coming under his sway. And that was how he had done it for years, before she'd even had a chance to be a grown woman. An influential and powerful and very sexual man and she a kid, beautiful, yes, but feeling scrawny and bewildered. It hadn't been easy breaking off with him. At times she experienced moments of great power, staying Nyia, staying thirty-year-old woman in his presence. And then this feeling of shrinking would come over her, she'd feel adolescent and unformed again. Afraid, even.

Here was another: Nyia at twenty in a white nightgown on the balcony of a hotel in Paris. These pictures were like tiny outtakes, vignettes of erotic melancholy. They had fallen in love each time they'd shot a film together. Mirina had known all about it. She tolerated, even encouraged, Leonard's affairs. So modern of her.

So European. She had her own loves, Nyia knew. Leonard had liked the mother-of-pearl buttons on that nightgown. He'd kissed all the buttons on the gown as he'd unfastened them.

Yacht off Majorca, just three years ago. Distance and silence. She wanted love to continue, that was all. She had honored his relationship with Mirina—my God, she loved Mirina as a second mother. But if that was all it was ever going to be, over and over, some repeated melodrama in his personal inferno, she couldn't take it. The seduction and reunion, betrayal and breaking. Each time, it was worse for her. She was older then, not some little girl. And she'd finally come to realize it was all story for him. She was a character in his life. A role, not a person. She wanted him to leave Mirina and marry her. It would never happen.

That hotel in Barcelona, Leonard naked at the window, smoking. She didn't need a photograph to remember. She could picture him perfectly. Drinking from a bottle wrapped in raffia, thin moonlight across the wooden floor.

"This is the last time," she'd told him. "Because for you it's all a fiction, so you can work more intensely. Love and sex and creation and art, it's all bound up for you, but not for me. Not anymore."

He'd laughed. "Don't be dramatic," he'd said. He, who was addicted to drama.

"I can't be your creation anymore, that's all. I'll always love you, I'll always work with you."

And that had been it. She'd left him that night, folded clothes quietly into a small suitcase, asked the concierge for another room. She had been with him from the age of fifteen until she was twenty-seven. He was still bitter underneath, she knew, though he had no right to be. Still tried to get to her, old tricks. *Play the scene with me, I'm directing you, this is my method. Creative tension.* And always acted as if it had been her betrayal.

.

But he had Mirina, he'd had her all along. He would never understand. Nyia had come to accept that it was beyond him.

She fingered the contents of her briefcase, lifting things out and arranging them back in order, the envelope of snapshots and studio stills, a birthday card, a plastic bag with a squashed faded rose inside. Matchbook from a hotel in Aix-en-Provence, napkin from the Ritz. A small African coin Leonard had given her. He had one like it, carried it with him always, like a charm. A small gold pocket watch that didn't work, a green fishing fly tied on a bent hook, a tiny wind-up duck that pecked and hopped around on tin webbed feet.

But this is what she was looking for, the packet of letters she kept in the back compartment of the briefcase, bound together with red string. All of them written on the same kind of paper, tissue-thin, blue airmail letters, French, PAR AVION in thin red script across the front. The kind that folded over and glued shut, both letter and envelope in one. This is what she wanted to show Harm Bohland in a few hours, the fan letters, love letters.

Just holding them she felt a black heat in her chest. "All my love," the letters were always signed. All from the same person, nameless, anonymous. The heat in her chest was not love. The early letters hadn't been strange, but they had changed. She pulled the most recent letter out from under the red string. When had she received this one? Forwarded in a pile of mail from her manager's office, two, three weeks ago. Working out of town these past months, Nyia had lost track. She opened the envelope and read the end of it again.

". . . . When I close my eyes I see you in my mind. You exist within my imagination. What you feel as an impulse is my will. What you see in a dream is a message from me. What seems to be accident, serendipity, happenstance, coincidence, is all planned by and foreseen by me. I don't have to do anything to bring these things about. They simply occur. In a strange way this is the intimacy I have always dreamed of. A pure realm. In my mind I make you do things. 'Bad?' you'll want to know. Lovely bad things, darling.

"In the *Interview* article you sounded so lonely. You said you were tired of being visible but not really seen. In your fear you surround yourself with protection—security, managers, agents, entourages of hangers-on. Someday you'll be able to step out of all that you fear and experience true freedom. You will know freedom beyond your face. It is exactly your face that keeps you so separate. And the more well-known that face becomes, the more separate you will feel. You must be very, very careful about your face.

"Isn't it odd that just when you become someone else, when you are acting a part, you feel the most satisfaction and fullness in your life? The rest of the time you are afraid. Because you just can't be sure.

"I know we will meet one day without artifice or mask. My only worry is that I have built you up too much in my imagination and that you could never live up to the image I have of you. To keep it from becoming too perfect I try to picture you doing ordinary things, taking a bath for instance and putting on your silk robe. There I go again, dreaming up stories. It's probably terrycloth. Or plaid flannel. But no—that was back in Denver, wasn't it, the plaid flannel? You're way beyond all that now.

"Perhaps it will be in New Mexico. Watch for me there. I'll be the one in the audience never wanting the scene to end. I watch you over and over, rewind, and watch again. Freeze the frames I like best. I'm often with you. I long to be with you as we were meant to be, but this is close enough for now. You exist in my mind. Your actions every moment reflect what I am thinking. All my love . . ."

Nyia folded the blue envelope back in on itself. It was postmarked April 27th, San Francisco. She placed it back with the others, slipped the whole bundle of them into her purse.

After checking to make sure the cabin door was locked, she walked the path to the big house along the *vega* fence that surrounded the pasture. She was hungry. Leonard had driven out to the site where they would begin shooting tomorrow. At least he had told her the scene they would begin with: the lovemaking scene, the honeymoon scene, Christine and Hank in some shabby motel. Mirina had said the site was perfect, an old thirties adobe motel up near Española, rusty metal lawn chairs outside each door, flaking paint on wooden doors, nineteen-thirties Coca-Cola machine outside the motel office right next to a ripped Naugahyde couch, salmon-colored. It was so perfect, Mirina had said, that a set designer couldn't have invented it in more detail.

Just inside the door of the main house, on a parson's table under an oil painting of Taos Pueblo, she saw it. Over the years she had gotten good at spotting them quickly, a blue corner in a pile of bills and magazines. She riffled quickly through the other mail and pulled out the airmail envelope. Chicago postmark, ten days ago. The letter had been sent to her manager, Suzanne Scolfield, and then it had been forwarded here.

Strange it should come today, just now, just as she read the last one, just as she was thinking of them, getting ready to show them all to Harm. Then, she thought, not strange at all. She turned and leaned on the parson's table, slit the envelope open carefully with her finger and glanced across the foyer at the image in the mirror of her white, white face.

FOUR

"DEAR NYIA,

"There is a scene from *Dead Heat* that I watch over and over, the swimming scene in the grotto. Jacobs really knew where to set that one, that half-built concrete hotel on the green shore, looking like some Mayan ruin, some modern eyesore temple to tourism and destruction of third-world culture. The small boat you dove from, your face hidden, just your eyes showing through the glass diving mask. How he filmed you down in that murky water, struggling to come up for air, the waves pushing you back toward the sharp rocks, as if something were actually there beneath you, the undertow or something caught around your ankles, sucking you down. The terror in your eyes as you came up out of the water, spitting and coughing and clawing for air.

"I admire the way you do not use a double for

those sorts of scenes. You enter fully, even the most dangerous ones. It has made me realize how much I, myself, hold back, do not push fully into the moment. Always the splitting off, as if my whole life were a movie and somewhere in myself I'm always watching. Unable to enter.

"This has led to a decision on my part of which I need to inform you. While up until now I have kept my feelings for you limited to your performances and admiration for your beauty and artistry, it is time I step out from the artificial limitations of the watcher and the watched. I need to leave my imagination and meet you in the real world. There is some destiny between us to be created, but I haven't yet decided what it should be.

"Watch for me. Just thinking of it, I could die.

All my love . . ."

Nyia read the letter twice, folded it, and walked out, past the adobe wall of the compound that held the big house, the pool, the garden. She walked north in the lengthening shadows of the foothills along the creek bed. She knew of others in the business who'd been harassed by weird letters, there were always those obsessive types who didn't know the difference between your character and who you really were: a person with a job. But her "fan," as she sometimes thought of him, for years had seemed merely an attentive admirer and a good critic. *Oh, more than that and you know it,* she thought. Why had she kept the letters at all? She'd have to tell Harm that, show him all the letters. Who she really thought was writing them.

Dead Heat. Tess Juran had been the first one hired to play the lead in that movie. Nyia had been under contract to do two more films with Leonard and Mirina, but she'd gone off to do other things. *Pursuit* was to have been a grade-B horror film. Suzanne had pushed it; *You've got to get out of the European, arty little things that play only on college campuses. This will show your range and your face. You can be big,* Suzanne had said. And then the surprise of it, a summer sleeper that grossed millions, a cult favorite and suddenly everything Suzanne had promised came true. Immediately, Nyia shot *Gun Law,* playing the sharpshooting wife of an undercover cop who's been undercover a bit too long and may have disappeared; another commercial success. She was bankable. "You have a face." Suzanne had beamed.

His late-night call had come a few weeks before she was to be on location in Brazil in the supporting role in Manuel Moravio's film, *Wings.* She hadn't spoken to Leonard for several months. He'd called then to borrow a dress of hers for a costume in his upcoming film. His voice was familiar as though they'd just been together days ago.

"Nyia, you just won't believe this."

"Leonard?"

"I'm sitting out on this veranda—I'm down in Manzanillo—bougainvillea in moonlight, the ocean only steps away and the moon is like a tipped over, lopsided thing seen through the branches of a palm tree, and in the middle of the night a man walks by selling hats. I mean, it's what?—two, three in the morning. Straw hats! And way down the beach from this outdoor café comes a guitar and trumpet, some out-of-tune mariachi band and loud singing. Are you there?"

"It's the middle of the night, Leonard."

"Should I hang up?"

"No," she'd said. That was her mistake, right there.

"Nyia, I need you."

"Sweetheart, we can't even talk about that, that's out of the question. Need, want, any of it."

"You called me 'sweetheart.'"

"You know what I mean, Leonard."

"But that's not what I mean. It's gotten crazy down here. The usual messes, last-minute financing, some controlling son-of-a-bitch from the backing studio down here overseeing everything, but what's happened is that Tess Juran has had a nervous breakdown."

Nyia had sat up in her bed in her Laurel Canyon home, dark night, Leonard Jacobs on the phone calling from Mexico after so long. In the absence between them, after all the pain had drained away, of course they were friends. There was no ending anything. You went on but the love just stayed there inside you like the ring of a tree. Or scar tissue.

"What do you mean, nervous breakdown? Do people still have those? Are you sure it wasn't an anxiety attack?"

"No, she just lost it, won't get out of bed. She calls me, says she's sick, she can't breathe, she's hyperventilating. I send over a doctor, the doctor calls and says she's gone in a major way. She can't work, she can hardly walk. It's part exhaustion, part anxiety, part God knows what. So she flew home this afternoon. Just up and out of here on a chartered flight to San Diego. Sayonara. Adios. Good-bye. We were to start filming tomorrow. In about three hours, to be exact. Only, I have no lead actress."

"So what are you going to do?"

"Okay, so there's casting—there's a list of names, of course. There's everyone's manager, agent, lawyer; there's flying back up there to have people read for us; there's insurance covering the lost time; there's paying everyone to stay down here sitting on their asses while I try to cover mine. In short, there's a big black hole and I'm sitting in it up to my neck in quicksand."

She had been silent then, touching the cool sheets, the air-conditioner humming in the dark room. She knew what was coming. She didn't even mind.

"You know the script, Nyia, from three years ago

when Mirina was first writing it and we'd sit around at night doing cold readings. You know this character, you helped invent her." He'd paused for a moment. "The mariachis just stopped. I can hear the surf from here. But the ocean is total blackness. I sit here at night and it's like the ocean is just breathing."

"What are you saying, Leonard?" Nyia had asked.

"Oh God, Nyia," he'd sighed. "I need you to come down here and take over the lead. I know, I know, we're through and all of that. It would be work. Only about three weeks or so. You'd save my life. Will you do it?"

"I'll call Suzanne and see what's what," she'd said. It was as if the whole thing were already decided.

"We have a boat down here," he'd said. "At a marina by a resort that looks like a Greek hillside with Turkish minarets."

"The boat is out, Leonard."

"But you might come?"

He'd known she would.

When the phone had rung again seconds later, Leonard went on as if he'd never hung up. "Another thing," he'd said. "The character Tess was playing—Jane. She's down in Mexico, she's left her husband, and she's going crazy. She hears voices. Mirina has written them in as voice-overs, her own voice instructing her what to do with her life. *Nyia, the character has a breakdown.*"

Nyia had been silent, thinking of Tess Juran, a young actress just coming into prominence, having a nervous breakdown at a hotel in Manzanillo, walking out on Leonard. "Was she just getting too far into character?" Nyia had asked. She wondered what else was going on down there.

"It's an intense part," Leonard had said. "Can you handle it?"

"I've never been more sane," Nyia had said. "And my life has never been more separate from the plot of a goddamned movie."

* * *

The plane landed on a thin green strip of land between the brown mountains and the sea. Manzanillo was an old fishing town with a small harbor, the airport only recently open to big jets and tourism. She stepped out of the plane into the rippling air, the heat shimmering off the tarmac. Just inside the terminal she saw Jack Drieser lift his hand in a wave. He wore all white and a straw hat, a two-day growth of beard.

Nyia checked through customs, then Jack came over, embracing her in a friendly hug. They'd worked together on several of Leonard's films over the last ten years. He was an odd-looking man who became beautiful before a camera. Up close he was ordinary, even a bit strange-looking with his scoop-shaped nose, close-set eyes that seemed too pale for his dark hair. His hair was thinning, but the beard became him, gave more definition to his face. He was a short man who seemed large on film, a quiet man who became animated and extroverted. It was always disconcerting seeing the footage from a day's shoot—the odd-looking Jack became the handsome lover. He was calm, intelligent, and gentle, and Nyia had always enjoyed working with him, a respite from Leonard's intensity.

"You are a godsend, Nyia," said Jack. He took her bag and they headed for a pile of luggage in the glass-doored lobby. "Tess just freaked. I talked to her the night before, we were going over a scene and she was all puffy-eyed like she'd been on some crying jag. The next day she split without a word to the rest of us."

"But why? This was Tess's first real lead. Was she strung out on something?"

Outside the airport terminal, hot wind surrounded Nyia. They stood in a crowd of tourists jockeying for cabs. "I don't know if she was using," Jack continued. "She was skinny as hell, she didn't really look good. Pasty-white and staying out of the sun so she wouldn't fry lobster-red. Over-sleeping, missing cues. Yeah, all the signs were there, but I never saw her high or drunk. I think it was psychological pressure. Maybe the part was just too stressful, too much for her."

"Her character, Jane. *My* character now," Nyia added. "She has a breakdown, experiences hallucinations. Did Tess just get too wrapped up in it?"

Jack squinted through his sunglasses at the long double row of palms that lined the road up to the airport, the dry mountains beyond. "To tell you the truth I don't think Tess could get far enough in. I think Leonard was pushing her hard, going over scenes with her, working with her privately, relentlessly. One theory is that he forced her to walk."

"Fired her?" said Nyia. "He told me it was definitely Tess who abandoned the project, not the other way around."

"Who the hell knows when it comes to Leonard?" asked Jack. "Anyway, you should know all about those late-night rehearsals, one-on-one with the director."

Nyia blushed and pushed at Jack's arm. "Hey, I was a kid, what did I know? I thought it was method acting."

"Some method," teased Jack. "But you know what I mean."

"So he was fucking her."

Jack shrugged. "Only the shadow knows. All the rest of us know is that Tess is gone, you're here, and I, for one, am delighted. We were all in this big zero-limbo wondering if the whole damn film was going to fold. Hell, I even called our esteemed manager, Suzanne, to see if there was any TV work coming up just in case. Then last night at dinner, Leonard announces, 'Our worries are over, Nyia Wyatt is stepping into the part of Jane and our only limitation is that we have to finish in three weeks so she can go to Brazil.' Anyway, you look great. And I am very glad you're here."

Jack hailed a cab outside the airport and they drove out a paved road through a palm plantation, then took the winding mountain road toward Manzanillo through scrub mountains, decrepit, crumbling adobe shacks with tin roofs giving way to scattered developments of condominiums and hotels as they neared the sea. The cab driver sang along with the radio in Spanish. Lurid pictures of a thorny Christ, protected by Ziploc bags, were pinned to the roof of the cab above their heads.

"You're a miracle," said Jack.

"Hey, it's a job, right? Anyway, I wanted Leonard in a position where he owed me. Just in case."

"Just in case what?"

Nyia shrugged. She didn't know.

They pulled into a private development called Club Santiago, surrounded by a high wall, and checked in with a sleepy guard in a white uniform sitting in the open-air booth at the electric entrance gate. Club Santiago was a few acres of land next to the sea, nudged up against a mountain, across the harbor from the small fishing city of Manzanillo. It consisted of a hotel, several pools, and two or three separate condominium areas, each with their own decor and theme—one was white stucco with violet bougainvillea and terra-cotta tiled verandas. The other featured more modern, adobelike structures with black wrought-iron balconies, vines hanging down like Spanish moss, modern cement foundations with sculptures in the center. Jack drove her to a ground-floor unit in one of the white condos, unlocked the door and handed her the key.

It was cool and dark inside, a ceiling fan circling over the clean room. Inside everything was white, except for a heavy Mediterranean-style table on which a copy of the screenplay had been placed with a note from Leonard: "We start tomorrow. After you've had a chance to rest, please join Mirina and me for dinner at Los Hadas."

She left word at his hotel for him to call, and when he returned the call later that afternoon, she refused his invitation. "I'm doing this as a favor to you, Leonard. But I don't want to socialize. I'm just not comfortable getting all chummy with you and Mirina again. Please understand." He said that he did, but she knew he was angry. Well, that was just too bad. She couldn't afford to get sucked in by him again. Business. That was all it would be.

The first few days of filming went brilliantly and she was happy. In the evenings she'd walked with Jack and Robin Reese, Leonard's assistant, Dan Howe, and some of the other actors and crew members down the miles-long beach toward the more populated area where small seaside bars and open-air cafés were huddled together. At white wooden tables they drank Dos Equis beers and margaritas and watched the sun set over the Pacific.

There was some concern at first in makeup that Robin and Nyia looked too much alike. "I could go red," the flamboyant Robin had suggested. They were both small, with straight blond hair, shoulder length. Connie, the makeup assistant, devised a French braid for Nyia; Robin's hair was left long, unkempt. The character Robin would play would wear red lipstick, while Nyia's Jane would have a face in muted tones as she increasingly disappeared into the madness of her second voice.

It had been good to see Robin too. They'd been together in one of Leonard's early films, and Nyia found Robin refreshing in her zany lippiness. She was gawky and silly off-screen, but, like Jack, transformed before a lens, all serious, sucked-in cheeks and sultry, smoky voice. Off-camera she was a tomboy dressed up, tongue-in-cheek, as a beautiful girl. She was only nineteen.

While Leonard and Mirina huddled over the script at night, inventing the next day's story, Nyia, Jack, and Robin, Gino, the cinematographer, Connie, and Dierdre Fine, a journalist who wrote about many of Leonard's films for *Vanity Fair*, danced at a jazz club in Manzanillo and ate grilled lobster at a café next to the sand. Multicolored Christmas lights dangled from wires slung between palm trees, while locals from the town of Santiago hawked blankets, jewelry, and puppets, then congregated under the dark trees, sitting quietly with their wares, looking at the moon.

One afternoon a group of them sat drinking at the outdoor café just down from where the parasailors took off. Robin wore a short red sundress, movie-star rhinestone-studded sunglasses with pointy rims, pearl-pink lipstick in a heart-shaped smear on her mouth. Her hair was tucked up under a straw cowboy hat.

"What's with all this synchronicity bullshit, Señor Jack?" Robin asked. "I mean, that wasn't, like, a major theme in Leonard's other films, was it? Is this some kind of in thing with Leonard? Like the closer you are to him, the more your life leaks into the film? Or what?"

"Just how close to Leonard are you?" asked Jack, poking her in the side with an extended finger.

"Oh, give me a break," Robin had protested. "What—a ménage à trois with Mirina taking notes from the side and Gino filming us in overhead mirrors? Oh yeah. I'm real excited about sleeping with my director. Isn't that just too classic Hollywood circa 1940 or something? Hey, my mother warned me about that sort of thing. Besides," she said, camping over the top of her glasses and assuming a Southern accent. "All I need is mah talent. I'm very well-bred, you know."

Nyia glanced down the beach toward the market, T-shirt vendors in the shade. Robin had gone on just a bit too long in her defense. Diversion. So it was Robin he was sleeping with, not Tess. Maybe there had even been some kind of competition going on between Tess and Robin. Her eyes followed the tiny dot of a parasail far out over the sparkling water. So what? Nyia thought, pushing it all away, Leonard and his women, his protégées, his so-called techniques. Thank God that was behind her now. Just another part she'd once played. A role. One that had lasted twelve years.

The next day during a script conference with Leonard prior to shooting in the market, Nyia read the words describing how her character, Jane, begins to break down, to hear voices coming to her clearly from far away. *Will appear as a voice-over signalled by gull's cry on soundtrack: In this scene she pursues a woman she imagines is her double, with the idea that she is actually searching for herself.*

"Double?" asked Nyia.

"It's a new direction. You and Robin look so much alike that Mirina has decided to play on that and work it into the story."

"Is this synchronicity backwards?" she asked.

"It's all the same, Nyia. That's what I've tried to tell you for years. The world enters the story, the story enters the world. You want to separate things, make them so complete unto themselves. The film, then a big cement wall, then your life. Like you work in a factory or something. Like you punch in and out on a clock. Don't you understand? It's permeable."

"It's just that it was too permeable before, that's all."

"It was only that way for you," he said.

It was one of those scenes Leonard loved: Nyia had been—Jane had been—shopping in the crowded aisles of an outdoor market filled with straw hats, jewelry, blankets, flipping through a stack of cotton dresses folded on a table in the blue shade of an umbrella. She heard the gulls and went deeply into character. The sound was her trigger. Under the third shirt, bright floral embroidery, a black blot moved. She pushed the dress back and Gino came in with the camera as a small scorpion scuttled to the edge of the material. Nyia gasped, nearly broke character, and held, held, knowing Leonard would want her to use this. She stayed in, Gino's camera close, Leonard in peripheral vision, ecstatic with her, she just knew it.

She backed away, pushing back against a wall of puppets, papier-mâché heads rattling against a board. The scorpion lurched. The vendor woman, not understanding the import of the moment, shook the dress off, telling Nyia in Spanish not to be afraid. Just then, the timing perfect, Robin came through the crowded aisle of the market in her white dress and sunglasses. Apparition. Nyia watched as she passed, stepping over the scorpion without seeing it was there. Leonard called cut and the crew cheered, broke into applause. The scorpion scurried under a table into a pile of sandals and straw purses.

Leonard blew a kiss to her with both hands. *You are in,* she thought. *All the way in, when the world begins to enter the story in that way. It was true. It was always true, just as Leonard had taught her.*

That night, after showering in the condominium she put on her silk robe; the window was open. Outside, a truck rattled by with hotel workers singing. She pulled back the sheets and shrieked. A huge inches-long centipede with its hundreds of legs rippled over the sheets, stopping, frozen near the pillow.

Did that count? she wondered. *She knew it did. Story alive in the world. But which direction was it moving to, world to story or story to world?*

After that, the synchronous moments came quickly. Robin made fun of the whole thing, humming the theme from "The Twilight Zone," but it was uncanny, the repetition; and the more trivial the double images were, the more mysterious and unsettling it seemed. Robin's character was called on to break a glass, and leaning to pick it up, to cut herself, the camera lingering on her slit finger. The blood was all makeup. It took several takes, and on the last one she really did cut herself. Of course, that was the take Leonard thought was brilliant.

That night, the group of them dined together, rowdy and slightly drunk, playing American rock-and-roll on a café jukebox. The waitress brought a round of drinks, pale margaritas, no ice, tequila in thick shot glasses. They all saw it, the glass fall and shatter. Small thing, nothing really. Robin had said, "No way am I picking that thing up." She dared anyone to. Finally the waitress bent down, all of them watching her as she cut her hand on the ragged glass as if she'd practiced it for hours and got it in one take.

The next day they'd gone for the afternoon to an open-air café in Manzanillo to wait while a boat scene was being set up in the harbor. Down the street Nyia could see the white fountain at the center of town, two men playing a wooden xylophone on the sidewalk. At one point, the screenplay called for some lines of argument about an order of food that was wrong. *I like the food at the hotel:* that was the line Robin was to whine twice in an upcoming scene.

Some Americans were seated behind them at a table, the woman complaining in a Texas accent, "But I hate green chili peppers." Her husband, sick of her, snapped, "Then why the fuck did you come to Mexico?" She sniffed, "I like the food at the hotel." Robin turned to gape at them, taking off her rhinestone glasses. The woman repeated the line as if on cue: "I like the food at the hotel."

"Let's get them into the movie," Robin whispered. "I want them to have walk-ons. They're too perfect. You couldn't cast them if you tried."

"They're already in the movie," said Jack.

"It's too much."

"No, it's perfect." Jack drank from a bottle of mineral water. "It's exactly right."

"It's like some kind of cosmic script and everyone is auditioning all the time."

"Exactly right." Jack smiled.

Later, out on the boats, the wind high that afternoon, Leonard and Gino, the cinematographer, were busy, and sullen. The light was too bright off the water and maybe they would have to wait until dusk. Leonard sent a small boat back to the pier, angry that the fishing boat hadn't arrived for the scene. It called for a boat full of gutted fish to cruise alongside at a certain point, and just as he was yelling about it, Dierdre Fine, who'd been allowed out on the boat that day to shoot pictures for *Vanity Fair,* nudged Nyia. "Why is he complaining? Here comes the boat right now." But, of course, it wasn't the movie boat, it was a real boat, just happening along.

Exactly. They'd begun to say that whenever a moment appeared from the screenplay. *Exactly*. The white boat rode low in the water as it rumbled by, the long fish in the sunlight, sharks, their gray-white skin slit neatly open, the men lying back, arms behind their heads. Leonard tried to flag them back to the boat, see if he could hire the real boat, the real fish, the real men instead of the late movie-set boat that still had not come.

It became a kind of game then, and they started to watch for the moments. Nyia began to suspect that someone was setting them up; it was too perfect. Too exact. But the moments were so fresh, they defied prearrangement. There was a scene later in the film that hinged on a woman being buried in the sand by her lover, playfully at first, but then it turned mean. She and Robin watched one morning as a group of local children played near the multicolored umbrellas on the long beach near Santiago. One child couldn't have been more than eighteen months; the Mexican mothers sat nearby while the other children dug a hole, setting the girl in the hole naked, covering her. She laughed, then fretted, then screamed as the sand covered her arms. And the mothers laughed too. Nyia wanted to run to the baby, pull her out, carry her back to her condominium in a plush bath towel, steal her away from the cruelty of the other children and the neglectful mothers who thought it was funny. Perhaps it was at that moment she felt afraid, like a taste under her tongue, an edge in her stomach.

That night they were out on Leonard's chartered yacht in the small marina harbor in front of Los Hadas, a resort complex with hundreds of condominium units stacked up the hillside next to the sea. For once Leonard was cheerful. Nyia had avoided him as much as she could; Mirina too. She was friendly, but she kept apart and noticed that she felt much closer to the other actors, to Jack and Robin and the others. The scene Jack had shot earlier that day had been one in which he had leapt off the side of a boat to pull Nyia in. She had not been able to get her bearings, snorkling near the rocks, going under in the high waves.

That night they sat drinking in the dark on the yacht with the lights strung up the mast, when Dierdre Fine, who stood six feet in slippery white sandals, stood, held up her drink and slid back against the railing, laughing, almost as if she'd meant to—had she? on purpose?—fell back into the black water, screaming, whooping. Jack pulled his shoes off and flung himself into the water, grabbing her large body. She was sputtering, flailing toward him. Someone shone a light down into the waves, then threw a life preserver down, white *OH* in the black water. Back on the boat, Jack pointed at Leonard, drunk—all of them were drunk: "It's too fucking much, man."

Leonard just said, "I had nothing to do with that. Did anyone see me push her in? I'm telling you, the story takes over. It has a life of its own."

Robin whispered to Nyia, "The story, starring itself. Jesus. He really does believe in it, doesn't he?"

"Don't you?" said Nyia.

Robin shook her head, downed her margarita. She shivered in the night wind. "There's no place like home," she said.

"What do you mean?"

"Well, when we leave here. Leave the film. Things will just be what they are again. Not twice something."

Jack dried himself off with a towel. "Who wouldn't want to live twice?"

Robin answered, "Living once is trouble enough."

The filming had continued for several weeks. Leonard was pleased with how quickly it had come together considering the trouble at the start. He praised Nyia for her professionalism. The next day they were to film the climactic scene. Leonard had left this scene for close to last, though it occurred two-thirds of the way through the script. Almost every scene had now been completed and there was a feeling of both relief and agitation among the crew.

Back in her condominium that night, the ceiling fan blew the long white floor-length curtains. Nyia found a plaster figurine on a side table in her living room. It was crudely painted, four little skeletons dressed as mariachi figures, playing guitars and saxophones, xylophones and drums. She picked it up. Now, where did this come from? Had someone dropped it off? She'd heard of the Day of the Dead, a Halloween-like celebration, everyone masked in skull faces. Maybe the maid had brought it in. A decoration, a knickknack for her room.

Later, after Nyia was asleep, Robin knocked at Nyia's door, barefoot, hair wet, dressed in a bathrobe. Nyia opened the door a crack, then all the way. "What time is it?"

"Sorry," said Robin. "It's goddamn late. I can't sleep."

"I've got the scene tomorrow at the bar, it's the big one, I really need to rest," said Nyia.

"My air conditioning is out. All my electricity is out. Can I sleep in your extra room?"

Nyia had been given a two-bedroom unit. Robin entered, sat on the couch and picked up the skeleton figure, fingered one of the tiny grotesque faces. Nyia watched her for a moment. Robin was young, very young. This was her second feature film. She looked shaky, thought Nyia, as if she'd been drinking heavily and the room was swimming.

"Hey," Nyia said. "You better take it easy."

"You used to be with Leonard, didn't you?" asked Robin.

Nyia rolled her eyes. "I should have warned you to stay away from him, Robin."

Robin looked down at her hands. "I know—he's married and everything. Is that why you broke up with him?"

"In a nutshell."

"He's confusing. First he's all over me right in front of her, then it's got to be kept a secret. I mean, I know it's crazy."

"It is, believe me."

"But he is so sweet when he's on."

"Yes, he is."

"I'm sorry," said Robin. "I shouldn't be talking to you about this."

"It's all past," said Nyia. "What he does with his life . . . But you're right, I don't want to hear about it."

She brought Robin a blanket from the spare bed. Already Robin was lying on the couch and it was clear she wasn't getting up. Nyia covered her. The girl was blacked out, gone. She'd probably wake up and not even know what room she was in.

The following day Nyia waited for a taxi in front of the hotel, sweating in the late heat, the palms shimmering above. They would begin shooting those final pivotal scenes in a bar in Santiago. Then her character, Jane, who had been wandering around in a dream state, following the woman who appeared to be her double, would go out into the barrio night, chasing her down a deserted alley. Her husband, who had been searching for her, would run after her and shoot her.

The taxi came and Nyia climbed in. As she leaned forward to give the driver instructions, she saw the figure, *la muerte*, on the dashboard, the skulls on little springs, bobbing as the taxi pulled out into the brick street. Nyia put her hand to her chest, her heart wild there under her palm. She didn't want to play the game anymore. It was starting to feel crazy. But maybe it *was* just coincidence. Images circled around. That was all there was to it.

Jack was relaxed that evening watching the filming, involved in the bar scene. He was playing an American expatriate, a painter who befriends the runaway wife. They would dance together in the bar. The scenes went exceptionally well, but still Leonard called for them to be shot again and again. He was harsh and critical to the extras and the actors, yelling commands at the cameramen. Then they were all expected to turn on a dime, smile and dance for the camera. Even the little band of musicians were getting irritated. The scene acquired a quality of forced gaiety on the surface with an undercurrent of hot, retentive anger just below.

At one point, Nyia couldn't stand it anymore. She approached Leonard, looked right at him. "You've got to back off. Everyone is too uptight, we're losing the party, we're losing the pleasure."

"That's exactly what I want," he snapped. "I want the illusion of a smile, with hatred right underneath. Because next you go off into that street to be killed, you got that? This is your last moment on earth and you know that at some level you blew it. You left your husband and it didn't cure your unhappiness because it wasn't his fault. And I want everything in this scene to convey that conflict. You got that, Nyia? You understand my motive for directing this scene?"

Nyia just glared at him. She wanted to grab the collar of his white shirt and shake him. He was a genius and just now hateful. They shot the scene one more time. It was perfect, of course.

It was then that she felt herself go totally into the dream. The next scene was to be shot outside, in lights, in the street behind a grocery store. In the scene, she would run out, take off her shoes, look back once. See her husband for the last time just before he shoots her.

Nyia stepped toward the set, her high heels sinking into the dust, wearing a black dress that Leonard had bought her in Paris years ago. Leonard came over to her. "My preference for this scene is to take a straight shot. One time. It's a scene of release for her. She understands her death is stalking her in the form of this other woman. There's some feeling of relief as she accepts what is going to happen to her."

Nyia breathed deeply, then walked out around the corner of the mercado. The small side street in Santiago was barricaded and the set was crowded but quiet. Floodlights threw garish shadows on the pink-and-green stucco buildings. Townspeople had gathered to watch the *norteamericanos* make a movie in their dusty little town. Big money in it, all the cafés and hotels full, big tippers too. Nyia walked into the dark street, then stopped, turned. There was a moon, a Cheshire cat grin. That's beautiful, she thought. The husband appeared; she glanced at him with love, then turned away. The gun fired off a blank and she staggered forward, letting her body fall without catching herself. Her arms flapped down next to her in the dirt.

After a few silent moments, Leonard said, "Stay there, Nyia." Connie came over with the blood, dabbing it on her head. There were several takes of her body lying there, facedown, first this angle, then that.

"Perfect," Leonard proclaimed.

Nyia did not know why she took the dress back to Club Santiago with her. In the trailer, Connie had helped her take it off, shake out the dust. They commented how clean it was, how much like new. No fake blood on it. They had even laughed. Perhaps that is why Leonard wanted only one take, to save the dress. Nyia had wrapped it in dry-cleaning plastic and took a taxi back to her white room.

Robin had stayed with her again that night. And the following day, Nyia decided to stay at Club Santiago to rest. She was finished with all her scenes. All that was left to be shot were a few final takes between Robin and Jack.

She was sitting on the veranda reading, her feet up on a cowhide table, shaded by bougainvillea when Robin returned in the afternoon.

"Party at Los Hadas tonight," Robin said. "Seafood and salsa on the balcony at sunset. Mirina says, *'Le filme est fini!'*"

"I don't know if I'm going," said Nyia. "I'm still beat." She looked for a while at Robin. She looked better, thought Nyia. You could bounce back quickly at nineteen.

"Look, I appreciate your advice," Robin offered. "About Leonard, I mean. It's not like I'm in love with him or anything."

"Just using him, eh?"

Robin smiled and shrugged. "Yeah, maybe. Do men ever sleep with women in power, I mean does it work that way?"

"Ask Mirina," Nyia said.

They both laughed.

Nyia took a last swim in the pool behind the condominiums, the stone fountain offering the only sound, the dark mountain fading green in the west and the salt smell of the Pacific nearby. As she swam laps, some part of her ached like a swallowed stone. She remembered the laughing about Leonard. The ease with which Robin could let go, see through him, move on, while she still held on in some secret place in her heart she was ashamed of, the place where she still loved him totally in spite of every betrayal. Perhaps in imagination and longing, love was perfect.

Exactly.

Turning off the light that night, she thought something was not right about the room, but she hadn't been able to think what it was, even after she turned the light back on. It wasn't until morning that she'd thought, *the dress. Now, where is that dress? I'm sure I draped it over that chair.*

The knock at the door came as she was boiling water for coffee in a small saucepan. She wasn't even dressed yet. Leonard burst in, agitated. "It's Robin, it's Robin," he stuttered. "Something's happened. The police called."

Nyia threw on jeans and sweater; the taxi was waiting by the hotel. They bumped over the clean, rinsed morning streets, chickens scattering in the dust as they pulled into Santiago. The police were already there, no red lights flashing, only small white cars with black stripes. Leonard strode over to them, spoke in halting Spanish, then covered his face with his palm.

Nyia entered the alley where they had shot that final scene. She could see the police hovering near the side of a building by some trash barrels. Leonard turned from the police and came to her side. "Robin's dead, Nyia. Someone shot her."

Nyia was still a moment, and heat broke through her body like a fever. Then the tears came up and the urge to vomit. She coughed the crying out like it was a sickness, bent over at the waist. Leonard grabbed her arm, pulled her tightly into his arms and she let him hold her in the breaking of it.

Sometime later, the police wagon arrived. In the commotion, Leonard had dropped his coin. Nyia spotted it at the edge of a puddle, picked it up and handed it to him. A brown wool blanket was pulled off the body for a moment as they lifted Robin. In that moment Nyia drank it in: Robin's eyes blank as stones, mouth open, yellow hair loose; the black dress with the satin bodice, the bare shoulders, arms stiff now, the body curled in on itself. The back of her head matted. Dark clotted ropes of hair saturated in blood.

"She looks like me," Nyia whispered to Leonard.

"What?"

"She's my double. She's wearing my dress. She's playing Jane. That's my scene."

Nyia stayed with Leonard throughout the day while Mirina went to the airport to wait for Robin's parents. She was with Leonard again for a time after that; they could not seem to help it. Back in L.A., the film was edited to completion. She went on to Brazil to star in

Manuel Moravio's film. The next time she received a letter from her fan, she was in the Amazon delta, playing a bird in a dream.

Nyia headed back to Leonard's ranch from her silent walk along the creekbed. She glanced at her watch. Nearly time to meet Harm Bohland, show him the letters.

She opened this most recent one, still folded in her pocket. The black dot of a hawk drifted in the wind above the foothill. *Just thinking of it, I could die,* the letter said. He was coming, he may already be in New Mexico.

So what am I doing here? she thought.

WHEN HE SEES THE ARTICLE IN THE SANTA FE *paper,* The New Mexican, *he realizes he's made a terrible mistake. He never should have involved another person. He just doesn't think sometimes, he gets carried away by the idea of the scene and he doesn't think about the consequences. It was just a small article, sniper fires at cars on road, not even mentioning who it was that was shot at. Anyone having information about this should contact the police.*

As he drives out to Madrid, it is with the idea that he will talk to the person who drove the pickup, who agreed to let him ride in the back, who agreed to follow the car to Albuquerque that night. As he drives out to talk to him, he is thinking that what he will do is give the man some money to stay quiet. But he knows in the back of his mind, that is not what he is going to do.

He's brought the video camera. He's going to get all of this down.

In his body he can feel the difference between thinking about it and doing it. Doing it feels better. Stronger. It is this following through he has been waiting all his life for. Don't hold back. He tells himself not to hold back.

The man lives out of town in an isolated area. A shack with a corrugated tin roof. When he pulls into the yard, scrub pine, mountains behind, he films the house. A dog on the steps looks up, doesn't even bark. The man comes from around the corner, wiping his hands on a rag.

"What are you doing with that videocam?" the man yells. His voice is loud. "What are you taking pictures of, man?"

He realizes that he won't have much time. He puts the camera in the car and reaches for the rifle. He remembers for an instant all the times he did not follow through and the one time he did, but it was the wrong person. How he was always fucking up.

The man shouts again. "What do you want, anyway?" It's like he knows something is wrong, but nothing is obvious yet. That's the way to do it, keep it low-key.

So he just stands up straight then, wheels around, and fires the gun into the man's chest. The man is knocked back a little by the blow, that weird instant of total confusion, not knowing what is going on. He has enough life left in him to touch his chest where the bullet entered, the man steps back once. He almost fires again, but then the man falls. He waits a minute. The dog trots over to sniff at the man. He shoots the dog.

He picks up the empty case ejected from the gun, wipes the gun off and puts it back in the car. The air around the house is quiet and full of the wind. No one is coming, but he hurries anyway, dragging the man into the house and into the bedroom. For some reason he puts the man in bed. He goes around the house smashing things up—it's a mess anyway, what difference does it make? There's a bird in a cage by the window, some kind of pigeon or dove. He used to watch his grandmother on the farm with the chickens, twisting them in a sudden jerk. He knows how to do it and he does.

The place looks good, just right. Authentic. He wants to

remember how the scene looks. There still seems to be no one coming. He runs to the car for the camera and films the yard again, the dog, the trail where the body dragged over the dirt. In the house, filming the mess. The man in the bed. Filming him there. For a minute he's afraid the man is still alive. There's a gurgle in the man's throat like he's trying to speak: Maybe he is trying to speak.

He doesn't know if the man is alive or dead. He puts a pillow over the man's face and presses down. When he checks again after a few minutes the gurgling has stopped.

He films the bedroom and the man's face.

As he is closing the front door, he thinks of something he wants to take with him. It will be a gift for her. There is a good knife in the kitchen drawer and he goes to the bird cage. His grandmother also taught him to do this.

The door locks behind him. He decides he can just leave the dog there. It will look like a burglary. But the trail in the dirt doesn't look right. He rips off a pine branch and sweeps over the path the body left. There. That looks better. Just before he leaves, he films the scene again.

This is much better, he realizes. No more walk-ons or script consultations. It's becoming a sort of documentary.

Then he drives back north, past Santa Fe to Tesuque, to the road that goes past the ranch, and waits there. He feels better just seeing her return from a walk along the creek. He's not going to let her out of his sight now.

FIVE

HARM BOHLAND REACHED FOR A TACK IN THE open desk drawer and knocked the cup onto the floor, where it broke sharply in a few pieces, coffee splashing across the linoleum onto a pile of file folders. He'd had the cup over ten years, his FBI cup, cracked though it was. It had almost jumped off the edge of that goddamn desk. He thought better of picking up the jagged pieces, and swept them into a dustpan instead. He didn't want to cut himself.

He returned to the empty bulletin board behind his desk, where he was tacking up index cards inscribed with *the facts*. That's how he liked to think of them. He had an appreciation for pieces of indisputable information, significant or trivial, it didn't matter. A case often began with a few significant facts, the trivial ones followed. Watch the trivia, he reminded himself. Things were likely to be hidden in insignificance.

He would stick the cards up on the board, square white islands separated by a sea of cork. More squares would be added as he investigated, then more, until a pattern, a grid, a connection would emerge.

It gave him a feeling of accomplishment to see the case growing on the wall behind his desk. It was proof of something; he knew a few things, one or two at least. Stare at that bulletin board and then at the traffic on Cerrillos out the storefront office through the glass, streaked in the afternoon sun. His accounting background had trained him to be logical, but he knew the real discoveries in this work happened in the spaces between facts, in that distance between one truth and another.

Side by side, the cards read:

November 4, 1988—Robin Reese killed—Manzanillo, Mexico. Shot in the back of the head while on location to film *Dead Heat*. Weapon used: Winchester .30-30 rifle. Soft-point bullet recovered from body, helical grooves on bullet jacket indicating type of weapon used.

April 17, 1989—Nyia Wyatt assaulted by intruder in her Laurel Canyon home during week of grand jury investigation into Robin Reese murder. Person: male, masked. Weapon used: Probably a .38 revolver. Six unused live cartridges recovered on premises.

Monday, June 25, 1990—Nyia Wyatt's car shot at on Turquoise Trail, Madrid, New Mexico. Weapon used:

He'd left that final weapon question unanswered. That information would be supplied by Americo Quintana of the Santa Fe Police Department. His friend, Buddy Hirsch, of the Los Angeles Police Department, might be able to ferret out additional

information about the Laurel Canyon break-in. He and
Hirsch had worked together on a number of cases in
which the FBI and the LAPD had cooperated. Bud
would be surprised to hear from him. Harm sat back in
the creaking swivel chair and read again the articles
Leonard Jacobs had copied for him.

At first, Mexican authorities had considered Robin
Reese's murder a mugging; later the Manzanillo police
surmised it might have been drug-related. She was
found without purse or shoes, facedown behind a row
of stores in the small barrio of Santiago where the film
crew had been working that day. Her purse and shoes
were found later in garbage barrels outside the club
where she had been drinking. The killing did not
involve a sexual assault. The gun had been fired at a
range of approximately one hundred yards, the bullet
entering the back left side of the lower skull.

That didn't sound like a mugging, Harm thought.
Shootings that occurred during muggings were usually
up close and body wounds, not head wounds. In execu-
tion-style killings, the gun was most often placed at
the temple or forehead. Someone had fired at Robin
Reese from a distance; she'd been a moving target.
Perhaps she'd been running away, her back turned
toward her assailant. Perhaps the person had been
following her or driving by. But how likely was that in
an alley?

Her death was publicized in a number of articles in
the file. Harm read through them quickly. No new
information, but they'd sure kept it in the press. There
had been a lot of coverage, the murder and the film taking on some kind of cult status. Next were clippings
regarding a suit filed by the woman's family claiming
Leonard and Mirina Jacobs and Visionfilm Studios were
negligent in the death of their daughter.

Jacobs had included a *People* magazine article featuring a photograph of Reese's parents on their living
room couch in their Pasadena home, holding a high

school portrait of Robin between them. Their faces revealed two bitter, grieving parents searching for someone to blame. They admitted that Robin had once been in treatment for alcoholism, but to their knowledge was not a drug user.

A photo on the next page of the magazine showed Nyia Wyatt on Leonard Jacobs's arm at a Hollywood fundraiser for literacy. "Nyia Wyatt escorted by longtime companion, director Leonard Jacobs," the caption read. Harm paused, read the caption again.

So they were lovers, he thought. *Of course.* He remembered how Nyia had sat in Jacobs's office chair, so comfortable there in an intimate way. Legs crossed, leather dress up to her thighs.

Motive. He wanted to leap ahead to that. From facts to motive. From what happened to why. Sometimes the why came to him first and he had to work backwards to the facts. He decided to start a question file and wrote on a white card: "Are Nyia and Jacobs still lovers? Does Mirina Jacobs know? What did Robin Reese have to do with any of that?"

A final article in the *Los Angeles Times* reported that the Reese case had been dropped. *Variety* ran a piece about the difficulty in getting insurance for making movies. Liability costs were forcing independent filmmakers out of business.

Suddenly he felt frustrated being here in Santa Fe. He liked to interview people, and if he were in L.A., he'd drive right out to the Reeses' in Pasadena; he'd look up this Sand character, who'd served time after Jacobs testified against him. But that would have to wait a few days, a week even, until the filming of *Trial and Error* was complete. In the meantime, there was Nyia Wyatt herself to interview, Quintana, the officer who'd delivered her back to the ranch last night, and the Jacobses themselves. Harm felt uneasy and he wasn't sure why.

The phone rang and he yanked it up to his ear.

"Bohland and Associates, Accounting and Investigation," he said. There were no associates, but it sounded better that way.

"Yo, Dad. It's me."

"Hey, Nickie! Are we all set for Friday?"

"Yeah, but I got a baseball game tomorrow night. Can you come?"

Tomorrow, tomorrow: the Jacobses' dinner party. What time did that start? Nickie was nine, summer and baseball were eternal, and he'd gotten the kid a new mitt for his birthday last March. "I could come for at least an hour, how's that?"

"Only an hour?" An exasperated sigh followed.

Harm had moved to Santa Fe a year ago just to be with Nickie more. His ex-wife, Sandy, had been pissed. *Moved out here to get away from you, not to have you follow me around the rest of my life. It's not you I want to see,* he'd said. *Seeing you at all just hurts,* she'd said. He thought so too. But it hurt more not seeing Nickie. He couldn't bear being away from his kid. And he'd been devoted, probably saw him more now than when he lived with him, the hours he'd worked before, the weekends, the evenings.

"It'll have to be an hour," he said. "But Nick, my new case, the people are making a movie. Maybe I can get you on the set. Would you like that?"

"Yeah. Sure, Dad."

"Are you mad I can't come for the whole game?"

A silence. "It's okay. I'll make you pay."

Harm smiled. *There's the kid.* "Oh, yeah? How?"

"I challenge you to a two-hour Mega Man Nintendo duel on Friday night, and you can't say your eyes are blurring out."

"Deal," said Harm.

"The game starts at six."

"Be there."

"Or be square," said Nickie. "Later, Dad."

Harm Bohland glanced at his watch. He should

have time to make it to the body shop where the Mercedes had been towed and to the Santa Fe library before he met Nyia Wyatt. He placed Jacobs's file in his briefcase, turned on the answering machine and looked once more at the index cards on the bulletin board. Soon there'd be more.

When the next call came in, he let the machine click on, waiting to see if it was important before answering. The woman's low voice sounded both authoritative and sexy. Slight Southern accent, Carolinas maybe.

"Mr. Bohland, this is Suzanne Scolfield calling from Santa Monica. I'm Nyia Wyatt's manager. She just called about this shooting and I am extremely concerned and would like to speak to you directly about this matter."

Harm picked up the phone, interrupting her taped message. "Bohland here," he said.

"Oh, thank God, a human voice. I just have a thing about a human voice answering a phone. It's such a relief. Anyway. I'm just very concerned about Nyia. Leonard Jacobs, true to form, is not returning my calls; Nyia tells me they've hired a detective, namely you, and I just want to know what in God's name is going on. I want to be kept apprised of the situation." The woman spoke clearly and slowly.

"To tell you the truth, Ms. Scolfield, I've just been hired this morning. I've been reviewing the case. I'm just heading out now to take a look at Miss Wyatt's car and then to meet with her."

"She said she was shot at."

"Her car was shot at, that's correct." He'd have to be careful here, confidentiality and all. And the fact that Jacobs wanted even more discretion during these initial days of investigation.

"A sniper, Nyia said."

"The police think that's a possibility. I don't have a lot to go on at this point. By tomorrow, Nyia could have some more information for you." Noncommittal. Throw it back to Nyia. He wondered what this Scolfield knew about Robin Reese. "Seems like this kind of thing has happened before during Visionfilm productions," he said. "Tell me, was Nyia Wyatt your client during the making of *Dead Heat* down in Manzanillo?"

"Oh, that was so tragic. Personally, I thought Nyia should have stayed away from that film. This one, too, for that matter. Nyia's big now, these Visionfilm projects are far too small for her. But she was under contract to do two more. *Dead Heat* and *Trial and Error* fulfill her contractual obligations to Visionfilm. Then she'll be free. Free as a bird. There's just always some kind of trouble around Leonard Jacobs, has been from the start."

"What kind of trouble?"

"Well, financial, of course. Visionfilm almost went belly up—Leonard made sure his partner took the hit for that fiasco. I don't know where he got backing for this one. Of course, Nyia Wyatt is money in the bank now and he knows it. Then there's just the whole area of, shall we say, personal relationships. Visionfilm is known for being practically incestuous—and just when my client gets straightened out about all that, back she goes into the snakepit.

"I just don't understand it, frankly. She can work with Lumet, Bertolucci, Wender, or any of the commercial studios. Disney is interested in a whole series of things with her. I tell her she's wasting her time with these avant-garde things. But a contract is a contract and maybe it's just as well she gets it out of the way now. I just don't want her to get caught up in anything dangerous. That's my concern."

"Did you feel Nyia was in any kind of danger prior to her coming out here to do this film?" Harm asked.

Scolfield paused and he heard the hiss of a match,

then the exhalation of cigarette smoke. "Let's just put it this way. Leonard Jacobs is known for pushing everyone to the limit and sometimes that has a detrimental effect on the people involved."

"Robin Reese's family thought that Jacobs was directly responsible in some way for their daughter's death. What do you think about that?"

"Responsibility and negligence—that can be a fine line, can't it, Mr. Bohland?" answered Scolfield. "What Leonard does is create a whole dark little world around his films. And some people just lose it in that world. Lose themselves. You know what I mean? I think that happened to Robin. But as far as Robin's death, I guess it couldn't really have been Leonard's fault. Not directly. Why was Robin out wandering around the back streets of a Mexican town in the first place, playing a character outside the time they were actually filming? You know? It was like she just didn't know when to stop acting. You could say she stepped into some pretty dangerous circumstances because she lost sight of the difference between her character and her own self. I guess Leonard can't really be held responsible for what adults do, but he definitely sets the stage for psychological distress. That's what I think and you can quote me on it."

"Well, Mr. Jacobs does seem to be taking steps to secure the set down here and to look into the situation," said Harm. "I'm sure he'll be happy to keep you posted on any developments regarding Nyia's welfare."

"Mr. Bohland, Mr. Jacobs and I are not on speaking terms. We mostly communicate through lawyers. That's exactly why I'm calling you. I just want you to get in touch with me day or night if anything, anything at all, comes up that puts my client in a compromised position. Will you do that?"

Scolfield was assertive under that lilting Southern voice. He bet she was a good manager, the watch-dog type.

"Why lawyers?" asked Harm.

"It's a long story. Let's just say that at one time Leonard Jacobs more or less owned Nyia Wyatt, lock, stock, and soul. She wanted someone else to manage her affairs and it took him a little while to get used to that. I guess that's all I can say about it without going too far."

"I understand the need for confidentiality," he offered.

"My other concern is the media," said Suzanne Scolfield. "They're just going to be picking up on this thing like wildfire."

"Mr. Jacobs is also concerned about discretion," said Harm. "I don't think he's going to want a lot of media coverage on this. I think he's going to be keeping a lid on it."

"Well, just tell him that Dierdre is coming out to cover the story," said Scolfield. "Dierdre Fine. He'll know. Now, here's my answering service number, call me day or night, twenty-four hours. I do not want to be left out in the cold. Are we clear on this?" she demanded.

Harm jotted down the number. "All clear," he said. Then hung up, rubbing his ear. Jesus. Yes, ma'am. He wondered if Nyia had any trouble being managed by such a strong personality. There was definitely tension between her director and her manager. It was obvious that Nyia must have been caught up in the middle at some point. It wasn't until he was in the Jeep, halfway toward the plaza, that he realized Scolfield had seemed both concerned about media coverage and setting it up. Who was Dierdre Fine, anyway?

Serrano Body Shop was only minutes from the plaza at the center of downtown Santa Fe, but it could just as well have been at the outskirts of any small New Mexico town. The gravel yard was surrounded by a high cyclone fence, the garage building set back from the street. In the open yard, cars with missing wheels were set up on cinder blocks. Men in sleeveless shirts sat around on milk crates, taking a break. An old refrigerator tilted out in front of the office, and in the center of the yard in the shade of an old cottonwood sat a single yellow dinette chair. Metal clanged and a motor revved in the dark garage.

Inside the office, Harm nodded toward a man with a big belly, wearing a clean white shirt. "I'm here to look at the Mercedes," Harm said, opening his identification for the man to see.

The man glanced at the ID only briefly, then nodded toward the back. "Sure," he said. "Go ahead and take a look. We haven't had a chance to work on her yet." He handed Harm a key on a wire with a cardboard tag.

The Mercedes was parked out back between a Porsche and a rusty pickup with half a paint job. The safety glass in the windshield had held around the bullet hole in a web of shattered glass. Harm unlocked the front door and peered in at the cream-colored leather seats. The man in the white shirt came up behind him. "Yeah, the cops dug that bullet out already. See where it went through? Right there." He pointed a brown leathery hand.

Damn. Harm would have liked to have seen the bullet hole before they ripped into the seat. But even so it was pretty clear geometry: windshield hole to mid-front seat, straight down the middle. This car had not been shot at by some sniper on a side hill. He could see right off that the shot would have had to have come at more of an angle in that case, even in through a side window. Unless she'd been on a very sharp curve, ninety degrees maybe, and the gunshot coming from somewhere slightly raised, directly in front of her.

No. He would bet anything the car was fired at from a vehicle in front of the Mercedes at a range of fifty to a hundred feet. But there was nothing about another vehicle in Jacobs's typed report.

Harm glanced in the back seat and picked up a single sheet of paper.

Christine: it read. *Did you sleep with her? Just answer me.*

Hank: What—on the day of my wedding? Did you ever hear of something called human decency?

Christine: It's the first time I heard it mentioned in regard to screwing around on your bride of four hours and thirty-seven minutes.

Hank, looking at watch: Six. Six hours and twenty-two minutes. And I can hardly wait for the rest of my life to unfold before my very eyes.

Harm slammed the back door of the Mercedes and the windshield sagged a little further inward.

"Thanks," he told the man in the white shirt, handing him the key.

The Jeep was already hot and he drove quickly toward the plaza, pulling over to park near the Galisteo Newsstand. He'd walk the rest of the way to the library from there, cut through the plaza. He liked the walk.

The square plaza at the center of Santa Fe was bordered by the Palace of the Governors on one side and rows of adobe shops on the others. An American flag and the flag of New Mexico, yellow with a red zia, hung over the large building, and on the sidewalk under its portico, Indians from the pueblos sat in the shade with silver and turquoise, pottery, dolls, and beadwork spread on blankets before them. There was an obelisk at the center of the square with a spiked fence surrounding it, the whole plaza a pattern of patio stones and brick slate walkways angling across, leading to the center.

As Harm Bohland crossed, a flock of purple pigeons lifted off and circled over the plaza in formation, coming to rest simultaneously in a tree near the art museum. The white pillars on the veranda of the Palace of the Governors stood out against the dark shadowed archways, curved shadows from the *vegas* extending from the portico. He smelled fried food and it made him hungry. Above the town, the mountains were blue in the June light of late afternoon. God, this was a pretty town. There was even a chance he could be happy here. He knew it occasionally, but it was an unfamiliar feeling and he pushed it away.

The Santa Fe Public Library was several blocks off the plaza in a rosy building. Harm went to the basement and sat before a microfilm machine for a half hour, sliding the little arrow around and squinting at the blurry print. He was curious to see what Leonard Jacobs might have left out of his file of clippings. It appeared that he'd included every article the *Los Angeles Times* had run on the Reese murder and the subsequent grand jury investigation.

Back upstairs he checked references to both of the Jacobses and Nyia Wyatt in *American Film, Vanity Fair,* and *Vogue.* It looked as if there was a good article on Leonard Jacobs in *Los Angeles Magazine,* but the Santa Fe library didn't carry that one. He'd have it faxed from L.A.

As he read, he found himself starting a third pile of index cards in addition to *Facts* and *Questions.* These cards were notes on filmmaking; it came to him that as of tomorrow on the set he needed to appear as something of an expert on post-modern filmmaking technique, about which he now knew approximately three things: video was taking over .35 millimeter as the technology of choice, image often took precedence over plot, and scripts were considered gestalts of character study, not rigid maps of lines to be read, whatever the hell that meant.

The *Village Voice* had an interesting profile on both

Jacobses, printed a year or so back. A photograph portrayed them looking tender in their Paris apartment, embracing on a small balcony, the roofs of Montmartre below.

Mirina, the article noted, was an expatriate Czech screenwriter who had once been Leonard Jacobs's professor at NYU. Little-heard-of outside film circles in America, she was revered in Europe, considered a grande dame of elegant, sexy movies with subtitles. She was almost fifteen years older than her husband, in her late fifties now.

The article commented on Leonard Jacobs's use of heightened emotions, fragments, and dissociation in editing. A cubist of films, the writer called him. Made movies by breaking things down and apart, both in the finished product, and in the process of making the film itself, in the way he pushed the actors and altered the script as the film progressed. There was some controversy about his methods after Robin Reese had been killed.

But, apparently, this experience was common to other filmmakers, not just Leonard Jacobs. The writer quoted a *Vanity Fair* interview with Angelica Huston, who commented that her life often followed the plot of movies she'd made. After playing a character whose husband has a child by another woman, her lover, Jack Nicholson, did exactly that. Harm read, "'It's odd,' says Huston over lunch in a favorite Italian restaurant, 'how circumstances in my life run parallel to my work in film. You start to deal with guns, and guns come up in life. It *does* invoke something. You have to be careful; you really have to be careful.'"

But the Jacobses, it seemed, were known for making much more of this mirror effect, playing off it during the actual making of the film. Harm stretched and rubbed his eyes, looking briefly over his notes. All this would help him carry on a coherent conversation at the

Jacobses' cocktail party tomorrow, but what about the case? He thought of the other actors in the Visionfilm ensemble, those who'd also been down in Manzanillo. He went upstairs again and checked cross-references on Jack Drieser and Tess Juran.

Skimming an article in *Variety,* his eyes rested on a small headline CONTRACTUAL DISPUTES PLAGUE VISIONFILM. According to the article, Tess Juran had been hired as lead in *Dead Heat,* but had emotional problems that left her unable to work. Nyia Wyatt, longtime Visionfilm ensemble member and Jacobs's protégée, was brought in to take over the lead. So Jacobs had not originally intended to use Nyia in *Dead Heat.* Interesting. It was Tess Juran who was to have played the part. Tess Juran was also in *Trial and Error,* this current film, playing second lead to Nyia. Tess Juran, who was to have been picked up by Nyia at the airport last night. Tess Juran, who didn't show up at the airport, leaving Nyia to drive back to Santa Fe alone.

Juran. What did he know about her? He read further. She was young, mid-twenties. Respected as an actress, but emerging. Still breaking into adult roles, wanting access to good lead parts. Did a couple steamy things that bombed. Desiring the prestige of being associated with Visionfilm, even if the movies weren't major moneymakers. And now Juran was back in a supporting role. Her second chance, but not as lead. He'd have to ask Nyia if there were any hard feelings between them after she took over the lead in *Dead Heat.* He would no doubt meet Tess Juran on the set tomorrow and he'd sense quickly if there was any animosity between the two.

There was something about the magazine photographs that struck him, though he couldn't figure out what it was. He flipped through the pages that showed Tess Juran in a studio still, then Robin Reese in a clip from *Dead Heat.* The *People* magazine article, Nyia on Leonard Jacobs's arm. It was the dress, thought Harm.

All three women are wearing the same black dress, white satin off-the-shoulder straps, fifties style.

What was it, some dress fetish of Jacobs? Did they borrow each other's clothes? Maybe it was just because it was a costume, a dress the characters all wore. They all looked good in it.

Harm made photocopies of the articles and returned the magazines to the shelf, then walked upstairs and out into the street. Just one night until he had to go into his role as free-lance writer doing a scholarly piece on post-modern filmmakers, featuring Leonard Jacobs, master of improvisational, cut-and-paste cubistic erotic mysteries. Harm did not feel prepared for his part and doing some homework had only made him feel even less secure. Now he knew how ignorant he really was.

Strolling back across the plaza to his car, he realized he had time to kill before meeting Nyia Wyatt at the Pink Adobe. He still felt uneasy, jumpy feeling in his gut. He pressed his arm to his side to feel the gun he sometimes wore strapped inside his faded jeans jacket. He hadn't worn it today.

Pool, he thought. That and the index cards, that would calm him down. Knock a few balls around, things came together in his thinking. He drove over to the Velvet Cushion Billiard Hall across from a shopping mall, only a few minutes away from where he was to meet Nyia.

Inside he nodded to Juan, who sat behind the linoleum counter, paid for some balls and went to a table about halfway back, his favorite table, the one by the Old Milwaukee clock. In the corner, the electronic zip of a Goldwings video game. He came here often with Nickie, and the kid stuck his face in that game and didn't come out for an hour. Along the white concrete walls chairs were set up for spectators, but there weren't many today and not many players. The Velvet Cushion sign on the wall stated the rules of the place:

"Don't sit on ashtray stand. Don't sit on floor. No drugs or pushers of dope allowed in here. No radio music thanks."

Harm Bohland racked the balls and busted the rack. The balls scattered down the length of the table, and then it hit him—what the anxiety in his gut was about: stage fright. Acting. An undercover role required acting and that had once nearly been the end of him. He clenched his teeth as he thought of it. It was funny—his original inspiration to join the FBI had been an actor, Robert Stack as Elliot Ness on "The Untouchables." Hell, half his boyhood had been spent in that fantasy.

He'd started out after college as an accountant, then a CPA, adding an MBA on after that, night school yet another way to keep busy, stay obsessed with work. After he'd testified for the government in a wire-transfer embezzlement case, he got hooked on the idea of working for the FBI. They'd recruited him, said he had a good mind for that sort of thing.

He should have known better, of course. He'd pictured the job all intrigue, sneaking around dark corners, flipping a badge out of a suitcoat pocket. Unfortunately, he'd ended up in the division that investigated white-collar and organized crime by auditing tax returns. So what else was new? Irregularities in expense accounts, phony loopholes, money-laundering schemes, bogus business, too many accounts in the Cayman Islands. Very large losses on feature films never made by foreign companies with no office. Names like Frère Brothers—in French: the Brother Brothers. Sure.

For years in the L.A. office he'd dreamed of doing fieldwork, strapping a snubnosed .38 under his arm in a thin leather holster, trailing some guy downtown while the sun shined. Then he'd gotten his chance. He was called in on a case that required a financial expert at a meeting with crime figures out in Arizona. It was an undercover operation, a sting involving a group selling arms, then diverting profits into a chain of motels across the western states. In fact, the code name of the sting was "Operation: Blue Motel."

The federal government was arranging to buy the motels, then they'd seize the books and arrest the participants. Harm's job was to be the expert government witness—incognito. No one knew the feds were the buyers. He would review the books and records of the proposed sellers, and if the evidence was juicy, he would indicate it to the waiting agents filming the meeting through a hole in the motel wall. But everything went to hell.

He still remembered the odd euphoria he'd felt when he didn't know he'd been shot but heard the blast. He'd slid down to the floor as federal agents and crooks in expensive leisure-wear traded gunfire across the parking lot. He remembered reaching behind him to touch the pool of blood on the tiles. The blood was warm and that had made him stupidly happy. The last thing he had noticed before he blacked out was how dry the scraggly palm trees looked outside the motel door. By the time they got him to the emergency room, he was almost dead.

He'd recuperated in a hospital back in L.A., recovering from a ruptured lung. One afternoon when his wife came in to visit him, she announced she was moving to Santa Fe, filing for divorce, and taking Nickie with her. Said she was sorry about the timing and all, what with his getting shot at, but that he was an absentee father anyway, never home much and Nickie would be better off having actual visits with him than growing up with a father who was just a ghost. Said he had an intimacy-avoidance problem and was a case of arrested growth and that life was not just a list of numbers that could be perfectly added up. Logic taken to an extreme would always equal chaos, she told him.

Harm Bohland had celebrated his fortieth birthday by himself in a deer blind up in Big Sur. Shivering in an early snow in the dark pines, he'd just looked straight at his life and saw it, for an instant, as it was. His by-then ex-wife had been right; he'd fucked love up bad by forgetting it was there. He'd pushed hard those years just to sit in an office with a calculator in a left-brain daze and dream of being an investigator, and what had he gotten for it but a hole in his back and child-support payments?

So he gave notice, sold most of his possessions, except his record collection from the sixties and he didn't give a damn if turntables were becoming obsolete. He drove out to Santa Fe pulling a U-Haul, opened his office, and started all over again in the beauty of the sage and the chamiso and the big blue vault of that giant New Mexico sky.

But the thought of acting again was making him a little sick. Tomorrow he was going to have to act around a bunch of professional actors and he was going to fucking blow it. The last time he had tried to be anything but Harmon E. Bohland, he'd ended up on that motel room floor in a lake of blood watching the earth shrink to the size of a pretty marble. Floating out there in the black spot of the hole in his chest waiting for an angel. Who, by the way, never came. None of those shining lights and beautiful voices greeting him at death's door. Just a blue marble and a black spot. And the thought, *That's all, folks,* straight out of his cartoon childhood.

He lined up the shot, drew back his cue, and the balls scattered, rebounding off the rail. Then he thought of Nyia in her purple dress—the strange realization that she wasn't a generic face on a magazine cover. She couldn't be reduced to a photo in a grocery store magazine. She was a human being, a frightened one. She had a story to tell and he was going to hear it in less than an hour. He broke another rack and listened to the cold balls clack together in the empty hall.

SIX

THE FEELING STRUCK HER AS SHE BENT TO LOCK the rental car. That sensation of someone looking over her shoulder, or quietly entering a room behind her, turning to see a shadow move just out of sight. A knot at the back of her hairline unraveled across her shoulders and back in a quiver. Last night when she had felt this, the shot came just after, and the car flew off the road.

Nyia slowly turned to face the parking lot, peering toward the round state capitol building, then over a crumbling adobe wall in front of the car. The parking lot was deserted; she was alone. She came around the corner toward the restaurant, surveying the street one last time, San Miguel Chapel along Old Santa Fe Trail, shops closed in early evening. Story coming alive in her: Leonard's good sign. Those days were gone. Now the halo glow around the story suggested a migraine vision, anxious pressure in her skull. Cars parked up and down the block appeared empty. For some reason she blew a kiss, as if to an invisible lover down the quiet street.

Her cheeks were hot as she entered the courtyard between the bar and dining area of the Pink Adobe. She saw it now, how she could flip into acting, creating, in a single instant, whole imaginary worlds. Maybe her entire life had been imaginary until now.

That feeling of being watched—the truth was, she'd always loved it. Being at the center, turning to kiss the fear, push into the scene and improvise, darling, improvise. What was acting but that?

She took a seat by a window, set down the packet of letters and ordered a margarita. When it came she squeezed the triangle of lime into the foam and licked her fingers. Through the two rows of skylights, the dusk was cobalt. At the corner of the heavy wooden bar a tree extended up through the ceiling. The bar, crowded at cocktail hour, was decorated in folk-art dragons, a large, wild yellow-and-red face grinned through the piano jazz on the stereo. She stared out the small arched window by her table and was startled at his voice beside her.

"You look completely different." Harm Bohland had walked in through the French doors that faced the courtyard and come over to her table. He pulled out the chair opposite her and sat down, signaling the waitress. "It's your hair. And the glasses, the lipstick. So, is this the real you?"

Nyia's hair was combed back tightly into a French braid. She wore a smear of wine-red lipstick and black wire-frame glasses, baggy gray pants tucked into short brown boots and an oversized stretched-out black turtleneck belted low at the waist.

"More me than strapless leather, you mean? They're all me. I've got a lot of costumes. That's my job."

"I can see that."

A small candle burned in a glass between them. She was surprised that she felt so attracted to him. He wore a denim shirt with western snaps; his blond hair was a little long, falling over one eye; he pushed it back with his big hand. What was it about him? He was nice-looking in an ordinary way, chin stubble, kind brown eyes. Maybe it was the calm she felt in him, steady like a good doctor. She trusted him. People outside the business were who they were. No duplicity, no acting. No using their faces to get something. For a second, she wished they were just two travelers meeting in Santa Fe for the first time. Another fantasy, she thought. Just stay real. His gaze was direct and he did not look away from her.

"I'm very relieved Leonard agreed to hire someone to look into all of this, but all day I've been thinking—why did I wait for him to do it?" She ate some of the popcorn a waitress had set on the table. "I have to admit I wish I'd just hired you myself."

"Why?"

"It would be simpler. I want you to work for me, not Leonard."

Harm looked at her quizzically.

"I feel that to some extent Leonard sees these 'incidents,' as he likes to call them—incidents such as being shot at, someone breaking into my house and assaulting me, not to mention murder—as someone trying to sabotage his films. That hiring you is one way of protecting his business interests and also as something that will pacify me, take care of my state of mind, so I won't screw up. But I think the whole thing is much more simple. I believe someone wants to kill me." Nyia found herself smiling. How incongruous, she thought. And knew then how nervous and scared she was. Harm Bohland took out a legal-size tablet and wrote down the date at the top of the page.

"Things just start to add up," Nyia said. "A good

friend of mine was killed wearing my clothing. We looked so much alike, we were cast as doubles in the film. My house was broken into, I was assaulted. Last night I was shot at again, twice. Now I'm supposed to calm down and complete my final week of filming so my director won't go over budget."

Harm shoved a file across the table and she opened it—newspaper clippings faxed from Visionfilm's L.A. office. She'd read them all before.

"I've been reading about Robin Reese all afternoon," said Harm. "What can you tell me that's not in these? And what's this about the clothing? It wasn't this dress, was it?" He pushed three copies of photographs of Tess Juran, Robin Reese, and herself all wearing the black dress. Nyia picked up the *People* magazine photo. She'd forgotten that she'd been photographed in that dress, that it was a matter of public record.

"That's the one," she said. "Leonard bought it for me. A few months before he started filming *Dead Heat*, he asked to borrow the dress. He pictured the lead character wearing it. I gave it to him, I didn't want it anymore. It went into costume. But of course, it was still my dress. I guess that's why I brought the dress back to the condo with me." Nyia told Harm about Robin staying with her that night, wearing the dress without asking the night she was killed. "Some part of me has always thought it was supposed to have been me that was killed that night. The shrink I was seeing said I was compensating. Trying to relieve my grief by thinking it was my fault. Like, if I'd never brought the dress back to where we were staying . . . . If she hadn't been staying with me . . . If only I had worn the dress . . . He said that if I could accept the blame for her death, then some part of me could think I could go back and prevent it. It was some way I kept from accepting reality. He was probably right."

"What else?" asked Harm.

"All the 'incidents'—Robin's death, the break-in and assault, and what happened last night—all exactly parallel scripts I'm either working on or reading. As if the scenes in the screenplays are acted out in real life."

Harm was looking at her oddly. Please believe me, she thought.

"Have you heard of it?" she asked. "Synchronicity? It's a Jungian concept—that our lives have underlying patterns much bigger than what we perceive, that connections are made between random events and that's what creates meaning in our lives. Like you come across a word you've just learned the definition of—now you see it everywhere. Or you have a dream about a red car. The next day someone picks you up in a red car. You read an old love letter. Suddenly after years of not hearing from her, your old lover gets in touch with you. Hasn't anything like that ever happened to you?"

"Maybe," he said. "But if it did I probably didn't notice it. Once when I was playing pool at a bar my last ball went in just as the Broncos scored a touchdown. Do you want another drink?"

She shook her head. "Just spring water, please. Otherwise I'll look puffy for the camera. Hazards of the job."

"Sounds like one of the lesser hazards to me. So you're saying Robin's death paralleled somewhat the plot of *Dead Heat?*"

"Not somewhat. Exactly. The character—my character—argued in a bar with a man, left the bar, and was shot in a back street."

"Did anyone else besides you see the similarity?"

"Everyone did. Leonard and Mirina—they all saw it but they also denied it. They couldn't afford to admit the connection was so obvious. And this film we're doing now—there's violence in it too. Tomorrow I do a scene where a kerosene lamp falls over in a motel room and there's a fire. Later, a car stalls on a train track and is destroyed. Do you see what I'm getting at?"

"Tell me about this break-in at your home," Harm said. "The clippings Jacobs gave me on that were pretty scanty. Was anyone ever arrested?"

She shook her head. "It happened during the grand jury investigation into Robin's death. I was supposed to have gone to a dinner party that night, but I didn't feel up to it. I'd been with lawyers all day and I was reading a script I really liked. All I wanted to do was go home and read. I have an office at my house, a little reading room with a couch in it and a desk. I fell asleep there, with the script across my chest. When I woke up, this man . . . he had no idea I was in there—the couch faced the window away from the desk, and he was behind me rummaging through my desk and shelves. I didn't even think about hiding or staying still. I sat straight up and looked at him."

Nyia stopped. Story, she thought. She could go into it again, that quick. Replay the whole thing. Enter it. She breathed in, exhaled slowly and went on.

"He wore a ski mask and a long, dark-green raincoat. When he saw me he ran out. There was another door through a small bathroom that led into my bedroom and I snuck through there. I kept a small can of mace in the drawer beside my bed and I went for it. Just then he came at me from behind. He got the mace, of course, got me in the face with it. I was screaming, my eyes burning from the chemical. He pressed his hand over my mouth so hard my lips were bleeding. He had gloves on, brown leather gloves. I stopped resisting and just lay quiet. I was afraid he was going to rape me. I acted like I'd passed out, all limp, my eyes closed.

"Then I felt the gun. Against my temple, like the cold end of a pipe, and you know what? It wasn't anything like they say—your whole life going before you in an instant. I was just exactly where I was in this stupid bedroom at the very last moment of my life and all I could think was, what a fucking waste. Then he pulled the trigger three times. Loudest sounds I ever heard in my life. More like a clank than a click, like a huge torpedo just dropping right into my brain. One, two, three, calm as you please. Click, click, click.

"Obviously, the gun did not fire. It was like somebody playing Russian roulette with my head instead of his own. Suddenly he just let go and disappeared. I fell back to the floor and lay there, blind, really, until I was sure he wasn't coming back. I waited a long time. Then I felt for the phone up on the nightstand and called the police. I had an automatic call on the phone for 911."

"Did he take anything?"

"The office was a mess, but nothing was missing as far as I could tell. I kept thinking there had to be something missing, but I didn't know what it was."

"What about a security system?"

"It was deactivated. It had just been installed a month or two before that. I didn't make good use of it. I only turned it on when I wasn't there."

"It sounds as if you interrupted a burglary attempt and scared him off."

"That's what the police thought. But here's the thing," she said. "A week later, after everything quieted down, I finally got around to finishing reading that script. In one of the final scenes a man holds an unloaded gun to a woman's head and fires three times."

Harm squinted at her. "Who had access to that script? Who knew you had it?"

"Leonard, Mirina, practically everyone at Visionfilm, a man I was dating, a lot of people at United Artists—they were considering handling the financing—Vestron Video, the woman who wrote the script . . ."

"If the person had actually intended to kill you, don't you think they would have loaded the gun?

Leonard told me the police found the live cartridges out on the driveway in front of your house."

Nyia looked at her palms. "Okay, so maybe he was just trying to scare me. Or he was just some completely demented person. Should I be any less concerned?" Nyia finished her water. "And what happened last night, the car getting shot at, that's all in the script we're working with now. It's the same thing. Exactly the same."

She pushed the packet of letters across the table to him. There must have been fifty or sixty of them. For an instant she kept her hand on them. "Then there are these. This is what I really wanted to show you. Nobody knows about these. Nobody."

"What are they?"

"Fan letters. Love letters. All from the same person. I got the first one, let's see"—She pulled the first letter out from the packet—"1987—about three years ago. At first I thought they were just beautifully written. You don't get many fan letters that really give you something intelligent. The person who wrote them was witty, a good critic. Knew the history and theory of film. Theories on the connections between film and painting. And then . . . I don't know . . ."

She watched as Harm read the first one, nodding as he listened, silently moving his lips.

"But the last few letters have taken on a very weird tone. They cross over into some obsessive kind of thing. People just don't realize you're not your characters. I just got this one in today's mail."

Harm read the two letters quickly, scanning the pages. Nyia bent over the candle.

After he finished reading, he flipped through the envelopes. "They're postmarked from all over the world," he said. "He writes to you fifteen, twenty times a year? London, New Orleans, Toronto. He sounds vaguely psychotic. You have no idea who they're from?"

Nyia fingered the braid down the back of her head. *Okay,* she thought. *Let it go.* "The reason I kept the letters is because at one time I thought they were from Leonard. We were lovers for many years. I thought he chose to write to me in this voice because he couldn't really express his love to me in any other way. I don't know. I imagined it was him, I wanted to think it was him, I suppose. My fantasy. I began to receive them right after I broke up with him.

"Besides, he always seemed to know where I was. The letters were sometimes forwarded by the production company or the studio backing the picture or my manager's office. But sometimes they'd come directly to where I was staying, to a hotel or a post office box I'd taken out in Key West one winter. But I suppose there are a lot of people who could find out where I am at any given time."

Harm slipped the final letter back in the envelope. "Do you mind if I read through all of them?"

"Go ahead."

Harm leaned back in his chair. "So you think these separate 'incidents' are tied in with these letters, that the person writing the letters might well be Leonard Jacobs, the man who has hired me to find out who shot at you last night."

Nyia didn't want to say it out loud. She held back. She'd never even really said it to herself, not that clearly. What was she doing? He was her former lover, her friend, her teacher, her director. When had she first felt it? After Robin was killed. Finally she nodded, yes. "Maybe it sounds crazy. I don't have any proof Leonard really wrote the letters. They're all typed, there's no signature. But it all seems connected somehow. At least to me."

Harm put his hands over his eyes for a moment. "Yeah," he said. "You should have hired me yourself. This definitely complicates things."

"There's something else," said Nyia. She took a videocassette out of her bag. "I received this from my 'fan' about six months ago. Do you have a VCR? If not, there's one out at the ranch."

"I've got one." He stood. "Let's go."

The bar was crowded and dark as they made their way to the door. He said he lived close by, that he'd walked over. Nyia offered to drive and they walked in silence to her car. "Something else I need to know," he said, slamming the car door. "Does Mirina Jacobs know about your affair with her husband?"

"All the way along. She accepted it. She had her own affairs, that's the way they did their marriage. It was an open arrangement. He had other affairs after I broke off with him, he was involved with Robin Reese briefly down in Mexico, but I think she was pulling out of it. I don't think it was anything serious for either of them."

"And what about this other actress, Tess Juran? Was there any involvement between her and Leonard, is that why she left *Dead Heat* or was asked to leave?"

"The circumstances of her leaving were pretty obscure, but it's definitely a possibility."

"Who knew you were going to Albuquerque last night to pick up Tess Juran?"

Nyia glanced over at Harm in the dark car. He indicated to take a right up Acequia Madre, the street named the "mother ditch." "Just about everyone here on the production crew. We've all been waiting for Tess to come in."

"Turn here," said Harm. She pulled the car up next to an adobe wall surrounding a small house. They got out and Harm unlocked his front door, pushing it open for her. "Make yourself at home," he said. "I'll get this set up."

She liked the way he didn't wait on her. And she liked his house full of ramshackle wicker rocking chairs, brightly striped Mexican blankets tossed over a worn-out couch, books piled next to a leather chair and ottoman. She wandered down the hallway, peering in his bedroom, futon mattress, down comforter, lava lamp on the floor beside the bed. In the bathroom there were plastic Mickey Mouse figures along the edge of the tub. She hadn't realized he had kids. No wedding ring though, and no sign of a woman in the place. No creme rinse. Good, she thought, then felt suddenly shy. She was drawn to him. It felt safe here. She picked up a Donald Duck figure, then set it by the sink.

Harm called to her from a room farther down the hall. As she entered, he inserted the videocassette in the VCR slot and stood. "The entertainment suite," he said. "It's not Paramount, but it's home." He smiled. "I'm sorry, I've got to say this. I can't get over the fact that it's you. This happens to you a lot, I bet. I think if I say something about it, I'll be able to relax. Doesn't it make you mad when people get nervous around you?"

"It's kind of lonely, actually."

"I never thought of it that way."

"People don't. One day I might quit all this, go buy a ranch out in Montana or something. Write my memoirs and ride horses. Run a bar with a Wurlitzer jukebox and make french fries. Don't laugh! I really might."

"Nyia's Bar and Grill?"

"I even have a name for it. 'The Memory Lounge.' Do you like it?"

"It's good, but I don't know if it'll play in Billings. Maybe you could wallpaper the place with old articles from *People* magazine."

"And show my old movies."

"Yeah, but then you'd be you again, the famous you."

"You're right. You know, I could use you, Harm. You're kind of smart."

"Kind of?"

She smiled but felt sad for some reason. He sat down on a small sofa and she sat next to him, brushing his shoulder. She didn't pull away and neither did he. "This is the only video he's ever sent," she explained.

"And if it wasn't made by Leonard, it's someone who knows film. It's pretty sophisticated."

Harm snapped on the TV and VCR and the room filled with gray, humming light. The video opened with home movies of Nyia as a little girl, dressed in a cowgirl outfit, riding a hobby horse in front of a suburban tract house. Quickly, black-and-white snapshots: Nyia in ballerina costume, standing beside her mother with a birthday cake.

Harm paused there, held the frame still. "She looks familiar, your mother," he said.

"Carole Wyatt. 'Family Time,' 'Off and Running,' 'Been There.' Do you remember any of those old shows? Late fifties, early sixties. She did a couple of movies, one with Henry Fonda, but no one remembers her in that one. Mostly television."

"She did game shows, too, right? I didn't realize that was your mom. So you followed in her footsteps."

Nyia liked the way he said "your mom." It made Carole sound so homey, as if nothing wrong had ever happened between them. Home sweet home. "Well," Nyia admitted, "it was more like she dragged me in her footsteps. Quintessential stage mother."

Harm started the video up again. Leonard as a young director, whispering to Nyia on the set of her first film. These were her mother's home movies, transferred onto video tape. It was artfully done, stretches of black between reels, images blinking on briefly, then black again: birthday cake, her bedroom. Haunting cello music beginning now in the background. Snapshots again. Mirina and Nyia in front of the Eiffel Tower in wool coats, arms around each other. Nyia was seventeen.

Nyia spoke over the music. "Some of the photos are studio shots, pictures published along the way in various magazines. The family snapshots—there was a BBC special a few years ago on Leonard's work, he was directing a film in London at the time. He asked me for childhood pictures and I got them all from my mother. It's all public material."

A mission-style stucco house with palm trees went by in a blur from a car window. "That's where I lived with Mirina and Leonard in L.A. I was nineteen, going to method acting classes."

Harm laughed then at soundless clips of Nyia in a series of horror-movie clips, cringing back against a wall, running from a hand that held a dagger. Screaming in shot after shot, hiding in a closet.

"My exploitation period," she said. "The movie was *Pursuit.* I was trying to break from Leonard. Get into mainstream, American films. Jesus, these are awful, aren't they?"

There were more photographs, more clips that showed her developing from a thin girl with too much makeup into the face she recognized as herself now. Then back to childhood photos.

Christmas: Sitting cross-legged in front of a tinsel tree with a brand-new doll, wearing the plaid flannel robe her mother had sewn. The only thing she'd ever made for her. Denver, must have been '67 or '68.

Cut to the "Arsenio Hall Show," applause as Nyia strides out and kisses Arsenio on the cheek. She had brought him a present, a bird cage with a yellow-green parrot inside. She described it by its Latin name, *Amazona brasiliensis,* then talked about her new movie, *Wings,* shot on location in Brazil, in which she was transformed into a tropical bird in a dream sequence. She opened the door of the delicate cage and took the bird out. It perched on her hand, then flew up. The video froze there, a closer shot of the bird, blurred.

The film went to black space. Harm reached for the remote control, but Nyia put her hand on his arm. "Wait. There's more. Okay, this last bit, this is a flash-back to Cannes, two years ago. I'm meeting Leonard for lunch. We'd broken up, but we met from time to time when neither of us could stand it. So there I am waiting in that little café, right? Do you see? I mean, who knew I was going there? Who knew I would be waiting? Only Leonard. And he never came. That's what made me think he made this."

"Just a minute," said Harm. He turned the VCR back on and rewound the videocassette a few seconds, clicked it on again. The film focused in on her as she took off her jacket and sat by the café window. A garçon brought a small white menu.

"Do you see it?" asked Harm.

"What?"

"The dress. You're wearing the black dress."

Nyia looked more closely through the glass, reflections of passing cars. God, he was right. Yes. Off the shoulder, the band of white moiré at the top of the bodice. Had Leonard asked her to wear it? Had she decided on her own?

Suddenly Nyia stood. "If this is a conflict of interest," she said, "or if you don't want to do it, I just better hire someone else. Maybe you can recommend someone. I've put this off way too long. I should have done this right after Robin was killed. I just didn't want to face it. But after last night . . . You know, when I woke up today I found glass in my hair." Nyia looked down at him. "I have to do something, Harm. Will you help me?"

She watched Harm's face for an answer. The video slipped to gray static.

"That's what I'm being paid to do," he said.

WHEN THEY LEFT THE RESTAURANT, HE HAD *considered following them. He'd been watching them at the table by the window, she leaning toward him, showing him something. They were across the bar, it was crowded, he couldn't really see. He stayed hidden back by the hanging plants, exhausted from what he'd done earlier in the day. His back ached. The body had been heavier than he realized. The evening paper had no news of it. Apparently no one had found it yet.*

It's a short ride back to Tesuque. He parks up the road in a cul-de-sac and walks back along the dirt road, dogs barking behind fences and high walls. Through the corral, the high grass dry underfoot. Her cabin is dark. The door is locked, but easy to open with a knife and a push. Inside, he waits, he can smell her in this room. He sits on the bed and thinks about being with her, here in the dark. She may come soon, if she doesn't stay with the stranger.

He opens the closet and takes out her robe, spreads it out

*on the bed. He lies down next to it, puts his face next to the
material, rolls over on top of it, aligning his body to its empty
outline. Imagines her in it.*

*It's really you I want to stop, he thinks. Sometimes I
think it would be enough to stop* him, *the one who can't seem
to forget you no matter how hard he tries. That would put an
end to it forever. Kill who loves you. That might free everyone
concerned. Unless you're preparing to love someone else now.*

*It might be better, he thinks, if there is a light on. She'll
come in and think,* how nice, someone is here, waiting for
me. *She'll think it's him, of course. She'll be surprised.*

*So he unhooks the latch, the window open now for air, just
a crack, white curtains pulled across so there's privacy. Then he
lights the kerosene lamp on the table by the window, turns the
flame low.*

*The knife in his pocket juts against his leg when he sits
down on the bed beside the robe. Not the blade, it's a buck knife,
folded shut, but he takes it out anyway, snaps it open and
inserts the tip into the dark-green silk, pressing down hard.
Then he slices through it, the sound of the blade in the silk like
a quiet zipper.*

SEVEN

NYIA CIRCLED THE BACK OF SANTA FE ON THE
Paseo de Paralta and headed out toward Tesuque along
the dark foothills. She was relieved that she'd given the
letters over to Harm, let go of them. There was some way
she felt vaguely ashamed of having kept them secret so
long. It was all tied up with Leonard, she knew. She'd
invented some kind of imaginary realm in which she
could still love him, her own fiction. Her own falsehood.

A pickup's high beams flashed behind her and she
found herself veering off sharply to the shoulder, heart
slamming in her chest, but the truck cruised on ahead
into the darkness without incident. Nyia let out her
breath, pulled over onto a wide turnout in the road, cut
the lights. It was so quiet. The stars seemed exceptionally
large and white in the summer night sky. She rolled the
window down to smell the sage, wet after a late afternoon rain.

For some reason she thought of a train ride back to Paris from Barcelona. Another night journey, a leave-taking. How she'd come alone with a basket of cheese and bread, leaning against the black window of the train, the glass rain-smeared, her own vision blurred from crying. Leonard had gone on to Italy without her, to rejoin Mirina, of course, assuming Nyia would come back to him. He hadn't taken her all that seriously. Just another of Nyia's interludes from which she had always returned.

But this time she did not return. She thought about commitment on that dusty train. How it was impossible to have that with Leonard because he already had it, such as it was, with his wife. So there was only one commitment she could make in this case, one to herself. A commitment to hold to her decision against all waves of emotion, loneliness, second-guessing and stupid hopefulness. She had wished, on that bleak ride, for an ally in her decision to leave him forever.

Back in Paris, she encountered not an ally, but an enemy. Her mother, Carole. In her suite of rooms in the pension, Carole had been drunk. When Nyia told her what had happened, Carole had laughed, flopped down on a velvet divan, poured herself a glass of pre-lunch sherry. It was not yet noon.

"Don't you remember those gorgeous statues Michelangelo never finished, the ones in Florence?" Carole had asked. "That's what you remind me of, Nyia. A beautiful hunk of half-formed rock. You leave Leonard Jacobs now and it's like a stone walking away from Michelangelo."

"I'm not a rock, Mother. I'm not somebody's raw material. Not yours or Leonard's."

"But you are in *formation*, sweetheart. You are in progress, you're a rough draft, you're a blueprint, you're . . ."

Nyia had turned and looked at her mother in her black stockings and red suit, her pinkish hair and puffy eyes, that wide mouth smeared with lipstick and lined with pencil. Her suite of rooms, her masseur coming that afternoon, her tickets to the symphony that night. All paid for by Nyia. Nyia had been supporting her mother for some time now. While her mother controlled her, discounted her, insulted her, and erased her.

Carole rattled on, pleased with her own words, listening to them like some dazed politician on a roll. "Why, you are unfinished business, Nyia, and if you choose to leave yourself in this half-formed state and abandon your one and only chance for salvation, you are not merely being stupid, but silly."

Nyia backed toward the door. Her mother shrank before her as if she were looking at her backward through binoculars. Small as a plastic doll. She wanted for one instant to rush toward her, to drag her mother toward those open windows and the little, black wrought-iron balcony that looked down into the courtyard, and push her over. A moment of epiphany—no matter that most people cut from their mother at age thirteen or fourteen.

Her mother stood and stubbed out a Gauloise in a crystal ashtray. Bells were ringing in the rainy spring sky outside the pension. Noon. Must be time for more sherry, more drinks. And the oddest thing was her mother's smile. She said the most hateful things, then smiled. *I love you.* Leonard was married. *I love you.* There would be no one certain day in which it became imperative to become oneself. Nyia picked up her bag from the table by the door and left as her mother was touching up her lipstick in the gilt-edged mirror. It was exactly like that moment in the hotel room in Barcelona with Leonard. Realizing that she did not really exist to these people. She was their idea and she corroborated in being other people's ideas of herself, and she was done with all that.

On the way out, Nyia informed the concierge that payment for the suite would be discontinued as of a week from today. Madame would be paying for her own room after that. She had lunch by herself at a small café, and while her mother was out that afternoon, Nyia packed up her things and took a room at a hotel.

It was when she was getting settled that she found the business card of a woman she'd met a few weeks ago at a party in Cannes, Suzanne Scolfield. It was actually Leonard who'd introduced them. She was a personal manager, specializing in career direction in theater and film, officing out of Westwood in L.A., but in Cannes for the film festival, then off to Paris and Rome to meet with Europeans in the industry. New talent, fresh faces.

Nyia had remembered Suzanne Scolfield well. She was not a beautiful woman, but strongly handsome. Her face was narrow, with sharply defined brows and pale gray eyes in constant movement. She glanced over Nyia's shoulder as she spoke to her, scanning the room as if she were listening in on several conversations while she carried on this terribly important one with Nyia. Now that was a talent. Her striking features were oddly changeable, depending on how Nyia looked at her. Softly feminine and nearly pretty when viewed from the front, from the side she looked angular, anxious. She wore her hair long, nearly waist-length. It draped in a sleek brown sheet over her white tailored suit, swung in a shiny ripple as she turned to grab a glass of champagne from a waiter's tray. Elegant gold jewelry clinked at her wrist, a complex gold chain hung at her open throat; she had clear skin and a thin, teasing smile. She was talkative and intelligent, animated, the bracelets jangling as her hands circled the air around her talk. Somehow Nyia had thought Suzanne's looks at odds with her lilting, musical voice. She was so professional, so poised, yet her voice was seductive, even girlish, and she leaned toward Nyia as she spoke, pulling her into an easy intimacy as if they'd known each other at some Southern boarding school and had both come from Kentucky horse money.

When Leonard introduced them, he'd raved about Nyia being the next Isabel Adjani. "But she'd never need to get rid of her accent," he told Suzanne. "A European star who's American; it was brilliant, wasn't it?"

Of course, Suzanne told them both, she had long been aware of Nyia's work in Leonard and Mirina's French films. Had long been a fan. What promise Nyia Wyatt had shown, even as an adolescent. The natural sexuality, she said, combined with the intense emotional presentation and tenderness and restraint. Of course, Suzanne deferred, much of it was due to Leonard's marvelous directorial talents. His eye for discovery.

Leonard had suddenly become territorial, warning Suzanne not too subtly to keep her hands off, that Nyia was supremely satisfied with the way Leonard was managing her career—*aren't you, darling*—arm around Nyia, pulling her close though they'd hardly been speaking that day. "Nyia," announced Leonard, "has absolutely no need of career management because"— he laughed—"her mother and I run her life for her. It's all handled in the family." He'd laughed, drawing Nyia off to meet some Italian financier in an Armani suit.

Later, Suzanne had managed to pull Nyia off into a corner while Leonard was hustling big wine money on the terrace. Suzanne had slipped her a card, speaking to her in that low caramel drawl. "So if you ever get tired of hearing that line about your mama and him running your life, won't you call me? Oh, that Leonard, he's so possessive. I've known him for years. Doesn't he just love to have the illusion that he's running everything in the whole wide world? You're not really managed solely by relations, are you, Nyia? An actress of your talent should really be seen in America. You should have a much wider audience than what you're getting from Visionfilm. Don't let your mother or

Leonard Jacobs hold you back. You could have a brilliant career. Don't be afraid to branch out, take some chances. Sometimes this whole European scene is just too *très* arty for me. But then, I do like my clients to have income, know what I mean? Guess I just believe in the old American dream. And in getting people's gift out to the big world. So do call if you ever want just to talk things over."

From across the room, Leonard had seen them huddled close and he'd nearly charged over to them, scooping Nyia up, asking her what bullshit Suzanne had been feeding her.

"Why don't you like her?" Nyia had asked him.

"She's a vulture," he'd answered.

Sure she was, Nyia had thought. But with incredible grace and good humor. And that's what made her good at what she did.

Nyia glanced down at Suzanne's business card, set it on the edge of the bureau in her hotel room, looked out across the Paris skyline, the red rooftops, the gray grid of streets, and the pigeons circling the chimneys. Heard the honking of Citröens in the narrow street below. She'd called Suzanne Scolfield's office that afternoon in California, leaving word with her answering service. Suzanne returned the call the following day. She was back in Paris, it turned out, had just come back from Rome. And yes, she'd be delighted to meet with Nyia.

They walked all afternoon by the Seine, up through Montmartre, past the flower markets and tiny bookstalls. Suzanne wore her hair back in a tight chignon that day, pearl earrings iridescent in the afternoon light accenting her thin face. She swung an ivory wool cape over her shoulders. As they talked, Nyia realized Suzanne wasn't much older than Nyia, but seemed so much more sure of herself. So self-possessed and worldly. She had talked of scripts she'd love Nyia to read, promised her fees far over what Nyia was getting from

Visionfilm. "And creative control," Suzanne had stressed. "Don't limit yourself to being Leonard Jacobs's fantasy. You could end up playing the same role until you're forty. You're past ingenue age as it is."

In addition, Suzanne assured her, if Nyia signed on with Scolfield Management, she could even develop her own projects and have access to a far wider range of roles, comedy, suspense, drama. "And a chance to work with people much more well-known than the actors he limits you to in his ensemble, brilliant though they are. You've got all the prestige you need now with these French things. Come home, Nyia. Haven't other people just taken control of you for too long? And there is no reason to do it all on your own or have your mother running your business. To tell you the truth," confided Suzanne, "it sounds like they're all living off your genius, not to mention your money. They need you. You don't need them!"

Everything Suzanne said had been like some incredible, harmonic chord she'd been straining to hear for years. The truth sang through her with a sense of relief and excitement, saying, Go! Be gone forever from this whole dissonance you've been so caught up in for so long: Mother, Leonard, Mirina. Though it was Mirina, oddly, she would miss the most, the one who pressed on her least, who gave her room to move, who let her be, who wrote for her.

Nyia found herself spilling out her story to Suzanne that afternoon in Montmartre. It was the next week that Suzanne gave the party for all the young actors and actresses she'd met in France on her European foray. Some hopefuls, wishing they could sign on with Scolfield Management, and some Suzanne hoped would sign with her. A jazz trio played in the corner of the small *appartement,* glass windows thrown open to the street. Nyia had worn a short black dress, her blond hair chin-length then, brushed back from her face. Dark lipstick but little makeup. Suzanne had breezed out into the party in a pink cocktail dress as puffy as a prom dress gone wild, her hair in some sixties beehive swirl.

That night Suzanne was at her best, all business at the center of her salon of the brightest young film people in the French industry, yet stylish, even fun. It was her tremendous empowerment of Nyia's potential to go it alone that convinced Nyia to sign on with her, yet what she loved most about Suzanne was her gossipy backroom girl-talk manner, her conspiratorial laughter that pulled Nyia close, that made her feel both protected and independent for the first time in her life. Suzanne was like the beautiful older sister Nyia had never had.

Nyia had first met Jack Drieser at that party. Suzanne hauled him over by the arm in his shiny tux and wire-frame glasses, hair falling over one eye. An earring back then. "You two should meet, my two favorite brand-new clients. Just don't go falling in love with her, Jack, she's on strict orders: No love whatsoever." Jack had rolled his eyes. "I just mean, she doesn't need any complications in her new and improved life, do you, Nyia? But I will allow the two of you to go dancing, I will agree to that."

Nyia had felt a world opening to her that evening, new friends, new possibilities. She'd been with Leonard so long, she hadn't realized what a shadow-figure she'd become. If she was unfinished, as her mother had criticized, it was only because she'd let them all keep her that way. Out of Leonard's dark grasp, his power and manipulations, she could say what she wanted, not be interrupted, corrected, told how to perceive, what to think. Out from under her mother's disapproving eye and her own anger toward all of them she could laugh and breathe. She felt the whole weight of her childhood drain out of her that night, dancing to a sweat with Jack, laughing at his mimicry of various people at the party and of Suzanne herself. *Queen Tulip,* he called her.

"Doesn't she just look like one? I don't know how a woman can be so smart and look so dumb. I mean she's usually so restrained in those designer clothes of hers. But then sometimes she lets go and you just see this Lexington debutante at a coming-out party with a rhinestone tiara and Junior League golf lessons."

She and Jack were together often after that. It turned out he knew Mirina, had taken a class with her at the Sorbonne. There was the relief of just being friends with a man, maybe the first she'd ever had. They rode bicycles, drank espresso at cafés and wore glasses, reading James Baldwin and Marguerite Duras, smoking Gauloises and listening to American jazz in late-night clubs. Here was the Paris she'd missed totally in her mother's shadow.

There was even that week in the Pyrenees, where they'd taken the train. Jack's friend, Dan Howe, had gotten him reading Hemingway, and Jack had become enamored of a basket of trout laid in cool ferns and the idea of drinking local wine next to rushing streams. This was all long before Dan came to work for Visionfilm. Dan wore that khaki fishing vest even back then, the hundreds of pockets all stuffed with cigarettes, rolling papers, pens, and the funny little fishing flies he tied in his spare time, tiny feathers and multicolored threads, copper hooks, busy as a woman knitting when they'd meet at cafés to talk. Dan Howe had waxed on so lyrically about the poetics of trout that they'd bought train tickets and left that very afternoon, fishing long days in streams so clear and cold, it hurt your bones to step in them. They slept in small inns and ate hard bread wrapped in white paper. The red wine gave Nyia a permanent hangover, but she didn't care. There was a deep vein of grief opening inside her by then, in spite of her happiness, a crack in her heart where Leonard Jacobs had always been lodged. Jack filled in that place. It wasn't that she loved Jack, not at all. It was just the ease of his stupid jokes, his intelligent talk, his love of literature, his simple presence and companionship.

It wasn't true they'd been completely platonic. There was a night that she had been in his room, talking, and she'd asked him to hold her. The room had been dark, the window open. Laughter and music came in from a tavern down the street. His body was so different from Leonard's, muscular and condensed, his face smooth, hair rough and short. He had wanted to make love, his hands cool on her breasts, gently touching her thighs apart. But she had frozen. His hardness felt foreign next to her thigh, the shape of him unfamiliar and odd. Her body ached for Leonard and she couldn't accept this other man, no matter that they were friends and she was so tired of being alone. In the dark she had recoiled from Jack. She couldn't sleep with a man whom she did not love and she still loved Leonard and would for a long, long time, no matter how wrong it was.

She had turned away, held her breath in until the urge to weep had passed. And whispered to Jack the truth. *Forgive me. There's something wrong with me. It has nothing to do with you.*

He stroked her back, said it was all right, he understood. He smoked in the black room. Together they'd watched the red point of the cigarette flare to brightness with his breath, then fade. Sometimes acting with Jack, when things became strained, one or the other of them would remember that night, how they had wisely chosen not to be involved with each other, how it was the purer form of the male-female configuration. How it allowed them to be together on camera without the troublesome history they might have had.

Not long after that trip, and before Leonard and Mirina returned from Italy, Nyia went home to the States alone. Her mother attempted to sue her for a percentage of her income from the new films she went on to make under Suzanne's management, but Carole

Wyatt got nothing. Leonard wrote and called, Mirina wrote and called. Nyia would have nothing to do with either of them for months, although she was aware she was under contract to do two more movies for Visionfilm. Finally, Leonard and she had lunch, but it was painful to see him. Now and then like some outtake of a previous film she'd been in years ago, she and Leonard would meet and make love, an afternoon at a beach house, a hotel room somewhere, the outcome of a chance meeting. It was always tender and they would part with sadness. Her sadness, anyway. Apparently it was just the way he wanted it.

She and Jack had ended up working together in some other films, including *Dead Heat,* against Suzanne's protests, and other projects as well. Dan Howe had gone on to work as Leonard's assistant. You could leave the city where your heart had died, your life left like some white-chalked outline of a murder victim, only to find the same old ghosts in new towns, new forms. But the hurt was less now. Mostly the hurt was less.

When a car pulled in behind her at the turnout, Nyia turned the key in the ignition, glanced over her left shoulder and pulled back out onto Bishop's Lodge Road. She drove slowly, savoring the sad memory of other nights of rain long ago. When she arrived back at the ranch, the yard lights were on behind the house, the red chili Christmas lights glowing on the wooden railing of the veranda. She parked and crossed the garden toward her cabin, looking back to see Mirina through a back window of the main house, bent over a typewriter, working on the script late into the night, her hair loose on her shoulders.

Mirina's work was her lover when the filming began. She would let Leonard go off into some other love for the duration of the film. Maybe it was just so he'd leave her alone to work. It had been some sort of drug between the three of them for years. Mirina never seemed jealous and Nyia had never understood how their marriage could be bigger than the affairs either of them had. What sustained them?

But the truth was, finally, that Nyia felt used by them. Hype up the love and intrigue so that art could be dramatic, mystical. She could act now, damn it. Pull it out on her own without all that crisis.

Nyia went the long way around the house, past the *vega* fence by the small corral and the horses, their great flanks twitching, patches of dark in the starlight. Voices then, quiet laughing. The pool was lit, rippled shadows lacing across the trees overhead. From a distance, Nyia stood watching Leonard and Tess Juran. So Tess had arrived this afternoon from Los Angeles. Leonard must have sent a limousine to get her. Watching them, Nyia thought, *that was my role*. She wondered what had gone on between them before Tess left the Mexico film.

It wasn't until she turned back toward her cabin that Nyia noticed the dim light inside. Had Mirina readied her room for her, turned down the bed, brought fresh towels? Nyia walked silently through the grass and pushed the door open, pausing only slightly with the realization that the door was unlocked. There was a moment, then, an instant when she thought, *no. This isn't right*. But then she was inside.

It must have been a dry gust that blew the unlatched window inward on its hinges, knocking against the kerosene lamp. She watched as the lamp tipped off the edge of the table and shattered on the plank floor. In seconds, the spilled kerosene ignited in a burst of flame with a sound, the fire jagging up toward the curtains. Nyia screamed, tore the quilt from the bed and something clattered against the wall. She threw the quilt down on the flames, slapping and stamping it down, smelling burnt cloth and fumes.

Scene eighteen, take one. Her palms were covered with

ash, her finger cut from the chimney glass. She put her hand to her mouth, tasting the blood.

Leonard was yelling her name as he ran toward her cabin. "What's going on?" He shoved in through the door, looking around the cabin, at Nyia kneeling on the floor.

"The window blew open and knocked it. Someone left the lamp burning in here."

Leonard stepped past her into the room and Tess came in behind him, shivering in a towel. "Are you okay, Ny?" Tess bent to look at her hand, her dark hair dripping.

"Why was this door unlocked?" Nyia demanded of Leonard. "Did somebody get my room ready for me tonight?"

"This isn't a bed and breakfast," he snapped. "The help just cleans, there's no one even here at night. The door was open?" He bent toward the door jamb, examining the lock. He wore his swimming trunks, a black sweatshirt. "I don't see evidence of someone breaking in," he said.

"I know I locked it. And the window."

"Stay up at the house tonight," said Leonard. He glanced at his bare wrist. "What time is it? I'm going to make a call."

Tess stayed with her as she packed things into a bag. Nyia threw her a sweater and Tess slipped it on over her bathing suit, toweling her hair dry, her long, thin legs crossed as she sat on the bed. Tess was a tall, bony woman in her mid-twenties, with wild, dark curls and pale brown cat-eyes, her face angular and dramatic. Though her voice was loud and sometimes seemed too big for the close space of a room, her movements were elegant as a dancer.

"Is this how it happened before?" demanded Tess. "Down in Mexico?"

Nyia nodded.

"That's your first scene tomorrow, isn't it—the fire in the bedroom? Doesn't the scene even call for an actual kerosene lamp? I hope this isn't Leonard's idea of some fucking joke, because I'm not putting up with it. I don't give a shit if it creates dramatic tension among us. Where's Jack, anyway? Is he here yet?"

"He's supposed to come in tonight, I think. He's staying up at Bishop's Lodge."

"Do you think Leonard unlocked the door on purpose? I mean, set this whole thing up like some little scene of his? What's the point—to get you emotionally prepared for tomorrow?"

"Maybe it was Mirina," said Nyia.

"Well, it's too weird. I'm not putting up with someone breaking into my room, I can tell you that."

Nyia felt in the corner of the closet on the hook for her robe, then searched the floor among the boots and shoes, but it wasn't there. "Something's missing," she whispered. "My robe's not here."

Tess joined her to look, but they couldn't find it. Nyia bent to look under the bed and pulled out a worn espadrille. "Maybe you left it somewhere," Tess suggested.

"I haven't gone anywhere. I think someone came in here and took my robe."

"So what is it, a laundry service? Some weirdo has a lingerie fetish, I mean what the hell?" Tess shuddered. "I got to go get in some dry clothes. How many days of filming have we got left?"

"Leonard says six."

"Has anything else like this been happening, Ny? Synchronous things?"

Now it felt strange not to tell her about the shooting last night, about Harm. It even felt unfair. Nyia wondered how long she would keep it from Tess. She couldn't lie to her. She said nothing. And knew it was a terrible lie of omission.

"Let's talk to Jack about it tomorrow," said Tess.

Nyia turned off the light in the cabin and they walked back to the main house together. Tess began to stalk on ahead, but Nyia took hold of her arm. "Wait, there's something I've got to ask you. We've talked about what went on down in Mexico and you always said you thought it was your gypsy blood that made you leave, but what was it really? Was there something between you and Leonard?"

Tess turned back to face Nyia. "You really want to know? I threw a tantrum. You know, I just couldn't stand his controlling, big-shot attitude. Granted he was the director. Is. I just rebelled. I wouldn't do anything he wanted, I had my own vision of the part. I couldn't get into the whole ensemble spirit."

"And what about now, Tess?"

"I'm two years older. Two years hungrier. It was hard to get work after that. I had a lousy rep, I felt I had to redeem myself with him. But not with this kind of shit going on. What about you, Nyia? You put up with all this for so long."

"It wasn't like this back then. No one got killed."

Tess glanced around the yard, out toward the corral where the horses stood still in the darkness, watching. A car slowed on the road at the front of the ranch, nearly came to a stop, then sped on ahead, tires kicking up the gravel.

"I'm going to see about staying up at the inn with Jack," said Tess.

Nyia blurted it out. "But are you involved with Leonard now?"

Tess laughed. "What, right under Mirina's nose? Do I look that stupid?" Tess began to walk on ahead toward the house, then turned back, facing Nyia.

"I thought you were . . ." Tess hesitated. "You're not still . . ."

Nyia shook her head.

When Nyia said nothing, Tess whispered, "Let's not get all paranoid between the two of us, okay?"

* * *

It was Nyia who let Harm in when he arrived half an hour later. Leonard was down the hallway in his office, waiting for them. She assured Harm, in a whisper, that she wasn't burned, she was all right, just shaken.

Leonard stood when they entered. "Looks as though we had an unwanted visitor on the premises, Bohland. Took a souvenir. I thought you'd better have a look at the cabin."

"Where's Mrs. Jacobs?" he asked.

"She's already gone to bed. I asked her if anyone had gone out there and she said not that she knew of. She said she would never have left a lamp burning in an empty cabin. Even with this rain, it's too dry out here."

"Who has access to the cabin?" asked Harm. "Keys?"

Leonard led them out of the house, back across the garden. "That's hard to say. It's one of our guest cabins. Whenever people come out to the ranch for a stay, we give them a key. We're always having new ones made, and out here, half the time, we don't even lock the guest cabins. It's New Mexico."

"I'd like you and Mrs. Jacobs to compile a list of names of people you know stayed in any of your cabins."

Leonard nodded. At the cabin, Nyia followed Leonard in and flicked the light on. The room still smelled of smoke and kerosene. Harm checked the lock with a flashlight, then aimed the beam into the corners of the single room, shining it up into the closet and drawers. "Get Quintana out here to fingerprint tomorrow," he said.

Harm was searching on the other side of the bed now, reaching back behind the mattress near the bedstead and pulling out a dark-green sash.

"That's the tie to my robe," said Nyia.

"It was caught behind the bed." As Harm lifted the

mattress and pulled the bed away from the wall, there was the sound of something clattering down through the springs to the floor. When he stood he was holding a black buck knife, folded shut.

"This yours, Nyia?" Harm asked.

She shook her head. Leonard said he'd never seen it. Harm wrapped the knife in a tissue from the bedside table and pocketed it.

The quilt lay in a heap by the door. Harm picked it up, shook it out and spread it on the floor, then bent down. It was ripped down the center in a perfectly straight line. Nyia knelt beside Harm. Someone had cut through the quilt, clean through the triangle pattern. She felt the sickness again, like the night her house had been broken into. The violation of someone being here, cutting her bed open, taking her clothing.

As she straightened, Leonard came over to her and put his arm around her. Without thinking she leaned against him, then hesitated and backed away. Harm flipped the quilt over to examine the other side.

"Nyia, you'll be safe up at the house," Leonard said. And to Harm, "I always wanted to keep the place like a little ranch. You know, not L.A. or New York with guard dogs, alarms. This place was my retreat from all that."

"Not anymore," said Harm.

Nyia turned and looked deeply at Leonard. Did you do this? she thought to herself. Could you? She saw how ridiculous it was, the thought of Leonard Jacobs sneaking around his own property, cutting blankets up and stealing bathrobes. He'd hurt her, yes—emotionally—but this wasn't like him. Maybe he'd written those letters, but this, this couldn't be Leonard.

Harm stood by the front door as Leonard went back into the main house. "Are you sure you feel okay, staying out here?" Harm asked Nyia. "I could drive you into town and you could check into a hotel."

"My room is right next door to Tess Juran. Leonard and Mirina are two doors down, if anything happens."

"You could be bedded down at the La Fonda in fifteen minutes."

She thought about it. "I think I'll be okay here. At least for tonight. Some of the others are staying at lodges up the way, I could see about staying somewhere else in the morning."

"I highly recommend it," said Harm.

Nyia leaned against the open door and didn't want him to go. Come in for a drink, she thought. Stay and have tea. His whiskers had grown in, his chin dark. His blond hair was curling over the neck of his jacket.

"I started reading through the letters after you left my place," Harm said. "And you're right—they are very well written, very literate. You're also right that the strange tone doesn't really come in until the last few, but looking back you can kind of see it all along. Have you had any thoughts that this could be some anonymous person, someone who's seen all your films many times, has studied your past, might even have files of material on you, clippings? You know, a fan. A disturbed fan."

"You mean some random person, not Leonard?"

"It's just a gut feeling. I'd like you to read back through the letters and really look for references to things that only Leonard could have known. In the meantime, what I'm going to do is send some of them off to a crime lab in Albuquerque. The exterior of a letter is full of every fingerprint in the world—every mail carrier or postal service personnel who touched it—but you can print the inside of a letter and sometimes there are even hair samples in them. Another thing is that you can check to see if there are any imprints of other sorts of writing done on top of a letter. Phone numbers, signatures. It's called indentation analysis. I want to see if the letters themselves have any more to tell us. And first thing in the morning I'm meeting Quintana to check out the site where your car was shot. I'll have him fingerprint the knife too."

He was silent, studying her face. "You don't really look like a movie star up close," he said. "You really look just like a human."

"Why, thank you, Mr. Bohland." Nyia smiled. He made her feel relaxed. She kept thinking, he has only one channel. There's only one level here and it's straight ahead. She didn't feel she had to read past anything to get to the truth of him.

"Why don't I come out here and pick you up tomorrow? I'll drive you to the set," he offered.

"That sounds good. I want to hear what you find out from Quintana."

He paused at the door, said good night, then turned and got into the Jeep, pulling out the long driveway. It was an odd pause, like at the end of a date, wondering if you're going to kiss the person. But that doesn't make any sense, she thought. This isn't a date.

The red lights of Harm's Jeep disappeared at a bend in the dark road. She wished she'd gone with him, back into Santa Fe.

Nyia pulled the brass sliding-lock shut on the bedroom door and climbed into bed. The house was still. She dialed Suzanne Scolfield's number in Los Angeles and waited several rings for her answering service to pick it up. "Oh, Miss Wyatt," the service said. "Miss Scolfield isn't available at the moment, but she did leave word—she is planning on being in Santa Fe tomorrow night for the Jacobses' dinner. Can I take a message and have her get in touch with you in the morning?"

The service hung up and Nyia stayed on the line a moment, thinking about calling Harm once before going to sleep. But as she reached to press the button for the dial tone, she heard a squeak on the line, a slow rhythmic creaking sound, almost like something whirling. She listened, then placed the phone gently back in the cradle.

At first she thought it might have been the line itself, the long-distance connection. And for an instant, she'd thought, no, it's a tape recorder. But just as she hung up she realized what it was. She reached up and snapped the light off and the room went black. Whoever was on the line, listening, was sitting very quietly, rocking back and forth in a rocking chair.

EIGHT

WHEN THE PHONE RANG, HARM REACHED FOR
the receiver on his cluttered desk. Over the tops of
buildings across Cerrillos, the Sangre de Cristos were
plum-colored in the morning light.

"Lieutenant Buddy Hirsch, Homicide, Los Angeles
Police Department, returning your call. Man, it was good
to hear from you yesterday, you got this great mañana
overdrive kind of lilt in your voice from sitting around on
your ass watching sunsets and eating huevos rancheros."

Harm spun his chair to face the wall where the
index cards were posted. "So how is everything in the
real world, Hirsch?"

"How long now since you moved out to New
Mexico? Less than a year? How can you even consider
calling L.A. the real world?"

"It's all a matter of degree," said Harm.

"So what's to this breaking and entering I'm digging

out of the files? This is very pricey clientele you're pulling in your first year in business, Mr. B."

"Yeah, it's all very discreet, too, you know what I mean? There's an undercover element to this gig, Hirsch."

"Don't you wish. Just tell me one thing."

"What's that?"

"Is she mythical?"

"She's mythical."

"Yeah." Hirsch cleared his throat. "You born-again son-of-a-bitch. Get left for dead at the shootout at the OK Corral, then rise again to become a guardian angel. You hurt me, Mr. B."

"Hirsch?"

"Yeah?"

"Just give me the report."

"Yeah. The security system on her house in Laurel Canyon was installed just prior to the break-in. The order was put in and paid for by Leonard Jacobs and billed to his company, Visionfilm. The report indicates Miss Wyatt failed to correctly activate said security system the evening of the assault. Stated she'd only had it about three weeks, didn't like it, didn't want it in the first place and basically blew it off."

"What kind of residence are we talking here?" asked Harm.

"This ain't no Bel Air mansion, Mr. B. More like a cottage. Was a carriage house in the twenties. Up on a steep hillside, overgrown gardens, a small pool, but modest by L.A. standards, for a movie star anyway. Miss Wyatt reported that apparently nothing was stolen, but the man left behind his bullets. Says here the assailant fired an empty piece at the side of the woman's head. Appeared that he actually emptied the weapon before entering the residence."

"Does the report show that the shooting was an act similar to one in a script she was reading?"

"Yeah, it says she called that in about a week later.

Turns out there was a piece in *Los Angeles Magazine* about a particular script, mentioning that she was probably going to be doing the part or was interested in the part. Even mentioned that scene specifically. Let's see, it's right here, interview with the screenwriter who says, quote, 'One of the ways you create a compelling story is to go against the expectations of the viewer. In a scene in a screenplay now being considered by Nyia Wyatt, a gun is fired three times at the character's head, but the gun is empty. So it's not violence per se that creates suspense, it is expectation and surprise.' Unquote. You see what they're getting at? What happened, it was written up in a magazine. Like somebody read the article and got the brilliant idea of making Nyia Wyatt audition for the part or something."

"Can I get a copy of that report and the name of the screenwriter who was interviewed in the article?"

"You got a fax?"

"Send it to the copy center over by the library and I'll pick it up. It's called Paper Tiger. Here's the number."

"Man, when are you going to enter the twentieth century? How come a big-time operation like Visionfilm hires some guy in an office next to a video store can't even afford a fax machine? How come they don't hire some swank security operation out of Beverly Hills, knows their way around a film set?"

"I got low overhead."

"Yeah, yeah. Hey, Mr. B—good luck with this. I'm glad to hear you got good business out there in adobeland. Send me some business cards, I'll keep you in mind. Call if you need anything else."

"Thanks, Bud."

Americo Quintana appeared to be a thoughtful man. No, he had said, no problem taking Harm out to the site where Nyia Wyatt's car had rolled. They stood now in the arroyo below the road, a creviced, dry mud-bank down below hills covered with twisted piñon and sage, still fresh in early summer. Harm could see the marks in the red dirt the car had made as it was dragged up the embankment by the tow truck.

"But you're right about the angle of that bullet," said Quintana. "Right down the center into the seat. It did go more or less straight in." Quintana turned in the direction of the road above. "But see that hill up ahead toward Santa Fe? Road turns real sharp right there. Could have been somebody up there, that's what I thought that night. But there's nothing up there, I looked around yesterday. I can take you up if you want, but there's not so much as a track, an empty case, or even a beer can." He fingered his mustache. "Nothing but natural things."

"What about the possibility the shot was fired from a vehicle in front of her car?" asked Harm.

"Yeah, we thought about that, but she didn't report any other vehicles. Said she felt totally alone on the road. All darkness. Maybe ask her again, see if she remembers anything different now. The car would have had to be right in front of her, slowing for that sharp turn up there."

Harm picked up a stone, tossing it from palm to palm.

"And somebody breaking into that cabin last night?" said Quintana. He squinted up at the sun. "It could be a connection, could be a coincidence. That's a ritzy neighborhood, out Bishop's Lodge Road. And the Jacobses don't have a wall or a fence around their place. Not even a guard dog like a lot of places out that way. Anybody could have wandered onto the property and gotten in there. But I told Mrs. Jacobs we'll send a few people out to the film set today and have somebody driving by their place every half hour or so, keeping their eye on things. Somebody's out there this morning, checking for prints. I can let you know if we find anything on that knife." Quintana paused, then started up the embankment.

Harm followed him, and as he reached the road, Quintana was leaning in the driver's window of his car, holding a mike to his mouth. Harm heard the static on the car radio. Quintana straightened. "Something going on out here, I just got another call. Why don't you come with me? Might be connected. Some crackpot wandering around, shooting at any old thing."

"What is it?" asked Harm.

"Dog. Mailman called it in. Out a back road a few miles from here. Dead dog in front of a house. Owner's usually home if the dog is out." He nodded toward the west. "Why don't you follow me? It's only a few minutes."

Harm arrived in the dry yard as Quintana got out of his car and bent over the dog. As Harm got close, he saw the flies in a swarm on the dog's belly where the gunshot wound had bled.

"Must have happened since yesterday afternoon," called Quintana. "Mailman came out around noon and said everything was okay then."

A short distance down a side road, a white pickup truck was parked next to a wood pile, both doors open. The back of the truck was half-filled with split wood. It looked as though a job had been interrupted. Quintana stood and moved toward the house, Harm just behind him. The door was slightly ajar and Quintana pushed it open. The house was in chaos, the couch and chairs tipped, television smashed, books, papers, junk scattered everywhere. Quintana reached to his hip and unsnapped the holster over his gun and took it out. Harm followed him into the trashed house.

It was quiet and Harm could smell death inside. It wasn't really even a smell, but he felt it come into him in the air. Quintana went directly down a hallway off from the living room, giving a bedroom door a shove with his boot.

"*Madre de Dios,*" he said under his breath.

He approached the bed where the dead man was tucked in, covers pulled up to his chin, the brown stain coming through the blanket. The man's face was turned toward the side, gray-blue now, frozen in an empty mask, the eyes stuck in that last focus that said fear, surprise, and no. *No, not this.* Harm could see it on his face, like some imprint of his last breath.

Harm spun quickly, glancing behind him at nothing, then turned back to the bedroom. The windows were open, floral print curtains blew in. Quintana did not need to take a pulse at the man's neck. He flipped the blanket back long enough to look at the massive chest wound, then carefully covered the body.

Harm walked into the kitchen, not wanting Quintana to know he felt light-headed. It came back in a second, that motel room in Tempe. He'd seen, for one brief flash, his own face in that blue face back there.

There was food scattered around, drawers emptied, utensils, forks, spoons, egg beater, spatulas, knives. In the corner there was an old-fashioned wire bird cage tipped onto the red and black linoleum. Harm called for Quintana. A dead bird, a mourning dove, had been thrown against the pantry door and lay among a pile of brown paper bags. As Harm walked over to look at it, he saw that the bird's legs were cut off. Somebody's fucking crazy here, he thought.

Quintana followed Harm's gaze and put his gun away. "Shit," said the dark-haired officer. "Things have been nice and quiet so far this summer. Nice and still." He turned for the living room, making his way over soup cans and boxes of macaroni. "I'm going to call this in," he said. "You can stick around if you want."

The dry wind rattled the venetian blinds in the next room. But Harm knew he had to get to Nyia.

* * *

Harm pressed hard to get up to Tesuque, but it still took almost forty minutes from Madrid. As he drove, the arc of sky over him seemed oceanic, the red land going for miles to the farthest reaches of mountains as far away as he could see. It wouldn't be good, he decided, to tell Nyia right off about what he'd just seen. Not until he knew if there was any connection between the grisly scene in that shack back there and her car, and the cabin last night. At least wait a few hours, until Quintana had processed the prints. But an intuition passed through him like a wave, and as he felt it, he pulled out to pass a slow truck. *Don't leave her. Stay with her.* He had not been hired as a bodyguard, no. But it wasn't right for her to be alone. That much he knew in his gut, and it took little logic to affirm it.

He pulled up into the dust of the Jacobses' driveway and the front door was open. Nyia must have heard the Jeep; she stepped to the door and waved. Each time Harm saw her, she looked different. This afternoon she was scrubbed, shiny-faced, her yellow hair uncombed. Her round wire-frame glasses diminished the intensity of her eyes. She wore a jeans jacket, black leggings, and green leather boots and she was smoking a cigarette. She coughed as she exhaled and put the cigarette out in a clay ashtray on a table just behind her in the foyer.

"The police just left about a half hour ago. They were out back dusting for fingerprints and asking everyone a lot of questions," she said.

"Did you get any sleep?"

She shook her head. "I made a call last night to L.A., to my manager, Suzanne. After I hung up, I was sure there was someone on the line, listening. There was this funny noise like a squeaking in the background, and after a while I decided it was a rocking chair. I felt completely paranoid all night."

"With good reason," he said. "So who was it?"

"I think it was Mirina. She has a study in the wing at the other end of the house. I looked all over for rocking chairs last night and the only one is in her room. I don't know if she was just about to make a call or what."

"Did you ask her about it?"

"No," said Nyia.

"I will."

Nyia checked her bag and said she'd be right back, heading down the hall to her room to get something. Harm waited in the foyer and saw a pile of mail, magazines, and newspapers on the table placed under a painting of Taos Pueblo. Half-hidden under a copy of the *Wall Street Journal* was an appointment calendar. He lifted the newspaper up: it was Leonard's. Harm flipped back a page or two, not looking for anything in particular, but something caught his eye. *June 25, Southwest #563, 8:30 P.M. N./L. pick up Tess/Albuquerque.* Leonard had intended to go with Nyia that night to pick up Tess, but she had gone alone. Why? Why had he canceled?

Nyia appeared beside him. "Ready?" she asked.

They walked in silence to the Jeep. Harm sensed an odd stillness in her, a blankness. Filming today, he thought. A scene with fire, just like in the cabin last night. But maybe she was always like this just before she worked. He pulled the door open for her and she climbed in, sweeping gum wrappers and cassette tapes to the floor.

"Sorry I'm not taking you out there in a limo," he said. "I was going to clean this up, but—"

She held up her palm. "I'd rather ride in a messy Jeep any day." She pulled out a pack of Vantage cigarettes and fumbled with some matches.

"I didn't know you smoked," said Harm.

"I don't. My character does. Do you mind? Little props, cues—something to get me over into the mindset of the story. Transitions." She blew the smoke out, turning her face toward the window. "Thanks for coming all the way out here to get me, Harm. I really do feel better knowing you'll be on the set today."

Harm backed out onto the road, and the Jeep jolted into gear. Nyia held a bound copy of the screenplay in her lap.

"You really wouldn't want a limo though?" he asked. "I mean, surely Jacobs would pop for a white stretch-mobile with a great stereo system. Isn't that part of the fun?"

"Yeah, for a party in Beverly Hills. A limo to the Golden Globe Awards. But right now I've got to think about being a young woman in a drab Southwestern town eloping with this sweet *On the Road* Kerouac-type guy and staying at this funky motel on our honeymoon night. So a big white stretch limo would totally throw me off. Don't you see?"

When Harm next looked over, Nyia was pulling a wedding veil over her head, the lace shadowing her cheeks.

"I don't think I can go through with this," she said quietly. "I'm afraid."

"Yeah, me too," said Harm. "We've only just met. I think we're rushing it a little."

Nyia Wyatt smiled, lifting the veil. "Hey, are you sure you don't want a part in this movie? That sounded real natural. You might have a future in this."

"Who, me? I'm just an academic, Miss Wyatt. Remember?"

"Oh yeah, I forgot. You're on today too. Good luck. What are you, some professor making a documentary or something? Is that why you brought a video camera?" She gestured toward the back of the Jeep.

"Very observant," he said. "Maybe you have a future as a detective."

"We could go into business together," she said. "Instead of acting in films, I could do undercover work for you."

"Fantastic. I'm a lousy actor."

"You know something? That's one thing I really like about you."

Nyia lit another cigarette and they drove out past the red foothills. "I am pretty nervous today. Not just about all this weird stuff going on. Leonard always starts right in with some major scene right off the bat. We're talking major eros here, the honeymoon love-making scene. It's not that I'm shy with Jack. We go back. We're old friends." She turned and looked out the window at a line of willows along a creek. "And we've been working together ten weeks now. But that's how Leonard works. He likes to jump in at the point of greatest dramatic tension. Makes you go right to the heart of it."

"A love scene can't be that tense. It sounds like it would be kind of fun."

"Yeah, but the characters—Hank and Christine—they're both pissed off in some way that they got married. They're making love and the kerosene lamp is knocked over—just like last night—but Hank won't let up. Christine tries to get away, there's a fire in the room, on the curtains. He thinks it's funny, see. But she's scared. Finally he stops and throws a blanket on the fire and after that she doesn't trust him anymore. It's like a sign to her."

Harm clicked on the turn signal and accelerated to pass a low-rider. A white van at the side of the road was selling chili ristras, dried heart-shaped wreaths of red chili peppers, and dried cattle skulls, O'Keeffe clichés for that New Mexico decorator touch. They drove in silence past Camel Rock, a sign advertising Pueblo Bingo, a dusty ranch yard with a hand-painted sign that read, BABY PIGS FOR SALE. As they neared Española, they passed an abandoned adobe shack. JUSTIN LOVES AMBERLEE was scrawled in spray-can paint across the side.

"How far back do you and Jack go?" asked Harm.

"We met in France three years ago. He's been a good friend. One summer we traveled all through Italy and Greece. We did a lot of fishing."

"Were you ever involved with him?"

"Strictly platonic."

"What about your friendship with Tess? Was there ever any anger on her part that you took over the lead in *Dead Heat?*" Harm asked.

She flipped a page of the script over, sliding her finger down the edge of the page, but said nothing so he went on. "I mean, do you get along with Tess? Did she ever hold that against you?"

"Are you investigating?" Nyia asked. "I can't get into all that just now. I need to concentrate, okay?" She shut the script and closed her eyes. A dirt road led off from the highway and Harm spotted the line of RVs and trailers parked in a line across from a shabby motel. The set itself was blocked off by red-striped roadblocks and Harm parked behind them in a jumble of cars. One car had a California license plate that spelled out MOVIE. Around the edges of the set there was a scurry of activity, cameras being adjusted on dollies and hoists. He glimpsed Leonard Jacobs conversing with a thick-chested man in a stocking cap.

Nyia stepped out of the Jeep and stood still for a moment in the bright midday light. The wind hissed through the dusty trees overhead. "Stay close, will you?" she asked.

Harm nodded, watching as she turned toward the motel and lit another cigarette, reading the script as she walked.

Suddenly he realized that at some point during the ride out she'd shifted into character. Emptied herself. It was almost a physical sensation.

"Professor Bohland?" A young man with a clipboard approached him. He was muscular and short. Over an aqua T-shirt that said Visionfilm in small black letters, he wore a khaki vest covered with pockets. "I'm Dan Howe, Mr. Jacobs's assistant on the set. I'm to make sure you're at home here today and be available to answer any questions you might have. So you're writing a textbook on film technique?"

Harm pulled the video camera bag from the Jeep and stuck a small notebook into it. Shit, he thought. No lines. No lines. Finally he muttered, "Not a textbook exactly. More of a scholarly piece. Critical. Post-modern improvisation in film and its relationship to cubism, jazz, and psychotherapy. I know that sounds a little bleak—but that's the ivory tower for you." Jesus, Bohland. He coiled into a square knot inside. Try harder to sound like an asshole, why don't you? Wear a sweat-shirt that says impostor on the back.

"Where do you teach?" asked the assistant.

Ask me for my *vitae*, too, he thought.

"The University of Minnesota. But I'm on sabbatical right now," he said. Better to leave it all a blank, if he could get away with it.

"Would you like to tour the set?" Howe asked.

Harm followed him over to the small motel. Its sign, HORIZON MOTEL ROOMS, creaked on metal hinges in the wind.

"So you'll be getting some video coverage on the filming today?" Howe asked.

"It's just a way of taking notes," Harm said. "I may use some of the footage in future classes. Jacobs has been so cooperative about all this. Actually, we'd like to get him out to do a residency with our department at some point."

"Leonard Jacobs cooperative?" Howe looked sky-ward as if pondering the remark. "That's generous of you. But then you just met him recently, right? I guess I shouldn't talk like this. You'll quote me in your piece and I'll be fired."

"Would you be willing to talk more about him if I promised you anonymity?"

The young man laughed. "I better check with my lawyer. But yeah, maybe."

Howe walked off toward the motel, a long, single line of rooms, brown adobe, sitting in the middle of a gravel yard under a giant cottonwood. The mountains spread out in a perfect vista behind the motel, the Sangre de Cristos in their blue splendor. He could see why they'd chosen this spot. The motel was straight out of the thirties. A shiny Harley-Davidson was parked at an angle in front of one of the rooms. Off to the side, in the shade of the cottonwood, Nyia was sitting now in a metal folding chair. Harm lifted the video camera, flicked it on, watched her through the lens as she adjusted the bridal veil.

Then he panned the set, taking in the preparations for the shoot. There was a tension, a quiet businesslike stir, and everyone seemed to have a clipboard. At the door to the motel unit the cinematographer was arranging lights and conferring with Jacobs. Nyia sat passively, slumped in a wedding dress with a big hoop skirt, like a prom dress from the fifties, cocktail length. A black-leather jacket was draped over her shoulders and one foot was bare. She dangled the other white pump from her toes, swinging it. No stockings.

Harm stole another shot of her, and moved in close. Her eyes were half-closed. She said she didn't practice lines so much as she emptied herself before a scene. Turned herself over to Leonard's wishes. Harm walked over to the motel building and watched through a door as Dan Howe placed a kerosene lamp before an open window.

As Harm circled the camera back toward Nyia, he felt a flash of fear for her. There was no way she could really be safe. Not with an undercover investigator, not even with a full-time bodyguard. He saw the vulnerability in her face that drew every eye. It made her a target. He settled the lens on her, a close-in shot: Nyia breathing, creamy bare throat, her upper chest rising, falling.

For an instant, Harm experienced her split. Outward persona: film-star; musical name; odd, intense beauty. Child actress who'd never had a permanent home, a receptacle for her pushy mother's failed dreams. Guarded woman who wasn't safe even in her own home, whose friend and colleague had been murdered. And even aside from all of that, something else entirely, just a human being, intelligent, lovely, funny, struggling like anyone to make sense of it all.

Harm watched as Jacobs cued Nyia, took her arm, led her to the motel, room number three, whispering to her. She nodded, nodded again. Jack Drieser leaned on the motorcycle outside the door, straddling the glossy Harley. At last the lights were properly adjusted. Leonard spoke briefly to Drieser, then glanced through the camera again to check the shot.

He didn't say, "Action." He called out, "Prepare for camera. Begin."

Nyia lit the kerosene lamp with a farmer match. The set was absolutely quiet. Jack came up behind her and slipped the leather jacket off, kissed her bare shoulders and unzipped the bodice of the wedding dress.

"Stop," said Leonard. He moved in to speak to Jack. Jack, head down, listened. How strange it must be, thought Harm, to be in such a private moment, not just because it was sexual but because it existed primarily in the imagination. Nyia seemed in a trance, an empty vessel, waiting.

"Take two. Prepare camera. Begin." That one small movement was repeated and repeated again, unzip, kiss. Unzip, kiss. Harm pulled the video shot in close to Nyia's face as she waited between takes. Jack seemed nervous. Leonard made him take a couple of deep breaths. Then Nyia went over to him, took him aside, and whispered something, moved up close and kissed him on the mouth. Glanced at him flirtatiously. He laughed, touched his growth of beard and looked up, rolling his eyes. He gave her a big friendly hug, nodded back at Leonard.

The next shot was a take.

The shooting progressed in tiny filmed moments. Harm hadn't realized how long it took to catch several split-second shots on film. Floodlights were adjusted for the fading afternoon, the sun heading down toward the mountains. Jack unzipped Nyia's dress for the sixth or seventh time and it dropped to the floor. Crinoline. Leonard insisted on a close-up of the skirt around her ankles, stiff on the wooden floor, petticoats holding it up like a crushed, white bell.

Between takes, Harm panned back toward the set and the observers. Nothing unusual, no weirdos lurking. Everyone seemed respectful, grateful to be allowed to watch. Along the highway he noticed several squad cars at the entrance to the parking lot, but no red lights. Just a presence. Good, he thought. Under a cottonwood, seated in the chair where Nyia had been, was a small man in a fedora, wild gray hair curling from under the brim. Occasionally Leonard stepped back and talked to him. He folded his arms across his chest, seeming to give Jacobs advice. That seemed odd, Jacobs taking advice from anyone. Harm wondered who he was. Mirina was nowhere to be seen.

Finally Dan Howe cleared the set of almost everyone except the principals. He asked everyone to move back to the trailers, that coffee would be served back there, and he'd be happy to answer questions if anyone from the press wanted information about today's filming. The next scene, he announced, was to be shot without observers. Harm balked; he didn't want to leave her.

Howe saw that he hadn't moved and started back

toward him, gesturing for him to come, but suddenly Jacobs was at his side. "It's all right," Jacobs called to Howe. "He can stay."

Harm felt among the chosen. He stood in silence at the edge of the set, peering in from the motel door. It was like being inside a magic circle. Two women in black jeans stood by with fire extinguishers. Leonard spoke again to Jack and Nyia, explaining to them that he only wanted to shoot this scene once.

"It has to be there. Right there," said Leonard. "Perfect one time. Because of the light. Otherwise we'll have to wait days before we can shoot this again. Are you clear? Are you clear?" he repeated.

Jack began to make love to Nyia, standing there in front of everyone, pulling the dress gently down, folding his hands over her breasts as she stood at the window. She bent back toward him, arching her neck, then turned into his arms, sliding her hands up under his shirt. She rode up his body, and he lifted her, her thighs wrapped around his waist as he carried her to the bed. The white shoes dropped to the floor.

Harm wanted to step in, say, "Stop that, not right here in public." He felt embarrassed and excited. They lay down on the thin mattress in the shabby motel room. Harm lifted the video camera and framed them in, brought them into focus. Then it was all right. They were in a movie then, surrounded on four sides by a frame and the feeling of time caught on a straight line of film. The lovemaking in front of all of them was all right then. Harm wondered what shots the cameramen were taking. He swung his camera toward them, at Jacobs's intense gaze taking it all in, and then the man in the black hat just behind him.

He'd always wondered if they actually made love in movies. He couldn't tell. Jack and Nyia were wildly erotic under the white sheets, but discreet. Surely the man was hard, though. Did that bother her—or was it just what she needed to get into the scene?

Just then Harm heard the glass break, and kerosene ignited across the wooden table with a sound of an exhalation. Flames shot up the white curtains. Harm's first impulse was to run in, throw his shirt across the flames, but then he remembered the fire extinguishers. Nyia let the sheet drop, and she sat across Jack, bare thighs pressing against his flanks. His hands on her bare back, shadows of flame across her shoulder blades. Harm's camera jerked back and forth between the fire and her naked back.

She began to struggle in Drieser's hold, his fingers pressed into her arms. Laughing, he flipped her over and they wrestled briefly, she was whimpering, then calling, "Stop it. Stop it, Hank." Then she went limp. He laughed, leaping off her, throwing the blanket on the flames.

At that Leonard cried, "Cut! Magnificent!" and the fire was sprayed out with foam. Jack grabbed the sheet and threw it around himself like a toga, bowing toward the few people watching. Nyia just lay there on the bed, facedown. Finally she rose, stepping into a robe a woman was holding open for her. The woman gave her a lit cigarette from her own mouth and escorted Nyia from room number three across the parking lot to her trailer. Jack sat down on the edge of the bed and Dan Howe handed him a Coke.

How could they just stop there? Harm wondered. He wanted the scene to go on. He wanted them to finish making love and curl together under the sheets, their thighs crossed and wet. He wanted to feel her cool shoulder against his mouth. He'd gotten totally lost, he knew it. Suddenly he craved a shot of tequila and a bite of lime. There was a strange smell of ammonia in the air and the late afternoon was blue and cool. He'd never seen anything like it. Not in person. Not unless he was a participant.

Dan Howe announced over a small bullhorn that filming was done for the day, that they would review footage but that Leonard thought it was a wrap and that he was extremely pleased with everyone's performance on this first day back to work in a new setting. Harm overheard Jacobs talking to the cinematographer and the black-hat man. "Original, perfect, spontaneous." Jacobs grinned and made a fist.

Harm knocked on the door of Nyia's trailer and a woman answered and let him in. Harm made a note of her, too, and wondered how many people had access to Nyia on the set. Costume people, makeup, assistants. Inside, Nyia was perched at a brown plaid breakfast nook wearing a gray sweater and her black leggings. She held a knife in her hand.

"Harm, come on in. Thanks, Connie." The woman clicked the door shut behind her as she stepped out of the trailer. "So what did you think?" asked Nyia. She seemed herself again, not her character, Christine.

Harm leaned against the tiny kitchen counter. "It was hot," he said.

"Hot. That's brilliant, Harm. You're a real critic, you know that? You're going to put Siskel and Ebert right out of business."

Without thinking, he lifted the video camera to his shoulder and clicked it on. Nyia moved a small, brown-paper package toward her on the dinette table. Harm pulled the lens in close as she slit the knife into the folds of one end. She looked up at him, staring into the camera. Slowly she raised her hand and gave him the finger.

"Will you put that fucking thing down?" Nyia whispered. "Haven't I had enough for one day?"

Immediately he lowered the camera and when he looked up at her, she seemed closer. No lines framed her face.

"This is real, you know," Nyia said. "This is really my life at this moment, not some goddamn movie. The movie stops back there on the set. That's one thing nobody seems to understand. I don't want to be on camera every waking minute."

"Sorry," Harm said. "I got carried away. I'm into this thing of making the documentary, being the professor and everything. I didn't know when to stop."

"Nobody does. What, do I need a sign that says *off duty*? A light on my head like a cab? Please, Harm, don't film me when I'm not on a set, okay?" For several minutes she was quiet, slowly unfolding the brown paper covering the package. Then she said, "Look. I'm sorry I snapped at you. I'm exhausted."

But it was true, he thought. Just the act of filming her with the video camera made her seem slightly unreal. A character. He felt ashamed that he wanted to film her anyway. That he would look at the video of her lovemaking scene with Jack again and go to the movie a hundred times, saying he knew her. He shook his head. So it was that easy to exploit her.

He was setting the camera back in the case when he heard her draw her breath in sharply and then her cry. As he stood, he saw the small flat box she'd opened, filled with a mat of cotton as if for jewelry. Displayed on the cotton were two bird claws, curled back, red-scaled, the sharp nails extending from the curved talons, the ragged mutilation of the stick-legs where they'd been severed.

Nyia covered her mouth and pushed the box away and Harm grabbed it. No mistake. They were connected, the blue man this afternoon in the shack out by Madrid and this sick gift. He thought of the buck knife, the slit quilt on her bed. Now he'd have to tell her.

She reached out for him, and he held her against him. She was holding her breath as she buried her face in his chest.

"Where did you get this?" he asked. Releasing her, he examined the brown paper. No address, no stamps.

"It was just sitting in here on the table when I came in," she whispered, as if someone could be listening.

QUESTIONING THE MOTIVATION FOR CERTAIN KEY scenes. *For some reason, for some obscure reason, he had first imagined the lover killed in her presence. But why? Perhaps that would clarify things for her. Or clear the way for a new love to enter her life. He has always known that she loved the man, and had never stopped loving him, even though she was not seeing him anymore. Yes. To be rid of him—that would change everything.*

The first time he tried, though, it was a terrible failure. Santiago, following them that night out of the bar. He'd been waiting outside for a long time for her to come out, and when she did, there was the man with her, the lover, his arm around her, kissing her hair, feeling her ass in that dress. So they were together again, just as he suspected.

He followed them at a distance into the alley, wondering why they were going there. The man had her pressed against the wall, lifting her skirt; her hands dug into his back, clawing at his shirt.

I got him in the sight, but it was dark. Too dark. Pictured him crumpling at her feet in the middle of lovemaking like that. Perfect. I couldn't hold back anymore, squeezed off the shot. It blasted through the narrow alley and there was a scream, but not a woman's scream, not her scream. A man's low yell, then stifled, choked into silence. And then it was she who fell. He dropped her, let her slump down on the dirt next to the building and he turned briefly, staring in my direction, not seeing, the dark was thick. He turned and ran the other way.

I lifted the gun to my eyes, but he was gone. I ran then, too, back down side streets, streaming with the rush of it and knowing I'd fucked up, missing him completely. Shot her instead. But maybe, maybe it was just as well. Meant to be. In keeping with the order of things. Maybe now I could be done with her, with the churning pain of her in my mind, some endless repeating mantra of desire, some thirst like an ache that never leaves.

But it wasn't her at all. Wild blond hair, black dress, in his arms. It could only have been her. And yet it wasn't. That was how wrong everything had gone.

After that he withdrew into himself for many months, and the feeling went far away, far under. Sure, somewhere inside, he knew that he had done it. He wasn't totally mad, that was the thing. The strangest thing. There was some place of total clarity inside him that knew everything. But on some other level, he dissociated, yes—that was it. And the woman's death was something he learned about, but had nothing to do with. And for many months he accepted that as true. Told the therapist he simply wished she had been the one who'd died.

Hostile fantasies. Impotent aggressive wishes. Something about hating his mother.

Until slowly it came to him that the images deeply buried were not fantasies. They were memories. He began to understand how deeply he had failed. That he had not accomplished his goal. Began to plan again, see new scenes so clearly in his mind, how the lover would have to die in her arms. That was the way it would have to be.

But what about the motivation for the scene? He no longer knew, it didn't matter. The story began to have a truth of its own, a momentum to be honored. Obeyed. So he waited for the next time. And the next time came.

NINE

NYIA WAITED IN THE JEEP WHILE HARM CALLED
Quintana from a phone booth at a gas station on St.
Francis. Santa Fe looked golden in the late afternoon
light. Suzanne Scolfield would be at dinner tonight;
Nyia wanted to talk to her about pulling out of the rest
of the film. What would the legal consequences be? She
just wanted out. That was all. It was out of control now,
even more so than in Mexico.

Driving back from Española, Harm had told her
about the man they'd found that afternoon in the shack
out by Madrid. She pulled her jacket close around her
now and watched the traffic in the side mirror. *Dead
man, dead bird,* she thought. *Sitting duck.*

Harm climbed back into the Jeep, pulled the door
shut with a clank. He closed his eyes for a minute before
speaking, rubbing the bridge of his nose. "They found a
receipt from a local sporting goods store in the man's

garbage, dated the morning of the day your car was shot. They also found quite a bit of cash squirreled away in places that weren't all that secretive. That makes it look as though burglary wasn't the motivation. They didn't find a gun on the premises, but they're looking into whether or not the man could have purchased one that morning. Maybe that's what was stolen. Quintana's sending someone to my office first thing in the morning to pick up the claws, see if they match the thing we found in the guy's kitchen, although I don't think it can be anything but.

"Asking around town, questioning neighbors, seems the guy was a loner, kind of odd. Hung out at a bar in Cerrillos pretty regularly. Then people would go days without seeing him. Did odd jobs, carpentry, sold wood, handyman type of thing."

"Was he the one who shot at me?" she asked.

"Could have been. But if he was, who shot him? Who else knew about it? Maybe somebody who knew he fired at you wanted him silenced. Permanently. That's conjecture. I don't know. Nyia, I've got to say, though, that I don't see how this could be Leonard Jacobs." He looked directly at her.

"Are you saying that to make me feel better?"

"No, it's just a gut feeling. He's got too much riding on you, he depends on you too much. I don't think he'd go this far."

"But on other films, he did things purposefully to create tension, make everyone feel crazy, dangerous, off-center. He could easily have lit that lamp in my cabin, he could have hired some guy to shoot at my car. Maybe not to kill me, maybe just to scare me."

Harm thought for a moment, taking that in. "And then murder the person he'd hired to do it? Would Leonard Jacobs really go that far to create dramatic tension among his crew?" Harm turned toward the west, then pulled his jacket up at the wrist to check his watch. "Damn. Would it be okay if we didn't get to the party right on time? There's a promise I can't break."

"Take your time. I don't really want to go back to the ranch anyway. I can't stay there now, Harm. I'd feel better if I could stay someplace where you were nearby. Very nearby."

His hand rested on the stick shift. She found herself putting her hand on his, she didn't care. He didn't pull away, he just looked at her palm on his, then at her face.

"Do you want to stay at my place?" he asked. "Or you could check into a hotel."

"I don't want to stay at a hotel. Are you sure it's okay?"

"It's highly irregular." He smiled. "But I think it can be arranged." The Jeep lurched out onto St. Francis. "Do you like baseball?" he asked.

She wouldn't have to sleep with him. That wasn't why she thought of staying at his place, not at first, but if it happened, why not? He was smart and attractive and low-key. He seemed absolutely the most natural man she'd ever been with in her life. He wasn't dazzled by her, or if he was, he knew it and stopped it and came back to someplace from which maybe no one had ever related to her, at least not a man. Something like friendship but with that nice buzz between bodies, that warmth like electric wires running from his shoulder to hers as they drove through town. He felt so damn safe to her. But it was more than that. And even if that was all it was, she thought, that was a lot. She looked over at him, took her time. Blond, slightly graying hair, long at the back of his neck, beard stubble, dark brows with a few wild hairs, strong profile, chin a little wobbly. No iron man. Belly round over his belt. He wasn't a movie star, thank God. But he was handsome in his own way, sexy, safe, real. Yes. That was a lot. A whole lot.

* * *

She sat on the bleachers, a styrofoam cup of coffee in her hands. Harm had run out onto the field to coach third base. When his kid came on base, the skinny one with the shaggy blond hair and the thin curl of a tail-braid down his neck, Harm leaned down to whisper in his ear, then clapped him on the back.

When the team ran in, Harm walked beside his son, arm on the kid's shoulder. Both laughing. He steered the boy toward Nyia, and Nickie squinted up into the sun. His squint became a shy scowl.

"This is Nyia Wyatt, Nickie. She makes movies."

He gave her a gap-toothed grin. "Were you in *Batman?*"

Nyia shook her head.

"Dick Tracy?"

"No, that wasn't me."

"Any comic strips?" he asked.

Harm told Nickie he'd be right back with a root beer and headed over to the refreshment stand. The kid looked pained. "Are you my dad's new girlfriend?" he asked.

"Not yet," said Nyia. "Do you think he needs a new one?"

He wiggled his tongue out from the hole in his teeth, feeling the space, thinking. "Yeah. My mom's getting married to someone else now. A lot of my friends have a whole bunch of different moms and dads. But it's not so bad."

"Why's that?" asked Nyia.

"We got more people to come to the games?" He stated it as a question, his brows raised. Nyia thought he must be pondering what good reason the adults in his life could possibly have for living such complicated lives. Harm returned with the root beers. They stayed one more inning, Harm hanging on the backstop with Nickie. The boy swayed next to him rhythmically, bouncing gently off his father's side.

Cheerios. Mickey Mouse and baseball. Far cry from

a moonlit room in Majorca, Nyia thought. The mountains glowed saffron now in the sunset. It was a nice town. She found herself hoping nothing too awful would happen here, in case she ever wanted to stay. Then reminded herself, stay in the present. Don't future it to death, she thought.

They stopped briefly at Harm's, where he changed into a suit. Actually black jeans, black sportcoat, denim shirt, black leather tie and snakeskin cowboy boots, his hair slicked back wet from the shower. She nodded in approval.

"Very nice," she said.

"L.A. togs," said Harm. "I haven't dressed like this since I moved out here."

On the drive back up to Tesuque, he told her he was going to speak to Leonard about the undercover status of his investigation. Said he felt hampered by it and that it made him nervous, anyway. He didn't say why.

Nyia stood briefly at the mirror in Leonard and Mirina's living room, listening to the clink of wine glasses on the patio outside, a man playing meandering jazz on an electric piano on the veranda by the pool. In the reflection of the room, there was that migraine shimmer at the edges of things. *Story alive in you. Story alive.* In spite of everything, the filming had gone exceptionally well today. And she knew she wasn't completely out of character. She would have to stop trying to resist it. Just let go into the story and give everything to it. That was how it had to be. There came a time when you finally entered and there was no turning back.

Leonard came up behind her and put his hand on her bare back. "You were incredible today with Jack," he said quietly. He touched her face with his palm, looking deeply at her in the mirror. "Ah," he said. "You're all the way in, aren't you, Nyia?" He smiled approvingly. "You're wide open."

"Am I?" she asked.

He touched the edge of her lower lip as if adjusting the line of her lipstick. But when he spoke it was as a friend, and that's what always got to her.

"Be careful, Nyia," he said. "Save it for the camera, won't you?"

She nodded. "I'll try," she said. Then thought: *That's better. In the past he'd have said, 'Save it for me.'*

Leonard strode out across the patio into the dusk. The yard was crowded now and she watched him move through the dinner guests, greeting them. God, she'd be glad in some way when their lives could be forever separate. Just not see him, all behind her. Closed book. Leonard went to Tess and handed her a glass of wine. Tess edged up against his white shirt. Where was Mirina?

Fat crows sagged the branches of the cottonwood, cawed and flapped, swooping at the hors d'oeuvres platters set on the cowhide tables. Nyia watched their bird-feet as they hopped down to the edge of the pool. Shimmering black things.

"Nyia." She turned toward the voice behind her, gruff and sweet, its tinge of Southern belle locked behind straight white teeth. Suzanne's sleek brown hair was pulled back into a careful chignon. She wore an off-white knit suit, probably Anne Klein, thought Nyia, and her signature gold jewelry, simple but expensive. Suzanne's executive demeanor was counterpoint to the innate Southern charm of her past. Nyia had heard stories of her years as a Tulane sorority girl, magnolia wrists and mint juleps on shaded verandas. She carried the well-to-do South in her equestrian poise, but her style was both haughty and playful. Nyia was relieved to see her.

"Suzanne! Your service said you'd be here, how did you get Leonard to let you come?"

"We have our little ways. Besides, I have to keep watch on my clients. I just talked to Jack out by the pool and he said you all had an excellent day. I just wish you were putting all that talent into something that was going to make some more money for you, sweetheart. Not to mention me." She smiled.

"Maybe this will."

"Only because you're in it. How are you? What's going on with this investigation? I want to meet your detective. That's the other reason I came out. I want Leonard and Mirina damn well aware that if even one hair on your sweet head is so much as breathed upon, lawyers will be descending from all directions. Nyia, I just want you to feel protected. Now, look. I've got the names of some security outfits that could fly someone out in a day, if you feel like you need somebody with you besides—what's his name—Harm Bohland? Which one is he now, anyway?"

Nyia tried not to roll her eyes. Suzanne was a great manager. Bossy and mothering, at times. Those same qualities made her occasionally intolerable, but she took care of business. And she was nothing compared to her own mother's controlling. Nyia had always been able to tell Suzanne when to back off, and they had a good relationship. "He's undercover, Suzanne. Don't blow it. That's him in the black jacket and jeans."

"You know, I think this is ridiculous, don't you? This undercover thing? I'm talking to Leonard about it as soon as I can get him off in a corner somewhere. A detective's presence would be a great asset to this entire situation, give a clear message to any idiots that the set is well-protected. Undercover," she nearly hissed under her breath. "Just another one of Leonard Jacobs's endless little games."

Nyia wanted to blurt everything to Suzanne, but the

place was filling up now. One of Leonard's producers came over to talk to her, pulling Suzanne away by the elbow to meet someone. Maybe she could get her off by herself later, take her back to her room to talk. Suzanne called back over her shoulder as she headed for the patio, "Oh, Nyia, by the way. Did you see Manuel Moravio? He was looking for you."

Manuel? she thought. She had no idea he'd be here. There he was, wearing his famous black fedora, sitting on the far side of the pool, huddled in close conversation with Mirina. Perhaps he had a new screenplay for her. Suzanne would certainly find out.

Nyia had played the bird in his story, the changeling, the dream-image of a woman flying. Though the air still felt warm, suddenly she shuddered. Thinking of the claws in that box. Wondering if there could be some connection between her role in *Wings* and that awful package. But what would it be? Some creep sending her images from her previous film roles? Great, she thought, remembering the knives in *Pursuit*, the armory of weapons throughout *Gun Law*. That was all she needed.

And where was Harm? She felt relief roll through her when she saw him, his head bent in close conversation now with Tess. She'd moved right in, hadn't she? Thin, wiry, seductive and gorgeous in that red dress. Leonard at her other side, hovering. Tess deferring to his power and presence. Oh Tess, thought Nyia. I should tell you some things. Okay, so she was jealous. Two men captivated: one her former lover, one her next.

But the truth was that, in spite of herself, Nyia liked Tess. She wanted to dislike her, seeing her with Leonard, but she didn't. Tess was like a great, smart, feisty, long-legged foal. She developed her own scripts, acted in children's television, had been a star athlete at some Ivy League college. A diver, maybe? Or was it a runner? Nyia couldn't remember. Tess's cousin was a playwright who'd gotten her strong, early roles as a wise-ass young thing in off-Broadway plays. It would be easier to hate Tess if she were just vacant space surrounded by a cap of black curls. She wasn't.

Nyia watched as Harm smiled back at something Tess said. Research, Nyia told herself. He's on the job. He looked properly professional with a posture of attentive intelligence.

Jack Drieser had joined them. Nyia crossed the patio and sat at the edge of the conversation in a leather chair. Jack was explaining to Harm: "Actually, working with Leonard and Mirina is much more like being in a play, because the script is being developed the whole time we're filming. It's not static. The actors have a part in the creation of the thing. Or Leonard is damn good at making you feel that you do. It's so much more than simply reading lines."

One of the producers had also joined the group, a tall, graying woman wearing southwestern turquoise.

"But what's wrong with lines?" the producer asked. "Chekhov wrote lines, Shakespeare wrote lines." Nyia knew she was playing devil's advocate. Actually she was a great admirer of Leonard's methods, was one of his longtime backers.

Jack spoke again. "Hey, if you wanted a secure thing, you wouldn't be in a Jacobs film. Am I right? Are any of us really in this for stability? Christ, Paulette, I know you have to watch the bottom line, but even you. I mean, you could invest in gold boullion. Or real estate. There you go. Now, land is real. There's something stable."

"Jack, you've been in New York too long," said Tess. "Haven't you heard about the death of the family farm? You're romanticizing dirt again. I'll tell you what's stable if you want an investment. Viruses. Put your money in drug companies researching cures for viruses. Viruses are stable."

Harm had been taken up by the group, Nyia could

tell. They were all in love with the idea that they'd be written up in somebody's scholarly research. Nyia relaxed in the late shade under the portico and looked around. She used to love all this, feel so much a part of it. Just now she felt like a guest. An actor in her own life. She closed her eyes and listened to Jack pontificate.

"What Mirina does," Jack said to Harm, "she lets you know the story of the film bit by bit. She keeps retelling it along the way as it changes. She'll do it tonight, at dinner, won't she, Tess? But halfway through the actual filming she'll completely change her mind. She'll start to flip things a hundred and eighty degrees. Tell you your character is a brother now instead of a husband. Okay, what does that do to the story, since in the last scene you made love to this woman? Nothing is ever what you expect. That's where all the brilliance lies, in the unexpected changes.

"The camera work is another signature," he went on. "The cameras work up so much closer than in most films. The way Leonard directs the cameraman to walk right into the scene, circle you, right up in your face. He's twenty years ahead of his time, using video technology and transferring it to thirty-five millimeter. It's exactly that home-movie roughness that makes it so powerful. It suggests an intimacy, a loss of control. Like life. And that's what moves people."

Nyia watched as Harm listened, absorbing everything. He was doing all right, Nyia thought.

"Doesn't it ever just disintegrate from lack of planning?" asked Harm. "Don't people fight all these changes in midstream? Don't they just get pissed off?"

"Of course," Jack said. "People go nuts, they break down. They throw tantrums and call their agents. Leonard loves it. In psychological circles, I believe it's called acting out. Bringing all the reactivity and rage up to the surface. He cracks people open so they give everything, past control of ego. Everyone is on edge. Hey, aren't we? Aren't we all just about to fucking lose it? I know I am." Jack looked over his shoulder at Nyia sitting in the shadows. "Nyia, I could hardly make love to you today! Am I right?" Jack toasted Nyia in the shade, laughed, and downed his drink. "Now you know I'm losing it."

Harm pressed on.

"Wouldn't it be easier if everyone just got along?"

Tess Juran spoke up. "But what we'd be doing is pushing all our darkness down. If we were all just nicey-nice, and oh-so professional, the dark stuff would be there, but it'd be repressed. The way Mirina and Leonard work it, everybody's wild, demon energy comes out in the making of the film. They make you show your throat to the camera. You have to be willing to die for it, right, Jack?"

Tess tossed her hair back. Nyia could tell she thought she was being profound for the professor. Not remembering that in *Dead Heat* someone had.

Nyia hung back on the patio as the crowd was called inside to the long table. Harm approached Nyia and she shook his hand. "How do you do, Professor Bohland? Leonard has spoken so highly of your work." She smiled, dropping her voice. "Is that what I call you?"

"Professor will do. How are you doing, Nyia?"

"Will you sit by me at dinner?" she asked. "I mean, will you be my date tonight, Harm? You know, flirt with me. Tell me I'm prettier than Tess?"

"Do I have to pretend or can it be the truth?"

"That's real good, professor. You're a natural at improv, you know that? I do think you should get a screen test." Nyia looked up at the crows. "I'm spooked," she said quietly. "I just need you to stay right by me."

"Absolutely no problem."

She took Harm's elbow and they turned to go in to dinner. Nyia looked down the row of faces, many of whom had been down in Manzanillo at a similar dinner. Grilled lobster had been the feast that night. Shrimp in cilantro and salsa. Mirina narrating the story, all of them spellbound as the Pacific sun had set over the balcony and Mexican boys had brought flowers to the table for the women. But Robin had been with them that night, alive and laughing, creamy and drunk in a sequined dress, at Leonard's side.

Leonard came in just then and sat down next to Tess. Mirina stepped to the head of the table, Moravio at her side, raised her glass and sat down.

TEN ⭐

"THE STORY OF THE FILM IS VERY SIMPLE, REAL-
LY. It is a triptych, three separate stories. The characters are very different in each one, but all are played by
the same ensemble, this very gifted group of actors."
Mirina gestured down the table with a sweep of her
hand and leaned back in her chair. "In each story there
is the tension of a pattern. Mindless repetitions of dra-
mas lived out over and over again until one is fully con-
scious of them. In each story, two people love each
other, but one of them is inadvertently responsible for
the death of another. I suppose the theme is this: we
don't mean to, but when we love, we destroy one another. It happens in the smallest of ways."

Harm took out a small tablet and jotted something
down. Good, thought Nyia. Very in character.

"The first two sequences have already been
filmed," said Mirina. "The first in New York. Lower East

Side. A sculptor and an artist's model fall in love. Of course, she's really a waitress who lives with a fellow art student from the New School. The sculptor comes often to her restaurant; he loves chicken. He sculpts these huge pieces that resemble white bones. The model cooks for him in his studio and he begins to create more fleshlike pieces. His bones take on flesh. Love fills his work. But she grows thin, as if the work is taking her very body from her. Her roommate warns her away from him. The model accuses her roommate of being jealous.

"The sculptor and the model dance in dark clubs, they fuck on the studio floor in the white dust from the stones. He buys her a hat at a flea market, she wears it when they make love. It is a very thirties-style hat, black net down over the eyes. She tells him she will always wear this hat. She says, 'Without this hat I don't know if I love you or not. It is a magic hat. If I wear the hat, I love you. If I don't wear the hat, you know we're through.'

"'Then if you lose the hat,' he tells her, 'I will have to leave you.'

"'That's silly,' says the woman. 'You started the game,' he says. 'I am only playing it.'

"One day the roommate borrows the hat without asking. She goes out walking in SoHo, she meets up with the sculptor. They drink together at the Prince Street bar. Drunk, they go back to his studio. The model is working at the restaurant that night. The roommate and the sculptor make love. It is all because of the hat, he thinks. It is the hat's fault.

"The model never learns of the indiscretion. But one night the sculptor and the model are walking on the bridge. The hat blows off, it lands on a ledge just out of reach. 'You can't lose that hat,' he tells her. 'You know what will happen without it.' He reaches for it. She is afraid. She holds him back, promises she will love him with or without the hat.

"'Forget the damn hat,' she cries. Now he is dancing on the ledge, the river black below in the night. She begs him to get down, he is drunk. Finally he does get down. 'Now it is my turn,' she says.

"'No, you don't,' he begs her, but before he can say anything she has climbed out on the ledge. She reaches down for the hat. You only see his face to know she has fallen. But no—she comes up laughing, the hat in her hand. A semi thunders toward them on the bridge. 'I am tired of this damn hat!' she cries. 'It's not a diamond, it's not a gold ring. It means nothing to either of us. It is only a hat.' She throws the hat in the road. The sculptor runs for it and she throws herself after him, to push him from the path of the oncoming truck. They stumble in the traffic, slowly falling. He makes it to the other side of the bridge. In the final shot, you see her thin body thud across the hood of a car, a blur in the tail lights. He is holding the hat. He stands in traffic and the traffic goes by."

Mirina sipped from a fluted wine glass, then set it down. No one spoke. Harm put his arm across the back of Nyia's chair. Mirina began again. "Second story. Two couples, old friends, are camping in the Canadian wilderness. This was actually filmed in northern Minnesota in the Boundary Waters Canoe Area. It is raining. It is cold. One of the women is angry. The other is very sweet, always trying to cheer everyone up. The men are old friends. The angry woman would rather have gone to the Caribbean, a resort, anything but this. The sweet woman cleans the fish and gathers wood for a fire. The angry woman says, 'What are you, a slave or something?' The sweet woman scrapes the fish scales off with a knife; she splits wood. At night in the tent while the sweet woman makes love to her husband, she hears a bear rummaging about the campsite. In the morning it is a mess, but the sun is shining. The rain has stopped. As they clean up the debris, there is much talk about long marriages. Each couple has been married nearly twenty years. The sweet woman says the secret is to take what pleases you and ignore the rest. The angry woman says, 'I want more. I deserve to have more.'

"In the sunny weather the angry woman cheers up at last. She suns naked on a rock. Her husband goes fishing again. When he comes back he paddles the canoe out from shore and dives into the deep granite water. But he does not come up. He has tricked her. He has swum to the edge of the rock and there is an overhang where he has hidden. He pops up, laughing at her. She is angry again but he keeps laughing, climbs out, they make love in the forest, back from the rocks beneath the pines. 'It is always like this,' she says afterward. 'Just when I hate you, you make me laugh.'

"That night he goes out to look at the moon, smoke a cigarette. The sweet woman, his friend's wife, is sitting there in the moonlight. It is very beautiful, many stars, more than you can ever imagine. He tells the sweet woman about how he tricked his angry wife earlier in the day by hiding under the ledge. The sweet woman says she is jealous of them sometimes, the other couple. 'You are unhappy with each other, but you are passionate. Perhaps I am just too safe. I get up early and start the fire, while your wife sleeps and complains, and the two of you go fishing. Perhaps I will take a chance someday. Do something outrageous instead of always being so good.'

"He dares her to strip naked in the moonlight and dive into the glacial water. She agrees, starts to undress, then shivers. 'No,' she says. 'See? I hold back.' 'I don't,' he cries. He throws off his clothes and dives in. He does not come up. She calls out to him, knows he is hiding under the ledge. Still, he does not come up. She waits and waits. He does not come. She rouses her husband, slumbering in the tent, and tells him what has happened. Her husband says, 'He is tricking you. He probably swam down the shore and got out there. Stay here with me and keep me warm,' he says.

"In the morning the sweet woman gets up early and goes down to the water with a bucket. She leans out over the rock ledge and looks down to see the blue-white body of the man, down in the clear deep, a gash in his head, seeming to stare up at her with vacant eyes. The sweet woman sets the pail down, splashes water on her face, then walks quietly to the campsite and begins to build a fire, very deliberately, twig by twig."

Two men cleared the soup bowls from the long table and poured more wine. Nyia drank her glass quickly. This was Mirina's hour, Nyia could listen to her all night. She leaned forward on her elbows, listening carefully, and her shoulder brushed Harm's. He put his arm around her. She glanced down the table. Leonard was staring at her, watching her. Nyia let her gaze rim the other faces, all rapt before Mirina's narrative power: producers, cinematographers, actors, some crew members, makeup, wardrobe and set assistants, a few people from the press.

Any of them could have written letters, anonymously, over the years, she supposed. Could have forced the door on her cabin last night, lit the kerosene lamp, stuck a knife in her bed. The ranch was an open place, not some walled fortress; any of them might have stayed in the cabin themselves at some point. They might have hired some drunk met casually in a bar in Madrid, paid the man to follow her to Albuquerque and back, shoot at her rented Mercedes on a black road. But why? Why all that? And why go back to kill the man? What more had the dead man known?

She tried to picture which of them had been in Manzanillo when Robin was killed. Many, she realized. Leonard worked with an ensemble company; he gathered people up over years, not only actors but crew as well. She returned to Leonard's face, having circled the table, and his direct gaze was still on her. For many years he'd benefited from controlling people, creating scenarios both before a camera and in his life. She still felt he could have something to do with all of this. Even the murder. Perhaps it was creative control gone crazy, his vision become deadly, like cells multiplying too fast in the marrow of a person's bones. He could have simply lost the edge between what movie he was actually directing, an actual one or some internal drama dreamed in a sick mind. He used to direct her life. He could no longer do that, so what was he doing with that thwarted impulse? She smiled at him; she was acting. Their old game: who would look away first? He smiled back. Nyia noticed his hand was under the table, probably on Tess's thigh.

Someone had interrupted Mirina with a question about revising scripts as she went, but now she was back to the story, the New Mexico sequence. Nyia knew some parts of it, but only a few scenes. The burning lamp. The honeymoon scene they had filmed today. She was anxious to hear the whole story, even if everything would be changed as they filmed in the next few days.

"Now the last story. Are you still with me?" Mirina asked the group. "A young couple from Los Angeles is taking a road trip through the American West on a motorcycle. They stay for a few days at a motel, arguing about whether or not to marry. The woman does not want to. She feels that marriage will ruin what they have, but finally she agrees. They go to a justice of the peace; the young woman has found a wedding dress at a secondhand store. That night in the motel room, as they make love, the kerosene lantern is knocked over and the curtains go up in flames, but the fire is put out. The woman is frightened but the man thinks it is funny. That night the woman cannot sleep. 'It is a bad sign,' she thinks.

"At a bar the following night, the new bride gets

drunk and dances wildly with another man. Her new groom is despondent. He goes back to the motel, goes down to the office and gets a can of soda. The woman who runs the motel is in the back room of the office, watching TV. She invites the man to join her. She seduces him, a quick, heartless fuck on the couch with the TV going. You can tell by the man's face, he is sorry he is doing this. Afterwards the motel woman smokes. 'You don't have to worry. I won't tell your wife.' He asks her if she does this often. 'Wouldn't you?' she asks, looking around, 'if this was your life?'

"That night the bride has a nightmare. She dreams the motorcycle explodes as they are riding it.

"Because of the fire and the dream, the bride is now very afraid. She says these are omens, they must sell the motorcycle. They argue terribly, but the man agrees. In the morning he rides the bike back down into Santa Fe, sells it, and buys a wonderful old car as an exchange. They take it out for a drive and as they wind through a canyon, a gunshot echoes through the rocks. They pull over to examine the car. There's a perfect bullet hole through the side window. Up above on the foothills, a teenaged boy stands with a rifle. When they see him, the boy shoots the gun straight up at a crow, but he does not hit it.

"Later, back at the motel, the bride can't find her husband. He is with the woman who owns the motel. Not in bed though. Just sitting at a table playing cards. The bride comes in on them and knows in an instant they have been lovers. But she keeps it to herself, she says nothing.

"They begin the drive back to L.A. and she complains about the hole in the otherwise perfect car. The man says, 'You have already in two days ruined everything about my life. I am married now and I no longer have my bike.' He says, 'I will never forgive you.'

"'And you,' she says, 'have slept with another

woman on the second day of our marriage and I will never forgive you.'

"He reaches over and touches her leg. 'So we're enemies then forever?'

"She says she guesses they are. The car comes to a railroad crossing. A train is coming but very slowly— or so it seems. The red crossing lights are blinking, but there is no black-and-white railroad crossing gate. They are free to go over if they want to. He urges her to drive across the tracks in spite of the train and she does. The car stalls. She tries to start the motor up again. He gets out of the car and yells at her to jump out. It is as if she doesn't even hear him. She will not leave the car. She screams out that it is the only thing in the world that they own, she is not leaving the car. He races to the car in front of the slow but ever-approaching train, which is sounding its loud whistle. He tears her from the car as the train bears down on them, shoving the car, crumpling it like a little can. They roll down into the arroyo and lie there, holding each other as the train roars past them."

Great, thought Nyia. She had known about the train scene vaguely, but not the part about having to leap out at the last minute with an engine bearing down. In her mind, she pictured a big, red X, some mental charm of protection against Mirina's imagery.

Gunshot, bullet hole, fire and train. She wondered what would Mirina change about these scenes? Surely she would not leave a happy ending for the newlyweds. Tess was cast as the motel woman. Nyia, of course, the bride. The cheap ring still there on her finger. *Rita and Sam.*

Mirina pushed her chair back. "There is an epilogue, very brief. The camera follows the train and now it is years later. Our sculptor is walking down the aisle of the dining car. At the last table he spots a beautiful, older woman, eating alone. She is wearing a small black hat, exactly the kind you once saw in the thirties. Exactly the same sort his lover wore before she was killed. He introduces himself and asks if he can join her. It is the sweet woman from the fishing trip. By chance they have just met, their stories converge. They discuss their adult children, their several divorces, their various journeys. They go back to her private berth and make love, ponder whether or not chance meetings are the purest form of love. The sweet woman says she learned long ago that it is important to take chances. She says she never used to, but now she does. Afterward, after lovemaking, the train passes slowly through a small town. They lift the shade and peer out into the afternoon. The train passes the town dump, where a black bear paws through the remnants of dismantled households. A dog runs barking along-side the train, a crow alights on a pile of black tires. Backs of buildings. Yards. In one backyard, a woman is hanging out laundry on a line to dry. It is the bride, now aged twenty years. The groom is tinkering with a motorcycle in back of the house. The woman looks up briefly, stops what she is doing and watches the train go by. She waves."

Mirina finished and touched her empty glass; gesturing to the server for more. Jack Drieser began clapping, his applause cracking the silence.

Tess Juran pushed her chair back from the table. "That's beautiful, Mirina. Very symbolic," she said. "But why tell us the story when the whole thing changes once we start filming it? In the first two segments, the ones we've already filmed—originally they were much different. The angry woman, *moi*—I was the one who was supposed to have drowned, but it became Jack as we filmed. And the roommate was supposed to marry the sculptor in your first script. So why do you tell us these stories at all? Why set us up with expectations?"

Mirina looked up as a young man cleared her soup bowl away. "We have to begin somewhere, don't we? To give up our expectations, yes. But first we must have some. And who knows—perhaps sometimes the story does turn out exactly as we all expect it to and love prevails."

A man pushed open the door from the kitchen and carried out two plates. He served Nyia and Harm first. As Nyia took a drink of wine, her eyes came to rest on her plate: roasted quail on a bed of chard and pine nuts, garnished with grilled red peppers and green grapes. Plates were served around the table, people exclaiming over the elegance of the meal.

Nyia put the cloth napkin to her mouth and glanced up at Harm. Suddenly she felt repulsed by the meal, the small brown bird so artfully prepared. Excusing herself, Nyia hurried down the long glass hallway and out onto the dark patio. Above the foothills there was a slice of melon-colored moon. Someone had left a jacket draped over the back of a cowhide chair. She slipped it on and sat down. Nyia had felt the breath pulled right from her lungs when Mirina had launched into that part about the kid shooting from the hillside. That had not been in the script two days ago. Did it ever occur to her to check with Nyia as to whether or not she felt okay about facts from her own true life appearing in the movie? And it didn't even fit. It wasn't an organic part of the story. Except to say the bullet hole had ruined the car.

And then there was the bit with the train. Fabulous. She could hardly wait to have Jack drag her from a car parked on a track with a locomotive bearing down out of hell. Fuck that. That was a stunt scene; she wasn't going to do it. They could hire a double for that, she'd talk to Suzanne about it. That's all she needed, to be frozen in a car stalled on a train track.

He appeared behind her without a sound and she spun in the shadows to face him.

Her eyes focused on the shape in the dim light reflected from the pool.

"Nyia, are you avoiding me?"

"Christ, you scared me, Manuel," she said. "I didn't hear you until you were right here. How are you? Come, sit here with me."

The writer had taken his black hat off, his thin graying hair wiry and wild. He was a small man, thick-chested yet sinewy, with bright Spanish eyes and a melodious voice. He spoke in perfect English, had lived many years in London, but still with the accent of his country. He sat down next to her, took her hand and kissed it.

"You totally ignore me at the party."

"I apologize, Manuel. You were talking to Mirina, I got pulled into conversation with Tess and Jack. I heard you were on the set this afternoon."

"Ah, I tried to remain hidden. I know how you get when you are working. I know you're in a trance state and can't see us mere human beings!" He laughed, his eyes dark with magic. He looked out across the garden by the pool as the wind rustled the leaves, voices and glass sounds drifting out to them. "But you stay too distant. You are a difficult woman to get close to. You are a cool fire. A blue flame."

"Manuel, you're so poetic. But I didn't mean to slight you. I'm preoccupied, it's true."

Again he took her hands, both of them this time, in a courtly gesture as if they were preparing to stand and promenade in some folk dance he'd learned in his boyhood. He was an odd one, flashes of great joy, some childlike brilliance, then for days downcast, troubled, not speaking much. She hadn't minded these qualities when working with him on *Wings*. When he coiled into himself, she had time to develop her own relationship to the character. In his creative despondency, she had room to move. Once, though, when he had not spoken to her for several days, she had thought it strange. Had she displeased him in some way? Finally she'd felt too disconnected and had confronted him.

"But you have no scenes on these days," Manuel

had told her. "And if you have no scenes, I forget you exist. I forget you are not Sonia. And you Americans need attention all the time in order to know you are there! I tell you what. We will go dancing. Dancing will solve this dilemma."

That wasn't quite what she'd wanted, but she hadn't minded the way he had spun her stiffly in his arms, dancing the merengue and tango, smelling of lemons and garlic.

Now Nyia gave his hand a squeeze, then pulled away. "So, how is it you are here?" she asked. "I didn't think you'd ever even met Mirina and Leonard."

"Your precious Suzanne got me the invitation, actually. But Mirina seems to have welcomed me."

Strange the way he put that. Moravio was already a world-renowned author when he made his novel *Wings* into a film. His directorial debut had garnered international praise and numerous awards. He was far more well-known than either of the Jacobses, and Nyia could tell Mirina was terribly impressed with herself for having him as a guest, seated right next to her at dinner.

Manuel Moravio went on. "Mirina has even given me a room here at her home, what a wonderful place." He looked overhead at the stars through the cottonwoods. "But I came to see you. I'm writing a sequel to *Wings*. I never imagined it at the beginning. Actually, now I feel it may be a trilogy or a quartet. In each story, Sonia's life progresses. *Wings* took her up through her mid-twenties, to her wedding day. This next one will be her story through age forty. This may sound silly, but since you played the part of Sonia in the film version of *Wings*, you have become my muse for her character. I felt stuck in my writing and I thought if I saw you, watched you work, it would free me up in some way. I called Suzanne and she arranged with Mirina for me to come to Santa Fe. It is my first time here. Mirina and Leonard have been more than gracious. They have welcomed me into their home."

Well, they ought to, Nyia thought. He reached up and touched her face and she thought of Harm's unpretentious touch, his hand in the Jeep this afternoon. With Manuel, as with Leonard, she was not really herself. To them she was a muse, a projection, something imaginary, an archetypal force. Manuel was touching Sonia's cheek, not Nyia's. His hand lingered there, warm against her face, and this time she didn't pull away, as if she might be able to know, through his touch, whether his unexpected presence here had anything to do with the bizarre events of the last days.

"Manuel, will there be a bird again, in this new story?"

"No," he said. "You know, I first pictured Sonia as an animal of some kind. In her youth, Sonia was a bird, she was flight, she was transformation. But after her marriage, she can no longer fly."

"What do you mean? Is she damaged in some way?" Just be direct, Nyia thought. Confront him. "Have you cut off her feet?"

Moravio laughed. "What a strange question. Do you mean, have I bound her feet? Or removed her wings?" He tilted his head. "What do you mean?"

"Nothing. Go on." Blank response, she thought.

"No, her totem animal, her metaphor in the sequel will be a horse. A black mare. I bought her at an auction in Rio. I have her on my ranch outside Rio. I watch the trainers work with her every day after writing. I named her *Duende*."

"What does it mean?"

"I hope it doesn't keep people from betting on her. The word can mean soul. Or it can mean something like the presence of death."

Nyia sat slowly upright in the chair.

"No, no, it's not what you think. Its meaning is like

that sudden flash of intense life you feel when you realize your mortality. It is no different from what Leonard creates as he makes a film."

From inside the house, the voices had grown louder. Nyia wanted to go back in, to Harm's side. As she moved to stand up, Moravio grabbed her wrist. "It would be so important to me if we could spend some time alone together, Nyia, while I am here. I know you are working. But we could have dinner one night."

She drew away from his grasp, but he kept hold of her hand.

"May I bring a friend?"

Moravio looked almost alarmed. "No, of course not. I mean, I didn't come all this way to socialize with you and the rest of these people. I came to talk with you about Sonia. I need your help."

Nyia knew she didn't want to be alone with him. Then why was she sitting out here on the patio, out of Harm's sight? The wind moved among the flowers, rippling the surface of the pool.

"I am staying right here at the ranch. Mirina has prepared her small studio for me as a bedroom and you are staying downstairs. Perhaps there is simply a time to sit out here by the pool after filming one day. Or have coffee in the morning."

She didn't want to tell him she wasn't going to be staying here anymore. Suzanne had not just come out from L.A. to oversee this investigation and check up on Leonard. She had arranged for Moravio to be here, it would be necessary to spend time with him. She would be expected to help Moravio write his book, and of course, she would be invited to play Sonia in return, the role for which she'd won the Academy Award. Nyia knew all this, but she stood and stepped away from the writer back toward the lights of the house. Perhaps there would be some way to spend time with Manuel, but to have Harm nearby. Seated across a room at a local restaurant. She didn't want to be alone with

Manuel. Not with anyone, she realized. Not even with someone for whom she had enormous respect.

"Of course we'll have time to talk, Manuel. Let me arrange it with Suzanne, she knows my schedule."

"Are you angry with me?" he asked suddenly. He palmed his hair, nearly bowing to her.

"Of course not. Please don't take offense," she said. "You know how actors get toward the end of filming. It doesn't have anything to do with . . ."

Just then Dan Howe, Leonard's assistant, opened the patio doors and spotted them down the veranda. "Coffee is being served, Nyia, Señor Moravio. Mirina asked me to send for you."

Inside, people were milling around, standing by the fire in the living room, drinking coffee from Mirina's collection of china cups. Harm came up behind her. "Don't go off like that," he whispered into her hair.

"I was just outside the door."

"I know where you were. I was on the other side of the pool watching you from behind a fence."

She turned to face him. "I didn't even see you."

"Of course not," he said. "You're not watching the edges. I am."

"Thank you," she said. "But I was doing some investigation of my own and I found out something. Manuel Moravio is staying upstairs in Mirina's office. But I don't think he arrived until today."

Even though she'd had coffee, Nyia was tired. She motioned Harm over from his conversation with Moravio by the fireplace, and told him she was going down to her room to pack up her things, that she wanted to leave soon.

"There is one thing I forgot, out in the cabin," she told him. "It's way back in the closet, an old leather briefcase. Could you go get it for me?"

He excused himself from the party and Nyia returned to her room, folding her clothes into a bag, then a notebook, alarm clock, and paperback novel she'd not had a chance to read. Her back was turned when someone opened the door, then knocked; an afterthought. She glanced over her shoulder as Jack Drieser shut the door.

"Where are you off to?" he asked.

"The La Fonda," she lied. "It just gets too weird staying here. With Leonard and all. You know . . ."

Jack smiled, hands in his pockets. "I just wanted to thank you for today . . . for helping me get through that scene. I just couldn't seem to get all the way in. When you made me laugh—well, thanks."

"Now you can help me if I can't get in."

"You're always in, though. I mean, you seem to be able to get into a part and stay there through the whole filming. I envy that. Although it takes its toll, doesn't it?"

"What do you mean?" she asked.

"I don't know. You get so involved, intense about everything. Are you seeing Leonard again? You've got that glassy, kind of distant feel to you."

She shook her head. "No. You know that's over, Jack."

"These things are never black and white, though, are they?

"No," she repeated. "I've made a clear decision about Leonard. It's been over for quite some time. If you were a tad bit more observant, you'd see he has a new attachment."

"Tess?" he asked.

"Bingo, baby."

"Goddamn," Jack said. "One of these days, I'm going to take up directing. Great benefits, that job." Then his face was serious again. Nyia zipped the bag up and looked around the room. "Why didn't you tell me about the fire in your cabin last night, Nyia? Tess filled me in."

Nyia sat at the edge of the bed. "I didn't have a chance, Jack. I didn't see you until we were on the set today."

"You could have told me then. You could have come to my trailer, we could have talked. This is the same kind of shit that happened down in Mexico. I deserve to know if we're heading into Strangeville again, don't I?"

She looked down at her hands, spread her palms open. Which one was her life line? she wondered. Someone had once told her she had old palms, many lives. "I'm sorry, Jack. I'm pretty shook up about it, to tell you the truth."

"Well, so am I. Could you please keep me posted, if you notice other things going on?"

First Tess, then Jack, unable to speak truthfully to either one. She felt cut off from them, from everyone, not even trusting Moravio just now at the party. The secrecy of it all. Harm undercover. Was it all just some way for Leonard to carry on, create dissension and separation between them? She longed to tell Jack what was going on. *Check with Harm first,* she thought.

"I will, Jack."

"And let's just go out or something. Hang out like we did down in Mexico. We don't have to get so serious about it all, do we?"

"There's some other stuff going on," she said. "It's not just the film."

"Ah, the professor then?"

"What is this, Jack, twenty questions?"

"You know I have to keep tabs on you."

"He's not bad, though, is he? It might be nice to date a professor."

Jack leaned back against the door. "Well, it was nice making love with you today, Nyia."

It had been nice, in its own strange way—though they really hadn't made love, of course. Just the feel of skin against skin. Lonely, she thought. When all you got was love play-acted in front of a camera. Worse yet, when that's all you really wanted because the rest was too complicated.

"You mean Christine," she said.

"Yeah. Christine."

There was a knock at the door and Jack opened it. Harm stood there with the briefcase, looking surprised, then angry, all in an instant. "Your briefcase, Miss Wyatt." He set it down and turned to walk back down the hall.

"I was just leaving," said Jack. He brushed past Harm toward the living room.

Harm returned to her door, but didn't speak. He picked up her suitcase and the briefcase and she followed him out to the Jeep parked in the circular drive in front of the house. There was a thick silence between them. The peacock moved between the cars, in the long shadows of a floodlight. Up the drive, near the road, Nyia saw a squad car parked. Security, she thought. Just keeping an eye. She felt relieved.

Harm didn't speak until they were nearing town, coming down Bishop's Lodge Road into the close streets of Santa Fe, lined with lilacs and adobe walls.

"Look, it's none of my business," said Harm, "but I'm trying to look out for you. I didn't feel comfortable with you going off to talk to Moravio. Then I find you alone with Drieser. Door closed. I want you to try to stay out in the open, where there are other people around you. Can we agree on that? Don't go off with people."

"But these are all people I know very well," she said.

"That doesn't mean shit. You know Jacobs, too. You don't trust him, do you?"

"I can't become a total paranoid."

"You don't have to, but don't be stupid either."

"Don't talk to me like that. You're working for me."

"I'm working for Jacobs." He kept his eyes straight

ahead on the winding road. Suddenly she realized he was a little jealous. "So which hotel do you want to go to?" he asked.

"The Bohland Inn," she said. "If there's still a vacancy."

HE BECOMES OBSESSED WITH THINGS HAPPENING *in pairs. When there are two of anything, it is some kind of sign to him. Like the two women in Mexico, the two who looked so much alike, the two dresses, they both had the same dress, the black and white, opposition and parallel. Two horses in the corral, two o'clock in the afternoon, two of a kind, good things come in pairs, tea for two, too much, too little, too soon.*

Perhaps, he thinks, he has gone too far in the world itself. There is a safety in imagination, if he stays in that realm with her—fantasy, ideation, he can see it all, control it. So he pulls back, yes, he feels afraid. He can see that in the world there is outcome, there is reaction and the loss of privacy that his fantasy world contains. For instance, out walking tonight, looking at the lit house across the field, he saw the squad car parked on the dark road to the house. Because he had gone into her room last night, because he had been there, tonight there are police. Causality.

So he contents himself with imagery, promises himself it will stay at that level, go no further.

Idea for scene, possible dream sequence: They are dancing, she in the black and white dress. No, better yet, the wedding dress, the strapless lace dress that she wears in the film. Bare shoulders, neck, the thin bones of her spine. But in the hand he has at her back, as he dances with her, as he leads her, he holds a knife. She does not see the knife, but she feels it, he presses her more closely to him, pulls the knife up through her hair as if with fingers, combing the black knife through her hair as they dance, and she tilts her neck back, feeling it then, trying to back away from him with a sudden thrust. Expertly, she spins in his arms and when she faces him again she is holding the blade.

No. I don't want that. Why did that picture enter? It is getting more difficult. There is no control even in the fantasies. Why is she holding the knife? She should not.

Then he realizes, curses under his breath. He left it there. Idiot. When he ran out last night to get the camera, he left it there on her bed. Took the robe, left the fucking knife. For an instant a hot wave of shock goes through him. But then he remembers, he wore gloves. Of course he did.

But she has it now, he is sure of it. Has some part of him. And for a moment he is afraid he is losing power. But then he remembers that things always happen in pairs.

ELEVEN

SHE APPEARED AT THE DOOR AS HE FINISHED spreading a blanket on the fold-out couch in the back room where they'd watched the strange history-of-her-life scrapbook video last night. She'd changed out of her violet leather into black cotton leggings and an oversized white T-shirt. No makeup, the crimson heart lips and shadowed eyes washed clean now, her natural face, open and radiant, but not plain. It occurred to him that her natural face might be just another persona, another layer. She was a complex person, always shifting. It was like looking into a kaleidoscope: you knew it was the same view, it was all done with mirrors, light, pretty colored glass, all angles and perception. It was beautiful.

"I almost forgot," she said. She lifted the briefcase he'd retrieved from the cabin and spread it open on the bed, parting the accordion compartments, peering into the slots, pulling out junk as she searched for something, dropping the objects back in. "I found another letter, one that must have slipped out of the pile."

Harm watched as she held up an old corsage in a plastic Ziploc bag, a postcard from Aspen, a tiny plastic baby doll, a birthday candle, snapshots. Finally she found it, the blue tissue letter, and handed it to him.

"What's all this stuff? Props to get in character with?"

She snapped it shut, looked embarrassed. "Never thought of it that way. Actually it's to get out of character. It's the original Memory Lounge."

"What do you mean?"

"Look around here at your place, this room right here. School photos of your kid, a trophy for what— racquetball—over there on that shelf. Calligraphy on the wall of some Zen saying you like. I mean, you can do that with a home, all your trivia right there to remind you of who you are. Reflect you back to yourself. So when I travel I carry this with me. It's just mementos, souvenirs, keepsakes. In lieu of an attic, I guess. I'm on the road so much of the time. Go ahead." She motioned with her head. "You can snoop. Nothing in there is valuable."

He fingered through the trinkets: programs to awards dinners, mother-of-pearl button, matches from a hotel. Harm lifted out a packet of photographs, some familiar faces. Nyia sat next to him on the fold-out bed, peering over his shoulder as he flipped through the pictures.

"That's Robin in Manzanillo," she said quietly. "Mirina, taking a nap. Jack and Suzanne at a benefit for the homeless. This is an old one." There were several Polaroids of fish spread out on ferns and leaves on some black rocks.

"Good catch," he said.

"Jack caught those. We had quite a feast."

A handbill for a summer stock theater in Oregon—

her mother, Carole Wyatt, in the role of Amanda Wingfield in *The Glass Menagerie*. Harm put the photos back in the briefcase and clasped it shut. He was aware that Nyia was sitting very close to him, looking down at her hands curled in her lap. He read the letter quickly; it was an older one, not threatening or strange in tone. Yet the elements of fantasy were still there. *Picture this . . . I imagine that . . . Sometimes when I'm almost asleep, I think of you. . . .*

Someone who thought of himself as a character in her life. Leonard? It was possible. A random fan? Even chaos had pattern. Random motions of wind and movements of gnats in clouds when documented on computers showed repetition, some kind of plan. It was always a question of watching long enough, closely enough, to see the intelligence in the activity. To see the reason.

"There's got to be some logic to what's going on," he said.

"There does?"

"How long since you and Leonard have been involved?" he asked.

"Three years. More or less."

"What do you mean, more or less?"

She looked down at her hands. "It's hard to break off totally from Leonard. You have to be a stone or something."

"Are you still in love with him?"

She shook her head immediately. "We have a long, long history. And I care deeply about Leonard. Mirina too. But I'm not in love. I've sorted that out. What about you? Have you ever been in love? You know how it is—how it's never really over, but it is? What about your ex-wife, do you still have an attachment to her? Does it come up sometimes and grab you and just pull you down?" She looked at him through a tangle of hair.

"You mean Sandy?" he asked. "Yeah, there was a bond, eleven years' worth. We had good times. But by the time we split up it was gone for us, and it had been like that for a couple years. I don't know where it went. We numbed out. Or I did. So, no, there's no lingering attachment. Sometimes when I see her, I wonder how come I ever did love her. Who did I think I was? Who did I think she was?"

"So you were really able to move on, then?"

Harm thought about that. *Into what, though?* he wondered. If he'd truly moved on, perhaps he'd have been able to attach to someone new. But he hadn't. The women he'd been with had been interesting, dull, passionate, shallow, smart, a little cold, fun, serious, but none of them had taken hold. He hadn't opened. Did that mean he was still attached to Sandy?

Finally he said, "No, I don't think I've really moved on. I'm not with her, but there's some other way people get stuck. Some stay hung up on the same person from their past, some just numb out. I think I was asleep with her. Maybe I still am."

"Do you think you'll ever wake up?" Nyia asked. "I hope you don't mind me asking. Seeing you with your boy today, I just got to thinking."

"About?"

"About men. About you," she said. Guileless. Perfectly open. He noticed his breath was thick in his chest and his thighs ached. He ran a fingernail under his thumbnail to avoid looking at her so closely. It was her eyes, he'd decided, the intensity of them. See through to the back of your head. Didn't blame Leonard one bit, he thought. And love? He'd once thought it meant comfort, available sex. That was a good definition for starters. One his ex-wife thought was pretty lame. He guessed it was, but he didn't know what else to think or was afraid to imagine. He looked up at Nyia Wyatt's eyes and thought, *night, night, sleep tight, baby.* He had to get out of there, the way she was looking at him.

He changed the subject then, to get the focus off

himself. "What about Mirina? Is there residual anger that comes up when you work with her, left from the time you were Leonard's lover?"

"I'm not with him, she knows that. Tess is. At least it seems that way."

"Maybe she knows you're not involved with him now, and she wants to make sure it stays that way. Like you said, there are still times when you're attracted to him, still times when you sleep with him—"

Nyia held up her palm. "Not anymore. Not for some time."

"When was the last time?"

Her dark eyes darted back and forth, as if she were scanning a page. Suddenly she covered her face with her hands. "Oh, God," she whispered.

"When was it, Nyia?"

She shook her head, then looked up at Harm. "It wasn't the last time we made love, but the last time we almost did. See, what happens is that there are times when we both seem to fall into it, the familiarity, a seductive, almost playful feeling. And I have to watch it really closely or I can be right back in with him without even knowing how it happened.

"It was a year ago last spring. I was seeing him a lot because of the grand jury investigation into Robin's death. That dinner party, I wasn't feeling well and he drove me home."

"Wait a minute. The night your house was broken into? Leonard drove you home that night?"

"Yes," she said. "He came in, and suddenly we were at it, but I pulled away. I couldn't get back into it with him, it was too painful. I'd fall in love so deeply and he was married, it was the same dilemma over and over. I asked him to leave."

Harm watched her eyes, again the quick, back-and-forth movements, her focus internal, bringing the memory up. "Yes, he left. And I lay down to read the screenplay and fell asleep and when I woke—"

Harm stood and stuffed his hands in his pockets. "Did you report this to the police after the assault, that Leonard had just been there?"

Nyia put her hand to her temple. She mouthed the word but didn't speak it: *No.*

"Why, Nyia? Didn't you think it might have been Leonard, coming back after you'd rejected him?"

"Why would I have thought that, Harm? He loved me."

He rolled his eyes at her.

"Okay, so it's obvious to you," she said. "But there are things you just don't see at the time. Love makes black holes in people. You said yourself you were asleep for years. I was too. But I'm awake now. Just barely, maybe. No, I never thought Leonard would break into my house, the house he'd just had a security system installed in, for chrissake."

"But why didn't you tell anyone he'd just been there?"

Nyia just smiled at him, an ironic, angry grin. He'd never seen her do that, and when she spoke, it was in some kind of accent, part French or part Eastern European, a drawl as if she were in a part. "We didn't want Mirina to know he'd driven me home, that we had just been together. It was a secret."

"You mean you agreed on that beforehand, that you wouldn't tell?"

Then she was back in her own voice. Odd, quick switching of selves. "Okay, *I* didn't want Mirina to know. *I* didn't tell the police he'd driven me home. *I* said that Leonard had a driver take me home."

"Goddamn it, Nyia. I mean, truth is truth. It's not like onion layers unfolding. How do I know if you're telling me everything?"

"I'm telling you everything I know. Everything I'm aware of knowing right now." She lay back on the fold-out couch and covered her face with her arm as if shielding her eyes from the lamplight. Quietly, she added, "What I've come to realize is that in your shame you hide things, even from yourself. And it becomes a habit. That kind of deception. Self-deception. I'm trying really hard to break out of that, Harm. It's hard to explain to someone who hasn't experienced it. Please understand, I got hooked into Leonard when I was fifteen years old. That double life, keeping secrets. Lying. Sometimes it's still like he's part of my psyche, not a separate person."

Harm watched her speak, still with her face covered. The way she put that sounded much like the letter writer. *I'm part of you. You're in me.*

She turned over then, pushed her face into the pillow and pulled the blanket up over her legs. "I've got to get to sleep," she said.

"Let's talk about it again in the morning," said Harm. "See if there is anything else you remember." He shut the door behind him with a click.

In the next room, lights out, fifteen or twenty minutes later, his eyes were still open, watching shadows barely move on the wall. Then she was at his door, knocking lightly, standing in the orange shadow of the nightlight he kept in the hall for Nickie, a shadow in T-shirt and bare legs.

"I can't get to sleep," she said quietly.

He sat up, waited. "I sleep real light," he told her. "I'll hear if there's any trouble. It'll be okay."

She shifted to the other foot, silent.

It had to be just his own lumbering desire, thudding awake like a stupid bear. It had been a long time. Yeah, he was making it up, but there was that ache that went silent through the air between people, and it felt like that. Too long alone, it made you weird, he thought.

Finally, she just said, "Have you got any ibuprofen?"

He brought it into the back room along with a glass of water. Stood there while she drank it down. It was she who acted first. She took his hand and pulled him down to her, the weight of his chest across her shoulders. He was afraid she wouldn't be able to breathe. He laid his body along hers, his cock swelling against her thigh. He lifted his face and moved her hair from her lips, put his mouth down on hers, awkward at first, her mouth too far open. She closed it a little, let him lead, followed him, very soft and full, her mouth, and their tongues reached in past teeth like some kind of blind, unintelligible language. She shifted her sharp hips up under him, her leg between his, forcing it softly up against his groin.

"This isn't a real good idea," he whispered and kissed her again, harder now, putting his mouth over hers.

"Yes, it is," she whispered. "It's not an idea."

"It might not be ethical," he said.

"Really?" she asked. "But you're not sure?" He slid his hand under her shirt and her breast was cold, the nipple hard, centered in his palm.

Her palm ran the length of his chest, down over his belt and jeans, holding him there, the tips of her fingers curving around him, her nails through the stiff cloth.

"Then don't do anything," she whispered. "Just lie here with me. We don't have to do anything. I just don't want to be alone. Will you hold me? Just stay here with me?"

He lifted her shirt, blue cotton against her white, white skin, just looked at her beneath him like that, chest rising in breaths, her mouth open. Sure. Just lie there, he thought. Do nothing. He looked behind him to make sure there were no candles burning, no kerosene lamps. Then reached up and snapped the light off, put his tongue to her hard breast.

When she slid around him, took him into her, he had the oddest feeling that today's scene with Jack had been foreplay. That she had felt unfinished then, with everyone watching. For a moment she seemed far away, far down in her body, gulping toward him, swimming against him in her waves. Then he thought, no, it was he who'd felt unfinished. He and probably everyone who'd watched them. But she was lovely, greedy and fast, said his name and then, "I'm here, I'm here for you," and she was. He let go then, too, followed her down.

Sometime in the night he woke, cold. She was pressed against him, holding him from behind, her arms circling his chest. He pulled the blanket around them and thought of her shame about almost sleeping with Leonard that night of the break-in and his judgmental attitude. But it happens, he thought. It happens that quick. She shifted in her sleep, her smooth skin cool against his back.

It didn't seem right to leave her there alone. Harm stood for a few minutes at the door watching her sleep, hair tangled across the crumpled pillow. Dawn-gray light came in through rice-paper shades. His office was a little over five minutes away down Acequia Madre, around Paseo de Peralta. Quintana had said he would meet him there to get the package left at her trailer on the set yesterday, see if the damn things matched the dove in the dead man's house.

And he needed to check for calls and messages before driving Nyia up to Española for the day. Fifteen to twenty minutes he'd be gone, at most.

Closing and locking the front door, he checked his watch. 8:10. He looked up and down the quiet street, lined with walled-in houses, high wooden and adobe walls, a dirt road only minutes from downtown Santa Fe. A black dog walked to an open gate and lay down. Otherwise the street was empty. He backed out and drove to Acequia Madre, then wheeled around and returned to the house, as if he'd forgotten something. Emptiness and tranquility. She'd be okay for a few minutes.

Six minutes to his office: he'd never timed it. The morning paper lay just inside the screen door and he flipped it open. It wasn't a top-of-the-page headline, but you couldn't miss it: FILM COMPANY HARASSED BY SNIPER, BURGLARY.

Great, he thought. So much for Jacobs's almighty privacy. It was bound to get out. He scanned the article:

Visionfilm crew members in Santa Fe to complete work on a feature-length film starring Nyia Wyatt have been harassed by a sniper's bullets and a break-in at the Tesuque ranch of director Leonard Jacobs. A car driven by Miss Wyatt was fired at by an unidentified sniper on Highway 14 between Madrid and Cerrillos at approximately 10:30 p.m. the night of June 25th. The following night a guest house on the Jacobses' ranch was broken into and vandalized. A small fire broke out, but nothing was reported stolen.

Police reports indicate the incidents are isolated and may have no connection to one another, but crew members working on the film expressed relief that Visionfilm has arranged with the New Mexico Film Commission for extra security on the set and at the Jacobses' home on Bishop's Lodge Road. During the filming of *Dead Heat*, also starring Nyia Wyatt, a young actress, Robin Reese, was murdered. There were no suspects in the case and the murder remains unsolved. A crew member who asked to remain anonymous stated that no one wants a repetition of what happened on the last film.

Auteur Jacobs, known for his iconoclastic filmmaking methods, insisted that the set, just south of Española on Highway 25, will be a safe and protected environment for the remainder of filming. The company hopes to complete work next week and return to Los Angeles.

Harm spread the paper out on his desk, folding the pages over. There in the second section, several pages in, he found it. CERRILLOS SLAYING BAFFLES POLICE. A name, finally: Howard Nims, woodworker, woodcutter, handyman. Forty-seven. As he read the article quickly, he noticed that key elements had been left out of each article. No mention of Nims's bird. No mention of the recovered buck knife or the shredded quilt. Quintana must be keeping things back from the media.

It was good Jacobs had arranged for added security. The location of the set up by Española had been given, as well as the location of the Jacobses' ranch. He shook his head. The set would be crazy today, he bet, full of gawkers.

He wondered if either of the Jacobses had been interviewed for the article. Security had been mentioned several times. Perhaps it was some kind of insurance. Let the public know the place was being watched. At the end of the article, Quintana was quoted as saying, "New Mexico has always been known for its hospitality to the film industry. But with public events, rock concerts, festivals, fairs, there is always the chance of disruption. We're here to make sure those types do not have access to the set. Security will be increased and only those with passes will be allowed in."

Harm played his messages back, jotting down names and numbers. Hirsch's voice came on: "Okay, Mr. B., here's what you wanted. John Sand was in prison July 1, 1987 through October 28, 1988. Over and out." The last voice was Suzanne Scolfield's. He'd chatted with her briefly at the party last night and found her more accommodating in person than she'd seemed on the phone.

"Mr. Bohland, Suzanne Scolfield here. Obviously we couldn't confer openly last night, but I'd appreciate being able to speak with you today, perhaps on the set. Or contact me at my hotel this evening at this number."

The screen door banged against the loose frame as Quintana knocked. He stuck his face in and Harm waved him in.

"What do we have?" Quintana asked.

Harm placed the package on the edge of the desk and Quintana examined it, nodding slowly, scrunching up his nose. The things had a faint odor of rotting flesh.

"It's got to be the same person," said Quintana. "I'll have the lab check these out. Guy definitely wore gloves; we didn't get any prints out there. Wore them in the cabin too. Very careful, very deliberate. Assuming the cabin break-in was this same person. There isn't anything yet that definitely connects them."

Quintana eased himself into a chair in front of Harm's desk. "Nims definitely knew something," he said. "I'm thinking this: Nims was hired to kill Wyatt. But he messed up. Didn't get the job done. Whoever hired him goes back and kills Nims to cover his ass. In order to follow her, Nims has to know she's going to Albuquerque, right? Has to be tracking her. Maybe followed her all the way from Tesuque, maybe just knew she'd be at the airport. Picked her up there."

Harm remembered the scribbled appointment book Jacobs had left on the table in his foyer. "Jacobs was supposed to have been with her; he'd planned to go," he told Quintana. "It was written on his calendar."

"So both Jacobses knew Nyia Wyatt was going to Albuquerque to the airport?"

"And possibly other Visionfilm staff. Howe, for instance, Jacobs's assistant."

"Who else?" Quintana asked, almost to himself.

"Well, Juran," said Harm. "Tess Juran. She left a message for Nyia with the airlines, saying she was taking another flight."

Quintana frowned. "Missed the plane, did she? That's funny. Doesn't sound right. Say Nims follows Wyatt to the airport, sees she's alone. No Jacobs, no Juran. Follows her back on the Turquoise Trail. Fires, misses. Twice."

"He didn't exactly miss."

"He missed her. Next day, boom, Nims is dead," said Quintana.

"And the next day Wyatt receives this pretty little thing." Harm nodded toward the claws.

Quintana stood abruptly. "I've got to get out to the set. Are you going to be up there today?"

"I'm driving Nyia Wyatt up there."

Harm checked his watch as Quintana slammed out the screen door. Twenty-five minutes he'd been gone. Damn. She was probably still sleeping.

He wanted to check the passenger lists of incoming flights from L.A. to see if indeed Juran had held a ticket for that flight. He knew the airlines would not give out that information, but maybe Quintana could get it. It was just something about Nyia driving all the way to Albuquerque to get a person who never showed up. Drive in and out alone on a dark road. It seemed like a setup. Had someone suggested she take the Turquoise Trail? If he could get close to Juran on the set today, he'd just ask her when and how she got to New Mexico.

Goddamn it, thought Harm, this undercover thing was bullshit. He couldn't really find anything out by staying in a false role. He couldn't question Moravio about his whereabouts the evening of June twenty-fifth. He couldn't question Howe about animosity between Reese and the other crew members down in Manzanillo. He was stuck making phone calls to L.A. and reading magazines in the basement of the library. Anyway, Quintana would be up there today—and he already knew Harm was a detective working for Jacobs. The whole thing was cloying, limiting.

Maybe that was just what Jacobs wanted, he thought. He remembered that Hirsch had given him shit on the phone yesterday: *Why not hire some top-rate security operation out of Beverly Hills?* Why him indeed, with his half-inch listing in the yellow pages that said, "specializing in accounting"? Maybe he wasn't *undercover* at all. Maybe he was just gagged. Made ineffective by his role, impotent. Take all the directness and power out of what an investigator does: *investigate*. But why? Why hire him and then make him powerless or at least operating at half-power? To appease Nyia, give her a feeling of false security?

Again he checked his watch, stood and rewound the answering machine, listening to Hirsch's message again, this time jotting the dates down.

It wasn't until he was nearly back to his house that he realized Sand had been released from prison less than a month before Robin Reese was killed.

Nyia turned as he came into the kitchen, twisting the telephone cord around her waist. She was dressed in black jeans and last night's white T-shirt, dirty white sneakers, and wire-frame glasses.

"So there's no way out?" she asked. "Isn't there some clause in my contract about working conditions or health? Mental health! Couldn't I be diagnosed by a psychiatrist? Say I'm unable to continue? Isn't that what Tess did down in Mexico?"

She was listening then. Interrupting once, "But, Suzanne . . ." then listening again.

"I know, I get it. Because the actual filming hadn't started when Tess left. Yes, I do appreciate it, Suzanne. You were absolutely right to come out and pressure him into getting added security. I don't know why he just didn't have it all along. So you think that will be enough, restricted access to the sets, and staying here with Bohland? Do I need a bodyguard too?" Silent again. Coiling and uncoiling the cord around her finger. "No, I really am going to lay low. Just work, then I'm out of there. Yes, he will be with me the whole time. Okay. Yeah. It feels like a comfortable arrangement." She looked over at Harm and smiled.

He knew she was part mirage and thought, *That's all right. As long as I don't forget it.*

Nyia said a few last words to Scolfield and hung up. "She arranged with Leonard to schedule all my scenes in the next three days, so I can get out of here. Condense my part of the work and move it up. She's convinced Leonard that without me on the set it's actually safer for everyone."

Nyia crossed the red-and-black tiled kitchen and stood close to him. "Thank you," she said quietly. She kissed him lightly on the mouth.

"I'm going to talk to Jacobs today about getting out from under cover. I feel boxed in," he said. "I can't really get into any kind of inquiry when I'm in this role."

"I think Suzanne would totally support you in that. She's furious at Leonard for setting it up that way."

"Maybe I'll talk to her first and have her handle it. She could demand it on your behalf. Sounds like she's got some clout."

"Yeah. She's muscular," said Nyia.

On the way out of Santa Fe, Harm stopped by the Galisteo Newsstand near the plaza and ran in to pick up a copy of the *Los Angeles Times*. Nyia rattled the pages in the wind as they drove out on St. Francis, out through the low foothills, past the site of the Santa Fe Opera and up a small rise, the vista of the Sangre de Cristos rising before them and the dry-sea emptiness of the landscape.

"Here it is," she said. "Entertainment section, front page."

So he'd guessed right, Harm thought. If it was in the Albuquerque papers, it was bound to be in the *Times*. There were a few press people at last night's dinner. They had to have seen the squad car on the road as they came in, and asked about it.

Nyia read out loud, "'Life is stranger than fiction on the set of Visionfilm Productions' Santa Fe-based location. Unsettling occurrences that plagued the production of the cult film *Dead Heat* in Mexico seem to be repeating themselves in Leonard and Mirina Jacobs's new picture, starring Nyia Wyatt, Jack Drieser, and Tess Juran.'"

"Leonard is going to go nuts over this," she said, then read on.

"The media might be a kind of deterrent," said Harm. "All the talk about increased security and all. Might be enough to scare the guy off."

Nyia folded the paper and stuck it in the folder of notes on her lap. "It feels the opposite to me. Like the spotlight is really on now. Who was the guy that wanted Jodie Foster to fall in love with him? I mean, sometimes it's exactly the media attention that crazy people want. Son of Sam? The Zodiac Killer? Okay, so now the world's watching our quiet little avant-garde film. This is what happened after Robin died. The press picked it all up and went crazy. You saw all the articles Leonard gave you."

"Isn't that good for business?" Harm asked.

"Yeah," she said. "If you live through it."

Nyia closed her eyes and they rode in silence. Nearing Española, he could see the traffic lining the road on either side near the set. Four or five New Mexico State Patrol cars and squad cars from Santa Fe and Española were parked along the road, one blocking the entrance into the parking lot across from the motel. In addition, there was a television van with a satellite dish on top—Albuquerque station KOAT, Channel 7. L.A. was next.

"What scenes are you doing today?" Harm asked.

"Look at this goddamn circus," she muttered. Harm pulled up behind a black van stopped at the police barricade.

Nyia turned to him. "I think it might be the wedding scene. But with Leonard, you never know."

She rolled the window down as they waited for the police to finish with the van. It was cooler up here and she pulled her leather jacket around her, lit a cigarette and blew the smoke out as she read her notes.

Harm glanced out at her through the privacy of mirrored glasses and he could feel her click into character. It was almost a physical sensation of her leaving, someone else there beside him. He wondered what she was like when she wasn't working. Some people thrived on crisis even while protesting it, and she'd lived like this for years. You couldn't really get hold of her, and that mystery was exactly what made her so fascinating. Moody, mercurial. For an instant he felt the blankness in her and knew it was something she was creating, a space for Christine to take over. Again he wondered who exactly he'd made love to last night, Nyia or Christine?

While they waited, he scribbled on an index card: *Mirina: What scenes with potential violence will be in upcoming shots? When will the train sequence be filmed?*

When he looked up across the parking lot, he spotted Suzanne Scolfield approaching the Jeep. She was wearing suede pants, a white shirt, strands of beaded Indian jewelry—her hair pulled back by a black headband, dark red lips, sunglasses. She smiled and motioned for Nyia to come.

Nyia touched Harm's shoulder. "You'll stay close today?"

He nodded.

"I didn't sleep well last night. Do I look puffy?"

"Yeah, a little doughy right over here on the left cheek." He poked her gently.

She smiled, then smiled again. "You don't know how good that feels."

"What?" he asked.

"Just cutting through like that. Teasing me. It gets so intense sometimes. Just to know someone is out there."

She got out of the Jeep and slammed the door.

"And where are you, Nyia?" he asked.

She turned back and peered in the open window, cigarette in the corner of her mouth. For a second, a frightened look washed over her face and then a dark scowl.

Christine, thought Harm.

"Who, me?" Nyia asked.

TWELVE

"HOW'S THE RESEARCH GOING?" JACK DRIESER'S hands were full of script pages, a coffee cup, a Walkman and cassette tape boxes, and a white motel towel was draped over one arm. He came over to where Harm was sitting in a folding metal chair, sat down in one beside him, dusted off the knee of his black jeans. "I think I'm getting married today," he said. "I'm not certain, but that's my guess. You never know exactly which scene they're going to shoot."

Odd choice for a leading man, thought Harm. Yes, he was charismatic, he had a certain intensity. Thinning hair, slightly overbuilt in the shoulders, as if to make up for his height. But Dustin Hoffman was short too. And wasn't Humphrey Bogart supposed to have been only about five-nine?

Jack was bouncing one knee nervously. "I get all twitchy right before a shoot. Energy. Too much coffee." He laughed.

"What makes you the most nervous?" asked Harm.

"Look at this place," said Jack. "Cops all over, television stations sending in crews—I hate this media shit. Filming up near Canada, we were completely alone. Out in the boonies at some lodge, we'd go out fishing between takes on lakes so clear you could spot agates six feet down in the water. Glacial, though. Fucking cold."

"What about the psychological techniques Jacobs claims to bring to this whole process? You talked about that some last night at the party—but does that ever get in the way?"

Drieser poured the coffee slowly out into the dust at his feet. "Tastes like dirt," he said, then sighed. "You bet. It can get troublesome, blurring the edges between the film and your life, you know? Plus, you never know how far he'll take it. What he'll do to create that effect."

"Are you saying he actually creates these parallels, sets them up?"

"That's my opinion," said Jack. "Basically, I think the man likes to live in his own movie."

"Do you think it's effective? Artistically, I mean."

Drieser rubbed his face with the towel. "It's kind of a hype. You know, it's Jacobs's *context*. I know Nyia really gets into it, but as far as I'm concerned it just adds to the heebie-jeebies. I mean, if you get into that shit, it makes the job feel fucking haunted, you know what I mean?"

"Is that what it felt like down in Manzanillo?"

"Oh yeah. It was too weird. But that's what Leonard does. He juices everybody into this high state of drama. But Robin—he didn't have anything to do with that. You know what my theory is about Robin? She had a death wish. Unconsciously or something. I'm not any shrink, but she pushed things to the edge, you know? Out in the middle of the night playing the part of the woman who gets killed in the movie. That's just stupid. She's out at what, two A.M. in a back alley, drunk on her ass, wearing the character's dress, you see what I'm getting at?"

"I'd think that too much melodrama on the set would be counterproductive."

"I'll tell you one thing," said Drieser. "Actors getting killed on the set is counterproductive. Sometimes I think Leonard does it just for publicity. It's his angle, his con. Mr. Avant-Garde. He's brilliant at it. Whatever is going on during the making of the film is cycled right back into the film as well as outward to the media. Look at them swarming around here today. They love to come on location with Visionfilm, because it's totally unpredictable. Look what Robin's death did to *Dead Heat*. It was like people went to see the film because of what happened during the filming. Its reputation preceded it, you know? There were even rumors that actual footage of Robin's body was used in the film. Another slanderous bit of information printed by your friends and mine, trash publications of America. Thank God you're writing a book no one will ever read. It will keep you honest. No offense. I mean, you're not writing for a tabloid, working class or highbrow, you know what I'm saying? *National Lies and Libel*. Here they come now, hungry little water bugs skating around on the surface of things, looking for something to devour."

Harm watched as a very tall woman strode across the dust to the shade where he and Drieser sat talking. She was well over six feet, in white cowboy boots, white shirt, and tight jeans ripped at the knees. She wore a large straw cowboy hat over peroxide-blond hair, black hatband with a small fan of feathers tucked in at the side. Silver sunglasses shaded her eyes. "Jackie!" she cried. "Good morning, Mr. Zip, Zip Zip!"

"See, man? They are story-hungry. Everybody wants a piece."

"Who is that?" Harm asked.

"Dierdre Fine. Writes for *Vanity Fair*. She's written about me and Nyia before, and she's mean. She'll find someone who knew you back in seventh grade when you got caught shoplifting at a mall. She'll track down your ex-wives and pay them for dirt quotes. She loves that shit. I thought I'd get good press if I slept with her, but it got even worse. Thought I'd try it again though, you never know." Drieser winked at Harm. "The woman is big."

"What time did you get up?" Dierdre Fine called to Jack as she approached. "Jesus, you people work strange hours." She took the hat off and handed it to Jack. "You left this hat in my room, John Wayne. And who might this be?"

Jack introduced Harm, then said he had to be getting over to makeup. Harm glimpsed Nyia heading out toward the set motel, oblivious as a sleepwalker and already deeply in character. Suzanne walked beside her, carrying her file of notes.

"Ah, so you're the other writer here," said Dierdre Fine. "We have to talk. You're doing Jacobs's biography, Jack tells me. It's getting very intellectual around here. I don't know if I can take it. Listen, you want to go into Española and get a beer before they start shooting? You can tell me everything you know from the ivory-tower angle and I'll give you the ultimate truth. What do you say?"

"Who am I to refuse the ultimate truth?" asked Harm.

Dierdre Fine stood with her hands on her hips and even after Harm stood to shake her hand, she was taller than he. He pointed out his Jeep and said he'd meet her over there, as soon as he checked with Leonard about something.

"You mean you have personal access to the gods too?" Fine looked skyward through silver glasses, pressed her palms together. "See you in two seconds."

Jacobs sat on the Naugahyde couch by the old

Coke machine outside the motel office. The cinematographer bent over his shoulder, looking at Leonard's clipboards. When Jacobs saw Harm, he raised his eyebrows, then stood quickly and came toward him, put his arm on Harm's shoulder and drew him into the shade of a cottonwood.

"It's getting crazy here. You see what I meant by wanting to keep things quiet?" Jacobs shook his head.

"Can we meet later, go over some things?" asked Harm.

Jacobs sighed. "Let's do it by phone. Call me tonight at the house."

"I need to find out one thing real quick. What airline and flight did Tess Juran come in on yesterday?" asked Harm.

Leonard Jacobs looked straight up into the cottonwood, where several crows sat in the shade. The leaves in the wind made a dry, clattering sound.

"Now, Bohland, that is one detail that I personally would have absolutely no idea about. Why don't you check with Howe, my assistant, about that." He paused. "Why?" he asked.

"Just trying to find out who arrived in Santa Fe when. Determining alibis, motive—"

"Tess Juran does not need an alibi. For all I know she came in on a private jet or drove her own car out from L.A. Let's not get off into side issues here, Bohland. We're talking about protecting Nyia here."

"Mr. Jacobs, my job is often about side issues."

"I think you're doing a fine job of just sticking close to Nyia. Have the police come up with anything else about that murder out in Cerrillos?"

Changing the subject, thought Harm. Patronizing too. He decided to press further.

"But Tess *is* staying at your house, isn't she? Surely you'd know if she came in on a flight yesterday, the day of the party?"

Jacobs lowered his eyes and seemed to look past Harm, over his shoulder somewhere. He nodded slowly. "Yes. Now I remember. She was up in Taos staying with some friends. Came out a few days early to get acclimated. She'd sent word through my assistant, but I completely forgot about it. I had arranged to go into Albuquerque to pick her up and Nyia offered to go instead. I completely forgot," he repeated. He gestured around the set. "I have a lot to keep track of on location, and my actors' personal flight schedules are not among my priority topics for any given day."

That sounded awfully strange, though Harm, when it so happened you were spending a good deal of time with that particular actor and when one of your other actors who happened to be your former lover was nearly killed while attending to said flight schedule.

"You're saying Tess was already in New Mexico?"

"Taos, yes."

"Where in Taos?" asked Harm.

Jacobs looked irritated and began to walk away. "Look, check with Howe," he said, holding up his hand like a traffic cop as if to stop Harm from proceeding toward him.

"One more thing," said Harm. "This undercover thing, it's not working. It seems counterproductive now that there is so much media coverage anyway and the papers have picked up on the shooting."

Jacobs stepped back to Harm in the cottonwood shade.

"It's really holding me back from being able to proceed on the case," he continued. "I'd like to be able to question people freely, openly. It might even be more protective to Nyia if people were aware, in general, that you were investigating these occurrences. In a serious way," Harm added.

Jacobs rubbed his beard with the back of his hand. "Good point, good point, Bohland. Let me sleep on it.

Stay as you are today. Let's talk about it later. I'll discuss it with Mirina." He turned and walked back toward the motel.

Everything went through Mirina. Harm watched Jacobs for a moment, then jogged in the direction of Nyia's trailer. Halfway across the parking lot, he turned. Leonard was conferring with Tess by the motel office door, his arm around her. She was nodding. Suddenly she glanced up and her eyes met Harm's. He's instructing her, thought Harm. He's telling her what he told me about her staying with friends in Taos. He felt as certain of it as if he'd had a tape recorder hidden in her purse.

"Harm?" Nyia appeared beside him. "I'm not on for another hour or so. I'm going to rest in the trailer and Suzanne is going to stay with me. In case you wonder where I am."

"That's good," he said. "I'm going to be doing some interviews. For my dissertation," he added. "My scholarly treatise." He glanced at his watch. Just after noon. "I'll check back with you in an hour then. Make sure Suzanne stays with you, okay?"

Española was a strip of town along the highway to Taos, lined with motels, fast-food restaurants, auto-repair shops, and small cinderblock houses set back from the dusty roadside. Low-riding cars—Impalas and Lincolns with back tires jacked up like cartoon speedsters—and rusty pickups cruised through the town, slowing at lights, then heading up to Taos or Los Alamos. Dierdre Fine indicated a right turn with her thumb. A small stand next to a bar sold apples, fresh green chilis, and wreaths of dried corn and straw flowers. In the distance, over the roof of the bar, snowy peaks rose in the bright noon sky.

Inside, the bar was dim and quiet. The only sound was of a soap opera, the TV hung at an angle in the corner. Harm stood just inside the door and let his eyes adjust to the darkness. Dierdre Fine strode over to the bar and returned with two Dos Equis. "My treat. You get the next round. Shoot a game?" she asked, heading to the back of the bar, where a pool table was lit by a hovering Coors sign. The green felt of the table was faded, ripped in one corner.

Dierdre Fine set her Dos Equis on a table by the wall and eyed her shot. Her cowboy boots made her even taller. She pushed white shirtsleeves up and moved a toothpick around in her mouth, pushing it from side to side with her tongue. The ball sped down the length of the table and missed the pocket. Dierdre shook her head.

"Okay. Ultimate truth time. First off," said Dierdre, "Nyia Wyatt was Leonard Jacobs's lover from the time she was fifteen years old."

"That's what I hear."

"Oh, that's old news to you? You have done your tabloid research, haven't you, professor? Tell me, how does that fit into a great filmmaker's creative process, I ask you? Don't forget to leave that juicy tidbit out of your textbook."

"Fifteen?" Harm asked. "So she was a minor when they got together."

"He married one older but he likes them young." Dierdre swung around the corner of the table, reaching for the blue cube of chalk. She eyed her shot, "Fourteen in the corner," she said, then continued. "He was arrested once in London years and years ago for raping a seventeen-year-old girl, but the case was dropped. The girl later appeared in a couple of his films, the ones nobody's ever heard of. That was before Mirina wrote for him. This was all way before Nyia, too, of course. The story is that Nyia was not coerced. Not only did Nyia eagerly comply, but her mother complied on Nyia's behalf. It was Nyia's mother who pushed the relationship from the start. Of course, you can always argue that at the age of fifteen, do you have much of a choice? Do you have a mind prior to the age of, say, thirty?"

"How do you know so much about all this?" Harm asked.

Dierdre Fine tilted back her head, gulping her beer, wound the chalk on the top of the cue, looked thoughtfully up at the ceiling. "Nyia told me herself in an interview about two years back. Down in Manzanillo. Before Robin Reese was murdered. Nyia's mother told me too. She lives in L.A. You know she's still working? Bit parts in television. Her face has been lifted so many times, the skin is like a fitted sheet. She has this snaky permanent grin. But she does play a great drunk. Of course, she doesn't have to act much to accomplish that. Her best stuff was on *The Twilight Zone*. They ought to have put her in some of those monster movies Nyia made all her bucks in. Eight ball in the side pocket.

"I mean, she is one strange lady. You ever heard that saying, you love someone to death? That's how Carole Wyatt loves her daughter. She really doesn't get it that her kid is actually a separate person. Nyia is the embodiment of all of Carole Wyatt's failed dreams. She lives in this apartment building in Santa Monica, Del Mar something, the TV on all day, and there's this tough old broad with that sleek, stretched-out face, cheekbones like knives, and the eyes—the eyes are so much Nyia's, you think you're looking at Nyia Wyatt in makeup. But Carole Wyatt is like a parody of beauty. She looks just like Nyia except for the silver hair and all her features pickled in years of booze. And she adores the kid. Idolizes her, except for one thing. She can't accept that Nyia made the break, you know? Nyia put her foot down a few years back and told her mother that she wanted to run her own life.

"Carole Wyatt pushed Nyia all through her childhood to become what she could never be. Ran her whole career, all the years with Leonard, everything. It must have been about three years ago when Nyia cut her mother off. Got her own personal manager—Suzanne Scolfield—you probably met her at the party last night. Cutthroat. Smooth as an ice sculpture and damned successful. She's the one got Nyia doing the horror pics. Told her that otherwise she'd always be arty and unknown. Show your face to America, Suzanne told Nyia. It worked too. Led right into the part in *Wings*. Moravio saw Nyia mutating into a hologram and knew she was the one for his Sonia. Next came the Academy Award nomination and the rest is your basic silver-screen history."

Harm bent into the light over the table and called his shot. "Seven on the side," he said. "What about the technique Leonard has of creating tension by promoting in-fighting on the set?" he continued. "Do you think it really amplifies the emotional content of the film?"

"In-fucking, you mean?" Dierdre laughed.

Harm wiped beer from his lip and smiled. He liked this Dierdre Fine. She towered over him, then bent to eye her angle. He wanted to quiz her, but at this point she was on a roll, full of secrets she was dying to tell. She went on, tossing the toothpick down in a clean ashtray on the table, retrieving it after her shot.

"See, Jacobs is basically what you call sexually addicted. That's the new term now for playboy, Don Juan, rogue, asshole, whatever. I don't mean he goes for prostitutes, porn, ties women up, or any of that. I really don't know what the man does behind closed doors. But he's always got some young thing on the fringe. He's never without a lover, a side dish to Mirina. Nyia Wyatt left him three years ago, same time she signed on with Scolfield. She broke with her past, with Leonard, with Mirina, and with her mother. She told me—again in that interview; exclusive, I might add—it was because Leonard refused to divorce Mirina and marry her. She gave him the ultimatum; he thought it was a bluff. In some weird way, he is completely devoted to his wife. Or dependent, it's all how you look at it. Angle," she said, eyeing her shot down the line of the cue, "of perception. Your shot."

Three years, thought Harm. Three years since the letters began.

"But what about Mirina?" Harm asked. "Where is she in all of this?"

"She and Leonard have *l'arrangement*," said Dierdre with a flourish and a French accent. "A creative partnership. Mirina is the brains, Leonard is the technician. Without his wife, Leonard Jacobs would run out of ideas pretty damn fast, and without Leonard, Mirina would have to relinquish control of her scripts."

Harm chalked his cue and watched as Fine shot the balls in one after another. "You want to play again?" she asked, flipping a couple of quarters in her palm.

"I'm going to order a burger," he said. "How about you?" When he returned from the bar, Dierdre was sprawled on the orange plastic chair, her sunglasses on even though the bar was dark.

Harm sat across from her. "Is it your perception that Jacobs deliberately gets involved with his leading actresses in the service of a more intense film?"

"You got it, professor. Take Manzanillo. Nyia had broken off with him and he was down there trying to get this film together and it wasn't happening. The juice just wasn't there, you know? He takes up with Robin, but Lord, she was young. She was cute, kind of eccentric, willful, really attractive—and she went along with it in a way, like a flirtation, but she really didn't take him seriously. Not like Nyia had. Nyia really loved the man. Robin was only playing around with him— same as he was with her. It pissed him off. He was used to total drama, total romantic immersion, triangling off Mirina and Nyia all those years. And here Robin Reese just wanted to mess around a little. Lay the director, basically."

An Eric Clapton tune came on from a muted juke-box in the corner, and Harm twirled the glass ashtray, thinking.

"And then she was killed," he said. "Just like her character in the film. Was there a connection?"

Dierdre took off her glasses. "Just like the character *Nyia* was playing, you mean. I'll admit it was damn haunting, the way Robin died, how it was so much like the movie. But a connection with Leonard? Like, are you suggesting he killed her because she wasn't taking him seriously enough?" She set the sunglasses on the table. Her eyes were pale gray, nondescript compared to the rest of her. "Pretty high price to pay, both personally and professionally." Dierdre scrunched her face up. "Nah. Not Leonard's style. But it's interesting. The cops said it was a drug deal going down. They never found out who did it."

"And what was Tess Juran's role in all of that? Why did she leave the film in the first place? Was she involved with Jacobs too?"

Dierdre leaned toward him. "You know, you don't sound anything like an academic, with all these questions. You sound like a cop!" She laughed. "Tessie, now she's a little hard to read. Very intense. Another baby. She's what—twenty-five? She's had some problems, some chem-dep stuff. Treatment a couple times, I think. Pretty volatile. But I don't know. I was never clear why she left *Dead Heat*. Conflicts over creative control, I heard. Nothing new."

Suddenly she sat straight up in her orange chair. "Say, here's another thing. Leonard Jacobs is on antide-pressants. Sometimes you'll see Mirina dishing out the medication. Like, 'Mom will take care of you, sweetie.' It's curious to watch them. I mean, you'd think she wouldn't put up with his womanizing for two seconds, but she's from Europe, she's older, she's devoted to him, she takes care of him. Who knows why people stay together, anyway?"

Harm shook his head. "You're a veritable font of information, Fine. I ought to do my dissertation on you."

"Hey," she said. "People love to talk. You're going to find out so much more than you could ever use in your textbook. You go ahead and write about the *noir* influence, professor. My question is, who is the new Nyia Wyatt? The survivor angle. Nyia, who survived this hellish mother. Nyia, who survived this controlling, obsessive-director kind of a thing. Nyia, who survived the murder of her close friend, where she easily could have been the one who was shot and not a few people thought it could have been a case of mistaken identity. There were whispers, anyway," Dierdre whispered.

"Could someone have wanted Robin Reese out of the way?" Harm asked.

"No." Dierdre was emphatic. "Not Robin. She was fucked up but very sweet. But when you think about it, there are plenty of people who would like to see Leonard Jacobs fall a few feet."

"Such as . . ."

"Well, let's draw up a list and invite them all to a party. Okay, such as . . . John Sand, Leonard's former partner, who lost a lawsuit to him a few years ago. Claimed Mirina and Leonard had developed properties that were his. Hell of a smart guy, but not smart enough to hold onto his money. Did time for securities fraud."

"I heard something about that."

Dierdre Fine raised the pool cue above her head as if stretching. Harm didn't think she was so bad. Of course, he wasn't being written about either. She played pretty good pool.

"But no one would be out to hurt Nyia Wyatt, would

they?" asked Harm. "Does Leonard hold it against her, that she broke up with him?"

Dierdre Fine paused. "I see what you're getting at. Nyia does have some air of doom around her, and she does play it up. I think it's the aura of the monster pics. But hurt Nyia? Now, like I said, Leonard I could see someone wanting to hurt. He's left a trail. But not Nyia. She gets press out of it all though. Why do you think I'm here?"

"To write some piece called, 'Death, Take One.'"

"Not bad, professor. Can I use that?"

"So Nyia's manager arranged for you to come out and do this piece for *Vanity Fair?*" asked Harm.

"I wouldn't say she arranged it. She called to let me know weird things were going on out here. Yeah. She likes me to keep tabs on Leonard for her. And anyway, that's her business, to put attention on Nyia. My business too." Dierdre shrugged, lined up her shot.

The ball slipped in, rattled down the hole in the righthand corner. Dierdre Fine straightened and pushed up her sleeves, then fumbled in a big leather bag, pulling out a camera, uncapping it. She focused it on Harm and flashed once, then again. He found himself briefly posing: *Tough-guy author/professor leans over table to make a shot.* In character, he thought. Yeah.

"No, really," she said. "I'm here to find out who Nyia's sleeping with now," said Dierdre Fine. "Any ideas, professor?"

"Not my area of research," he said, jolting the cue through his bridge, banking the ball off the siderail. The ball ricocheted back off the corner, rolled slowly back to the center of the green table.

Dierdre snapped several more pictures, then capped the camera. "But Nyia Wyatt *is* staying with you, isn't she? Surely she's not helping you correct papers. Come on. Didn't I give you some information for *your* research?" Dierdre Fine grinned.

Caught, he thought. Watched, observed, seen. He

recalled the video he'd taken the other morning of the couple on the porch, the strawberries. What goes around comes around.

"Come on, professor," Dierdre winked. "It'll be good for your book sales," she whispered.

Exploitation, he thought. And he saw what Jack had been getting at.

"DEAR NYIA,"

[He writes on blue paper.]

"It is getting very difficult to endure the feeling of holding back from revealing myself to you. There are those who don't want you to live, who have not wanted that for a long time. Sometimes I think I am joining them, because of the impossibility of holding the pain. It's in my throat now, like needles stuck there and salt water.

"But there are some things I want you to know before I decide which way the story is going to go. Leonard Jacobs has never loved you. He uses you, he is attached to you, but it is not love. I can't believe you don't see that, how he almost moves you around in his mouth like a stone. You're a figure in his dream-life, both much smaller and much larger than you actually are. Why can't you see that?

"Those in power are entreating me to close out on this thing. As if it were only a game. As if I could just do it that

☆ **219** ☆

easily. They really don't see the conflict. It is like a burn inside me—you know when you hold it under hot water and still nothing stops it? Doesn't love just feel like that?

"But one thing I'm sure of. I know I can't stand it anymore. And I don't think it will feel any easier if you are no longer in the world. That might relieve some of it. But not all. I keep thinking there has got to be some other way than this."

[He folds the envelope, licks it, presses it shut. There is another way and he knows what it is. It has been coming to him for days now. Ever since the man and the dog. How easy that was and without consequence. The lover has got to be the one to die. Then there might be some hope. He knows he is indecisive. Watches himself vacillate between his need to be done with her, and the other. The other need.

Possible idea for scene: He cleans his gun, sitting in front of a mirror.]

THIRTEEN

NYIA SAT INSIDE HER TRAILER ACROSS THE parking lot from the motel. Out the small window she could see Leonard conferring with the cinematographer about the last scene of the day. Jack was waiting by the motel, she could see him shifting nervously by the office door. He got like that when he was really on. He and Tess had been finishing up shots on the couch by the rusty Coke machine. The wedding scene was next. They'd film across the parking lot in an adobe building that had been made to look like a small law office. She could see the actor playing the justice of the peace approach Jack, the two of them laughing now. Suzanne had stepped out for a second to get some coffee.

She tried to keep her mind on the film, but the crows in the trees overhead were loud, their calls raking the stillness. How would they sound in the film?

Leonard must be working them in somehow. In spite of everything, she admired his work. Feathers, green and black. Crow feathers were dense, starlings had that rainbow glow when the sun hit them. She watched one hop to the gravel by her trailer.

The wedding dress hung in a skinny closet in the trailer's single bedroom. When she pulled it off the hanger, she noticed a dirty smear near the hem. She shook the dress out, dust puffing into the sunlight that angled in the narrow window. This is filthy, she thought. She wondered if the costume people had done this on purpose, dirtied it up, secondhand-store dress, wedding in a seedy lawyer's office in the middle of nowhere after riding in on a Harley. She slid into it, yanking it down over her head, and reached behind her to zip up the back. She brushed off more dirt from the lace skirt.

She was never quite sure what scene would be coming up, in spite of Mirina's nightly notes. It was Leonard who decided sequence. Keeping them all off balance was part of his whole technique. And she wasn't sure if they would do the bike scene tomorrow or the train scene. The Harley leaned outside motel room number three, dusty in the cottonwood shade. The sleek-finned white Mercury that Hank would buy in trade for the Harley was parked off to the side of the lot. In some dark, flat place deep inside, she dreaded getting into that car.

Just another chance for images to bleed through, script to actual moment, back again. But no, it was more than that. Something more, the fear she felt about the car. Nyia closed her eyes, thinking about driving back from Albuquerque two nights ago, the incredible stars as she'd cruised the Turquoise Trail. She'd been lost in them, not really paying attention to the road. They'd been like that up in northern Minnesota, too, where they'd filmed the camping sequence. You couldn't see stars like that in L.A. She would forget about stars altogether sometimes. It was like forgetting about God.

They had all thought the shot came from the hillside because of what that cop, Americo Quintana, had said about a crackpot sniper. Nyia closed her eyes and replayed it in her mind. Starlight. Mozart on the tape player. Boom. She had looked in the rearview mirror. Then another boom. No, wait. First there had been something else. She had looked in the rearview mirror just before the shot. Why? Because of the lights. Lights behind her, too bright, bearing down. That was why. She had been about to adjust the mirror upward when the car had pulled out to pass. It slowed beside her for an instant, same speed. But it wasn't a car, it was a truck, a pickup. The shot had come as the truck passed her, a split second after. That was what had been so scary, the thought she might veer into the passing truck. But at the time, she hadn't thought *shot*. She'd thought *backfire* and looked in the rearview mirror.

Nyia kept her eyes closed, trying to recall exactly the way it had looked. She'd glanced in the rearview mirror as the truck was passing. Then the second shot, the windshield a sudden blur of broken glass. What color was the truck? Some part of her body remembered what her mind had not taken in. White. Blankets piled in the back, feed bags. Maybe a dog. A dog on a feed bag in back of a truck and something else. A man. A man and a dog in the back of a white truck—not an odd sight in New Mexico. But she hadn't remembered them until now.

Someone had followed her from Albuquerque. Not an ambush from a foothill. She was sure of it, suddenly, shocked that she hadn't remembered it before as Quintana and Leonard and Harm had questioned her. It was as if the first way she had remembered it had solidified in her mind. The truck had burst past; someone had shot at her from the back of that truck.

There was a knock at the metal door of her trailer and Suzanne clicked the door open. "Dressed, Nyia? I brought a friend." Suzanne stepped up into the trailer, Manuel Moravio behind her, his hat in his hand. He bowed in a courtly manner, his wild gray hair springing out from his head. Sometimes she thought Moravio looked like a gnome. He bent toward her and kissed her cheek.

"What about tonight, Nyia?" asked Suzanne. "Moravio wants to take the two of us up to that wonderful restaurant in Chimayo near that little sanctuary. He says it reminds him of towns in Brazil where he grew up, tiny clay churches built in the middle of nowhere off dirt roads. And"—she put her arm around him, gave him a squeeze—"he's going to tell us all about the adventures of Sonia in the sequel to *Wings*."

Moravio gleamed at Nyia with his small, bright eyes. "So tell me, Beauty, do you want to hear a story tonight?"

Nyia looked back out the window at the crows. Moravio slid in next to her on the bench of the dinette table. He took her hand in both of his, cupping it. "I've come all this way, Nyia. I know you're tired. Surely—"

"Manuel, you don't have to convince her. She'd be delighted to come. Honored." Suzanne stood behind Moravio where he could not see her face, glaring sternly at Nyia. Then she cheesed a big smile, nodding her head in a pantomime of yesness.

It wasn't that Nyia didn't want to go. She thought of Harm, of the window open above the bed where they'd slept last night, tangled up like grapevines. "I need to check my schedule, Manuel. I might—"

Again Suzanne interrupted. "Nyia, Manuel thinks so highly of you. He's just been telling me—oh shush, Manuel, don't be embarrassed. Look, Nyia, you can rearrange something. Can't you."

It was a statement, not a question.

A second knock came at the trailer door, Mirina called her name. Suzanne opened the door and Mirina stood in the afternoon sun, squinting into the dark trailer. "Nyia, I've got some notes I want to go over with you. Some changes coming up in the next scene. Suzanne, Manuel? If you'll excuse us."

Moravio stood, pulling his theatrical hat down over his scraggly hair. He took Nyia's hand, kissed it as gently as a moth landing. She wanted to brush it away, his attention spreading over her like some thick ooze of adoration.

"I'll see, Manuel. If not tonight—"

Suzanne addressed Mirina. "I've got some coffee here. Mind if I stay and listen?"

"I'd rather you didn't, Suzanne." Mirina stepped aside for Moravio to leave the trailer and Mirina held the door open for Suzanne.

Suzanne just sipped her coffee from a styrofoam cup. "I'd just love to see what one-hundred-and-eighty-degree turns will be coming up in this next bit. What death-defying leaps, what numinous moments of surprise."

Mirina entered the trailer and leaned against the kitchen counter. "I know you don't really like the way we work here, Suzanne." For a moment Mirina looked tired. She fingered her silver and turquoise earrings. "But I really do need to be alone with Nyia."

Then it was Leonard's turn. Nyia could see him jogging across the parking lot, stopping to nod at Moravio. He cut through the bitter, restrained tone in which the two women were talking, ordering everyone out immediately. "Wedding scene is in five minutes. Nyia, I need to talk to you." He grabbed the folder of notes from Mirina. "I will do it," he told his wife.

Mirina left the trailer.

"Suzanne?" said Leonard. "Out, please. Two minutes. Privacy."

"I've been asked to stay."

"By whom?"

"My client."

"Is that right, Nyia?"

What was she, Nyia wondered, a rope in some awful tug? When she spoke, her voice was hoarse, cracked. "Just wait outside the door, Suzanne. It will be all right."

Suzanne pursed her lips, poured her coffee slowly into the tiny sink. "I'll be right outside if you need me, Nyia." As she left she gave the door a little slam. Leonard rolled his eyes.

"I won't say anything," he said.

"Good," said Nyia.

"I'm sure she's very helpful to your career."

"She is, Leonard. Come on. What's up?"

He sat down next to her at the dinette table, white shirt sleeves pushed up on his arms. A whole conversation took place between them in the air and the silence and the crows' racket and the whir of the cottonwoods in the dry wind. He opened the folder of notes, studied them, rubbed his beard, then looked up at her, studying her face. God, how she had loved him once. When he had come to her in kindness and intensity like this. Back when boys her age had seemed so stupid and shallow. Nyia took a deep breath. How could someone appear so open, eyes black wells deep as love could get? Yet finally be so closed you could never really enter. She took him in as deeply as she could. As director, not lover. Thinking, almost trying to say it telepathically, *Leonard, are you trying to hurt me?* Trying to see the truth of it there, if she could.

"You're so quiet, Nyia. You feel . . ." he paused, quiet. "I've never seen you so open."

"I'm not open," she whispered. "I'm full of secrets. It might be that I hate you."

They kept their eyes locked to each other's. She looked away first. She almost always did. "Good," he said. "If that's what you need."

She nodded. Then went into Christine, staring back at him, changing her eyes. Pulled the veil down over her eyes. He knew she had shifted instantly and he smiled.

"Beautiful." That was the moment he loved. When she exited herself. She rested there like a bird on a thin branch. Both she and not she. "That's it. You're radiant," he said.

He adjusted the veil, pulled it back again so her face was bared to his. Put his hand on her knee, pushing the lace up to feel her thigh.

That was how he used to do it. Make love to her a little in the trailer before she would go out on set, reach right into her, kissing her neck, making her wet. Take the energy out there, he used to say to her. Take the energy to the camera. Nyia pushed his hand away.

"You think you don't need me at all anymore," Leonard said.

Nyia nodded. "I don't."

"Tess is just learning."

She let it stand. Sure. Tess, that much was clear. Just learning. And he teaching.

"I'm not jealous of Tess. Go make love to her, Leonard. If that's what you want."

He looked down, smiling. "It's play, Nyia. It's all part of the play. You always took it so damn seriously. It's just a way of heightening the energy, bring Eros to the lens of the camera. You had to make it such a melodrama by refusing to just let go and play."

God, he was brilliant. Watching him do his own shift like that, even use her boundary against her.

"Are you sure?" he asked, leaning toward her, close to her face. She couldn't help it. She started to laugh.

"Oh, Leonard, I played with you for years. It's so old now! You almost destroyed me with it. I was a kid, you put me in your little play." She kept laughing, tears coming. He stood, grasping the door handle. He walked out into the sunshine, closing the door behind him.

She waited a few minutes, calming herself. Connie came in to make last-minute adjustments in Nyia's makeup. Nyia could see Suzanne pacing just outside the trailer. She felt vibrant in her skin, the scratchy lace of the bodice and the silky material against her legs. Every inch of her was alive now and she didn't need Leonard's Eros or any technique to heighten anything at all. She focused on Connie's red lipstick and the round yellow edge of her coffee cup. Details. She was ready.

Connie said, "You look great. Leave 'em for dead."

"Don't say that, Connie. Just say, 'Good luck.'" Nyia swished the crinoline skirt through the trailer's narrow doorway and stepped down the two metal steps into the dust.

As she came onto the set across the lot she could feel the tension. Harm was back, standing in the shade next to Dierdre Fine. He raised a hand, nodded to her. *I'm here now.*

Good, she thought. As she approached the building, Tess appeared in the doorway in a white wedding dress. Leonard stood behind her, pulled at Tess's sleeve.

Jack approached Nyia. "Trouble," he said, stopping her. "You're out of the scene. Leonard's putting Tess in as the bride. It's a brand-new story, babe. Surprise, surprise."

Nyia felt the heat rise up inside her. *No. This was her part.* Oh God, why had she ever agreed to work with him again? Oh yes, she remembered. She was under contract.

Nyia breezed over to Tess in her nearly identical dress. So this had been planned long ago by Leonard. Enough lead time, anyway, to get two dresses. "Say, don't you look pretty," Nyia said to Tess.

Leonard went back into the adobe building to check the lighting.

"Sorry," said Tess. "This wasn't my idea, believe me."

"Don't worry," Nyia told her. "This is just another of Leonard's little devices. You're not playing the bride. I am. He's just trying to make me mad."

"No, he's for real," said Tess. "I'm you now."

She understood so little, thought Nyia. The game, the way Leonard played it. Where was Suzanne?

Suddenly Tess moved very close to Nyia. "To tell you the truth, I'm scared," she said. "This thing with the dresses. The same dresses. I hate this shit. I like my part. I like being the woman in the motel."

"Settle down, Tess," said Nyia. "He's not for real."

Just then Leonard came back out and pulled Nyia aside.

"You're going to be taking a little break," he told Nyia. "We are going to use Tess in the bride part. Switch up."

"Leonard, this is very brilliant as usual, but it is in my contract that I play lead."

"Oh, you'll still have the lead. Mirina is revising now. That's what she wanted to talk to you about. We'll work out the details tonight."

"You just don't stop, do you?"

Don't lose it, Nyia told herself. Just get Suzanne. Let Suzanne handle it, don't even try to deal with him.

"You're off, Nyia. You get a day's break. We'll finish up the motel sequence and then we're going to do the bike shots on the road up from Chimayo on the way to Truchas. You know where it is, don't you? Be there around eleven A.M., day after tomorrow. You're free until then."

"Don't fuck with me, Leonard."

He turned to look at her. "Oh, I won't."

Nyia stalked back across the road to her trailer, trembling. She ripped off the dress and threw it on the plaid couch, pulled on jeans and T-shirt. Again there was a knock and Leonard entered, leaning back against the door.

"Are you upset, darling?" he asked.

She put her fist on the table. "Don't call me darling anymore. I'm going to try to be calm out of respect for our long personal and professional relationship. Leonard, I cannot have any more sexual or romantic energy between us for any reason. We agreed on this. We talked about it before we started filming. Our relationship is strictly business and if you do not respect this agreement I will file a sexual harassment suit against you. I've already spoken to Suzanne and my lawyer about it. I'm going to take this time off and when I return I expect you to reinstate me in the lead role of the bride, Christine's role intact. If you don't, you'll be in breach of contract. It is just as simple as that. And I'll just see you in court."

"We're going to go ahead and shoot the wedding scene, Nyia. And if you're not happy with the way things are going, just have Suzanne talk to me about it. We're not so far into this third story that we can't reshoot all your scenes with Tess in the part of Christine if there's trouble."

"Are you threatening to fire me?" Nyia asked. "You know this film is nothing without me."

Leonard opened the door and spoke over his shoulder. "The story is altered. Tess is the bride."

The door clicked shut behind him.

Nyia pulled on hightop sneakers, quickly tied them. She actually felt cleansed by the anger. Broken through into it. There was no way he could do this. Change the story, yes; put her in a supporting role, no. She scooped up a pile of mail that Connie had brought for her on the table and the notes Mirina had left. Nyia slipped the papers into a bag and stepped out of the trailer.

Dan Howe came around the side of the trailer, pushing his round wire-frame glasses up on his nose. "Let's talk. Don't go off half-cocked," he told her.

He ran his hand through fine, ash-blond hair, stuffed one hand in his vest jacket. Nyia took several deep breaths, trying to calm the racket her heart was making in her chest, pounding the anger up to her forehead into a glimmer of pain. Dan searched in his pockets for his gold watch, flipped it open, then snapped it shut. He looked the same as he'd looked for years, he'd even worn this outfit back in Paris, saying the vest was his replacement for a briefcase. He was a walking filing cabinet or bureau drawer. She didn't want to trust him or be talked out of her anger. But Dan had always been a calm, witnessing presence on the film sets. He was Leonard's assistant, but not his yes-man. And they'd always been able to talk, although she'd never felt as close to him as she had Jack.

Dan sighed, blinked up at the desert sun and leaned against the hot white metal of the trailer. "So we've been here before, right?" he asked. "This is the part where Leonard drives everybody to the brink to bring out all the deep shit and drive you nuts. Right? So what are you going to do, get all riled up on a personal basis or step back and see it for what it is, Leonard's way. His technique. Okay, so when he's in it, he doesn't really see what he's doing. He's going on instinct. Why do you think I work for him? I have to follow behind and remind everyone not to take it personally. Find the energy that's stirred up in your encounter with him and take it to the camera, Nyia."

Nyia watched her sneaker make an arc in the dust, back and forth, a moon-shape as she thought about what Dan was saying. There was truth in it. Or the sound of truth.

"There's only one thing, Dan. It's a con. An excuse for Leonard to get away with shit. You know, I just don't have to go nuts anymore in order to get it on with the camera. Besides, there's a level that goes on between Leonard and me that you know nothing about."

"Don't I? I was around when you and Leonard split. I know what went on between you two. Everybody does."

"Great. Nothing like a private life."

"You didn't choose a private life," he said.

Nyia looked away. Across the gravel, Leonard, Gino, Tess, and Jack were conferring by the Coke machine. Maybe she just felt rejected. Goddamn him, she thought.

"So are you going to let him get to you, or are you going to make creative use of whatever's bothering you?" Dan asked.

"I've got to talk to Suzanne," Nyia said. "Have you seen her?"

"She left with Mr. Moravio, went out to lunch, I believe."

Finally Nyia looked up at Dan, his thin face and hollow sculptured cheeks. "So I should take the point of view to just go with it for three more days and then I'm out of here and out of his life forever?"

"That's workable," he said. "Better than a nosedive off the deep end. Look, my advice to anyone who's about to see a lawyer is to go fishing instead. It's cheaper, for one thing. And when you step back, things change automatically. Your feelings, anyway. Why don't you get Jack and go snag some trout? I hear there's a good spot real close to town up by the ski area. Hey, you've got a free day off, expenses paid. Give Mirina time to work out the script changes and let it go, Nyia. Don't be such a star."

She smirked at him. *Fuck you.* "But Dan, what fun is it being a star if I can't throw a tantrum? Leonard gets to have all the fun."

"Hey, he's the boss."

"He's your boss."

"Yeah," said Dan. "And I'm only following orders." He smiled. "Here." He reached in his pocket and pulled out a tiny fishing fly, bright brass hook hidden in a mandala of feathers and one red bead. "I guarantee, a very major fish is going to fall in love with this sweetheart. Look around you, Nyia. It's the Land of Enchantment. Don't get so caught up in the Big L. He isn't the universe."

Nyia took the fly and put it in her bag. "Okay, Dan," she sighed. "But you can let Mirina know, and Suzanne will be letting Mirina know, that I will go with the proverbial flow as long as it's Lead Flow. I'll wear whatever costume Leonard wants, as long as my role is maintained. I don't care if he wants me to play Hank. Just have him take a peek at my contract and his handwriting on it."

"Yeah," said Dan. "Beautiful."

Harm was walking from under the giant cottonwood by the motel. She nodded toward him and headed for the Jeep parked at the roadside. He met her there. She climbed in the hot Jeep and looked ahead at the line of mountains where the blue became snow and then sky again, far above all this.

Harm climbed in and slammed the door.

She explained about the switch in roles and the day off, her concerns about sexual harassment.

"Sounds like you'd have a case," said Harm.

She noticed the inside of the Jeep was immaculate, no gum wrappers or pop cans in sight. She hadn't noticed when they'd driven out this morning. And he was clean shaven and wearing a white T-shirt under a faded baseball jacket.

Nyia reached over and touched his arm. "Want to go fishing?" she asked.

"Fishing," he said. "Sure. Hey, do you mind if Nickie joins us for a couple of hours? You could watch some father-son bonding—you never know, it could be research for a future role or something."

Nyia laughed quietly. That sounded fabulous. Then she thought, what did he mean by that?

It wasn't until Harm pulled out to pass a pickup south of Española that Nyia remembered the white truck. She recounted the memory for him, how the image had been superseded by her thought that her car had backfired.

"That definitely fits," he said. "Nims—the man who was killed—his truck was white. I should call Quintana. He was supposed to have been on the set today. That's something we hadn't thought of, that Nims was only the driver, that the person doing the shooting was in the back of the truck. Quintana's probably searched the cab of the truck, but he should check the back too."

The dry landscape spread before them, brown in the white heat of early afternoon. Nyia glanced over at Harm, at his tan neck and the shape of his hands on the steering wheel. He pushed in a jazz tape, warm alto sax oozing out softly in the silence between them. She wondered what he was like as a father. She wondered how he'd gotten into being a detective. She'd only seen him that once with Nickie and was glad suddenly for this time they'd have now, just a day out of all this, to go up into the mountains, ride horses, or hike in a canyon. Leonard had told her Harm was real smart, had an MBA from UCLA. How come he wasn't some CEO or something? But she liked him better this way. His jacket slipped to the side, she saw the thin leather strap of the holster and the black metal of the gun. Her heart felt hot and loud in her chest, just seeing it.

In Santa Fe, Harm headed for his office, pulled the Jeep up in front of a small adobe building next to a video-rental place, the large front window painted with Bohland and Associates, Private Investigators and

Accounting. Harm unlocked the door and pushed it open, and the screen door knocked shut behind them. He stepped over piles of papers next to the old wooden desk and sat down in the creaking swivel chair, replaying his messages. She couldn't help, in spite of herself, wishing that this office were some sleek TV detective's office with Eurostyle furniture, a thick Rolodex, and state-of-the-art computer. Harm didn't even have a secretary. Though the office was very neat, bulletin boards on the back wall with index cards meticulously tacked up, matching black file cabinets in a row against a wall, it was very unpretentious. Down-to-earth. *No, say it,* she thought. *Say it to yourself: The guy's a nobody.*

She walked over to the filing cabinets above which his degrees and certifications were framed. Licensed by the State of New Mexico. Well, maybe not a complete nobody. What kind of office had Philip Marlowe had, anyway? But somehow, without realizing it, she had wanted more. Behind that came this thought: *What a relief.* He wasn't what some interior decorator defined him as, or a degree or an address or a wardrobe. Then she remembered that that was exactly why she liked him.

Harm was busy scribbling the messages on a pink pad when Suzanne's low voice came on. "I'm actually calling with a message for Nyia. I realize I didn't get an address where you-all are staying, and it's imperative I see Nyia later today. I heard all about this business of the proposed script changes and I've interceded on her behalf. I'll be back from the set around six or six-thirty and will be at my hotel until eight or so. Please have her call me then. Thanks."

Harm looked up at her as he was dialing the phone. "Got that?" he said.

"Yes, sir." Nyia lowered herself into a chair opposite the desk. She held out her hand against her thigh, eyeing the cheap engagement ring. Rita and Sam.

Why, Rita, why did you get rid of it? She pictured Rita removing the ring in a fit, stashing it in the bottom of an old jewelry box, finding it years later and wanting to be rid of it. Rita at the pawn shop in La Cienega, counting the cash the bald man handed her, guitars overhead and TVs and stereos lined up on a counter behind him. Yeah, the diamonds were probably genuine zirconia. And the ring was probably jinxed.

On the credenza behind Harm were several pictures of his son at various ages, typical smiling school photos, one with missing teeth and a Garfield sweatshirt. She listened as Harm told Quintana about her realization that a truck had passed her, that there may have been someone riding in the back of the truck.

"So only the cab was dusted for prints?" Harm asked. "And there was no gunpowder residue inside the truck?" He hesitated, keeping eye contact with Nyia. "Well, let me know what you come up with. No, she's been given a day off, she won't be on the set tomorrow, I'll be with her. Thanks. Yeah, if I get anything else I'll call you too."

Without hanging up the receiver he punched out another call and asked for Nickie. "Big guy, what's up? Can you go fishing and have a bite to eat? Ask your mom." He waited, circling the tip of a very sharp pencil into a dark spot on the desk blotter. It must be strange, thought Nyia, to have to make a date with your own kid. Then again, maybe parents who lived with their kids never gave it half as much thought. Hers never had, not that she remembered. "Great," Harm finished. "Pick you up in ten minutes. Bring your tackle box."

Nyia leaned forward in the seat so that Nickie could scramble into the back. They drove out of Santa Fe quickly, up into the mountains toward the ski area, Nickie chattering excitedly about the plot of a movie he'd seen with his buddies, how he went off the high dive at his swimming lesson and did a giant cannonball and then got in trouble for swimming all the way to the end of the pool instead of going straight to the ladder to get out; and could they please, please, please, Dad, have dinner at Pizza Hut, because they're giving away these awesome soccer balls with any large order and they only cost $3.99 and Stevie Radman got one, but it went flying into a ditch when he was playing soccer with his cousins last weekend up in Taos and it landed on a cactus and the air went all out of it.

They came to a small turnout where a mountain creek gushed down through scraggly piñon in the three-o'clock sun. Nickie found himself a spot on a boulder and cast out, while Harm sorted through the confusion of lures and spinners in Nickie's tackle box. Nyia cut the hook off an extra pole Harm had in the Jeep, tied the fly onto the line, and stood in the shade where the creek pooled in a swirl. She dropped the line into the brown, mirror-like water; smelled the pine, sun-warmed. The water sound washed through her and the quiet, Harm's quiet talk with his son and the comfortable quiet between them.

Nyia stayed upstream, away from the two of them, but when she glanced over at Harm, he was looking at her. He smiled, sitting on the rock now behind the kid, then motioned her over.

When she got there, he rose, said he was going to get something from the Jeep.

"Getting any bites?" she called to Nickie.

"Nah. It's kind of a rotten time to fish. Morning is better. My dad knows that, but we came here anyway." He turned to face her. "It's like, a date where I could come, too, right?" He squinted at her, the sun in his face. Precocious kid, she thought. But sincere. He continued without her answer. "But that's okay, 'cause otherwise I might get left out. Right? I mean, like, if he took you or some other lady to Pizza Hut and I didn't get to go."

"Yeah," said Nyia, "and what if he, like, bought a soccer ball for $3.99? It wouldn't even be fair, either, 'cause I don't even play soccer."

"Yeah," said Nickie, "and one time he went back to California where, like, we used to live there when I was a baby before my mom and dad got a divorce. And, anyway, he brought me this gigantic stuffed alligator from Disneyland, 'cause he went there with some lady on a date and her kids got to go along and I didn't."

Nyia shook her head. "I hope you told him he blew it totally."

Nickie came over and sat next to her on the lichen-covered rock. He had a way of scrunching up his face so that the gap in his teeth was exposed and he resembled a little chipmunk. "No, I didn't even say a thing. You know—'cause of the alligator and everything. 'Cause, like, he tried."

"Aren't fathers just like that, though?" she asked. "Like, they try."

"Yeah, like so what?" Nickie laughed.

"Yeah, like a stuffed alligator instead of Disneyland? Give me a break."

They both laughed and she showed him the fly her friend had given her and asked Nickie if he'd like to try it. When he ran back down to the creek to cast her line into the water, she glanced around her to see where Harm had gone. The Jeep stood empty by the side of the road. A blue Caravan had pulled up behind the Jeep, and a man was leaning into the side door. It was open but facing away from where Nyia could see. Where was Harm? The man slid the door shut with a clank, walked around to the driver's side and got in. He yanked the van around one-hundred-and-eighty degrees and headed back down the mountain road. Nyia ran toward the road to see if she could spot the license-plate number, but the van had disappeared around a curve. *I'm that paranoid,* she thought. *Don't trust anything as ordinary any more.* She walked back to where Nickie was yelling, "Got one, I got a bite!" and pulling a tiny squiggling minnow of a trout up out of the water.

Then she spotted Harm upstream and on the other side. He stood in the pine shade, the video camera hoisted to his shoulder, arcing the lens back toward her. Probably zooming in now, she thought. For a second she wanted to scream at him, *I told you not ever to film me when . . .* but instead she lifted her hand and waved, smiled, and started back toward Nickie. For him, for him and Nickie, this was family photo time, not an intrusion on her private life. The camera meant something totally different to him. Nickie held the line up for Harm to focus in on, then carefully removed the hook from the silver fish and tossed it back into the rushing water.

Harm balanced on the black rocks over the creek, then walked down the thirty feet to Nickie and Nyia. She gave him a dirty look and her mouth was tight. "I told you not to film me, Harm."

"This is just for fun. Did you really mind?" he asked.

"You could have asked first. You didn't even ask."

"Do I need a contract?"

"Maybe," Nyia said.

"Hey," said Harm. "Get over there next to the kid and the two of you take off your shoes and wade across." He gestured upward. "Great vista, mountains, fat clouds, postcard stuff. It could be a souvenir. I'll make a copy for you. You can see what you look like when you forget who you are."

She was about to get angry, when she stopped, turning to face him in the striped sun shadows. She grinned, then shook her head. "You don't let up, do you?"

"You don't let me."

Nickie called to his father from the boulder. "Get a shot of me over here, Dad!"

Harm raised the camera, zoomed in. Nickie threw up his arms and yelled, "When do we eat?"

Driving back down into Santa Fe, for a moment Nyia imagined a simpler life: she could move to Santa Fe and open a children's theater company and school, teach mask making, mime, creative dramatics. Occasionally she would do experimental European films or produce small films directed by women and minorities. Harm would start a video company on the side and they would collaborate, make great children's stories based on Native American creation myths and African tales. She'd commute to L.A. once a month, glad to be out of that scene. Learn to bake cornbread from blue corn flour, live in an adobe house off Canyon Road, with wood floors and rag rugs, a big old dog curled in front of a fire, Nickie and Harm out back pitching a ball. They would marry on a yellow hillside in the sage and chamiso. Or better yet, in the *santuario* at Chimayo. Could you marry there if you weren't Catholic?

Stop it, she told herself. No fiction, no stories. Just what is. Daydreams were just another escape, and she was through escaping. Things were complicated enough as it was.

When they pulled up in front of Harm's, a burgundy Lincoln was parked in front of the house. Suzanne sat on a wooden bench, waiting for them.

FOURTEEN

"IT'S MORAVIO," CALLED SUZANNE.

Nyia climbed out of the Jeep. Suzanne looked dusty and tired, the white shirt smudged, shirttail coming out of the suede pants. Her hair was pulled back into a long braid that fell down between her shoulder blades, and strands flew out loose and windswept. The perfect makeup was faded, and she was sunburned.

She approached the Jeep as Harm got out, checking her watch. "Nyia, he's come all this way to spend some time with you, the plans were set in motion long before things took a turn for hell here. He's blocked. He has this notion that if he can tell you about his ideas for the next book, spend some time with you, it'll open him up. He asked me to speak to you."

"I just don't think I can get involved with him right now. Can't I meet with him back in L.A. next week?"

Nickie clambered out of the backseat and sauntered

toward the house. Suzanne glanced after him. "Yours?" she asked Harm.

"Since he was born," said Harm.

"Suzanne," Nyia continued, "I want to talk about filing a sexual harassment suit."

"We've got to talk," said Suzanne.

"Why don't you come in," Harm invited. But Suzanne took hold of Nyia's arm.

"I've made a reservation for you and Moravio for dinner. Give him two hours, Nyia. Think brilliant career. Think past all this trouble with Visionfilm. This is nothing compared to where we're going. Let Moravio build Sonia's character for you. It's the chance of a lifetime."

Nyia looked over at Harm, questioningly.

"Go ahead," he said. Then he turned to Suzanne. "And I want to talk to you about something. I spoke with Jacobs about taking me out from under cover and I'd appreciate your going to bat for me with him. I know you support me in that."

Suzanne rested her hands on her hips. Distractedly, she watched a speck of bird circle over the trees. "What we've got here is a very tender balance of powers," she said. "Now I see that it was something of a mistake to have Moravio here: he's threatening to Leonard, Leonard is pissed I'm here anyway, and all this pressure. Of course, in some way, it's just what he loves. I will bring it up with him. But the best thing for all of us may be just to ride this whole thing out for two, three days, however long it takes to get Nyia's scenes wrapped up. It's delicate. You know what I'm saying? But I'll see what I can do. Nyia, are you going to do this dinner—as a favor to me, if nothing else?"

"I'd feel better if Harm were there with me."

Harm shrugged. "I've got Nickie here."

"I'll drive you and pick you up," offered Suzanne. "You'll be in a public restaurant with him. Two hours, max."

* * *

Suzanne waited while Nyia showered and changed. Nyia dressed down, long skirt and sweater, black ankle boots, a felt hat pulled over her still damp hair. As they were leaving, Nickie bolted up to her, then stopped short, his sneakers squeaking on the tile floor. "Bye." He smiled, gap-toothed. Then, impulsively, he hugged her. She looked up at Harm and he walked back into the kitchen. *Don't get too close,* she thought, *if all you're doing is messing around.* Then she wondered who that internal admonition was addressed to: herself or Harm?

Nickie spoke in a rasping whisper. "If you guys do end up going to Pizza Hut sometime—"

"Kiddo," she said, messing his tousled hair. "That soccer ball is yours. Count on it."

"Yes!" He jumped up, slapping at the air, then ran back to the TV, crouched down and clicked on the Nintendo grid, oblivious.

They rode in silence a few minutes in the quiet, closed air conditioning of the car. Suzanne seemed very tense. Finally she spoke. "It's bad, Nyia. I've looked into this with the lawyer before. He told me your chances of winning a sexual harassment case against Leonard would be very slim. He says Leonard could tear you up in court and this type of thing could play out in the papers and rags for months. It's because you were with him all those years, the harassment thing just wouldn't hold up. It's not like you're the innocent, you know what I'm saying?

"Three days of filming and you're done. I've spoken with Mirina and she's guaranteeing you the lead, but in some altered form. Just go along with their game at this point, that's my best advice. This whole thing is getting totally out of control and the best we can do is just maneuver through it and come out the other side. Then you're done with Leonard Jacobs, done with

Visionfilm, and the past is behind us. The main thing working for us here is Dierdre Fine. She's far more protection for you against Leonard than Harm. Leonard knows she's taking notes, the darling. Taking notes and taking pictures. If we can just get through these next days without a mishap, she'll tell the world all about Visionfilm. You'll be on to bigger and better things and the publicity will help the film, even though it is Jacobs's." Suzanne parked in front of a restaurant near downtown Santa Fe.

"So the part I want you to play is demure, honey." She drew that last word out, sweet belle voice exaggerated. "Just play them out like fish, give 'em lots of line, lots and lots of line. Moravio, Leonard, they're yours for the taking. You use them, not the other way around. Got that? Think strategy."

Nyia nodded. Strategy. Okay. Suzanne was very terse and angry. There was no pink-prom dress Paris deb in sight here. But Nyia didn't like the thought of it, just going along with Leonard. Lie down and let him walk all over her. Go with the game. She didn't want to. She wanted to take him on for once, straight ahead. But she could see Suzanne's point.

Suzanne sighed and brushed strands of hair from her forehead, looked again at her watch. "I'll be back to pick you up in two hours, exactly. Call me at the hotel or call Harm if anything, anything at all, goes wrong."

Nyia had the odd sensation, as Suzanne pulled away, of her car being a boat and the restaurant an island where she'd been abandoned. She asked the maître d' for Moravio's table and he led her to a booth at the back. Moravio half stood, smoothing his wiry hair back, as Nyia slid into the booth. He leaned to kiss her cheek and she offered her hand.

"Moravio," she said, "let's talk business. Tell me

about Sonia and the new story and tell me how I can help you. Where are you stuck?"

"Stuck?" he asked. "Business? Sonia is not my business, she is my life."

"But she's made up, Manuel. And I want you to know that I'm not Sonia, I'm me." When he didn't speak, she went on. "You know that, don't you?" she asked. "Otherwise I can't speak to you about her character development. I can't be anyone's mythology."

He folded and refolded his napkin. The waiter brought a bottle of Fume and Moravio tasted it, approving.

"Well, of course, I know this is so," he said at last. "But the truth of the matter is, I don't want it to be so. I want to come to America, make this long journey and speak to the character in my head through you. I want to have dinner with Sonia. I want to dance with Sonia. I want to ... be with Sonia. You have guessed right, Beauty."

"That's exactly why you're blocked, then. If you think she's outside you, in me."

Suddenly, he laughed, his head rocking back against the banquette seat. He leaned toward her across the table, and took out his checkbook. He wrote Nyia's name on the check and looked up at her. "Play Sonia, then. Act her. For just this time we are together." Moravio slid his hand up her arm, took hold of her shoulder for a moment, then fingered the hair at her neck. "Improvise Sonia with me this evening. I hire you, I pay you, then it is all clear. Strictly professional, yes? I consult with you about character development. What is your fee? What does Leonard pay you for one week in his film? I pay you that amount for one evening."

"Moravio," she said, reaching across to touch his hand. "Can't we just converse? As artists?" The whole thing reminded her of prostitution, wear this black lace, lick your lips, act out his sex fantasy, be his black goddess, hourly fee. That's probably what he wanted anyway. Make love to Sonia. Fuck your character, then go home and write about her.

Moravio tilted the glass back and drank the wine, pouring more. Then he laughed. "You are a smart woman, Nyia Wyatt. This is actually helping me, your resistance. It really is. I hadn't realized how obsessed I'd gotten about Sonia, really thinking that somehow the key to writing her was you."

"It's not," said Nyia.

"I was even going to ask you to wear this."

Here it comes, she thought, garter belt and push-up bra, Brazilian style. Instead he brought a hat box up from the floor and set it on the table. He opened it and ruffled through tissue, bringing out the thirties hat, the one with the feathers, black glass beads, and the veil, the prop for the waitress in the part of the film they'd already completed in New York.

"I got it from costume. You would look lovely in it," said Moravio.

Nyia shook her head. He just didn't stop. "I like this hat I'm wearing fine," she said.

He fingered the hat almost lovingly, then replaced it in the box and set the box on the floor. The booth they were sitting in was very private and Nyia couldn't see the rest of the restaurant. She felt claustrophobic.

"You know, when I was growing up in Brazil, in Rio, my mother would send me during summers to stay with my grandparents on their plantation in-country. It was like a palace built in the jungle, their beautiful house set miles away from civilization. The journey took several days, by train and car. A treasure chest of a mansion, gardens, fountains, all carved out of this very poor rural country. My grandparents owned much of the land in that area. They were like king and queen, and everyone in the town worked for them in some way. There was one other family that also owned much land in that area. The people lived always as serfs to them.

"My grandmother would spend part of the year in Rio and another part in Paris and when she would come back to her home, she would become very depressed. Often she would become like an invalid, although nothing was wrong with her. She would take to her bed for weeks. She could never accept this was the core reality of her life. She would dress in fine clothes and walk with me around the property, surveying the land and the livestock and the hen houses and the horses, wearing her fine millinery and carrying an umbrella to protect her from the sun. Then she would go back to the house, undress, and spend the rest of the day in bed. Priests would come to visit her.

"I suppose I grew up knowing women who actually played out different parts in the 'sets' of their lives, and who had no single identity to call their own. In Paris, one persona. On her husband's land, another. But at the heart of it, rejecting who they really were."

"But maybe who she really was wasn't any of those things. It wasn't so accepted back then for a woman to have any identity apart from a husband or a father," said Nyia.

"And you think you do?"

"I have no husband, and my father died when I was seven. And I'm American and a modern woman. Not a turn-of-the-century Latin socialite."

"And you don't think that is just another role to play? 'Modern American woman.' You really believe that is you, the core truth of who you are?" asked Moravio.

Nyia didn't answer.

"You see, Nyia, your gift is that you don't really know. Exactly in that emptiness in you is a crack where you can become anyone you want. That's your genius. It brings you a great deal of unhappiness. You should actually treasure that emptiness, not try so hard to fill it with some idea of yourself."

"It's better to have your own idea filling you than someone else's," she said.

"Then you should be the writer of the script, not the actress."

He stared at her with dark eyes, glazed now by the wine into a dance of syntax and definition. *If a self fell in a forest and no one was there to hear it . . .* She thought suddenly of Nickie and Harm ordering pizza and playing ball. For some people life was actual, she thought. Not a verbal maze.

After that she kept the focus of the conversation on him, and on his writing process and on his ideas for Sonia. He got more drunk and was singing Portuguese folk songs when Suzanne arrived to join them for coffee and drive her back to Harm's.

He met her at the door and Suzanne took off, red taillights and dust on the dark street. Nyia stood listening for a moment before going into the house.

"I took Nickie back to his mom's."

She was disappointed, she realized. Had been looking forward to Cheerios with the kid and his toothy questions.

"To tell you the truth," Harm went on, "I just didn't feel comfortable with him staying here, with all of this going on."

Nyia stood in the dim light coming from the kitchen and took that in. *Not safe here. Not safe enough for the kid. Because I'm here.*

"It's all because of me."

"I'm not saying it's your fault. It's just the way it is. Besides, I try not to mix up my work and my life too much. I know that's an issue you can understand."

Nyia went into the dark living room and sat on the couch. Harm sat across from her in a wicker chair. He seemed distant. Maybe Nickie had said something.

"Why did you invite Nickie fishing today then?"

Harm shrugged. "You invited me. It was already set up that I would see Nickie."

"Which came first, the chicken or the egg?" asked Nyia. "What difference does it make, we were there together with you zooming that videocam in on us like a happy little family scene. Now it's 'keep personal and work lives separate?' Where do I fit into that? Which am I?"

He looked at his hand, studying it as if he hadn't really looked at it in a while. Finally he said, "Look, I mostly took him back because of the safety issue. If anyone were to try to get to you here—I didn't want him pulled into that. And the other thing is—" He stopped, stood up and went to the window at the front of the dark room, and looked out onto the small patio. He spoke, facing the window. "I don't know where you fit into it all. I don't know where the hell any of this fits. Do you?"

She shouldn't have pressed him. She knew this was a conversation that was way, way too soon for them to have and maybe one that would always be inappropriate, given their lives. Having Nickie there had made that clear to him. It had made her wish for another life.

Nyia went over to him, leaned against his back, hands at his waist, around him. "I hear you."

She stayed like that several minutes before he turned to hold her. It went between them like some pulse and she almost laughed. Their feelings were very real, but the context for them was wrong. Now, when had she ever felt that before?

She pulled away and walked down the hall toward the back room. Harm appeared at the door, holding a dark-blue steel revolver. "Do you know how to use one of these?"

"Is it a .38? I learned how to shoot when I was in *Gun Law*. I had to spend a lot of time at a shooting range so I could look believable and not jerk the thing around like a scared cowgirl."

"Yeah, it's a .38 Smith Wesson Chief Special." He swung out the cylinder and handed it to her, butt first, and she closed her grip around it. She saw that the chambers were empty and swung the cylinder closed.

Harm pulled a box of shells from a high shelf in the closet and set it on the bed next to Nyia. "Would you feel more comfortable if you had this in that bedside table right there?"

"Would you?" she asked.

He shrugged. "Only if you're confident you could use it."

"No problem," she said. "But I'd rather you did."

"No problem."

She reopened the cylinder and slid the cartridges one by one into the chambers, then clicked it shut. She opened the drawer and set the gun inside. "I'll be sure to unload it if Nickie comes over."

"I just don't think I'm going to have him around here until after you're all done filming."

"And gone back to L.A.," said Nyia.

Harm looked away. "Yeah," he said.

Nyia fumbled in her bag for her T-shirt, pulling out the script notes and mail that she'd gathered up from the trailer that afternoon. Her hand closed around a padded book envelope in her bag. Inside the envelope was a videocassette. It was unmarked. A wave of heat went black through her chest and Harm appeared behind her at the door.

"Another video," she whispered. "It was in my bag."

"Where did you get it?" he said. "Wait a minute." He appeared with a dishtowel and took it from her, protecting the thing from further fingerprints.

"I didn't have this bag with me tonight, with Moravio. It was in the trailer today all day."

He bent down and turned on the television and VCR, inserted the videocassette and clicked it on *play*. The picture blinked on, grainy, camera held jerkily, lens moving in: Santa Fe Plaza at sunset. Now the Pink

Adobe, dusk. Rosy light. Nyia walking toward the restaurant entrance, looking once at her watch, walking toward the courtyard, turning back to the street to blow a kiss.

"Did you know someone was filming you?" asked Harm.

Nyia could hardly breathe. "I had this strange feeling of being on camera."

In the bar of the Pink Adobe, the video camera picked up voices, clack and clink of glasses, jazz from the stereo. It zoomed in on them talking, leaning in over that candle, Nyia taking out the letters, passing them on the table. Camera in closer now as Harm opened a letter and read it.

He was right there the whole time, sitting at the bar with a video camera on his shoulder. How blind they'd been.

The film went blank then and Harm moved to click the *eject* button. "Wait," said Nyia, kneeling down beside him on the floor. "Remember the other video? There was something more."

The camera seemed to swing around a room, out of focus, then came to rest on a small plaid couch and dinette table.

"My trailer," said Nyia. "He was in my trailer." The camera wandered, focusing on a half-empty coffee cup left on the dinette table, her hightops on the floor by the tiny couch. It wandered toward the back of the trailer toward the bedroom, closet door open. Now the wedding dress, hanging in the nearly empty closet. Shot of the dress spread out on the bed. The frame went black again.

"Walking right into my goddamn trailer. I can't believe this. This has got to be someone who has no problem getting on the set, right?"

Darkness followed on the tape and Nyia could hear the wind. He'd been filming outside. Lights came on briefly and then the sound of tires roaring by. Again. Footsteps in gravel. He was squatting next to a road, holding the camera down low, filming the wheels of the cars as they whizzed by, flash of headlights.

As the next car's headlights lit the surface of the blacktop, Nyia saw the wedding dress lying in the road and the car's tires rolling over it. The dress flew up behind the car like a white rag, a piece of paper blowing away, a ghost in the wind.

FIFTEEN

WHEN HARM APPEARED AT THE BACK DOOR, she'd already been up for a while, sitting at a wooden table in the adobe-walled patio, drinking coffee. Already dressed in jeans, baggy turtleneck, hightops. And she'd already made up her mind.

"I want to go back to the set today," was the first thing she said to him. "I can't stand waiting around to see what's going to happen. I just want to stop in, at least talk to Mirina about where my part is going. I called the ranch earlier, but she'd already gone up there."

"Does Suzanne know about this?"

"Look," she said. "I've got an idea. Leonard's got a little cabin up in Taos. I've got the key for the place on the ring of ranch keys he gave me. We could go up there for the night and just stop in at the set on the way. Española's right on the way to Taos."

They went out for breakfast at a warehouse-sized café called Cloud Cliff, drank strong café au lait and read the paper, acting like any normal Santa Fe lovers who hadn't touched each other the night before, falling asleep in the silent hole between what's said and what's not said.

The drive up to Española went quickly, and Nyia watched the clouds move over the vast landscape in a white herd. The set was still well-blocked, but no one had left word to prevent Nyia from entering and the security personnel waved them through when he recognized Nyia in the Jeep. Mirina was seated in a lawn chair in the noon sun, large sunglasses nearly covering half of her delicate face. She wore her hair down loose over a long denim coat. Harm stood back as Nyia approached her.

"What happened to your day off?" Mirina asked, without looking up from her notes.

"I have to talk to you. I want to know what is going on with my part."

Mirina looked up at her then, took off her glasses. The skin around her eyes looked slightly swollen, as if she'd been drinking. She stood, motioning for Nyia to come into the trailer. Nyia sat down on a small built-in bench while Mirina stood, opened a small refrigerator and poured French table wine into a paper cup. "I shouldn't be doing this," she said, lifting the bottle toward Nyia. "I'll head down to Mexico in a week or so when we're all done here, to get away. From everyone." She nearly spat out those last words.

"I keep vowing, each film." Mirina sipped the wine. "This is the last time. Dissolve the corporation, Visionfilm; go back to Paris and simply write. Forget all this production. It's always a nightmare. It's getting worse each time. Nyia, didn't we have fun in the old days?" Mirina's face creased into a smile and she looked her age, the New Mexico sun drying the fine, weathered lines around her mouth, the dark lipstick edging into the cracks.

"What about Christine?"

"I'm working on her, I don't want to talk about it until I'm done. You know how I like to work. Things come to me at the last minute."

"Why can't my part stay the way it was?"

"Because the director has determined that there will be a change." Mirina sighed. "The dictator, I should say."

"Mirina! It's your story. Leonard can't control it, can he?"

She drank the rest of the wine, considered pouring more, then put the bottle back in the refrigerator.

"Will you trust me for now, darling? Somehow the process must run its course. This is how it works. He breaks it apart and frustrates all of us. He breaks my story open and in that place is where the best story comes. I can't explain. I hate it, yes. Some days I just want to make up the story and that is that. But that isn't the way we work. You know that. By tomorrow I will have it figured out, that's all I can say."

Suddenly from outside, voices erupted by the motel. Mirina peered out the small window. "I was afraid of this," she said.

Nyia followed Mirina out of the trailer across the parking lot. Harm was already there, next to Dierdre, who was snapping pictures.

Leonard grabbed Dierdre's camera, clicked it open, and yanked out the loop of film. "Give us some room to move, will you, Dierdre? To resolve our conflicts without being documented?"

She smirked at him. "Come on, Mr. Jacobs. Scandals are great press."

Leonard faced Moravio, who held his arms crossed tightly across his barrel chest. His dark eyes were angry slits. Suddenly Moravio threw his arms out, bellowing. "You are completely misusing her. You have no understanding of what you are working with here."

"With all due respect, my dear fellow, I am the director here and you are a visiting, albeit highly distinguished, guest. Please keep in mind, this is not a collaboration, Señor Moravio, and I'd appreciate your staying out of the directorial process."

"You are arrogant, you are ruining the story. If you don't keep Nyia as the bride in this final sequence the entire consummation of the triptych is destroyed. The dark wedding the lovers struggle toward, the dream of the flames between them, all this imagery is wasted if you take her from this part. Not only are you misusing her, you are mistreating her. Everyone knows this!" Moravio was shouting.

When Leonard saw Nyia, he yelled, "Did you put him up to this? You and Suzanne? What are you doing here anyway? I thought I told you to take the day off! Does everyone realize that they are about to be fired! Who is in charge here?" He opened his hands, turning around with his arms spread, palms open to the sky like some anguished Christ without a cross.

Leonard called to Dan Howe, who stood off from the group, over by the motel. "Howe, please remove Señor Moravio from the set. See that he is provided with transportation back to Santa Fe. Security!" Then he added to Howe, "And get Fine out of here too. Clear all press from the set."

Dan Howe came forward to take Moravio's arm, but the wiry man shrugged him off. As Leonard brushed past him, Nyia heard Leonard say, "Don't lose yourself in a woman, Moravio." Without warning, the older man lunged toward Leonard, pushing him back by the shoulders. Leonard lost his footing and slipped to the gravel. The set became extremely quiet. Dierdre had reloaded her camera and stood off by the giant cottonwood, snapping pictures with a telephoto lens.

Leonard sat up, brushing himself off. Dan Howe helped him to his feet and then two security personnel in blue uniforms were beside Moravio, escorting him to a limousine parked by the entrance to the set. Dan Howe followed them, Moravio muttering in Portuguese. As he got in the limo, he turned and spat in the dust at his feet.

Leonard came up to Nyia, brushing the dust from his sleeves. "And you," he hissed, "kindly absent yourself from the premises as I have asked you to do, or you will likewise be removed. Thank you." He stalked back toward the motel and entered the office, where he sat in a metal patio chair.

Jack was beside her. "Hey, that was just like a fucking fight in the high school parking lot!" He nudged her with his elbow. "You're a troublemaker, you know that?"

"All I want is to play my part," whispered Nyia. "Why does it have to be so melodramatic?"

"Mirina told me this morning that your part is pretty well intact and Leonard's just blowing off steam. She's only making some small changes, that's my understanding. Go on. Take the day off and get out of here. Let Leonard pull it back together. You can see he's lost it. Having you here only makes it worse."

"Thanks, Jack."

"No, you know that. You've got to find some way to play into it. Quit pushing against him." Jack took her by the arms. "Stop fighting him."

"You're siding with him in this, aren't you? You used to stand up for me."

Jack shook his head and smiled. "I don't take him so seriously," he said. "It's a job. Let go, Nyia. Jesus."

Across the parking lot, Howe slammed the limousine door and the long car pulled out. Jack was right, but she couldn't get the distance. There were things

Jack didn't know, about the car being shot at and that man killed out by Madrid. Nyia began walking back toward the Jeep. It was time she had a talk with Jack and Tess, let them in on everything, who Harm was. Stop the lie of it all. She was going to get out of here and let everyone cool off. Tomorrow, she would let them all know.

Dan Howe came toward Nyia, pulling a pencil out of his vest pocket. "Robin!" he called out, raising the pencil. "Hold up a minute!"

Nyia took a few more steps and then stopped dead at the sound of that name.

"Say, Nyia!" Howe called again. But that wasn't what he'd just said. Had anyone else heard it?

Howe jogged up to her, out of breath. Jack joined them. "We're going to be doing the bike scene tomorrow," he said quietly. "The script calls for you on the bike—unless Leonard informs me otherwise. But be there anyway, up past Chimayo. Here's a map I had copied for everybody."

Nyia took the map, stared down at it. "You called me Robin," she said.

Howe glanced over her shoulder, watching as the limo took a right onto the highway and headed back toward Santa Fe. "I said 'Nyia.'"

"No," she breathed. "No, you didn't. Jack, did you hear him?"

Jack shrugged. "Big deal."

Dan zipped his vest up with a jerk. "Did you have any luck with the fly yesterday?" he asked her. When she didn't speak, he cleared his throat, then again. "Yeah. I guess maybe I did call you Robin. Sorry. I'm pretty tense, I guess. Walking through a minefield here."

"Ego minefield," Jack said under his breath.

Dan went on. "It just seems like we're right back in a very familiar place in this whole process and—" He stopped. "It's just that sometimes you look so much like

Robin, it's like looking at a ghost. I'm not the only one who thinks so."

"Pull it together, Howe," snapped Jack. "This isn't Mexico, it's *New* Mexico. Everybody is going to have to pull it the fuck together."

Dan Howe fixed on some distant vista, lips moving slightly without sound, his brow lined in some inner conversation.

Harm was leaning on the Jeep and Nyia walked over to him. "Let's get out of here."

They drove through Española behind a cattle truck and headed north, veering right toward Taos. Soon the green mountains and the red rocks rose up on either side of the highway leading into the Rio Grande gorge, the river just a creek here in a gulch beside the road, then wider, gulleys and arroyos chiseled into the land like giant mud-cracks. In a crevice next to the highway a rusted car lay overturned, and Nyia shuddered, thinking of the car and train scene yet to be shot. Thank God they weren't going to do that one tomorrow.

Coming up over a rise in the blacktop, Nyia saw the wide mesa stretching below Taos mountain, the giant crack in the earth that was Rio Grande gorge—where the earth had shifted millions of years ago, broken open into that black crevice—miles of sage and cactus, the vast sky, the familiar blue profile of the mountains. Harm was contemplative and quiet as they neared the town.

They parked behind Taos Plaza. Nyia took Harm's arm as they came around the corner into the square at the center of town. Trees came up through the bricks of the plaza and a tiny American flag at the top of a flagpole whipped in the wind, so small it looked like a miniature. Teenagers lounged in a small band-shell across from Hotel La Fonda. Companions shared one skateboard, taking turns. Dried ristras were strung on the bandshell and street lamps on thick wooden posts lined the square in front of the curio shops and art stores, El Mercado and Hotel La Fonda. The shadows seemed soft here. They walked out through the plaza in the direction of the Pueblo, past curved shoulder-high walls and flowering bushes. Sudden gust in her face, grit of sand. There was still snow on Taos mountain.

Later they sat at a restaurant drinking white wine and looking at paintings by local artists on the walls.

"I'm thinking about those letters," Nyia said. "How they started coming after I left Paris three years ago. And it was definitely around the time I broke up with Leonard."

"And you also signed on with Suzanne Scolfield at that time?"

"Yes," she said. "How did you know?"

He shrugged. "I'm doing research, remember? So what happened—your mother managed your career up until then?"

"I was just sick of all of them. Leonard, Mirina, my mother. I was twenty-seven years old and was totally controlled by my mother and my lover. I know it probably sounds weird, but three years ago I had no idea who I really was. I was the roles I played, I was a product of my mother's fantasies, I was some kind of muse for Leonard. I just felt used. I signed on with Suzanne, left Paris and went back to California, did the horror movies, *Pursuit* and *Gun Law,* back to back. Everyone was aghast. Well, Leonard and Mirina were. But I loved it, Harm. It was fun, it was lightweight. I loved all the special effects and the fast-paced stories. It was just right. After that came *Dead Heat*—I owed Leonard. Then *Wings.* I'm in a prime place now in my career. But I had this one last film to do with Leonard and Mirina. It was in my contract with them."

"You've left them in the dust, Nyia."

She tasted her wine.

"There are quite a few people you've left behind as you've become your own person. I'm talking motivation, Nyia. Why anyone might want to hurt you, injure you, see you out of commission."

"But that's sick," she whispered.

"Yeah," he said. "Murder is a very sick thing."

They ate dessert in silence and listened to a man with a long red beard play a blue guitar. Nyia drank coffee and a few people got up to dance in the small restaurant. She touched Harm's hand. "Will you dance with me?"

"Has anyone ever said no to you?" he asked as he stood.

"Plenty."

"That's pretty hard to believe."

"Yeah? I looked hard for people who would say no, actually. That was my number. It took me a long time to figure that out."

"Well, how about a yes?" Harm asked. She rested her head on his chest as they danced and she felt safe, knew it was a false safety and didn't care. It was false because no one could protect her ever, false because no man could ever cure her life, false because there could never really be anything between them. They were from different worlds, she knew that. She leaned into him anyway, felt some hesitation in his body. A few minutes into the music, he gave in and moved with her.

After dinner they walked around the dark, nearly empty plaza, staring at trinkets and Southwestern art in the closed shop windows. It was cold now. As they peered in the window of the mercado at the cheap beaded belts and moccasins, he bent and kissed her neck, lifting her hair back with his fingers.

"Where's the cabin?" he asked.

Nyia tried to remember the way in the dark, several

miles north of Taos, then a right up into the mountains. They took one wrong turn, circled back, found the wood-and-stone cabin in a dark grove of pines. They kissed in the car, his jacket rough against her face.

The cabin was freezing and Harm rattled the fire-place grate, built a fire to a bright blaze. She brought some blankets from the small bedroom, spread them on the floor. The light from the fire threw black shadows over the furniture. He started to take his shirt off but she took his hand away, fingering the buttons. "Let me," she said.

She opened his shirt and pressed against his chest. He lay down and she rolled on top of him, pulling her shirt up to brush his skin with her breasts, and felt him harden against her. As she kissed him, she searched around in her heart for the meaning, then stopped that and gave in to the way the firelight licked at his long thighs rocking against her.

In the morning, the cabin was still cold. Nyia curled against Harm's back and he reached around to touch her. She fumbled on the floor next to the blankets for her watch. After eight. They should get going. She rose, pulling clothes on, her breath visible in the high country morning.

As she sat on the couch to put her shoes on, something crackled under the pillow. Reaching back, she pulled out a small paper bag. Inside there were post-cards, an Anne Tyler paperback, and a receipt from Los Llanos, a bookstore in Santa Fe. She pulled the post-cards out and immediately recognized Tess's writing. She turned over the postcard of Ranchos de Taos. It was dated June twenty-fourth.

Dear Ma,
    L's got this fabulous cabin in Taos and we're

taking a breather before the last gasp of production. Five days of pine and mountain before the rest of the crew flocks to New Mex. I realize I haven't had a vacation in a year. Hope to get back east in late summer, tell Gram Happy Birthday. Okay, I'll send a card myself.

Love, Tessie

Nyia felt the darkness go through her like heat. "Harm?" she said.

He threw the blanket back. "What's up?"

She fished in the bag for the sales slip, handed it to him and then the card.

"Look at the date on this sales slip. June twenty-third. And the postcard dated the twenty-fourth. Tess was in New Mexico at least two days before she was scheduled to fly into Albuquerque from L.A. They were up here, Leonard and Tess. Leonard knew all along she wasn't coming in on that flight."

Harm sat down next to her, read the card and looked through the bag. The other cards were blank.

"Who exactly made the arrangements for you to pick up Tess that night?"

Nyia thought a moment. "We talked about driving to Albuquerque together to get her a few days before that. Then he took off for a couple of days and it was just me and Mirina at the house, lounging, swimming in the pool. I think he said he was flying back to L.A. to meet with the studio people. He was gone for two days, I think. When it was time to get Tess, he wasn't back, so I just went. It was written in his calendar. I think Mirina reminded me. Yes. She did. She said, 'Are you still going to get Tess or shall I send a driver?' I didn't really want to go alone, but I thought it would be nice to have that time with Tess. So I went."

"So Mirina arranged it."

"Finally, yes."

Harm put the cards back in the bag. "The man's an out-and-out liar," he muttered.

"And so is Tess."

Sixteen

HARM PUSHED THE JEEP AROUND THE MOUNTAIN toward Chimayo on the back road down from Taos, slowing around steep banked canyon curves. A low-rider behind them honked and swerved past. Nyia had been very quiet since they'd left the cabin. He'd pulled over so she could call Suzanne from a pay phone at a gas station, but there was no answer at the hotel. The switchbacked road was lined deep in pines, and Harm slowed for the steep U-turns. As they came down toward Chimayo, postcard vistas appeared at every turn, a breathless panorama of rock and emptiness. He reached over and touched the hair at the back of her head, the collar of her denim jacket. She smelled of perfume and sex, she filled the car with it. She nuzzled his hand but turned toward the window, looking the other way. *Gone,* he thought. *Already drifting into Christine.*

"Are you going into character?" he asked. "Can you talk?"

Nyia glanced over with a trace of a smile and shook her head. "It's not that. I'm just so upset, there's so much duplicity. So much lying. I wish I'd been able to get hold of Suzanne, so I knew what was going down today. I just don't know what to expect."

"Which is how he always does it."

"Yes, but it feels so wrong this time."

"What do you think Jacobs is going to do?" Harm asked.

"If he cuts Christine out of the bride role, I'm walking."

"Can he really fire you?"

"He wouldn't be that stupid. Anyway, I've got a little surprise for him."

"Such as?"

"You'll see. There's an old Zen saying, 'Give up the struggle and there is no struggle.' You know, like in aikido? Instead of resisting your attacker, you accept the force of the attack and move with it, move the opponent right past you."

"I prefer an uppercut to the right jaw, myself. Very direct, very American."

As he swerved the Jeep around a sharp curve, Harm spotted the location site ahead, a gravel turnaround large enough for trailers and RVs, trucks and various four-wheel drive vehicles to pull over in a crowded, makeshift jumble. In a small meadow below the turnaround a helicopter was parked, the field speckled with wildflowers. On a flatbed truck angled alongside the road, crew members were anchoring cameras for the moving road-shots. Harm slowed, but Nyia said, "We're early. It's only ten. Keep going down to Chimayo, why don't you? I want to go to the *santuario*. Do you mind?"

"Going to say a few rosaries?"

"Whatever it takes," she said. Finally she looked back at him and smiled.

* * *

If you were daydreaming on the road, spacing out on the radio, or thinking about lunch, you'd miss Chimayo, Harm thought. A few winding turns past buildings the color of the red land and you'd passed through. But he remembered the left turn toward the *santuario*. He'd come out just before Easter with Nickie, telling him about the sacred dirt in the tiny folk chapel nudged back by a creek. How on Good Friday people made pilgrimages, walking all the way from Santa Fe for a whole day, leaving crutches in the room next to the altar, abandoning back braces, saying farewell to injuries and troubles. Christ Jesus would heal. Holy Mother. It was said the dirt in the sanctuary was holy and when touched miracles would happen in your life. Harm had stooped into the tiny room where the dirt hole was. Nickie had asked if he could touch the dirt. Harm had said okay, but the boy had turned and left the chapel and Harm had followed him. *No miracles. No faith,* he thought.

Harm turned in past the curio shop and parked. The small church was surrounded by a low adobe wall, its steeple seeming to lean against the sand hills just behind it. It looked like a toy church, a child's drawing, someplace in a tippy, slanting dream. Nyia got out of the Jeep, her yellow hair flying against the blue of her jacket. She paused for a moment, peering into the small shop that sold votive candles, plastic rosaries, and cellophane bookmarks with the names and stories of the saints.

"I guess I'll just go in for a minute," she said.

"Do you want company?"

"Sure."

Inside, she took a seat on a wooden pew in the back. Harm had never felt particularly comfortable in churches, but he liked this one because it was so kitsch. It was a folk-art relic, its altar jammed with numerous statues of Jesus, some plastic, some wooden, some glass, golden, white, blue. Some glanced down with liquid eyes of lambs, others gazed skyward, filled with grief. The crucifix held a thorn-topped Jesus with blood dripping down the side of his face. A table of terraced candles in red and white glasses flickered in front of the Virgin, her arms outspread. The church was nearly empty on a Friday morning, just an old man on his knees before the altar and a family over near the wall, the mother bent, her head covered in a scarf. Someone was crying quietly in the next room. The man got up and his boots echoed on the wooden floor.

"You want to go into the room where the sacred dirt is?" Harm asked.

Suddenly she stood, turned to go. By the time he followed her out she was nearly at the Jeep. "Let's split," she said, lightning a cigarette, puffing the smoke out into the wind.

Christine smoking, he thought. She'd gone in Nyia and come out Christine. Then she spoke lines he knew were written by Mirina: "I hate that bike. That bike has got to go."

It took them only minutes to get back up to the location site, park the Jeep behind the row of trailers. Mirina sat in a lawn chair against the side of a van, her head lowered over a sheaf of papers, scribbling.

"There's Mirina," said Nyia. "She could be rewriting my scene even now. All I want is just to know my part. I want one thing in my life that's going to be there for me. Maybe I should get a dog."

They walked together into the maze of cameras, cords, dollies, and hoists. Dan Howe approached them with his clipboard. He wore a black baseball cap and round glasses. "Bohland, there's a police officer here asking after you," he said. "Asked for the detective, but described you. Used your name. I thought maybe he had it wrong, but ..." He let his voice trail off. Shrugged his shoulders. "He's over there with the helicopter pilot."

Howe knows, thought Harm, and suddenly he felt exposed and stupid. *Fuck this,* he thought. *Jacobs is going to announce to the crew that I'm here and why I'm here. I can't continue with this role-playing. I'm no good at it. And something always goes wrong when I have to pretend.*

Quintana spotted him, took off his Stetson, and strode across the edge of the meadow to where they stood. "Miss Wyatt," he greeted her, putting the hat back on his short black hair. He nodded, then gestured for them to come closer. "Went back out to Nims's last night to check out the back of that truck. Found this." He handed Harm a brown bag. "Stuffed under some feed bags and some hay."

Harm opened it and looked in. "Computer diskettes," Harm said.

He started to take them out of the bag, but Quintana stopped him. "Going to have them finger-printed. Just to see. Funny. Doesn't seem like Nims, does it?"

"I certainly didn't notice a P.C. in the place," said Harm. "I've got something for you too." And he handed the wedding dress video to Quintana, told him what they'd seen. Then he filled Quintana in about the letters Nyia had received and her fears about them. "Some of the letters were printed on a dot-matrix printer," he said. Quintana was silent, listening, grinding his boot into the dirt.

Harm looked up and glimpsed Dan Howe in conversation with Leonard across the road, raising and lowering his arms. Tess sauntered up the road in a wedding dress and hiking boots, arm in arm with Jack Drieser. Jack spun her like a dancer and she laughed.

Harm nudged Nyia's arm. "Looks like Tess is ready for your part."

"Let's go see," Nyia sighed loudly, muttering under her breath, "Where's Suzanne?"

Harm ran ahead to Jack and Tess, meeting them as they came to the highway. From his jacket pocket he pulled the Anne Tyler novel Tess had left at the Taos cabin.

"What are you doing?" asked Nyia.

"Just wait," he said. "Tess, hold up a minute." Tess stopped, both she and Jack greeting Nyia and Harm.

"Where were you? Where the hell are you staying, anyway?" said Tess. "I was trying to get hold of you last night. Even Suzanne didn't know where you were. Nyia, none of this was my idea, you have got to believe me."

Jack was dressed in Hank's wardrobe, faded ripped jeans, white T-shirt, worn black-leather jacket, wire-frame glasses. He lifted his hands, palms up. "You just have to go with the flow, ladies. Didn't I tell you, Bohland? Improv. Personally, I don't let it bother me. You can't get sucked in, Nyia."

"He's not cutting you out of your part, Jack," Nyia snapped.

"Baby, you know he's not cutting you."

"He's cutting Christine out of me."

Jack reached over and held her shoulder. "We got to ride this one through together, Ny. You've helped me plenty of times. Can you let it go? It'll be a whole lot easier if you just go with it."

Nyia laughed, a bitter dryness to it.

Harm spoke up. "That's really a great place Leonard's got up in Taos. Say, we found your book up there, Tess. You had a nice lay-low interim up there, then, between the Canada sequence and this one?"

"Isn't it pretty?" she said, taking the book. "Thanks, I was looking all over for this." She kept her eyes on the cover, the gold wedding ring against the dark background. Harm could feel her get it, caught in her deception.

"You're so lucky you got a chance to go up there, Nyia," said Tess. Her voice sounded overly sweet.

"You too, honey," said Nyia. Half-Christine.

"Yeah, but I haven't been up there in months," Tess protested. "Must have been last fall when we were out here doing the planning for *Trial and Error*."

Harm squeezed Nyia's arm and broke in. "We thought you'd just been up there with Leonard."

"Oh," she laughed. "He borrowed that book as soon as he saw I had it. The sneak. I'm glad you found it. I sure never would have thought of going up there to look for it. The cabin? No. I went back to L.A. after Canada. You knew that." She gazed directly at Harm. "I always try to get home when I can. I feel so uprooted if I don't." With that, she turned and walked from the group to where Leonard was leaning against the flatbed trailer. By the time Nyia and Harm approached, Tess Juran was leaning intently into his talk. Nyia went right up to them while Harm stood off to the side.

"I hope you've reconsidered," Nyia said to Jacobs.

"You can see Tess is in the bride role," he announced.

Nyia did not look away. "What about the bride scenes we've already shot? The honeymoon sequence in the hotel?"

"The story is different now. Go talk to Mirina, she'll review the changes with you. I think you're really going to like it." He sounded excited, his voice high. "Christine is going to be Hank's *lover* now. They meet just before he's to marry Tess's character. When Tess finds out, she and Hank argue. Then she goes off on the bike to confront Christine back in town."

Tess said to Leonard, "No way am I getting on that bike. I hate that bike. I thought you said yesterday that Jack was doing the bike scene. Weren't you, Jack?"

"I can't keep it straight," Jack said. "First it was Nyia,

then it was me, now it's Tess. But Leonard's the boss, girls. Girls?" He rolled his eyes at Harm.

Nyia was suddenly very quiet. Harm could hardly hear her. She sounded like a child, whining. "But I wanted to be the bride, Leonard." There were tears, her eyes filled with them.

Tess lit a cigarette, looked away.

"You prepared me for that part," said Nyia. "We worked on it for weeks. We worked on it just days ago in the cabin, didn't we? Didn't we, Leonard?" The tears spilled over and her voice broke.

"That's good. That pain. Use it, Nyia. For Christine. Go into it."

She did. "I want to be married. That's all I ever wanted. You held it out in front of me and then you broke me, Leonard."

"Good," he whispered. Leonard glanced at Tess to see if she was watching.

Nyia knelt in front of him, where he had sat down in a lawn chair. She put her face against his shirt, her arms around him. He stroked her hair. Others were watching now out of the corners of their eyes. She was pushing it, she sobbed against him once, her shoulders shook silently. She raised her face and he put his hand against her cheek. Harm felt uncomfortable. No edge, he thought. This is how they were for years. No difference between real and character. That's how he'd trained her.

Tess stood and ground her cigarette into the dirt. "What is this crap?" she asked. "Some kind of technique? Is this what you call technique, Leonard?"

Nyia ignored Tess. She was totally in character and so was Leonard. She wrapped her hands around his neck, pressed her thumbs in. "If I were stronger, I swear I'd kill you," she whispered. Leonard smiled.

Harm watched them play-act the violence, Leonard holding his breath as she gripped his throat like that. What else had they played at? What were they still playing at even now? Maybe they'd gone so far into their game that others were being killed because of it. Robin Reese. Nims. He felt as he had when he'd watched Nyia making love with Jack in the honeymoon scene. He wanted to rush in to stop it, yet he wanted to watch to see where it went.

Nyia stood abruptly and walked away, brushing past Harm without looking at him, down the road toward the trailers. Harm started to follow, but Leonard came toward him.

"She's brilliant, isn't she? Watch. It's like a dance, she knows exactly when to take the conflict and fold it right back into the story. There is no one like her."

Then Harm remembered Nyia saying she had something for him. Was this what she'd meant?

"Leonard!" Tess called. "What the hell is going on here!"

Leonard leaned toward Harm, voice low, inspirational. "Tess is young. I don't know if she's truly receptive."

By her trailer, Nyia had found Suzanne. Harm watched as Suzanne took Nyia's face in hers, trying to calm her.

"Cast!" cried Leonard. "Listen up!" He opened his arms wide, addressing Mirina several trailers down, Suzanne, Nyia, Jack, Tess. Several cameramen and the cinematographer dropped what they were doing and listened. Where was Dierdre, Harm wondered. *Removed from the set.* Maybe she'd gone back to L.A.

"I announced yesterday at the script meeting that Jack would be in the bike scene, but we're making some changes now. We're into the random chaos now, where you have to let go into the story. You simply have to follow it now, trust it. Tess will be on the bike in this next scene." He instructed the cameramen who'd be on the truck preceding and following the bike, and those who would be on the road as she headed up the mountain. One more camera would be shooting from the helicopter.

"I can't ride the bike, Leonard." Tess bent her arms to her waist. "Isn't that a stunt act, anyway?"

Leonard almost growled back at her. "You get on the bike and you ride up the fucking road and the helicopter takes your fucking picture. You got that? *Comprende, señorita?* Drieser, show her how to start the thing up."

Leonard snapped around, facing Harm. "Bohland? I want you up in the helicopter with the cameraman. I want this documented. You got your videocam? This is exactly what I want in the documentary. This is exactly what your writing should reveal. This is where the text leaves off and the real work begins and every goddamn one of you knows it!" He was shouting now.

Mirina rose up from her chair and hurried over to him. Forcibly taking his arm, she led him back to the van.

Suzanne appeared beside Harm. "See how he gets? Mirina will calm him down, she knows how. Little genius baby. Tyrant," she muttered. "Can you believe Nyia put up with this all those years? Thank God this is her last project for Visionfilm."

"Did you confront Leonard about keeping Nyia in the bride part?" Harm asked her.

"She's better off going along with it at this point. I spoke with him at length last night. She won't be the bride part, but her part is still lead. He does have integrity, it's just that he's manic. Nyia's new part, as Mirina is writing it, is pretty damn interesting. I still hate his process though. Go on up in the copter," she drawled. "I'll stay back with Nyia. I've convinced Mirina that I'm sitting in on all script change meetings from now on. Go on," Suzanne insisted.

Harm ran back to the jeep for the video camera. As he climbed into the helicopter, the machine shuddered, revving its blades. It rose skyward in a loud sputter of wind and dust from the meadow, lifting magically into the blue air and planing out over the piñon.

Harm brought the set into view below, watched it grow as small as a bunch of children's toy soldiers staged in a sandbox. He glanced back for an instant. Nyia stood far below, hands to her eyes, shrinking as the helicopter sailed up. It went through him, then, in a sick wave. *I shouldn't have left her. This was a setup. I should be down there with her.*

He nudged the pilot, hollering into the blade racket. The pilot lifted his earphones briefly, shaking his head. "I can't circle back now, the cameras are rolling, see? This is it. Real thing."

A hundred feet down, Tess was clutching the handlebars, her hair blown back. In spite of her protests, it appeared that she could ride it well. The helicopter swooped down, hovering just in front of her. The cameraman followed her as she banked the curve, passing directly below. As planned, the flatbed truck pulled over at an overlook and Tess continued up, the helicopter circling her as she rode.

"Speed it up, Tommy," yelled the cameraman. "She's really cooking along there. I want to get another shot in front of her for a couple seconds, then just rise straight up for a long pull-out."

Harm felt a sudden exhilaration as the helicopter ascended, lifting away from the piñon and the blacktop. Below, Tess, on the shiny Harley, tossed back her head in the wind.

"Okay, she's supposed to turn around right up there and head back down. We'll hang up here and wait for Leonard to radio. He may want her to repeat the shot." The cameraman lowered his camera, but Harm kept her in his viewfinder.

Tess headed for the spot where the road widened, but did not slow down or stop. In the black-and-white square of his videocam, Harm saw that the bike did not diminish in speed as it approached the sharp curve where the arroyo fell down to a steep, rock-filled canyon. Tess flew out over the sand cliff as if she'd aimed the bike deliberately off the road. The Harley hung in the air for a second at the peak of its arc before Tess catapulted over the silver handlebars, the big Harley dropping away below her, toppling down. For a moment, Tess curled like an acrobat, pulling in on herself. Did she try to cover her head? Then she dropped hard, her head blasting into the jutting rocks, arms and legs flopping loose as she tumbled down, the bike crashing down over her, missing her, but it didn't matter. It didn't matter at all. Harm knew that.

"Oh Christ," the pilot cried into his headset. "Going down, going down." He dropped the helicopter so fast, Harm had to grab at the edge of the open door to keep his balance. He heard the pilot yell into the radio, "Accident. She's down. She's off the cliff. We're going down. Better get the medics up here goddamn quick. Get an ambulance. Oh fuck, it don't look good."

The pilot set the helicopter down on the rocks next to a gash in the sand, a small arroyo at the bottom of the canyon. The cameraman and pilot scrambled out before Harm. The blades threw spinning shadows over the red sand. The pilot turned Tess over, pulled off his T-shirt and pressed it to her scalp, which was open like lips; her eyes blue and full of some horrible wonder, her neck loose as rope in his hands.

"She's fuckin' dead," he shouted above the noise of helicopter blades, still pressing the T-shirt to her forehead. Blood was smeared on his arms and hands. He looked up at Harm helplessly. Harm could not help it. He raised the video camera to his shoulder and shot. No one told him not to.

The pilot lowered Tess to the sand, leaving his shirt in place, shaking his head. "It's no use," he spoke toward the video camera. "It's all she wrote." He put his head down to his knee, covering his face.

The cameraman stood over the steaming bike, not thirty feet away. "She never even slowed for that curve," he called. Harm turned the video camera on him.

"Hey, man," said the cameraman. "This ain't no movie."

Harm clicked the video camera off, pulling it away from his face.

The pilot stood over Tess for a moment, then started back to the helicopter to radio down to the set.

SEVENTEEN

HARM DUCKED INVOLUNTARILY AS THE
helicopter took off above him in a deafening whir,
zooming away, up over the mountain. The sputter of
the blades faded into the wind. The bike was smoking,
emitting a hissing sound. The cameraman took off his
jacket and covered Tess Juran's head and chest, spreading it across her. Then he stood, hands in pockets, not
knowing what to do. Harm walked over to the bike and
knelt down, examining a small copper wire at the base
of the brake pad by the wheel. *There: it was cut. The
hydraulic line to the brakes had been cut, the fluid drained out.*

Somebody had tampered with this bike. Harm
thought of the chaos back at the location, miles back
down the road, Leonard switching parts, Tess not wanting to get on the bike. Premonition, foreboding? He'd
heard tales of people knowing they were going to die,
feeling it in the air around them. Nyia would have been

on that bike if Leonard had kept her in the part of the bride. It would have been Nyia on those rocks over there, jacket over her face, the body seeming already whiter, bluer in just these few moments of death.

Who knew about that switch in roles? Everyone must have known the part was up in the air. Even Moravio could have been filled in by Suzanne. Someone had gotten to the bike last night and messed with it. But maybe it had been tampered with even before that. No bike scenes had actually been filmed yet. Maybe it had been fixed long before filming even began. And yet it was eerie, the repetition of events like Manzanillo. A certain doubling of roles, identity switches, and the matter of the dresses, black and white. Who was this death meant for? Harm asked himself.

Harm lifted the video camera and panned the arroyo, closing the lens in on the bike, the road above, and back to Tess's still body. Within minutes he heard the helicopter clattering through blue air. He could hear it before it tilted up over the pines. Whirling up the dry sand, it rested lightly several hundred yards away and Leonard leapt out, ducking beneath the blades. As he neared the body he slowed, then approached.

He knelt and removed the jacket, put his fingers against her throat, feeling for a pulse. Another man had jumped from the helicopter carrying a red bag with a white cross on it. He elbowed Leonard aside and also felt for her pulse, shaking his head.

"Can you do CPR?" cried Leonard.

The medic lifted Tess, feeling the spine at her neck, again shaking his head. "Mr. Jacobs, it's not her heart. Her neck is broken." He was silent, looking into Jacobs's dark eyes. "I'm sorry. There's nothing we can do now."

Jacobs put his hands beneath her head. The skull wound had bled profusely into the T-shirt. He cradled Tess Juran where he knelt in the dust. Just held her gently, mouthing her name. "Tessie. Tessie."

He set her down on the rocks, covered her again with the cameraman's jacket. The helicopter was silent now. The men stood in a semicircle in the piñon, watching. Leonard stood, walked away toward the arroyo, stumbled, vomited, gagged again.

Convincing, thought Harm. Plenty of affect. Jacobs was not reacting like a cold murderer, but among these people Harm no longer knew what was real, what was created.

Jacobs turned back toward them, finally spotting Harm. As he walked over to him, Jacobs stepped in a wide arc to avoid going near the body.

"This wasn't supposed to happen," he said quietly. He seemed dazed, his shirt smeared with blood. "I'm ruined now. That's the long and short of it. My life is over." He looked around at the mountains as if calculating the extent of his loss. How ruined, exactly, was he? "She was so beautiful," he whispered. "So young. What happened, Bohland? Did you see it?"

"She just sailed off, straight off. She never slowed down, never bent into the curve at all. I've got it on video. Quintana can look at it. I examined the bike, and the hydraulic line to the brakes was cut. This wasn't an accident. Mr. Jacobs, what about Nyia?"

He looked at Harm blankly. "She's all right. She's back down the hill at her trailer."

"But she was supposed to have been in this role today. You switched Tess to her part in the film."

Jacobs turned again and looked in the direction of Tess's body, glanced at his watch. There was a strange stillness about the man, and then Harm noticed he was shaking, a subtle shuddering to his head as if it were poised on a delicate spring.

"That's true," he said. "We got the idea for that yesterday; Mirina's been revising the script, that's how we do it, we—" He stopped. "You're saying somebody fucked with the bike thinking Nyia would be riding it today, is that what you're saying?"

Jacobs was shaking more visibly now as he faced the roadside above the arroyo where several cars had pulled up, one of them Quintana's. Quintana appeared at the edge of the canyon and began the descent, sliding down through the low piñon and sage, rocks tumbling before him.

Harm grabbed Leonard Jacobs's arm. The man was going into shock, Harm thought. He decided to push it anyway, or perhaps even because of that. "Leonard, I know Tess was up at the Taos cabin with you the night Nyia was shot at. I know you and Tess were lovers. Were you involved with Tess Juran down in Mexico? Was that why she left the film, some lovers' quarrel?"

Jacobs turned back to Harm. "That was part of it." He looked utterly vulnerable. Harm was shocked by his truthfulness.

"And then Robin, you were sleeping with her as well, isn't that true?"

Jacobs nodded. "Only once. I only made love to her once."

"Why did you send Nyia to pick up Tess at the airport if you knew Tess was already *in* New Mexico?"

"I didn't. Mirina checked my appointment book, saw I had Tess's flight penciled in, and sent Nyia because I was still up in Taos. I got down just before Quintana brought Nyia back after the car was shot at. I'd been up in Española and here in Chimayo with Howe, finalizing arrangements for the locations. Yes, I went up to the cabin. Yes, Tess and I were there together."

"Why didn't you mention this before? You should have come clean. How can I investigate if I don't know the fucking truth?"

Jacobs was shaking hard now, as if he were shuddering in subzero weather. He held up his hands. "You know how it is, Bohland. The wife . . . it's complicated, right?"

Quintana was examining the body now behind

them, looking up at Harm, waving him over. Harm called out to him, "I think Jacobs is going into shock." Quintana ran to them, called to the pilot to take Jacobs back down all the way into Santa Fe. There was no need for the helicopter to remain for Tess Juran. An ambulance was on its way.

"I was just trying to keep things separate," said Jacobs.

"The women, you mean."

He nodded. "It doesn't work."

Quintana led Jacobs to the helicopter. Shaking. Quivering of hands and head. Shock, yes, thought Harm, but something more. That kind of shaking was a side-effect to certain antidepressants. Especially those given to patients experiencing psychotic breaks. He wanted access to Leonard Jacobs's medical records. And the person he'd have to talk to about it would be Mirina.

Maybe Nyia wasn't the intended victim at all, he thought suddenly. Overhead a hawk spiraled in an air current, black wings spread in the bright air. Robin, Tess, Nyia. Murders or attempted murders. What was the common denominator? All of them were Leonard Jacobs's amorous pursuits. All of them his lovers, even if only once. *The wife . . . it's complicated.*

Mirina, who had hired him out of the yellow pages, not some fancy Beverly Hills detective agency, the detective with no ad at all, specializing in accounting, for God's sake. To placate Leonard and Nyia, Mirina had hired a detective, then kept him ineffectual by requiring him to be "undercover" as an academic writer who couldn't even investigate properly.

Killing off her husband's lovers? It was possible. It was the most probable motivation so far. But this was something more, much more. These were the actresses in their films together, Visionfilm Productions, their company. Mirina stood to be devastated financially by these women's deaths. Tess's death would open up a whole new investigation, a whole new insurance liability for Visionfilm. Personally there was motive. But professionally Mirina would be committing suicide to do it this way. She was a brilliant woman. Surely if she wanted to kill off Leonard's lovers she'd have had the brains to wait until the filming was complete.

Quintana was looking the bike over now and Harm ran over to him, telling him what he'd found examining the brakes. Quintana was chewing gum, snapping it loud in his cheeks.

"That's what it looks like," Quintana said. "What about Miss Wyatt? I thought she was with you in the helicopter." A crowd was gathering in the arroyo, coming down the embankment now from vehicles driven up from the location site.

"She's down the hill."

"You better go down and find her," Quintana said. Harm scrambled up the red rocks toward the road, video camera under one arm, grabbing the scrubby piñon for leverage with the other.

He got a ride down the several miles of blacktop in the back of a gold low-rider. Led Zeppelin's "Ramblin' Man" reverberated against the windows. He thanked the two silent drivers with their black ponytails and hopped out near the turnaround where Nyia's trailer was parked. He rapped hard against the thin metal of her trailer door and the door swung open.

Manuel Moravio leaned over the dinette table, straightened quickly and cranked his neck around to face Harm. He had bright, dark eyes, close together, and a thin, leathery face. "I'm waiting for Nyia," Moravio said. "Do you know where she is? I don't think she knows there's been an accident."

Accident, thought Harm. He doesn't know Tess is dead.

Harm stepped up into the cramped trailer. "How did you get in here?" he asked.

Moravio shrugged. "It was unlocked. I knocked, I tried the door, just as you did now. I know what you're thinking, that scene yesterday with Jacobs. We cleared it up. I lost my head, I'm afraid." He slid into one of the seats on either side of the small table.

Moravio pushed a blue envelope toward Harm. It was unfolded, open, the familiar typed words across the thin paper. "I shouldn't have," said Moravio, "but I read this. I snooped. I've received fan letters from all over the world, but never anything like this. How would one respond to such a letter? The devotion is skewed, don't you think? Of course, I'm not Nyia. What is the news from up the hill, then? Are there any broken bones?"

Harm didn't want to be the bearer of news. He looked the letter over quickly, eyes scanning the page.

"Dear Nyia,

"Don't you think you're taking this a bit too far? First you create one story, then leave it for another. I'm talking about your new companion, your new love. It is clear his role has begun to surpass its original intention, but perhaps all along that was meant to be. You really have moved on from Leonard, haven't you? I know it is silly, but I always imagined that once you had done that you would be free. For me.

"I am finally seeing how it is that I prevent myself from revealing my presence to you. In my mind, I feel that if we are still in the future, our love, our life together, it is entirely within my control. To actually put myself before you as I truly am, without pretense, is to let go totally. To leave it up to you to decide. And that I am not yet ready to do.

"The fiction of our love is still preferable. But it is provisional. In order to imagine loving you, I exit, leave my body slightly and watch off to the side. You know how it is: to enter the story, to act a part in a film, you dissociate from the central part of yourself. Can we be in the story together without leaving our true hearts? I admit a lack of trust in this process.

"You have a stubborn existence of your own apart from my thoughts about you. I see that now.

"For that reason I have decided on a plan. Destroying you might rid me of the object of my compulsion, yes. But it might only transfer my need onto another object. I think it more wise to give my love a final opportunity for consummation. That is, to go away together, see what might happen between us. I ask you if you are willing. But how can you say yes, not knowing even who I am? And yet I am afraid that if you know . . . .

"For this reason, I have decided that the going away cannot be something you have a choice about. We are going away soon, together. Please prepare yourself."

"You just found this here?" Harm asked Moravio.

"Right here on the table. I read it just now myself. It sounds as if the man is planning to kidnap her, Bohland."

Harm reread the letter, then looked up directly at Moravio. He wouldn't be stupid enough to stay for long in the trailer if he'd been the one to leave such a letter. Or open it to read it through one last time. Perhaps. One might perhaps, one who admired the sound of his own voice.

"I will tell you one other thing," said Moravio. "It is chilling to remember. One evening during the filming of *Wings,* we sat around talking, drinking, many of us. We agreed that the oddness of dreams came from their perfectly rational origins. So we all agreed to make up a story, beginning with a true event in our lives but moving out from there. Making it macabre or magical, whichever way we were drawn.

"Nyia told the story of a fan letter, a love letter. In time, the fan's letters became obsessive. The man was tragically in love with her, but only with his idea of her. He could not get close to her. She became afraid of him. Terrified. Finally she wouldn't even accept the letters. She recognized them by their blue envelopes and threw them away. She went to the police for protection, but since nothing wrong had happened, they could do nothing." Moravio stopped. "Professor Bohland, it was as if Nyia knew this would happen. But she never mentioned to me that she was actually receiving such letters."

"You said you were waiting for her," said Harm. His voice was loud, almost shouting.

Moravio answered quietly, "I couldn't find her. I thought perhaps she went up the mountain with some of the others to see how Miss Juran was...."

From the next trailer, Harm heard angry voices, muffled by the metal walls. He jerked the door open, calling back to Moravio, "Excuse me. I've got to find her."

He pulled open the door of the next trailer and Suzanne and Jack Drieser looked up, surprised.

"Where's Nyia? Have you seen her?"

"How is Tess?" cried Suzanne. "Is she okay?"

They don't know. Leonard had gone up in the helicopter but had not told anyone back here what was going on.

"She's dead." Harm stepped up into the trailer.

Jack sat down slowly on a small couch built against the wall. "Oh God," he said, then pounded his fist against the wall. "Fucking Jacobs. What did I tell you, Suzanne?" he yelled.

She looked at Harm in a posture of helplessness. "Jack wanted to leave the film too. I was begging him to stay, to finish—" She put her hand to her forehead. "I need a drink," she said. Only then did she think to ask, "What do you mean, she's dead? How can she be dead?"

Harm told them what had happened, the bike, the

arroyo, her broken neck. He left the details of the tampering to Quintana for now. Jack put his face in his hands and was breathing hard, a kind of frozen male crying, no tears. Harm put his hand on the man's shoulder.

Then he left the trailer, running from trailer to trailer, jerking open doors, asking for Nyia. Had anyone seen her, where had she gone? He ran to the flatbed truck, to a trailer for coffee and snacks, to the tarp strung on tent poles over some electronic equipment. Mirina was also missing. No one had seen her. As news spread throughout the location that Tess had been killed, people began hurrying to their cars. Harm heard a nasal announcement over a bullhorn. Howe announced in an urgent plea, "All Visionfilm crew and staff report immediately to the tent. Repeat, all Visionfilm staff and crew ..."

He had to go. She wasn't here. He had left her. He had promised not to leave her, to take care of her. Had Mirina taken her somewhere? Because even without entering all his notes and findings on index cards, it was clear: Mirina Jacobs had the motivation to kill her husband's lovers. Why she would do it in the context of destroying her own films, her own screenplays, was beyond him, but she had every reason. And it was the only reason Harm could think of.

As he turned to head for the Jeep, Suzanne Scolfield appeared beside him, grabbing the sleeve of his jacket. "Bohland. Here." She shoved him a check. "I don't know what your fees are," she said. "Your retainer, whatever. But I'd like you to stop working for the Jacobses as of now and start working for me. This undercover thing is totally bogus. It's a stupid setup to keep you from finding out what's really going on here. Leonard obviously has something to do with all of this and is trying to placate Nyia and the rest of the crew with the thought that he is looking into all of this. But it's gone too far. Find Nyia. That's all I ask. Find her and get her to a safe place. Will you do that?"

He took the check and stared at it. *Five grand.* He handed it back to her. "I may do that, Ms. Scolfield," he said. "I may just do that. Let me think about it. But one way or another, I am going to find Nyia. And who I'm working for doesn't make a goddamn bit of difference right now. I'll get back to you."

"Here's my card, my office number in L.A., and my service number. They can get a message to me at any time. Call me."

He nodded.

On his way to the Jeep, he stepped once more into Nyia's now-empty trailer. Moravio was gone now as well. He ruffled through some papers on the table. Nyia's script notes, a list of grievances against Leonard to be discussed with Suzanne, phone numbers with no names. He folded all the papers in half. He would go through them later when he had time. Right now he had to get back down to Santa Fe. She had a key to his house and he had an overwhelming intuition that that was where she had gone. The one safe place she had in Santa Fe.

As he slipped the wad of papers into his pocket, something fell out, drifted down to the floor under the table. He squatted to pick it up. A clear plastic square, a sleeve for a computer diskette. He stood holding it in his palm, trying to get it to speak to him, to tell him how it was connected with the back of Howard Nims's white pickup, a brown bag from an office supply store in Albuquerque, a pair of severed bird claws and a dead woman on a mountainside, her skull opened up and her life flown out forever.

☆   ☆   ☆

SHE WAS GONE.

She had disappeared and he could not find her. Some part of him knew that if he simply waited, she would turn up. Perhaps she rode up the mountain with someone to see what happened. Or walked off into the woods, across the field, into the pines. Maybe she stuck her thumb out, hitched a ride into Chimayo or back to Santa Fe.

He didn't know. He only knew he could not lose her, could not let her get away from him. She knew the plan now and he would have to follow through.

As the car pulled over to pick him up, he felt the gun in his pocket and thought, I'll wait until we get out to the highway. I'll drop the old man there. It was the old man in the blue shirt and faded jeans, the old man with brown face and white hair who told him, "Some girl died up on that road back there. Guess she went off on some motorcycle. Cars are backed up quite a ways, the road's all full of flares and some cops are *directing traffic. Said she broke her neck. I couldn't really get a look-see, but I thought I saw her down there in the gully. Took quite a fall, them rocks are hard. People just don't watch the road, they get all caught up in the scenery. What is this here, some kind of movie going on?"* the old man asked.

He'd felt the cold then. Felt it the same as he'd felt it down in Mexico that night, ice through him like liquid nitrogen, white smoke in his lungs. The story taking turns against him he had never planned. Going against the script, the way it had been written, the way it had been thought through. He'd never intended for Robin to be killed that night. It had never crossed his mind that Tess would die. The story was running things now, it was running him too. He would have to outrun it. It was like a maze and something was chasing him down. Not a person. The story itself, and he had to keep ahead of it before it got to him.

The man drove through Chimayo, past low willows along the Nambe River, leaning vega fences, dead trees with aching branches and no rain, the desert was making him sick. He didn't know how long he could stay in New Mexico now. Ravens flew up at the edge of the road and the landscape looked abandoned yet alive, a dry planet, the stripes in the rocks all white and slanted as if the ground had tipped here and risen up out of itself, locking at an angle to the sky. They passed a white cross on a high rock formation beside the road. Sun patterns flowed over the sand hills, rippling across the emptiness.

Just before the intersection he asked the man to pull over, and he did without asking why. He pulled the gun then and simply told the man to get out. Handed him a couple hundred bucks from his wallet. "For your trouble. You'll get the car back in a day or so. I'll leave it at the airport in Albuquerque." The man nodded, almost happy to loan the car out for two crisp hundred-dollar bills. Thinking, them crazy movie people, what they won't do.

He could only think of one place she might be. When he reached Santa Fe, he took the Paseo de Paralta around downtown, turned up Acequia Madre toward Bohland's house.

She'd be there, all right. That's where she must have gone.

The door was locked, but he kicked it open easily with a thrust of his boot. Little toy door, painted bright blue, shaped like an arch in a church. Not here, not here. He put on his gloves, he remembered that and also remembered he hadn't worn them in the car. He'd have to wipe the car down when he was through in here.

It seemed right somehow, though he wasn't sure why. He began by pulling books down off shelves, knocking over lamps, yanking out desk drawers, throwing chairs across the room. He was out of breath and panting by the time he was done. If only he'd brought the camera, could get this all down, show Bohland, I'm in your home, you are in her, you are not safe. None of you are safe. One by one you are gone. Get rid of them all. When they are gone, she'll be free. Bali, perhaps, he thought. New Zealand. Where no one would look for them, where they would have a chance. If, in paradise, without the past to haunt her, she could not grow to love him, then he would have to kill her. To free himself. Just to end it. Conclusively. It felt good to have a plan. But where was she?

He leaned on the kitchen counter by the phone. And there it was, the notepad and her writing. Ah. So that is where she had gone. Stroke of goddamn genius, lucky streak across his star-crossed palm. Propped up against the coffee pot, a letter to Bohland. He tore the page off the notepad and pocketed the letter.

Idea for a scene: A woman running away from someone gets on a plane, settles into her seat, watches as the ground falls away below, the tiny houses, the mountains. Believing she is safe, she closes her eyes to sleep. The camera pulls back, pans toward the rear of the plane, row by row, the ordinary faces, reading a magazine, drinking a cocktail, staring out the window at the sea of clouds.

A row or two from the back, he sits.

Waits.

EIGHTEEN

WHEN HARM PULLED UP BESIDE THE HOUSE, HE saw the open door. He hadn't been wearing his holster, but took the revolver out from under the front seat and got out of the Jeep. He left the driver's side door open to avoid making any noise. For a moment he stood next to the house, just listening. Wind, flick of cottonwood leaves, a dog barking, classical music coming from a house down the street. He swung around toward the living room, the gun held out before him, then stepped in, scanning quickly around the room that had been completely destroyed.

Harm stepped in over a pile of coats torn from a small closet, again listening, alert, receptive. Nothing. He felt his heart clamp down, twist shut. He might find her here, in one of these rooms. Go forward, continue. He swooped around the corner into the kitchen where dishes, pots, and pans had been swept from the cupboards in some kind of mindless vandalism. Not the act of someone looking for something. Just trashing the place. Bedroom, untouched. Bathroom, back room, all untouched. And empty.

He kept the gun in his hand but lowered it, walked again back to the living room, staring at the mess. Tantrum, he thought. Someone had been here for her—or here to leave him a warning. *I have access to you.* He'd been right to bring Nickie home the other night.

Again he walked back down the hallway past the bedroom and bathroom. Why had these rooms been left untouched? As he entered the back room, he saw that Nyia's things were gone. She'd hung some clothes in the closet, that purple satchel of hers had been there beside the TV. Her jewelry, bottles of creams and potions, a notebook, a clock, had been scattered across the table. All gone now. He sat on the fold-out couch, put his hand on the pillow.

Then he saw it; the briefcase, her portable Memory Lounge full of trinkets and weird keepsakes to make her feel safe and at home wherever she traveled. She wouldn't have left that here, he thought, if she really were leaving. She'd left it here for some reason. He reached over and slid it over to him with his cowboy boot, lifted it to the bed and clicked it open, riffling through its contents: matchbooks, junk jewelry, a tiny fuzzy dinosaur, ragged snapshots, a button that said *Rough Draft.* So many of these things were toys, he thought. Mementos from a childhood or from an extended one. There was even a picture drawn by a child on manila paper from grade school, fat primary crayon drawing of a girl's perfect fantasy house, smoke curlicuing from a chimney, flowers with doughnut-hole centers and ruffled R-shaped curtains at the windows blocked off in a T. Signed, in uneven letters, NYIA, AGE 7.

All he could ascertain from this pile of junk was that the woman couldn't release the past. Especially her childhood. He thought of what Dierdre Fine had told

him about Nyia's attachment to and break from her
mother. He didn't keep any of his childhood stuff
around in drawers. But his mother did, he realized. In
fact, she had a whole trunk of his things in the basement of their retirement condo in San Diego. In fact,
she was always trying to give him those things, or was
saving them for Nickie. *Someday you'll want to show Nickie
your Cub Scout Handbook.* Still, something about this
accumulation of artifacts was strange, the way she
hauled it around with her.

He leafed through the packet of snapshots, many of
them of Leonard at different ages, his hair long on his
shoulders, bearded, not bearded, the hair graying. Nyia,
in these pictures, looked alternately waiflike and elegant. If she was dressed up, she looked much older than
she was. This final one was of Mirina and Nyia, Mirina
behind her, arms around a young Nyia, Mirina looking
much younger, too, her black hair draped over Nyia's
bare shoulder.

It shot through him like a panic and he dismissed
it. Then let it spread, deepen as a question: Lovers?
Mirina and Nyia? Why the bond between the three of
them, why Mirina's tolerance of the long affair between
her husband and this young girl? But if it was so, why
hadn't Nyia mentioned it, even if it all had been long
ago?

Under the snapshots there was a pile of postcards,
a rubber band stretched around them. He flipped
through them quickly, turning them over to look at
the pictures of the Grand Canyon, Mendicino,
Prague, Leningrad, Jamaica. When he got to the one
that was typed, he set the rest of the packet down. Yes,
there it was, the same typing as in the early letters, the
p that jumped up a bit, the *t*'s and *f*'s and *h*'s whose
upper lines were dim, as if the ribbon were worn
there. An early postcard from her fan, the tone still
breezy. The card was from Key West, Ernest
Hemingway's house.

"Read recently that Hemingway would invent some terrible thing for a character in a short story but never put that thing into the story itself. Just his knowing that about the character would give his writing the charge of secrecy and emotion that he needed. Watching your films, I always have that sense of something you know that none of the rest of us can comprehend. You are mysterious and lovely and hidden. Never show your true face. Always hold something back. All my love . . ."

"Yes," whispered Harm. "Yes!" Across from the typed message and under the cluster of stamps was Nyia's address in London, written in block letters in black fountain pen. Written by hand. All the fan's letters had either been typed or printed out on a computer, the tissue paper inserted into a computer printer. Until this one, this card that she had not kept with the letters. *Yes, and yes again.* He would take this to a graphologist along with samples of handwriting to compare with it. He had Leonard's handwriting in that file of notes on Robin Reese. He had Mirina's handwritten notes to Nyia on the folded papers he'd taken from the trailer this afternoon. Again he wished he were in L.A. He'd worked with a fabulous questioned-documents examiner while he was with the FBI. Sally Beard was her name. This was the first break he felt he had toward a possible identity for the fan.

Harm stood and returned again to the living room. He couldn't think here and he needed to think. A game of pool did not feel apropos. Pulling the blue door shut, he saw that it had not just been left open, but had been broken open. He wiggled the latch and got it to shut somewhat. He needed to go to his office. He'd call Quintana later to come fingerprint the place. Perhaps in this manic act, the person had been careless about concealing himself. At the cabin at the ranch, he'd left that knife. Had Quintana checked for prints on that yet?

The phone was ringing as he unlocked the office door. As he lunged for the receiver he felt a surge of relief that his office hadn't been broken into.

"Bohland and Associates."

"I've been calling you for an hour. I'm back at the ranch. I've got to see you at once. I can come there." It was Mirina, breathless and hurried. Not her usual highly controlled and thoughtful European voice. "I can be there in fifteen or twenty minutes. Will you be there?" she added.

"Fine," he said.

While he waited he turned to the bulletin board where he'd pinned up the index cards, took them down and added them to the pile he'd been collecting in his briefcase. So someone was trying to kill Nyia—had made several attempts. He had a sense of drama or story about what he was doing, a controlling obsessive narrative of which Nyia was the center. The person had tried down in Manzanillo, but had shot the wrong woman. Mistaken identity. He had tried unsuccessfully at her home in Los Angeles last spring, but had been unable to go through with it. The gun had not been loaded. Nyia had perceived in that violence a parallel with the plot of the screenplay she'd been reading. Harm saw in it an imperfect, blocked attempt at murder. Someone was *acting out* murder, unable to bring himself to go through with it for real.

Then the shooting on the Turquoise Trail. Now this, the bike tampered with, prepared for Nyia's ride. The person was here, close to the making of the film, involved in it. The letters, the video, the claws. Someone who often knew where she was, who knew about film and video technique. The letters and attempts on her life had begun when she had cut Leonard off. Her occasional reconnections with Leonard probably only rekindled the fan's impossible attachment to her. Both

Robin's and Tess's deaths revealed a desire to kill Nyia and a failure to do so. To have the satisfaction of a death, but to have Nyia live. Purposefully or inadvertently. Consciously or unconsciously.

Then there was the other possibility—that Leonard had been right in the first place. That someone was sabotaging his films by killing off his lead actresses. Robin, Nyia, Tess. Attempts had been made on all their lives, two out of three had been successful. Nyia kept thinking that all the attempts at murder were meant for her, but maybe that wasn't it at all. Maybe they were exactly what they were. But that didn't make her any more safe.

Harm tried Quintana's office, but he hadn't yet returned. Outside the front window, Mirina's white Porsche jerked into place. She slammed out of the car and pulled open the screen door. As she removed her glasses he saw that her eyes were swollen from crying, her mouth bare of lipstick, lines creased around her lips, dry and tense. Her long hair was unbraided, wind-blown. She looked exhausted and every bit her age, but still had that fierce, dark beauty. Mirina lowered herself into a chair and put a cigarette in her mouth. "Do you mind?" she asked, holding the flame of a lighter out in the air. "Thanks. When I get really nervous, I smoke."

She opened her purse, took out her checkbook, and scribbled a check. Tore it out and slid it across the desk to Harm. Five thousand dollars.

"I'm furious that Suzanne Scolfield tried to hire you out from under me. This is a payment of expenses incurred so far and a bonus for your effort in remaining undercover. Of course, Officer Quintana informed me that he knew we hired you all along. But you really tried, you followed our directions. Now it doesn't even matter. Nothing matters but finding Nyia and protecting her." Mirina hissed out the smoke from between her teeth. "You are still working for Visionfilm. There will be an additional ten-thousand-dollar bonus for finding Nyia, in addition to whatever your fees are. Well? Are we in agreement?"

Harm straightened the edges on the index cards and set them next to the phone. "So far I'm still working for you, Mrs. Jacobs, but there is a whole lot that I need to know to be effective. There was an awful lot you didn't tell me when you hired me, most of which I've found out from Nyia herself."

"Such as . . ."

Harm folded his hands and leaned forward across the desk. "Well, all about her and Leonard's long romantic association over the years, beginning when she was a minor."

"That's been over for several years."

"You know, there is some reason to believe, Mrs. Jacobs, that you might have your own reasons to get rid of not only Nyia but Robin Reese and Tess Juran."

Mirina kept her gaze steadily on Harm's and did not falter. She inhaled deeply and sighed as she exhaled. "I know," she said quietly. "That's crossed my mind, that people might think that. But it's preposterous."

"Why?"

"Leonard and I have always had an open marriage, yet in our own way we have always been monogamous. In the heart. We have always been each other's primary love and somehow the other liaisons each of us have had have actually strengthened our bond. There was a certain stability, I will admit, when Leonard's interest was Nyia."

Interest, thought Harm. Nyia had suffered incredibly.

"Nyia accepted the primacy of our marriage and never tried to come between me and Leonard. Until the last year or so, when she was outgrowing the arrangement. It was bound to happen. She was growing up, wanting something primary of her own. Yes, it was hard on Leonard. But oddly, it seemed to have a renewing effect on our relationship. I suppose all this sounds rather complicated to you. I don't hold traditional views of commitment. I view sexuality as one of many ways of communicating with people. As long as the arrangements are clear and mutual . . . well, it works for us, anyway."

"So Nyia broke off from Leonard," said Harm. "But then she appeared again down in Manzanillo. Perhaps she was seeing him again, perhaps you were jealous. Or perhaps he was seeing Robin Reese. I know that he was currently involved with Tess Juran."

"Yes, I see your point. Of course. Jealous wife. Only, the trouble is that I'm just not. Don't you see? And these are my stars, the vehicles for my art becoming actualized. These are my financial investments, my living. Why would I kill any of them? Nyia most of all. I love Nyia. I practically raised her."

Some mother, he thought.

"What about Leonard? He uses Nyia, she rejects him, perhaps he is obsessed with her in some way, can't let go of her. He follows her in Manzanillo, a woman he thinks is her, shoots her. But it is a case of mistaken identity. He has killed Robin instead. In L.A. the next year, under the stress of the depositions, he goes to Nyia's house, again with the intention of killing her. But he is a sick man, he is on antidepressants, he has some history of mental instability. Again he can't bring himself to kill her, so he acts it out. He's lost touch with the difference between film and script and real life. Now, New Mexico, nearing the end of *Trial and Error*, his anxiety is at a high point. He hires a man to follow Nyia on the road to Albuquerque as she drives to pick up Tess. He knows Tess will not be on that plane because she is already in New Mexico. She is up at your cabin in Taos, she is his lover.

"But the man blows it. Nyia has nine lives. The man knows, however, Leonard's identity and must be killed, so Leonard shoots him. He's out of control now, he throws a tantrum in her cabin, slits her bed up with a knife. Starts a fire. He's obsessed with this idea of synchronicity, he's actually arranging for these things to happen." Harm stopped then. He had been watching Mirina Jacobs intensely the whole time he'd been talking, watching for some shift in feeling, some wavering of eye contact, shortness of breath, to indicate that she knew exactly what he was talking about.

Mirina had maintained eye contact the whole time, but was crying, tears running down her cheeks and into her wild hair. She made no attempt to brush them away as she tamped out the cigarette in an ashtray on the corner of his desk and lit another.

"There is absolutely nothing you have just said that I have not myself thought. It could all be perfectly true," Mirina finally said.

"Why didn't you talk to me?"

She laughed, bitterly, then whispered, "And lose my husband?"

"So you didn't really hire me with the intention of finding out the truth here? Do you want the truth now?"

Mirina nodded. "Now I do. I may not go to the police with the information. But I want the truth. And I would appreciate it if you could somehow conduct your investigation separately from Quintana. Is that legal?"

He shrugged.

"You could have hired some high-priced agency out of Beverly Hills," said Harm. "Instead you hire me, the smallest listing in the Santa Fe yellow pages."

"That's correct. I thought 'Accounting.' He does tax returns, he won't find much here. Leonard has been depressed for years and has been on medication. When he goes off, he does act strangely and I have to cope. I have to take care of him. He promises to stay on his medication during the filming, and yet he claims it blocks his creativity. Yet, creativity or no creativity, he can't even work if he doesn't take the medication.

"He becomes paranoid. You are actually the sixth detective I have hired for Leonard in so many years. I just go along with it, hoping it will placate him. When 'someone is on the case' it seems he can relax, put things out of his mind. When I called you I honestly thought that this was some crackpot sniper, as Quintana had said, and that Nyia and Leonard together were blowing it all out of proportion. I thought you'd look into it for a day or two, it would all blow over, and that would be that. I was wrong. You've heard of people who have some sort of compulsion to bring lawsuits? Leonard has a compulsion to have things investigated. Lost jewelry, stolen ideas for scripts, friends he's lost touch with. . . ."

"Mrs. Jacobs, do you think Leonard has had anything to do with the murders of Robin Reese and Tess Juran?"

At last she looked down. She cleared her throat, then stood, walked to the screen door and looked out at the traffic along Cerrillos, and at the Sangre de Cristos over the gas station across the way. Blue distance. She turned back to Harm.

"Now I need to know the truth," she said.

"Then answer just a few more questions. Where was Leonard the night of Robin's death? Was he with you?"

She looked down. "No. I was alone in our condominium that night and Leonard came in very, very late. He was sleeping on the couch when I woke in the morning."

"So neither of you had an alibi for the time of Robin's murder."

"That's correct. We were each other's false alibi."

"What about the night of the assault at Nyia's home in L.A.?"

"We were at a dinner party in Beverly Hills. Leonard left early. He called me from home and said he wasn't feeling well."

"Nyia was also at that party and left early."

"That's correct."

Harm put the diskette sleeve on the corner of his

desk. She reached for it, but he covered it with his palm. "Don't touch it. I will have this fingerprinted. Do you use disks of this size in the computer at your ranch?"

She shook her head. "My computer only has a five-and-a-quarter-inch floppy drive. I can't use the small ones."

Then he came over to her and showed her the letter he had found at Nyia's trailer today. "Have you ever seen letters such as these?"

She held it carefully and read the letter.

"Nyia has been receiving these for years. Fan letters. Only now they have obviously become something more. You lived in Paris. This is French stationery. Do you see what I'm getting at?"

"Oh God," Mirina whispered. "Oh God. This could be *my* stationery," she said. "I had a whole box of it, perhaps more than one box, in my office in Paris, years ago."

"How many years ago?"

"Three, four. And, in fact, I clearly remember that I could not find my supply of paper. And it was strange because I thought I had brought a box home with me. I know I had because I'd been writing Christmas letters in my bed and the entire box spilled out over the sheets. I'd put them back and . . . within days I couldn't find the box. We were going to San Moritz for Christmas, there was a move at the time. I lost track. But they were exactly like this. Of course, this is standard airmail letter paper. I'm only guessing that this has been written on my missing paper."

Mirina rubbed her temple, then the back of her neck. "I want you to find out if my husband has anything to do with any of this. Perhaps I have just been so blind. But it can't go on. Obviously. And I must protect Nyia. You'll continue, won't you, Harm?"

He looked at the check, slid it in his shirt pocket. "I'll continue."

Mirina stood to leave, extended her hand.

"One more thing. Truth," he said.

"Insofar as there is such a thing . . . ." she said. "What is it?"

"Were you and Nyia ever lovers?"

Again the bitter laugh.

Harm went on, "Nyia has a photograph in which her shoulders are bare, your arms are around her, cheek to cheek. I just wondered . . ."

"Our triangle only went in one direction," said Mirina. "Toward Leonard. That is: *No*. Can I see the rest of those letters?" she asked.

"I've sent them to a crime lab in Albuquerque," he said. "I'll show them to you when I get them back. Where is Leonard, by the way?"

"He's back at the ranch. He's been sedated and is sleeping. Will you want to question him?"

"I'll call you if I do."

"Thank you, Harm. . . . Find her, will you?"

She hesitated at the door, then left, stopping for a moment to stare at the mountains before getting into her car.

But where? he thought. He had driven the six minutes back to his house and stood in the living room, tilting a few chairs upright and straightening the bookshelf against the wall. He should call Quintana again.

At the kitchen counter, on hold for Quintana, he doodled a zia on the notepad by the phone. Colored in the sky with one of Nickie's colored pencils from the jar by the window. Looking down at the pad he saw it there in her writing, coming through the peacock-blue sky like a godsend. He pressed harder with the pencil until it came all the way through, the imprint of her writing from the paper that had been removed: *Southwest Flight #9407, arr. L.A. 5:20* P.M.

He hung up on Quintana's waiting line and dialed

Southwest at the Albuquerque airport. "I'm calling to see if a Nyia Wyatt has a reservation on flight 9407 to L.A. today."

"I'm sorry, sir, we cannot give out that information."

"Yeah, I know. I mean, I'd like to have her paged."

"One moment, please." He heard the tapping of computer keys. "Sir, that flight departed for LAX approximately fifteen minutes ago."

"What's the next available flight to L.A.?" he asked.

"We've got a flight leaving Albuquerque at six-thirty A.M. tomorrow."

"Nothing until tomorrow?"

"That's correct, sir."

"Six-thirty," he said. "Fine."

After making the reservation, he hung up and dialed his ex-wife's number to tell Nickie he would not be able to do an overnight this weekend. The Nintendo duel would have to wait.

NINETEEN

AS THE PLANE TAXIED OUT TO THE RUNWAY, Nyia watched the mountains, the brown landscape, open and empty. The engines revved up in a whir, then the plane shot toward the sky, pulled one wing down at a slant before heading west over the desert toward Los Angeles. Her head hurt as she pressed back against the seat. She was good at looking like someone else, her hair pulled back, no makeup, red wire-frame reading glasses. She hid her face in a *Vogue* magazine and didn't relax until the plane leveled off in a high blue arc and the stewardess came down the aisle offering wine.

She had been standing next to Mirina when the helicopter radioed that the Harley had gone off the road, the bike was down. *Accident*. Mirina had grabbed her arm hard. They'd waited several minutes. The second call came in, static over the mountains and Mirina in a hoarse whisper, "My God, she's dead. Oh, Nyia, Nyia." She lowered herself to a lawn chair.

Leonard tore across the turnaround to a Bronco and someone drove him up the hairpin turns. Mirina stayed a few minutes, staring off into the piñon, then said she had to go up, she had to see what was going on, couldn't stand it. Had to be with Leonard.

"Go ahead," Nyia told her. "I'll stay here." She had already known what she was going to do.

It wasn't difficult to find a car with the keys in it, one of the Visionfilm crew cars parked by the trailers. She had never gone back to her trailer, just slipped into the car and drove down through Chimayo, thirty minutes back to Santa Fe, to Harm's house.

Pushing the key into the lock, making sure to lock the door behind her, she ran to the back room. Threw her things into her satchel. Under a folded nightgown, she shoved the gun Harm had showed her and the box of bullets. She held it in her palm; its weight had frightened her, but she had wanted it then and she wanted it now. She couldn't take it on the plane with her. They checked all luggage with fluoroscopes now and it wasn't even registered in her name. She took the gun and put it back in the drawer of the bedside table.

Nyia looked at herself in the bathroom mirror, ran Harm's brush through her hair and picked up the Mickey Mouse toy from the edge of the tub. *Good-bye, little life. Little dream of a life.* Could it have worked out? A detective and an actress? Yeah, right. But he was sweet and funny. He cooked eggs, he was tender and generous in bed. The way he'd stopped in the middle and pulled out, kissing her again in her soft folds, no one had ever done that to her before, and she knew she might fall in love again sometime, knew she was getting over Leonard, that Leonard wouldn't always be the one she thought of, imprinted on him like some stupid duck.

She had called Southwest Airlines and made a reservation on the next flight to L.A. in the name of Elinor Wyatt, scribbled the flight number on the note pad, then looked for a bigger piece of paper to write a message to Harm. In a spiral notebook that looked like Nickie's she started two letters, ripping them out and throwing them in the wastebasket.

Finally she wrote, "Dear Harm, I'm scared to stay here. I see no one can protect me, not even you. I don't want to be all locked up in my life like a cage. I need to go somewhere to think. Probably home. I want to see you again, I know I will see you again because of all of this, but more than that. What I mean is, could I come back here sometime as a normal human being? We never had a chance to shoot pool."

After thinking for a moment about the word love, she signed the note simply "Nyia," then inserted "Love" above her name anyway. She went out the side door, locked it, and drove out of town toward Highway 25, toward Albuquerque in the high sunlight of afternoon. Fifteen minutes from the airport she realized she'd walked out without her briefcase. She could picture it sitting right by the TV in Harm's back room. He would keep it safe for her. It would give her an excuse to see him again. That junk didn't matter anyway. All that hanging on to the past. All the work to understand what had happened, why. It simply no longer mattered.

She must have slept, waking as the stewardess passed her a snack tray. Out the window, she glimpsed a red, barren landscape dotted with clouds and land formations that looked like the earth had boiled up, popped, then froze that way, puckered into a tiny black volcano. There were places you could be, she thought, where no one, no one at all would notice you, and the significance of your particular life, no matter how dramatic, would fade to nothing against rock and sky.

She wasn't sure of her plan. She was trying to let it form in her mind, but the main thing was to disappear. At least for a while. She would talk to Suzanne, her lawyer, her broker. Pull out enough cash to go away for a while. She couldn't stay near Leonard, near the film. They would have to hire someone else to complete the final triptych of *Trial and Error*. She would take time off, maybe as long as a year, she had enough money. Go someplace where no one knew her forwarding address.

Whoever had written those letters was very clear in his intention, slow and steady. He had tried in Mexico, but it had been Robin wearing her black dress. He had tried at her house last spring—but the gun had been empty. Tried on the highway outside Santa Fe. And today. That was to have been Nyia's character on the bike, and she knew without needing any facts at all that the bike had been messed with. She knew that the accident had been planned for her and in some way that gave her an odd and totally incongruous sense of peace.

Whoever is trying to kill me, she thought, believed that I would be on the bike today. And there were at least two people who had known she would not: Leonard and Mirina. They had decided Tess would be the bride, Tess would be on the bike. So it could not possibly be either of them.

From someplace down in her belly, frightened as she was, she knew that. It was far more likely to be some totally random person who had read about her in *National Enquirer* or *Vanity Fair*. Nyia pulled the shade down and closed her eyes. In one hour she would be back in L.A.

This was so much like the day Robin had been found in that alley in Manzanillo. How Leonard had come for her in the dawn, the taxi ride into the small town. She could still picture it all in her mind, even the smell of the ocean nearby and the sound of a rooster down the street.

And then it went through her like some truth she had always known, but which she hadn't had access to, a locked room in her psyche somewhere, opening now and telling her: *Leonard was with Robin when she was killed.*

Nyia opened her eyes, staring down the row of seats, confused for a moment at the strength with which the thought had ached through her. But why? she thought.

She pictured Robin's body covered, a heap near the pale-green stucco building. They had lifted her body into the back of a station wagon. Then Nyia had seen it, the gold glint in the dirt near where Robin had lain. She'd picked it up, handed it back to him, Leonard's coin, his African coin with the star on one side, camel on the other.

When she'd picked it up that day she had no suspicion, no thought of deception, only the intensity and horror of the moment, and so she had thought simply, *You dropped your coin, Leonard. Here.* Meaning: *You just dropped it, just now.* But no, it was lying almost beneath where the body had fallen. He must have dropped it that night. He had been there, with Robin. Yes, he had seemed surprised when she had given it to him, had first checked the change in his pockets, as if thinking, no, that isn't mine.

A shudder knifed through her. The plane trembled as it began its descent into the dark clouds. They dropped down, tossing in the wind, then cruised low over the gray grid of L.A. in rain, out over the Pacific where the plane tilted back toward LAX, the landing gear grinding down. *Home.*

The stewardess's sweet voice asked her to please have a pleasant stay in the Los Angeles area or wherever your final destination may be. *Right,* thought Nyia.

By the time the plane rattled to a stop, Nyia had a plan. She experienced an odd, distanced euphoria—then she realized what it was: relief. She left the plane in a slow herd of passengers. She had left "the story" behind. This was her story now, no one else's script or lines. She had a few things to do in L.A. and then she would leave for Brazil. When she had made *Wings* with Moravio, she'd made friends of her own down there. There would be places to stay, people to be with until the murderer was found. Even Moravio would not have to know she was there.

At the Pan Am counter she inquired about the availability of seats to Rio. A flight leaving in two days had plenty of room. She would not book in advance, would simply show up that morning. She would pay in cash.

Nyia stood at one of the stainless-steel phone booths along the concourse, dropped in twenty cents and dialed Suzanne's number in L.A. Her answering service picked up the call.

"Nyia Wyatt calling to leave a message for Suzanne."

"Oh, Ms. Wyatt. Ms. Scolfield asked us to page her if you called. She will return the call immediately. What is your number, please?"

Nyia pulled the glasses down on her nose to read the number on the pay phone. She waited several minutes, watching the river of people flow past her, and grabbed the receiver at the first jangle.

"Nyia? Oh, thank God, I've been worried sick. The place is a madhouse of police and media and then you take off. Harm Bohland has been sent to find you, but no one has any idea where you are. It's horrible, it's just horrible. Tess Juran's people are coming in from Seattle, Leonard's gone off the deep end, they have him sedated. The whole film is going down the tubes. I just don't know if they're going to be able to pull it off after this accident. Are you all right?"

"Suzanne, I just had to get out of there. I knew it would be a media witchhunt within an hour or two and I couldn't take it. But the main thing is this: I was supposed to have been on that bike today. Leonard put Tess into my role at the last minute.

Okay, it could have just been an accident, it could have. But first I'm shot at, then my bike goes off the road. Suzanne, it's not safe for me right now. At least for a while. So I'm going away. I wanted to let you know that I'm fine. I just need to protect myself right now."

"But where will you go?"

"I'm not even sure yet where I'm going. I just wanted to let you know I'm okay."

"So you're staying in L.A.?" Suzanne asked. "In case I need to get in touch with you?"

How did she know? Nyia thought. Then rolled her eyes upward. The answering service, the pay-phone number, area code 213.

Suzanne went on. "Because I *will* need to be getting in touch with you. For one thing, they're conducting an investigation. Actually, the police think it was not an accident at all."

"That's just what I'm telling you, Suzanne."

"The bike was sabotaged, and the only person who had access to the bike was Dan Howe. He had the keys to the storage unit. In fact, he was the one who purchased the bike in the first place. So, anyway, the police want you to answer some questions."

"Me? Why me?" Nyia's voice sounded high, echoing into the black phone.

"Nyia, they're questioning everyone. It hasn't officially been determined if it was a homicide or not. They're doing an autopsy tonight. But let's just say it just doesn't look good to run."

"I'm not running from the police, for God's sake."

"The police might not see it that way, honey. All they see is a woman dead after an accident, a motorcycle with the brake mechanism purposefully cut, and the sudden disappearance of the one person who had reason to want her out of the way."

"That's ridiculous!" Nyia cried.

"All I'm saying is a number of people reported that

you and Tess argued yesterday and that there was a tremendous tension because Leonard was putting Tess in your role. Do you see what I'm getting at? That's why you may have to come back to Santa Fe whether you want to or not. Now, where can I reach you if—"

Nyia followed the passersby with her gaze and felt pulled to move with them. "Suzanne," she said, "I just have to go. I'll be in touch."

Nyia placed the receiver gently back in the stainless-steel cradle.

They would be looking for her now. She couldn't go home. Not even to get her car. Especially to get her car. Anyway, she hadn't felt safe there in a year or more. Not since the break-in.

She picked up her satchel and joined the human river toward the baggage claim area. As Nyia walked out through the double glass doors, the Los Angeles twilight seemed strangely green, thick and warm. There was one place where she could go for a day or two where no one would think to look for her. She would get a hot bath, a meal, and a strong drink. She could even get her laundry done. And anyway, it had been too long; time to check in. It had been nearly three years, and if she was leaving the country she ought at least to say good-bye.

Traffic was clogged heading north out of Torrance. Nyia slept briefly in stand-still gridlock, waking when the cab driver changed the radio station from a talk show to the Doors' "Riders on the Storm." Marina Del Rey, Venice, exiting in Santa Monica, the mountains to the north were nearly invisible in the low clouds.

Nyia asked the cab driver to leave her off at the corner by Santa Monica Catholic High School. Even in the fading light the birdsong was profuse, the greenery lush and junglelike after the arid Southwest; jacaranda, yellow hibiscus, bougainvillea sprawling over fences and the acrid smell of tall eucalyptus swaying in the wind off the ocean only a few blocks away. Nyia inhaled the scent of fresh-cut grass, watched a homeless woman with a leathery face and an athletic build stoop to smell a rose. She walked several blocks past smaller mission-style houses until she came to an apartment building, pink stucco. *Mar Vista* curled across the front in green neon. As a man came out of the locked glass security door, Nyia slipped in, up the indoor/outdoor carpeted steps and into the central courtyard.

There was a small, square pool at the center of the courtyard. Old palms flanked the four corners, worn-out lawn furniture lined up toward the west, a tangled snake of garden hose lay unused. As she climbed the cement steps toward the second-floor balcony, she ran her hand along the white wrought-iron railing. The pool glowed from beneath with an aqua light and liquid shadows tilted across the palm trees. A few jacaranda leaves floated in the chlorinated water.

At the top of the stairs Nyia set down her bag and rang the chimes. She felt the footsteps approaching, and for an instant, as the door opened, she looked past the woman at the pinkish light of the television flooding the room.

She seemed smaller than Nyia had remembered and wore a white caftan, held a highball in one perfectly manicured hand, had a bronze-gold tan, her hair cut short, impeccably silver. Carole Wyatt actually gasped, stepped to the side and blinked back tears. But then, she'd always been good at that, it had been her specialty: spontaneous breakdown. Instant unhappiness on cue. She inhaled her Benson & Hedges and sniffed. "Oh, dolly, you look absolutely hideous. Get yourself in here. Nobody would know you were an Academy Award-winning actress. You look like a washed-out cocktail waitress. When was the last time you had a facial? You don't take care of yourself." She reached up and put her arms around Nyia, and Nyia held her tightly.

She really was crying, thought Nyia. Maybe it wasn't fake. I must be crazy to have come here. Well, maybe not crazy, just desperate.

"I knew you weren't dead," said her mother. "I keep up on you in all the rags, dolly. I even keep a file on you, I do. But still I ought to wring your little neck."

"Don't say that, Mother," Nyia pleaded. And went in.

Inside, Nyia realized it wasn't the television light that was pink, the whole apartment was pink. Pink couch, pink floral wallpaper, pink-checked wingback chairs, pink candles in glass hurricane lamps, pink silk flower arrangements. The room was awash in soft light like the inside of a heart. A giant mirror, centered over the sofa, took the place of any artwork. In the back of the room by a large window stood a tall golden bird cage, a white cockatoo inside.

"Somebody's trying to kill me," said Nyia.

"I knew it would take something like that to get you to come home. You waited until you really needed someplace to go, didn't you?"

Carole Wyatt turned and walked back toward the kitchen, raising her glass. "Vodka tonic, twist of lime, dolly? Put your stuff in the room, it's just like it was the last time you saw it three years ago. Nothing new."

Carole brought the drink to her daughter, set it on the bureau as Nyia put her bag on the floor next to the canopy bed she'd slept in as a teenager.

"I could be living a lot higher on the hog than this if you hadn't cut me out of your life. But I guess this'll do when you're on the run, huh? So who wants you dead? Leonard Jacobs, I suppose?"

Nyia felt the floor give when she said that. "Can we drop the hateful tone, Mother?"

"Whatever suits you, princess. I just live here." She turned and walked back into the living room and was seated in a recliner when Nyia returned. Carole kept her eyes on the show for a few minutes, then held up the remote control and snapped the television off.

She looked directly at Nyia. "I haven't forgiven you a single iota, but you can stay as long as you want. I'm not normally a hateful person, but you bring it out in me, dolly. I guess we've always been like that, haven't we? Well, you'll find your old ma has softened a bit. Lost some weight too. Don't I look swell? I'm taking ballroom dancing."

"You got a boyfriend, Mother?"

"I always have a beau," she said. "I just don't believe in being single, even though I haven't had a husband in something like twenty-five years. How about you, dolly? Fill me the hell in, why don't you? And what's all this about killing somebody? You've piqued my interest."

"Not somebody, Mother. Me."

Nyia told her everything, going back to Robin, her intuition about the coin, the shooting on the Turquoise Trail, the knifing of the quilt, the video, the letters, and Harm. Even Harm.

When she was finished, her mother got up, took Nyia's glass from her hand and went into the kitchen. She returned with two double-strength vodka tonics.

"So, who do you think is doing all this?" Carole Wyatt asked. She was looking over Nyia's head at her own reflection in the huge mirror, wiping at a line of mascara that had smeared under her eyes. "And why?"

Nyia just shook her head. "I just feel like it can't be Leonard and Mirina. They were the only ones who knew I wasn't going to be on that bike today. But I'm not sure of anything."

Today, thought Nyia. That road to Chimayo seemed miles in time ago, like a memory of a past life. It was only that morning. She realized she was exhausted.

"Leonard should be protecting you, not hurting you. You should have married him when you had the chance, dolly."

Nyia looked at her mother, incredulous. It was as if

the woman just had her own tape going at all times. She had since Nyia was a teenager and she'd first pushed Leonard toward her. She was still at it.

"Mother, there was no chance of me ever marrying Leonard Jacobs. The man is already married. Don't you get it?"

"You just never pressed the issue with him. You whined."

Nyia looked up at the plump halos the track lighting threw on the ceiling. "Give me a break."

"No, that's true. You lost him and he was the best thing that ever happened to you. You haven't been with anyone since, have you?"

"Harm."

"For what, all of two days?"

Nyia wiped a finger around the beaded drops of the highball glass.

Carole continued. "You know, it was humiliating for me when you broke off with Leonard and got rid of me too. I just need to tell you that. I'm expressing my feelings, that's what some expert on *Oprah* said was wrong with my generation. We kept too many secrets. So there you have it."

Drunk, thought Nyia. Carole was in her own little world, her own scenario, in the spotlight of the alcohol. Nyia wondered how many strong drinks she'd downed before Nyia had arrived.

"And for my part," said Nyia, "I have figured out that what you did was a terrible thing for a mother. I was a kid, you should have forbidden me to see him, not encouraged it. You saw he was using me, you saw it was a way to get me in film, you were living through me. I was just a vehicle for all your smashed-up dreams. You exploited me, Mother. I was an object to you and to Leonard. I was acting roles for all of you. I've only just begin to figure out my own life in the last few years."

Carole lit a long, brown cigarette and snapped the television back on, watching in intensity for a few minutes as if none of their conversation had ever taken place. *Crazy,* thought Nyia. *No wonder I was so crazy. She turned me on and off like that.*

Without looking at her, Carole spoke. "You're right, dolly," she sighed. "I guess you're right. But at the time I didn't know that's what I was doing. I thought I just wanted you to be happy. I had no idea you'd regret the fabulous success that's come to you because of all that Leonard and I have done for you over the years."

"That is so ripe, Mother. You are so good at that."

"What's that, dolly?" Carole's voice all charm and vodka.

What was the use? Nyia thought. No use. No use at all.

AFTER HE ABANDONED THE OLD MAN'S CAR NEAR
downtown, he walked up Bishop's Lodge Road toward the
big houses with glass windows built in the foothills surrounding Santa Fe.

*[Possible scene could show him running along the road,
might even use the helicopter for this shot, pan the mountains,
sunset shot.]*

Back at his room, he locked the door, undressed, tried to lie
in the dark and rest, his body idling like a car in winter, the
adrenaline and fear in him a vibration. He needed to find out
where things would go from here. He didn't know, and when
he didn't know he was afraid.

So she'd flown back to L.A., Southwest Flight 9407. There
were several flights tomorrow morning. Think, think. Could he
even find her there? But there would be one sure way to bring
her back. He thought about that for a while and sat up, turned
the bedside lamp on, took the .38 from the suitcase, then the

rags and solvent. He swung the cylinder out and inserted a small brush into each chamber.

In the mirror he saw himself, naked, gun on his lap, black metal against his skin. That was good, he'd have to get that shot. He took the video camera from the carrying case, flipped it on and panned the dark room. He set the camera up on a chair beside the bed, focusing it on the mirror, turned it on again. Then entered the picture, sat down on the bed, the camera filming his reflection as he held the gun, caressed it with the rag. Then he held the gun up to his reflection in the mirror. He wished he could cut the shot there. Instead he had to reach over and snap the camera off. Not perfect. Even so, that was a great shot.

Ideas were coming to him and he didn't want to miss the flow. He turned on the computer set up on the table across the room, inserted the diskette, and the screen glowed with green letters. Opening the document, he placed his fingers on the keyboard. After restoring his last document from the diskette to the hard drive, he entered his word-processing program.

"Further ideas to be developed," he typed. "One: He kidnaps her and changes her identity. After a while, she no longer even remembers who she is.

"Two: He finds them together, reunited, and kills the director in her presence. She willingly accompanies him after that. As his hostage.

"Another possibility: He realizes that his collaborator on the screenplay no longer trusts him. He begins to realize that his collaborator wants him off the project altogether. Wants it all, all the credit, all the control. This will not do, he realizes. It is his story, it always has been. The collaborator's job has always been limited to revision only. The collaborator does not seem to approve of recent turns in the story. The collaborator can no longer be trusted."

* * *

He stares at the blinking cursor. No more words come to him. Words now only seem to come when he takes action in the story itself. He cannot just stay locked in this room writing anymore. He dresses and goes out into the world to pick up where he left off. With the strange sensation that the story itself is hungry and needs to be fed.

TWENTY

THE DAWN WAS STILL COMPLETELY DARK WHEN Harm rose to make strong coffee, preparing to leave for Los Angeles on the six-thirty flight. Quintana had come to the house last night with two other officers, looked the place over, even helped to straighten up some. Told Harm he'd keep his eye on the place while he was in L.A. As Harm dumped the coffee grounds, thinking to take the garbage out at the last minute, he saw her writing on the crumpled paper in the wastebasket. *Dear Harm . . .* Only two or three sentences. She hadn't finished; had she decided not to leave a note after all? But she had thought of it anyway. This clearly indicated she had left on her own, had not been abducted. He smoothed the paper out, put it in his briefcase. On the ride to Albuquerque, the sun began to bleed crimson light against the edge of the sky, scarlet, fire-engine red, burgundy, violet, bittersweet-orange, changing by the second. He played an old Doors tape as he drove: "Riders on the Storm."

The flight left on time and he slept in spite of the coffee, woke feeling totally alert, Los Angeles spread before him like a computer board of fantastic proportions. It had been a while. He was not glad to be back.

He took the shuttle bus to Alamo Car Rental, rented a Chevy Cavalier, and drove first out to Nyia's house. He had called once before he'd gone to bed last night, and again this morning, always the same response. "Hi, this is Nyia. You can reach me through Suzanne Scolfield . . ."

Nyia's house was up in Laurel Canyon. He didn't really expect to find her there, but he wanted to see the place. He took a sharp righthand turn that led up to a steeply wooded hillside. The houses were balanced on the sides of the canyon, built over garages, protected by high fences and gates with blue security-system warning signs. Nyia's house was set back off the road behind a row of cedars and he nearly passed by the mailbox, which had no name on it. He pulled up at the gate that blocked the short driveway, and got out. Dried eucalyptus leaves crunched beneath his feet. The house looked like it had been lifted from the Atlantic seaboard and propped on a tiny plot of land in this California canyon. It was pale yellow with white trim. White roses were in bloom, sprawling across a trellis next to the front door. The place looked abandoned. A high iron fence surrounded the property. The front gate was locked and he pressed the button on the intercom. No answer to the harsh buzz. The pods and leaves on the driveway were thick, the Levelor blinds pulled down against the morning sun. A number of mail flyers were stuck between the spires of the wrought-iron gate. She'd never made it home, he thought. Home to L.A. maybe, but not here.

Harm drove back down to Sunset Boulevard and found a pay phone in a bakery that smelled of yeast and sugar. He looked up the addresses of James M. Reese,

John Sand, and the graphologist, Sally Beard, in the phone book. He called Beard first and she was in. Not planning on being around all Saturday, but for him, she'd schedule a special appointment. He thanked her.

The Reeses lived out in Pasadena. He decided to take the chance they'd be home—Saturday morning—and drove out without calling first. People usually didn't make appointments with detectives. Better to catch them off-guard.

He parked in front of a sprawling white colonial with a neatly manicured lawn. A trim man in his mid-fifties stood out front hosing down the driveway, pushing dried palm fronds toward the street. He wore a yellow golf shirt, stone-washed jeans, and bright white running shoes. He released the handle on the nozzle as Harm came up the driveway.

"Sir," called Harm. "Mr. Reese. If I could just talk with you for a moment."

The man walked back toward the house and turned off the water spigot. "Kathleen and I have been waiting since yesterday for one of you guys to show up," he called back to Harm. "Which paper are you from? If somebody hadn't showed up by tonight I was going to write my own editorial. What took you so long?"

"I'm not a journalist, Mr. Reese. I'm a private investigator. Harmon E. Bohland. I'm based in Santa Fe." He opened his identification wallet and Reese examined the picture ID.

"Bad picture." He grunted. "You look better in person. These things always make people look lousy. Santa Fe. So were you there when it happened, when Tess Juran was killed? We heard it on the news last night, and right away we thought, 'Here we go again.' Who are you investigating for? I should ask. Because I'll do anything in the world I can to see Mr. High-and-Mighty Leonard Jacobs in prison, so if you're working for that son-of-a-bitch you can get the hell out of here. Pardon my French."

"I'm working for Nyia Wyatt," Harm said. Half-truth. "And I'm also looking for her."

"Come on in. Kathleen will get us a cup of coffee.

"Has something happened to Nyia Wyatt too? The man should be prohibited from making movies. Everyone he casts is in danger. Kathleen!" James Reese yelled, pushing open the front door. The living room was all white furniture, white and glass and brass. On a glass étagère were several photographs of babies and children, a wedding portrait, and a black-and-white studio still of Robin. Mrs. Reese appeared in a turquoise jogging suit, and Reese introduced Harm.

"Why don't we sit in the kitchen," said Kathleen Reese. "If we're out on the deck, Ellen Jeffries is going to listen through the fence, although I don't really care what anybody thinks and as far as I'm concerned you can broadcast every word I have to say on prime-time TV during the evening news." She, too, seemed to have trouble discerning that Harm was a detective, not a reporter. They *wish* I was, he thought.

She poured a cup of coffee and handed it to Harm. He took it gratefully and it made him sad how good it always felt to be in a woman's kitchen. Maybe it was true that all divorced men near age forty were looking for home, for mom. That's what he'd been accused of more than once in his dating.

"I'm trying to find Nyia Wyatt. It sounds as if you've had news of the tragedy out in New Mexico. What do you know about it?"

"Just what was on the news last night and on the radio this morning—that Tess Juran was killed in a motorcycle accident—quote, unquote—on location outside Santa Fe." Kathleen Reese tore open a package of Equal and sprinkled it into the coffee. "And it was in the *Times* this morning. They knew each other, you know, Tess and Robin. We met Tess Juran at a party

Robin had when she graduated from acting school. And they were on the soaps together out in New York. We flew out to watch the filming once. She was a lovely girl. This is hideous, and that man should be put behind bars."

"Why did you feel Jacobs was negligent in Robin's death?"

"They tried to make it look like some crazed drug dealer did it," huffed Reese. "Made Robin look bad in the process just because she'd been through rehab. The girl was dry as a desert when she went down there to do that film. It was his so-called technique that was responsible. He was always trying to confuse the line between what was real and what was the film. Encouraging them to take their characters out of the film and live in them. Well, she was just a kid. That was just like giving a kid license to go nuts. Her character was a drinker, so next thing we heard she was boozing it up down there. We got a collect call from her, drunk, stoned, whatever. She told me, 'Daddy, it's for the movie. It's part of my character. I've got to push it to the limit and it's going to be good.'

"Said she had to inhabit the character, on and off camera, and that when the film was over she could come out. That's what she said. Well, I call that sick. It's only a job, you don't have to ruin your whole life, become a whore to play a whore, kill someone because your part calls for it. Where would Clint Eastwood be if he thought he had to inhabit all his characters, on-screen and off? Just tell me that.

"Next we hear she's dead in some back alley, shot in the head. I call it supreme negligence on the part of the director. We hired a good lawyer, but it just wasn't going to stand up in court. For one thing, there never was a proper autopsy. She was cremated down there and her ashes flown home. It was heart-breaking.

"And now this, Tess Juran, same thing, same goddamn thing. How many more will have to go, before this megalomaniac realizes he can't kill off all his actresses one by one for the sake of art?"

"Did your daughter ever receive any threatening letters?" asked Harm. "Any weird letters from fans, anyone obsessed with her, that sort of thing?"

Kathleen Reese shook her head. "Not that I know of. Did she, Jim? But she wrote to us regularly. I kept all her letters. I have a whole scrapbook." Kathleen Reese's eyes teared up and she stirred her coffee again.

"Now, honey." Reese put his hand on his wife's shoulder.

"No, maybe Mr. Bohland would like to see the snapshots Robin sent us from Mexico. Well, they were in her camera. We had them developed after she died."

"I would," said Harm.

Kathleen Reese led him to a den off the living room. She pulled a photograph album off a shelf and a shoebox from a wooden filing cabinet. Without speaking, she flipped open the album pages. "There were only seven or eight pictures on the roll," she said, pointing.

There was a group shot beside the pool—Nyia, Jack, Robin, and several others Harm didn't recognize. Robin and Nyia together on a patio. Nyia on a chaise lounge, covering her eyes. Dan Howe and Robin dancing. Connie applying lipstick to Robin on the set. Dierdre Fine, arms folded, toothpick in her mouth.

"Was this her boyfriend?" asked Harm. He pointed to the photograph of Robin and Howe.

"I believe she met that young man while she was a student at UCLA film school, didn't she, honey? I remember her saying something about how glad she was to know someone on the crew down there. You see, originally she intended to write screenplays, not act. She fell into acting in an improv class and found out she was pretty good at it."

"Was she ever involved with Leonard Jacobs?" Harm asked.

Kathleen Reese perched on the edge of a loveseat, holding the shoebox in her lap. "Involved? I wouldn't call it involved, would you, honey?"

Reese scowled. "Son of a bitch," he muttered.

"I think Leonard Jacobs escorted her to some things," said Kathleen. "That was the word she used. Not dating, not involved. In fact, she wrote me one letter about how she was trying to tell him to back off a little. After all, his wife was right there on location with them. I think Robin was infatuated with Leonard Jacobs, but she knew it was only a fling. And I always told her, 'Sweetie, be above reproach.' God, she used to hate it when I said that, but she knew the difference between real caring and messing around." Kathleen Reese looked lovingly at the shoebox as if it contained her daughter's ashes. "This was the last letter I ever received from her."

Mrs. Reese opened the shoebox and extended a blue airmail envelope to Harm. Tissue thin. *Par Avion.* Here we go, Harm thought.

"Did she always write to you on these envelopes?"

"Well, I never thought about that," she said. "I thought maybe it was just something she got down there. I never noticed until just now it was French. Should have been Spanish, right? Is there any significance to that?"

Harm skimmed the letter. Handwritten, not typed. She might have borrowed the stationery from someone. Was Mirina still using it then? When had Mirina lost that box of envelopes?

Harm read the section about Leonard carefully. "It's pretty heady going to a party with the director," Robin had written. "It's certainly getting me seen. But sometimes it feels kind of trashy, like I'm this little starlet trying to get known through him. I'd like to be known for the work I do. Plus, to tell you the truth, he's kind of creepy sometimes. I try to act the adoring young thing, at least while we're doing the film. This is a big step for me and I don't want to blow it by antagonizing him.

"Another really good thing is happening down here, though, that might lead to a real career break-through for me. I've gotten a chance to read a work-in-progress of what I feel could be a very important screenplay. One of the writers—I'm sworn to secrecy—is down here working on it around the edges of the filming of *Dead Heat*. And—get this—he thinks I might be perfect for the lead. At least I will get a chance to read for the part. It's fascinating the way he takes things that are really happening down here and feeds them into the story. It's like everything in life is inspiration for the work. I can't give too much away, but it's about an actress who is getting these fan letters and then, after a while, the person writing them is coming after her. It's very haunting and I'm excited to be able to see how a real writer works. I'm learning a lot."

The letter went on, but became chatty—what they ate, a sunset boat ride, snorkling in the murky waters.

"Did she ever mention to you who these two writers were?" asked Harm.

Kathleen squinted upward. Shook her head. "I don't think so. But some of the pages of the screenplay were in the things they sent back to us after she died."

Harm wanted to shout, but restrained himself. "May I see them?"

Kathleen Reese opened the cabinet, kneeled and fingered through several file folders, pulled one out and checked it. "Right here. Mr. Reese says I'm too much of a pack rat, but you never know when you might want to see some of the things from the past. If for no other reason than just to remember."

Even before he read the words, Harm recognized the dot-matrix printing on the screenplay. Same as the final round of letters, after the fan had abandoned the typewriter. It made sense. All this talk in the letters about the story. Whoever was writing the letters was writing a screenplay and using real life as the source of the story. Not just a psychotic imagination; an actual story. But as the last letters to Nyia showed, the difference between reality and fiction had dissolved for this writer, who believed the story more real than his life. He was living his story by acting it out.

Robin Reese's final letter to her mother said that there were two writers. A collaboration. That, he hadn't counted on. Leonard and Mirina? Mirina and Leonard? It kept making too much sense to be refuted.

Harm stood. "I'd like to borrow these, if I may. And the snapshots. I'll get them back to you."

"This was Robin's final letter to her mother," said Mr. Reese, protectively.

"I understand. I tell you what—I'll photocopy the letter and stick it right back in the mail to you today."

Kathleen Reese set the album on the desk, and the entire shoebox of memorabilia and letters. "You can take it all, Mr. Bohland," she said. "I sincerely hope something here can prove that Leonard Jacobs is a murderer."

TWENTY-ONE

NYIA SLEPT LATE INTO THE MORNING AND WOKE with a start in a bedroom she did not recognize, heard the television in the next room, felt the strange glow of a migraine starting. Coffee. She reached for the phone on the bedside table, fumbled through her address book to find Harm's number.

Answering machines took her messages at both his office and his home. "Harm, this is Nyia. I'm okay, I want you to know I'm safe. I just need to lay low for a little while, step out of it all. The film can wait, everything can. I will call you at six tonight, Saturday. Please be home. If not, I'll try again first thing Sunday morning, early."

Nyia showered, letting the hot spray rain down on the back of her neck; the anxiety was an ache inside her chest. She took deep breaths to calm herself. Maybe Suzanne was right, it didn't look good to run. But didn't they understand that she couldn't stay? Not for her contract, not for the police, not for Visionfilm, not even for Tess.

Back in the bedroom, she dropped the damp towel at the end of the bed and dialed Harm's number again. "One more thing," she said after the beep. "I've been thinking about you. I'm thinking Jamaica, a week in blue water. I'm thinking piña coladas and snorkling. I can't remember if you swim." She paused, then added, "I miss you."

Carole Wyatt was seated at the glass table by the windows, wearing white silk pants and blouse and white high heels with open toes. Her silver hair was perfectly jelled into place, her mouth outlined in opalescent magenta, her curved nails enameled in a matching color. She lifted the glass to her mouth. Bloody Mary, eleven o'clock on a Saturday morning, Nyia observed. Even a celery stalk, a sprig of parsley floating in the tomato juice.

Her mother's fine features had been mummified by repeated surgery and collagen injections. Her old beauty was like some mask she wore; the sadness and desperation showing through in the thick swelling under the eyes, puffy lids, lashes caked with cracked mascara applied too thick; too much sun, her skin orange-ish and powdery.

"You're in the paper," said her mother, shoving the *Los Angeles Times* across the table.

ACTRESS KILLED ON SW SET, read the headline. Nyia read it quickly. Tess's death was not yet determined to have been a homicide. Pending further investigation and the results of the autopsy.

Nyia put her head down on the quilted place mat. *Oh, Tess,* she thought. In some strange way it had already hit her that Tess had been killed. The fact of it: killed, the sudden shock of it, the error. But it was just now washing through Nyia that Tess was actually dead. That they would not see each other again, work on other projects, even finish the film. Tess was really gone.

And it was a terrible, terrible mistake. She was the one who should have been killed, she was supposed to have been the one. Then maybe everyone else would be safe.

Stop it, she told herself.

Her mother flipped the *Times* over to where the article continued on an inside page. "Read down to there, dolly. That's where you come in."

Nyia read out loud in a quiet voice. "'Several crew members and principal actors in the Visionfilm ensemble have fled New Mexico following Juran's death, citing the need for safety and privacy. Jack Drieser, who remained in Santa Fe, defended those who left, stating that the film location had been terrorized.

"'Violence and threats have plagued the film since the beginning of shooting several days ago. Police are reportedly seeking Nyia Wyatt for questioning regarding the actress's death, though police have stated that they do not have a firm suspect at this time. Wyatt's manager, Suzanne Scolfield, announced that the actress was in seclusion, recovering from exhaustion, and would certainly cooperate with the police when her health returned. A source who asked to remain anonymous suggested that Wyatt had checked into the Betty Ford Clinic for treatment of prescription medication abuse.'"

"Great," said Nyia. "So not only am I a murder suspect, I'm a pill junkie too. Just great. Goddamn fishbowl."

"It's free publicity, Nyia." Her mother ground black pepper into the Bloody Mary, tasted it and ground more in.

"I don't need publicity," Nyia said.

"The more action you've got going around the set of a film, the more people will go see it."

"That's so old-fashioned, Mother. That's your Marilyn Monroe fantasy: if you die, you'll be more famous. The more terrible it is, the better chance you have of becoming some classic tragedy figure. It's all in the marketing now, it's not what awful thing happened to your life. That's not what makes someone successful and respected."

"Look at John Lennon."

"Mother, John Lennon was famous and respected before he was killed."

"But people respect him a lot more than Paul. And you never hear anything at all about George, do you?"

Nyia closed her eyes, rubbed her forehead. "Make me a drink, Mother. You bring this out in me."

She stood and looked at Nyia brightly, clacking to the kitchen in her spiked heels. "And what about Ringo?" she called back. "I do happen to have some experience in this field, you know. Sometimes I wish I would have had *more* tragedies. But, then again, *your* life has been tragedy enough for any one mother."

"My life is not a tragedy."

Carole Wyatt bent into the refrigerator, raising her voice. "You can always talk to the police by phone, you know," her mother offered. "You could send a statement through a lawyer. An affidavit. In fact, that's exactly what you should do, see a lawyer. Are you still with Ernest Baum? If not, I've got somebody very good. I dated him last year, but it didn't work out."

"Mother, when was the last time anything worked out with you and a man?"

"I'd like to see *your* emotional résumé, darling: Why left last relationship; Skills developed in former position; Type of position now sought. You kids don't think the way we thought. What's 'working out,' anyway? For us, love is just love."

"God, Mother, you should hear yourself. You should be back on the soaps."

"I could in one second if I wanted to. Sid Harris said they'd love to have me on *Just in Time*. But I hate the hours, I hate New York. It's bad for my skin."

"You hate waking up."

"Well, I see you're up bright and early yourself. Dolly, you just walked off your job, under contract, and the police are seeking you for questioning regarding a possible murder, so let's not get into my life. Besides, I'm playing golf this afternoon with a man I met on a cruise. He's recently retired from the aerospace industry and he finds me captivating and vivacious." Her voice trilled. "He had a penile implant," she added.

"Mother."

"At seventy, that can be a real asset. It's actually quite erotic. You never know where your life will take you, dolly. You can't say I was dull as a mother."

"That's for sure."

"Nyia."

"What?"

"I'm glad you came home. You really aren't a tragedy. It's all just bad luck, I think. It'll turn. I just bet it will." Her mother just stood there across the kitchen, the fresh drink trembling in her hands. "Just take your time, honey, and think things through. Let me know if you need this lawyer's number. Nobody is going to hurt you."

Where had Nyia heard that before?

Nyia tried to finish the plate of scrambled eggs her mother had prepared. "Tex-Mex eggs with just that hint of cilantro," Carole said. "Would you believe this is a Weight Watchers' recipe?" Then Nyia excused herself and said she was going out.

Santa Monica Pier was a ten-block walk. Nyia lifted her face to the fresh salt wind. Crossing Pacific Avenue, she didn't see that the sidewalk was blocked off for construction. As she came to the opposite curve, a car swerved close, honking, and Nyia stumbled into a small hole where the sidewalk had been dug up for some kind of pipes.

She landed on her knees, palms flat on the damp sand. Standing up, her ankle hurt. She wiped the hair from her eye and dirt brushed her cheeks, grainy and wet. Nyia wiped it off with her sleeve, clapping it off her hands, then ran toward the bridge ramp that led down to the pier and the ocean. The sound of her sneakers was hollow on the rough wood planks of the pier. She passed Sinbad's and the Playland Arcade. 25-CENT SKEE-BALL, read the old sign. And there was that photo booth where she'd go as a teenager whenever she was staying with Carole instead of at the Jacobses' Beverly Hills home. Funny, Nyia thought. She'd never known exactly what skeeball was.

She walked past the bumper cars and Doreena's Fortunes, not open, and leaned against the wood railing. The surf rolled hard against the structure. Gulls squawked above the trash barrels. A purple iridescent pigeon joined her on the park bench at the end of the pier.

This morning, her mother's pink living room had appeared almost hallucinogenic. She noticed that the Spanish-speaking fishermen nearby were surrounded by yellow halos and she knew a migraine was coming. Up the back of her neck and into her eyes. But it wasn't the headache so much as what went with it, the feeling of being inside the story, that tension, both horrible and creative, an anxious glow.

She didn't even want to be Nyia Wyatt anymore. If only she could just become a blank slate waiting to grow a person. All her life she'd been controlled by others, and though she'd left them all, there was a way she still hadn't really let go. She hadn't gone on to create a new life. She'd been lost, wandering, draining out the attachment and the pain. And her life always went along all right until she saw Leonard. That was the killer, just seeing him. She fell in every time. So warm, so enmeshed. Finally, so incomplete. But some old part of her still said: *home.*

What she wanted to do was to grow a new story. It would have to be her own, not what anyone else wanted her to be. An actress friend of hers a couple of years ago had gotten sick of the whole Hollywood scene. She'd told Nyia, "Sure, I could make it here, but where would I be, even at the height of it all? A commercial property in a public life. That's not what I want." So she'd spun the globe, that old childhood fantasy, holding her finger to the whirling countries, red, yellow, green. Her finger had landed on Papua New Guinea, and she'd moved there, found a job with the new provisional government and ended up marrying an Oxford-educated tribal chieftain's son. She worked for an organization that created a Pan-Pacific Arts Festival, traveled widely in remote areas promoting the continuation of tribal music, masks, dolls, costumes, and dance as folk theater, maintaining the ethnic traditions as the country became modernized.

But all Nyia really wanted was this: something out of danger, with some meaning, the chance for love and love returned, clear and simple.

And impossible, she thought.

Walking back up the pier she passed the fajitas stand, inhaled the smell of grease and coconut oil. At another vendor's stand she bought a black baseball cap and cat-eye sunglasses, tucking her hair up into the cap. The vendor held a mirror up for her to look.

"Brand-new," said the small Asian man. "You look like brand-new girl."

"Thank you," said Nyia.

Passing the playland again, she glanced in at the merry-go-round. Even though it wasn't going, a small girl sat on one of the painted horses, holding the reins and waiting. Or maybe she didn't even care if it was stopped, thought Nyia. The girl was riding anyway and had the whole place to herself.

When she got back to her mother's apartment, there was a note for her. "Gone for a hot game of golf with Mr. Aerospace. Left keys to the Cutlass on top of the bureau. Probably be back quite late."

The plan had blinked on inside her at the vendor's

stand. She hadn't known where it was heading, or what it meant. It just felt right. Driving toward Beverly Hills, she stopped at two convenience stores and withdrew money from the cash machines.

Westwood Pavilion would be perfect, she thought. Not Sunset Plaza, nowhere on the Boulevard. That was her old stomping grounds, someone might recognize her there.

Nyia parked in the massive ramp of the three-story, blocks-long pavilion and called "No, thanks" to the valet who offered to wash and polish her car while she shopped. It was a relief to have a direction. It was gaining strength in her, she was riding it, and it felt good.

She came in on the second level by May Company, took the escalator down and walked the length of the mall. Skylights in the arched ceiling threw diffuse light onto dusty palms in big planters. Globe streetlamps all down the colonnade made the place look like someone's idea of mainstreet turned into a consumer paradise. Nyia wound through the columns painted colors like "seafoam" and "bisque."

There was so much merchandise here that, for a moment, Nyia felt a sense of vertigo. The possibilities and choices confused her. Go into any store, buy an identity. If you didn't have your own, you could borrow someone else's name: Georgio, Calvin, Paloma, Donna. With enough money, you could be anyone. Nyia found herself wishing she were that bored shopgirl, well dressed in her black-and-white houndstooth miniskirt power-suit, so intensely focused on her cuticles, waiting the forty-seven and a half minutes until her next break.

She had the sensation next to a shop selling bed linens (she'd grown up calling them sheets for some reason) that she might fall into the store, hurtle into the display of matching gray pillows and contrasting comforter, fall until she arrived on one of those beds, a sleeping mannequin, a dead princess.

Carlton Hair International had just had a cancellation and could take her immediately. Shawn massaged her scalp with suds, then set her up before an angled mirror. The salon was dark, with black glass and tortoiseshell trim. He surveyed her with an odd look and said what she'd been fearing since arriving in L.A.

"You're Nyia Wyatt!" he exclaimed, pulling back her hair.

Nyia fell instantly into an accent, slightly French. "And you must be John Malkovich!" she cried.

"No really, you are. You have to be!" said Shawn. "Come on."

Nyia thickened the accent. "No, I'm Ellen Barkin. Now, cut my hair short, very short. I want a black-reddish color with cellophane highlights. I want to look like a black-haired Annie Lennox. Eurhythmics. Do you like their music?"

"This is beautiful hair," Shawn protested, lifting her sun-streaked locks.

"But I need to be a brand-new girl, Shawn."

He squinted his eyes at her.

"Forget the business about the celebrities, will you, darling?" she said. "Why would Nyia Wyatt want to cut off all her pretty hair? Only a fool would do such a thing. I'm that fool. Now cut."

Shawn picked up his scissors and started in.

She liked the way she looked, it brought out the shark in her. She tried two lipsticks and bought one with a purple hue. South of France, she thought. Not South America at all, where everyone would think of finding me at Moravio's. Or worse yet, Moravio himself. A farmhouse in the south of France. I have enough money. First thing tomorrow, see my own lawyer, prepare a statement, liquidate my assets, move them to a

Swiss bank. A year in a farmhouse, Aix-en-Provence. I'll write. I have my own ideas for a screenplay, she thought.

After the salon, she tried on clothes at several shops, settling finally on a line of sophisticated cottons and knits in elementary colors, black, gray, ivory. Nothing at all like her green boots and jeans jackets, her purple leather strapless dress. The cherry-black hair, plum-red lips made her skin look very white. She slipped on the black chemise and ankle-strap sandals, the cat-eye sunglasses. *Yes,* she thought. *Brand-new.* She didn't look a bit like Nyia Wyatt. And no one would mistake her for Robin Reese either.

As she paid with her MasterCard, she was glad she'd kept it under her real name: Elinor N. Wyatt. Nyia was actually her middle name. Elinor had been her maternal grandmother. *Nora. Now that's a good name. Literary.* Nora Wyatt, a writer in a farmhouse in the south of France. Riding her bike to vineyards, wearing a straw boater's hat. A quiet year, two, five. What the hell difference did it make how long she dropped out? Anyway, she wanted a baby sometime in her thirties. That gave her ten long, slow years out of all of this craziness. She might never come back at all.

Putting her purchases in a shiny peach-colored bag, the clerk at the dress shop asked Nyia if she were from Eastern Europe. "It must be something, seeing all the changes in your country this past year."

Nyia looked at her oddly, then noticed she'd been speaking in that accent all along, as if in a character. Heat radiated through her chest and over her face as she realized the character she had been going into: Mirina. That's who she'd been creating all afternoon, the elegant writer in Paris and southern France, none other than her beloved Mirina twenty years ago when Mirina had first met Leonard Jacobs and fallen in love with him. *This won't do,* thought Nyia. *Not at all.*

Nyia exited the store and sat on a bench in the pavilion, listening to the murmuring voices of shoppers in the sunny, palm-filled cavern. All afternoon it had been coming to her. It had started with that vendor, *brand-new girl*. All right, here she was, no one would recognize her, she was saying, *I'm not who you think I am.* But it wasn't just a question of a new identity, going into hiding for the rest of her life, running away to Europe or Brazil in some self-invented witness protection program. Anyway, that would only fuel rumors that she had something to do with Tess's death.

No, there was something else that needed to be done. A creative solution. She was through acting the roles others wanted for her. And inadvertently this obsessive, demented person—*murderer,* she thought—was requiring her to do that. Pushing her back like a caged animal until she had no room to move, pushing and pushing until the only place she had left to go was to her mother's alcoholic kitchen.

I can't just keep being on the receiving end of his obsession. I'm tired of being in his movie, his videos spying on my life. I'm tired of him stealing my clothes, breaking into my rooms, watching me, seeing me in private moments. I'm tired of those goddamn letters and his weird notions of how I'm in his story and how the story is taking over everything. I'll give him a story to be in and it will be my story. You want me so bad, come and get me. My story is bigger than yours, I'm going to surround you and absorb you. I will be waiting for you to show your face. Come on ahead, she thought, kidnap me, take me away to your fantasy. I'll be waiting for you. I will enter your world and make it my own. The only way I'm going to survive is by playing my killer's game.

Back down the pavilion toward the parking ramp she'd seen an elegant stationery store. She walked there quickly and asked the clerk if they carried airmail envelopes, the kind that folded in on themselves. The young man brought her a box of them, and as she was drawing the money out of her purse she thought to ask, "You don't have the French ones, do you? *Par Avion?*"

"Why yes, we do happen to carry them."

He produced another box and she asked for a second just to make sure she had enough. She carried the paper and her new clothing purchases to her car, drove up La Cienega to a coffee shop, ordered a cappuccino and began to write:

My dear fan,

For years you have written to me, but it has been a very one-sided relationship. I have never been able to return my affection for you, or even my thoughts, but we both know by now that we have a level of connection that goes far beyond what either of us ever anticipated. It has become clear to me that only if I accept what you call your "story" can I truly live. It is your story itself that is the source of my life. Therefore it has become imperative for me to enter, without equivocation, the story of your love, wherein I will find my true purpose and identity.

I propose we meet to discuss the possibilities. I have no shortage of funds. I believe that I have survived all of this to be united with you and I know that is what you really want, not my death. Together we can create a totally new life. I will exist only for you and your story. I will be your creation. There is no reason for you to be so tormented, suffering this separation between fantasy and reality.

In a few days I will be back in New Mexico to tie up loose ends. At that time, I will be ready to leave with you, to exit my life as an individual entity and to serve only your will and your happiness. I send this in care of my dear friend, because I know you are near me and that your letters sometimes come in care of someone close to me. This will be the greatest acting job of my life, my darling, because it will be my life. My new life with you. Please contact me so that we can arrange a discreet meeting. I know that you will be able to find me. You always do.

Faithfully yours, Nyia.

She copied the letter over on each new page and folded them one by one. Her address book was in her purse. Visionfilm offices in L.A., New York, and Paris, the ranch in Tesuque, individually to both Mirina and Leonard. Manuel in care of Mirina and in Brazil, both his home in Rio and his country home. Suzanne Scolfield's home and agency. Paulette Joyce, Leonard's producer. Gino, Jack, Connie, Dan, other people on the Visionfilm crew. She addressed all the letters to "Nyia Wyatt," in care of them.

Nyia knew that if these letters arrived at home or office of anyone who cared about her, they would see that she got the letters unopened. She coded each of the letters so she knew who they were from, a tiny letter on the back side: V, L, M . . . As they were returned to her she could eliminate that person as the contact.

Across the bottom of each envelope she wrote in small capital letters, "READY."

If this person who was trying to kill her saw one of these letters in with his mail, he would recognize that it was not one of his. It was not even his writing, but the envelopes would be exactly the same. He would be curious and would open the letter. And would not be able to resist contacting her.

She would wait for his communication and then she would go to some remote place, perhaps the Taos cabin. Harm and Quintana could help her arrange the trap. She'd be there waiting with a gun hidden where she could get to it easily. They could put a wire on her or in the cabin, hear exactly who it was. They could set up hidden cameras and videotape the meeting. She would speak his name. She would engage him in conversation in such a way as to extract a confession. Then the police could move in. And if something went wrong . . .

Nyia licked the last of the envelopes. In the back of her address book, she had a page of stamps and carefully stuck one to each letter. *If something goes wrong,* she thought, *I'll shoot him. I'll have no other choice; it will be self-defense.*

She would wait a few more days at her mother's, until she was sure that most of the letters had arrived, at least the ones to New Mexico. In the meantime, she would arrange for Harm to be with her and to escort her back to the Southwest.

Driving back to Santa Monica, Nyia pulled over at a corner and dropped the letters, one by one, into the mailbox.

TWENTY-TWO ☆

HARM BOHLAND DROVE BACK OVER THE
mountains, dropped down into the yellow vat of air
that hung over Los Angeles. Sally Beard's office was out
on La Cienega, south of Santa Monica Boulevard. He
drove through the endless aisles of commerce, past the
Oriental rug stores and strip joints, then spotted her
sign above a medical clinic next to a tropical fish store.
He parked, crossed the street, and went up the carpeted stairs. Her door was open, and she stood talking on
the phone. When she saw him she held up one finger,
said good-bye, and gave him a big grin.

"Harm Bohland! So we've both gone free-lance.
What do you think? Were we idiots to give up that pension?" Sally Beard was a good-looking woman in her
late fifties, plump in faded blue jeans and a pink sweatshirt, auburn hair fluffed around her open, smiling
face. He'd always liked working with her.

"What have we got?" she asked. "Let's take a look."

She held one of the examples of writing up and then set it down next to the postcard. "You say the postcard address was written several years ago. Well, on the surface these examples look different, but I would say these were definitely written by the same person."

Sally handed him a note written by Mirina Jacobs. "See how the *t*-crosses are the same? The postcard address writing is very large and fast, written in a hurry. The notes here on the script are quite small—this would indicate a high degree of concentration, but the tri-zonal slashing is the same and there are many of the same characteristics."

Harm gathered the pages up. "Thanks, Sally."

"I hope that helps."

"It does."

"This isn't my specialty, but that computer dot matrix looks like an Epson printer," she added. "I'm having to develop some new skills here in this computer age."

Harm asked to use her Xerox machine to make a copy of Robin's letter so that he could return the original to her mother. He borrowed an envelope and stamp from Sally as well and she promised to mail it out on Monday.

He thanked her again and headed back out to his car.

Harm sat in the hot car for a moment, then rolled down the window, glanced at his watch, mentally mapping out the rest of the day. He had to get a place to stay tonight, maybe just a hotel over by the airport. He wanted to stop by John Sand's house, and thought it better to wait until late afternoon. People were often home on Saturday just prior to going out. And Dierdre Fine, he wanted to check with her too. He pulled out her business card, which had listed her home address: Venice Beach. There was a hotel that wasn't too bad right in Venice. His old neighborhood, where he'd lived when he was married and Nickie was just a baby in a blue umbrella stroller.

He got out of the car, jogged back across La Cienega and up the stairs, asked Sally Beard if he could use her phone for a minute. Dierdre Fine's answering machine came on and he was one sentence into his message when she intercepted the call, breathless.

"Bohland! I got to talk to you. Where are you?"

"I'm in town."

"Fabulous. I can't believe what's happened. I can't even believe I was stupid enough to come back here when Jacobs threw me out. I'm flying back out to New Mex tomorrow. But now you're in town. This is my lucky day. When can we talk? By the way, your cover is completely blown. Of course, I knew you weren't for real right off the bat. The professor bit and all."

"How did you know? Thought I had the ivory-tower act down pretty good."

"Howe. The University of Minnesota doesn't have a film department."

"Yeah. Well, that whole thing wasn't my idea in the first place."

"Listen, what are you doing for dinner tonight? I'm in an interview right now, but could we meet, say eight?"

"Perfect," he said.

"Rose Café? It's in my neighborhood."

"Rose at eight," he confirmed. Then asked, "You wouldn't be interviewing Nyia Wyatt, would you?"

"Thought she was at Betty Ford."

"That's just a line her manager is feeding the media. She's on the run, that's why I'm here. Listen, what I need is her mother's address. Didn't you say you'd interviewed her recently?"

"Yeah, but Nyia would never go there in a million years."

"I just want to ask her some questions. Can you help me out?"

"If you promise to give me something really juicy at dinner."

"Deal."

Harm heard pages ticking over, then Dierdre rattled off Carole Wyatt's address. Santa Monica. Perfect, he thought. Right close to Sand. He could check into the hotel in Venice, look up both Sand and Carole Wyatt, and rendezvous with Dierdre back at the Rose Café at eight. He thanked her, hung up, thanked Sally Beard again and returned to his car.

It was strange driving back into Venice. Nothing had changed. His wife had taught history at Venice High School. They'd lived in a rundown mission-style bungalow they were forever starting to fix up but never completed. As Harm got out of the car, the ocean air smelled sweet. A truck loaded with fresh vegetables was unloading in front of a health food store. He'd taken Nickie down the boardwalk on Saturday mornings while Sandy took her yoga class. Just looking at these streets brought back the taste of failure and defeat.

He checked into the Pacifica Hotel, dumped his things in a room on the third floor, showered, changed, and headed out again into the afternoon. Driving up Pacific Avenue toward Santa Monica, he knew he needed to stop and gather his thoughts before going to see Sand. Besides, there was the ocean rolling in bright splendor off to his left. He couldn't be back there without paying his respects to the water.

He parked on Pacific and walked along the grassy boulevard overlooking the ocean, palms flying in the June wind. On a corner across the street, he spotted a small bar that might have a pool table. As the traffic light changed, he crossed and entered the open door of Wind and Sun, stood there blind in the dark, smiling when he could finally see there was a pool table. He ordered a draft, dropped quarters into the table slots and racked up the balls.

A large TV sat at an angle to the bar and a rumpled map of London was tacked on the wall by the pool table. On the bar, clean glasses were lined up in a row on a towel and a dusty white pool ball was balanced on an upside-down shot glass. Battered Naugahyde lounge chairs were grouped around small tables, and the light inside seemed orange. A thin, drunk woman teetered into the bar in very high heels and perched at a barstool, watching Harm circle the table. "Hi, Larry," the woman said to the bartender. Regular, thought Harm. *Soused.* He hadn't thought of that word in a while.

He shot a rack, quickly setting them up again for another round. Went to the bar to order a second beer. The woman was laughing hysterically. "Look at this, Larry?" she slurred. "A quarter has fallen in my shoe!" Larry came around to peer into the woman's high heel. Now they were both laughing. Suddenly, they lapsed into speaking in perfect French. Larry drew Harm another draft. As he ran a ball down the rail he thought fondly of the Velvet Cushion Billiards in Santa Fe, of Juan Gonzalez, proprietor. He was glad he'd moved away from here.

It wasn't until after the third game against himself that he started to relax and think. He took one of the lounge chairs, found his index cards in his briefcase, and spread them out on the cocktail table. Based on Sally Beard's findings, he wrote, "It could be surmised that Mirina Jacobs wrote these letters that have been threatening Nyia this past year." Surmise and fact, however, were two different things. He knew that. At the very least, Mirina Jacobs had addressed one of them, the postcard. Does it follow that Mirina killed Robin Reese and Tess Juran? No, he thought. It does not follow. And what would Mirina's motivation for writing the letters be?

Where was Mirina the night Robin Reese was killed in Mexico? he wrote. Alone in her condo with no alibi. Where was Mirina the evening that Nyia's house was broken into? At a dinner party with numerous witnesses. Where was Mirina when Tess Juran flew off the canyon road into the desert? Waiting with Leonard back on the set. Who knew Tess would be on that bike? Only Mirina and Leonard? And Nyia, he thought, once Leonard had told her that Tess was replacing her in the role.

Harm looked back over his shoulder at the TV news. It was getting later than he thought. He took out a piece of paper and wrote Mirina Jacobs at the top and the three women's names underneath in little square boxes. Tess, Robin, Nyia. Obsession with story, with controlling others through story. It had kept looking like Leonard because of the love letter aspect of it. But if these letters had been written by Mirina, she'd written them through a character's point of view.

The screenplay pages that Kathleen Reese had provided demonstrated that "the story" was not just some demented maniac's internal fantasy life. "The story" was an actual screenplay. Robin had mentioned in her final letter to her mother that there were two writers at work on it. *Sworn to secrecy.*

Okay, second train of thought. What if Nyia was never the intended murder victim? Yes, she had been assaulted, her car had been shot at, she'd been harassed by the letters and videos. But two other women were the actual victims. What if, all along, it hadn't just been Nyia as primary target, but *anyone* Leonard was involved with? And suppose that Mirina's primary purpose was not to kill her husband's lovers, but to threaten and harass her husband? Thus it would not be essential to her actually to succeed in murdering the women, particularly in the case of Nyia, to whom Mirina was also very attached. She could be very cold-blooded when it came to Robin and Tess—but with Nyia she would feel a tremendous conflict. She could manage to be not quite able to kill her, but the threats would send a message that when Nyia became involved with Leonard, she would be in danger.

Mirina had alibis for some of the incidents with Nyia—but not all of them. But it would not have had to be Mirina herself who perpetrated the crimes. There were always people who could be hired to do such things—to play the part. *Actors,* Harm thought. A man in a ski mask with an empty gun, a local sharpshooter in the back of a pickup truck. A mechanic to tamper with a Harley-Davidson. Perhaps that was Mirina's ultimate screenplay—the one starring Leonard, herself, and all the women in Leonard's life. With one actress in the starring role, an actress Mirina had known since adolescence, an actress Mirina had trained in the business. The one, paradoxically, on which Visionfilm Productions' financial success was now dependent.

If that were the case, Mirina couldn't afford to go all the way with a death scenario for Nyia—she would lose her meal ticket. Not that Visionfilm movies weren't well regarded without Nyia, but they made little money without her. *Dead Heat* had been Visionfilm's first commercial success because it came out at the same time as *Wings.* And because of the notoriety surrounding the film after Robin Reese was murdered. Mirina and Leonard had trained Nyia to play the star in their movies and their lives. Without Nyia, there would be no money, no center to their work.

Or, it occurred to him, their lives. Some people actually needed the crisis, the drama and tension of affairs. Leonard was certainly one of those people. Sexual addiction, Dierdre Fine had called it.

Another possibility occurred to Harm. It was always when Leonard and Nyia had stopped seeing each other and he began to form a liaison with someone new that a woman was murdered. Perhaps Mirina's motivation was not to kill Nyia at all, but to kill her rivals-as-lovers. Harm wrote on a question card: *Why would Mirina want Leonard and Nyia to remain together?* Simply because it was familiar? Because Nyia—at least the younger, less individuated Nyia—was not an ego-threat to Mirina?

Harm didn't know. He flipped through this series of questions on the file cards and looked out the small, square window behind the bar at the scrap of ocean view.

Pattern; outcome, he thought. The outcome was that Leonard and Nyia were orchestrated into being together. Directed. Controlled. By Nyia's mother when she was just a teenager. Then by Mirina? But why would a woman orchestrate her husband's lifelong affair? What was the benefit?

Award-winning films, he wrote slowly on the napkin. *Commercially successful films.* Nyia starring in Visionfilm Productions plus Nyia and Leonard in an intense, unresolved relationship equalled a success formula for Visionfilm. But then why kill Nyia for it? *It is the other women who are killed,* he wrote. *Eliminated as Nyia's rivals.*

Then he read through several of the fan letters again, watching the sickness in them take form, the psychopathic imaginative enmeshment—Nyia as a character, not as a real person. The films, the letters, the videos, the murders—all were acts of fiction to this person, whoever it was. To this person with the slashing trizonal dynamics, the continuing *t*-cross and the big-ego capitals. To Mirina Jacobs. If this were the case, then Nyia was in more danger once the filming was completed. After *Trial and Error,* her contract with Visionfilm would run out. And there'd be no reason left for Mirina to spare her.

Harm put all his cards and papers back into his briefcase, paid his tab, and exited into the fading light. A swarm of bikers rode by with high handlebars gleaming, their engines screaming down Pacific Avenue. As he unlocked his car, a mylar balloon, partially deflated, drifted past him down the sidewalk. He was hungry and wished he'd eaten a couple bags of chips at the bar.

* * *

Sand's house was on a street thick with vines and foliage, large houses with thin strips of lawn, but homey, not mansions. Harm stepped over a kid's skateboard as he approached the front door.

A very beautiful, young Asian woman in jeans and a red blouse answered the door. The locked screen door was further protected by black wrought-iron grillwork. "Yes?" she asked.

"Who is it?" Harm heard a man's voice call. Then Sand appeared, pulling a suitcoat on over a gray T-shirt and black jeans. He was older, mid-forties, Leonard's age, but boyish, short-cropped hair jelled up in a semibutch, and a growth of whiskers.

Harm introduced himself, opened his identification, and Sand looked over the woman's shoulder. Harm noticed her pear-shaped diamond. A much younger wife. "Mr. Sand, I'd like a few minutes of your time, if you'd be willing to answer some questions about Leonard Jacobs. I'm actually trying to find Nyia Wyatt."

Sand hesitated, appeared to look past Harm, out onto the darkening street. "We're about to go out," he said. "But come on in. I've only got a couple of minutes."

He led Harm to a den off from the foyer and stood before a glass desk. The walls were lined with white shelves full of books. Above the desk hung a painting of a crumbling adobe and spiked *vega* fence throwing knife shadows across a mountain lion's back. A black crow was perched on the lion's back.

"Looks like New Mexico," said Harm.

"Got it in Santa Fe. Used to stay down at Jacobs's ranch quite a bit when we were in business together. Sit down, Mr. Bohland." Sand stayed standing, a reminder to Harm to keep it quick.

Harm folded his hands, looked up at Sand. "Mr. Sand, I know that Leonard testified against you in court and that you did some time for securities fraud. Do you harbor any resentments toward Jacobs for his role in your conviction?"

Sand brushed his hand through his spiked-up hair. He surprised Harm by saying, "I certainly did." Then he added, "Please note, however, the past tense. I did my time and I'm out. I'm into new projects, new properties, new marriage, new life. Len was subpoenaed, his lawyer advised him to save his own ass by testifying against me. Win some, lose some. But life goes on. I don't lose sleep over it. I learned some things. Funny. Prison was actually a sabbatical for me. Not a great way to take a reflective break during your midlife crisis, but there are worse places. Hospitals, for instance."

"You were released from prison approximately four weeks before Robin Reese was killed on the set of *Dead Heat* down in Mexico. Can you account for your whereabouts during that period of time?"

Sand laughed. "On parole. Check with my parole officer if you want. Look, are you suggesting that I had something to do with Robin, or with all this bullshit going on now in Santa Fe?" He laughed again, rubbed his neat growth of whiskers. "You work for Jacobs, don't you?"

Harm said yes. Then decided to surprise Sand, throw him off balance a little. "But to tell you the truth, it is becoming clear to me that he may well have something to do with the deaths of both Robin Reese and Tess Juran. This is completely off the record. It seems he was involved with both of them at the time of their deaths."

Sand walked to the chair behind the glass desk and sat down, picked up a perfectly sharpened pencil and twirled it through his fingers like a tiny baton. "That's not altogether true," he said quietly. "Did Jacobs tell you he was involved with Robin?"

"It came from other sources," said Harm.

"Well, they're wrong," said Sand. "My wife, Mary— she and Robin Reese were old friends. She told me Robin was involved with one of Jacobs's staff off and on for a year. Pretty tumultuous relationship, I think, but they were all very young. Dan Howe was his name. Robin appeared with Jacobs at some social functions, but that was as far as it went. I remember Mary telling me about it, I'm sure she'd tell you if you asked her. Robin thought Jacobs was a letch. Married and all. No, she was seeing Howe. Mary, sweetheart?" he called. "Could you come here a minute?"

The beautiful woman with the shoulder-length satin-black hair leaned into the study. "Dan Howe and Robin Reese, weren't they an item?" asked her husband.

She nodded. "They met in a screenwriting class at UCLA film school."

Harm slowly sat up in the leather chair.

"Howe studied screenwriting?"

Again Mary nodded. "He hasn't had anything optioned yet, that I know of."

"Mary's an agent," explained Sand.

Harm was silent for a moment, letting that reel through his mental index cards, throwing them all up in the air.

Sand stood. "We should be going," he said.

"Just one more question. You were Jacobs's financial partner, you knew the ins and outs of Visionfilm pretty well. How stable a corporation is it, do you think? Would anyone benefit from Visionfilm going under— let's say, if the company were ruined by liability issues, unable to complete projects . . ."

"I see what you're getting at, Mr. Bohland. First of all, let me say that I am completely out of it. I have no interests in Visionfilm whatsoever anymore, not even royalties. I sold my interest to Mirina Jacobs."

"Not Leonard?"

"Mirina offered a better price. Mirina Jacobs owns controlling interest in Visionfilm. She actually began the company with money from acting and filmmaking she'd done in Europe. When she met Leonard and divorced her husband, she invested all her money in Visionfilm and backed Leonard for years. Here's something you may be interested in. It's actually somewhere in the Visionfilm corporate structure, or possibly in the form of a prenuptial agreement between Leonard and Mirina: if Leonard ever leaves Mirina—leaves the marriage, that is—divorces her, he forfeits all financial rights to Visionfilm projects, both past and those currently in development. Isn't that incredible?" Sand shook his head. "But she was the one with all the bucks and the contacts, he was the genius pretty-boy, too young to think of getting a good lawyer. He signed and Mirina went on to make Visionfilm a success. He's done well for himself. But to tell you the truth, without Mirina he would lose everything he's ever made."

Sand walked to the door, pulled up his jacket sleeve to glance at a gold Rolex. "Ready, Mary?"

Harm followed Sand out into the blue of early night, shook his hand on the front steps, and thanked him for his help.

He only had about a half hour before he was to be at the Rose Café. Nyia's mother lived nearby; there was time. So that was the reason for Mirina and Leonard's oh-so-stable nonmonogamous relationship, thought Harm. *You can see other women all you want, but without me, you're nothing.* Mirina had Leonard in a box. How far would she go to keep him in it? And what would he do to get out?

SHE SAID HE WAS LIVING IN A FANTASY WORLD.

She said he had lost touch with reality.

She said that he had gone too far and that something would have to be done to protect him from himself.

Said he had become a danger to you. Had gone over the edge.

She told him to destroy all the writing, because it was incriminating. A search warrant for his room and he'd be locked up in prison with all kinds of free time to write.

He saw her point. He insisted he had nothing to do with the motorcycle. He knew he did not. But the way she pressed him, he began to have his doubts.

"Didn't you go out and shoot the driver of that truck?" she asked.

He admitted he did, yes.

"Then why should I—or anyone else for that matter— believe you had nothing to do with the brakes on that Harley?

For your own sake," she pleaded. "For your own good, destroy the writing. All of it."

But what, exactly, was she asking him to do?

She repeated it, clear as day: Destroy all printed copies of the manuscript and all the computer diskettes. Destroy any letters or copies of the letters.

So this afternoon, he had followed her advice. He put every page and diskette in a garbage bag and deposited them in a dumpster behind a convenience store. She promised him she would get rid of all her copies as well. She called back later to make sure he had done as she had asked him to.

He felt the death of it then, all his work, three years of it, gone. But it wasn't just the death of the pages. It was his own death. Without the story to be in, he realized, he did not exactly exist. The past was gone, thrown out like garbage, and the future was empty, like the blank screen on the computer. There was no longer a purpose. A core.

Minutes later, she called back again. Told him in no uncertain terms to stay away from you. Leave you alone.

And maybe she was right, too, he recognized that. That he had gone too far. Of course he had. So maybe he would have to give up writing about it, maybe it was obsessive, though at one time she had called it the strongest piece of new work she had seen in years and years. That's when he realized she had tricked him. Blackmailed him somehow.

He sat in the gray room thinking about that and about what he was going to do. There were two things. One: While the story might be dead, he was free to continue with his plan anyway. Possibly even more free to do so, without her looking over his shoulder all the time, suggesting revisions, rejecting his ideas.

And two: He still had the videotapes.

TWENTY-THREE ☆

NYIA FINISHED THE SECOND GLASS OF WINE,
paid the tab and walked back the several blocks along
Sunset Boulevard to the car. Early Saturday evening.
The shops had closed, but the cafés were crowded. All
the stores had names with V's: Venezia, Virago, La
Villanova. Mel Gibson and Goldie Hawn stared down at
her from a giant billboard advertising *Bird on a Wire*.
She passed the refinished Corvettes and Corvairs gleaming along the boulevard. Two mylar balloons, shaped
like lips, were tied to the handle of a Mercedes convert-
ible. She hadn't wanted to go back to her mother's, had
felt safer out in the city, wandering inside her disguise.
No one had recognized her. Men had looked at her, of
course. But she knew the difference between admiration and recognition. It had worked.

At six she had called Harm at both his office and
home. No answer. She left messages, would try again in

the morning. She debated leaving her mother's number, but was afraid. She wanted to talk to him first. After all, he did officially work for Mirina and Leonard.

It was dark by the time Nyia got back to the Mar Vista. She carried the shopping bags with the new clothes up to her mother's unit, unlocked the door and pushed it open. Carole was seated on the couch watching TV, a highball glass in her hand. When Nyia said hello, Carole held up her palm, not taking her eyes off the TV and said, "Just a sec, dolly. Just let me see this one part." But she glanced up anyway and let out a groan. "Oh God, what have you done now?"

"Got a haircut."

"You look hideous."

"Short hair is in vogue, Mother. I didn't want to be recognized."

Her mother went back to the show. "Then you should have been a telephone operator." She looked up again. "Your beautiful, beautiful hair. It was a trademark. You'll have trouble getting work now."

"For my last film I won an Academy Award, Mother."

"You look disgusting. Men hate short hair. But you're thirty, you're past caring about men." Nyia walked past her to the bedroom, peered through the curtain sheers toward the pool in the courtyard below. She slipped her clothes off and put on a black swimsuit. The evening was still warm and the thought of sitting there drinking with her mother and watching television made her sick. She missed Harm terribly.

"You're not going out again, are you?" her mother called after her.

"Just taking a dip, Mother."

"But I have a surprise for you."

"Save it," she called back, descending the green-carpeted steps down to the courtyard. She stood at the edge of the small pool, then pushed off into the water. The chlorine burned, but the water felt good, bath-warm from the day's sun, and she swam hard, four laps back and forth, stopping under the diving board, breathing hard. That was when she saw him, the hunched figure at the far end of the patio, seated at the end of a chaise lounge. The palm fronds overhead rustled. The man's head was bent down over his clasped hands.

Nyia's heart was wild in her chest, it had startled her to see someone there. She hadn't seen anyone when she'd come down the stairs. The man stood and came toward her into the rippled light reflected from the pool. Familiar silver hair and dark eyes, his face half in shadow, hands in his pockets.

"Carole called me last night to let me know where you were. I flew out this afternoon. I had to talk to my lawyer anyway. Nyia?"

Leonard stepped toward her. "I'm afraid," he said quietly. She remained still, treading the tepid water, clutching the cement ledge.

She told herself not to be frightened. *He knew you wouldn't be on the bike; it had to have been someone else who tampered with those brakes. Not Leonard, not Leonard.* But she found she was shivering, though the water was warm around her.

He came around the pool and crouched down beside her, kneeling in old jeans, a white shirt, expensive suit jacket, athletic shoes without socks. As usual he seemed incredibly attractive to her and outside the movie set he seemed smaller, calmer, more accessible. *Be a shark,* she told herself. Not a deer in his headlights, frozen. The rising moon over the palm tree was a lopsided crescent. Tinsel moon, fake moon. Fake town, she thought.

Nyia lifted herself from the water, wrapped herself in the towel she'd thrown over a metal chair. She dried her hair with a corner of it.

"What have you done to yourself?" Leonard asked.

"Haircut." *Couldn't they see?*

"But what about the continuity of the film?" He said

it slowly, as if it were the most important thing in the world.

She stared him down and he looked away. That's new, she thought. "What about it, Leonard? I mean, Tess is dead, isn't that a bigger continuity issue? I could wear a wig, right?" She sat down, the metal of the lawn chair cold on her wet thighs. He sat down next to her.

"Can I hold you? Are you still angry at me about switching the bride scenes?" His voice was very quiet.

"I'm alive, at least. I don't think I want you to hold me."

"Don't think?"

"Don't. Leonard, whoever tampered with that bike believed that I'd be the one riding it. Only you and Mirina knew about the script change regarding Tess."

"No." He shook his head, strangely quiet. "We had a script meeting after you took off that afternoon with Bohland. Mirina got really pissed at me for threatening you and arguing with Moravio. She said that neither you *nor* Tess would be on the Harley. She wanted Jack in the bike scene, that was where she wanted to take the story. Jack—Hank—would be concerned about Christine's dream. He'd be the one who'd make the choice to stay with the marriage, by giving up the bike, the symbol of his old life. That's what Mirina wanted. He'd be the one to ride the Harley into town and sell it.

"So that's what was decided at the script meeting that afternoon. And any number of people were aware of that, it was an open meeting. But the next morning, Mirina told me she respected my thoughts about the script after all. She went along with me and we put Tess on the bike. That's why everyone was so confused."

Nyia stood in bare feet. Now she was really cold. "You shouldn't be here, Leonard. I can't believe my mother called you."

"Can't you?" He laughed.

Just like old times, she thought. Old Leonard. Old seduction. It always felt the same going in with him, trust and sweetness high, heart open like an O'Keeffe flower, black center mystery throbbing, wanting him. But not this time. It felt different somehow, the spell was broken. She wanted Harm, she thought. Steady, even, three-hundred-and-sixty-degree view. Not the king of strobe, mask of Janus, Mr. Flip-Flop—loves me, loves me not.

"You have to go now," she said.

"Will you hear me out?" he asked, continuing on without waiting for an answer. "I've decided to complete the film. I've asked Katharine Palmer to come in and take over Tess's part—she's already in New Mexico, reshooting Tess's scenes with Jack. The triptych won't have quite the unity it should but . . ." He picked up a dried palm frond, held it while he spoke.

"The security will be extremely tight. The New Mexico Film Commission will assist us and so will the Santa Fe Police and the State Highway Patrol. Bohland will be with you at all times, not just as a detective, but as a bodyguard. You will do no stunt work of any kind. Doubles will take care of that, the car, the train scene. The set will be closed to outsiders and onlookers of any kind. The security will be absolute. We only have three days of filming left. Millions of dollars are at stake and all of our reputations. Come back, Nyia. Please."

"What about Tess? We just go on as if Tess hadn't died? What about a funeral, for chrissake?"

"There's a private memorial service for her tomorrow in Seattle. Closed to anyone but family. They feared a media deluge. As we did. Visionfilm is making a donation to Tess's educational film company. And of course, there will probably be a large insurance settlement. You will call the shots regarding your part. Christine's the bride, no problem. In addition, we will change your contract to give you a percentage of the film in addition to your salary. You're in control, Nyia. Just tell me what you want. Your terms."

"I'll have to talk to Suzanne about it," she said.

"I've already discussed it with her at length. Along with a lot of other things. Everything is different now, Nyia."

You've got that right, she thought.

Leonard looked up at the moon, silent a while. Finally he said, "I've left Mirina. That's why I went to my lawyer today. He's drawing up the papers so that I can file for divorce."

Nyia felt a space in her chest open like black wings beating.

Leonard went on. "I should have done it years ago when you first threatened to leave me. I never thought you'd pull away from me for good. Everything was always so tied up with Mirina—money, projects, properties, my creativity—I thought I couldn't live without her. She made me what I am. In my own dumb way, I didn't think I had what it takes to go it alone. Now I don't care.

"I've got enough to live on for a couple years and I own a couple good properties outright, separate from Visionfilm. I'm forty-five this year. I could still have a long life without her."

"I thought you loved her," Nyia whispered. "I thought you would never leave her."

He looked up at her, his eyes sad in the dim pool shadows. "I believe she killed Tess," he said, voice cracking. "I believe Mirina cut the brake lines so the bike would crash."

Nyia pulled the wet towel close around her.

"Getting back at me for trying to control the story: 'All right, darling, Tess can be on the Harley after all . . .' She knew Tess and I—" Leonard looked away.

"I know you were sleeping with her, Leonard."

"The last few years, things changed with Mirina.

We'd always had an understanding. But when I was starting to see Robin down in Mexico—"

"Tell me the truth, Leonard. Were you with Robin when she was shot?"

"Yes. How did you know?"

Nyia told him about the coin.

He took the coin out of his pocket, twirled it in his fingers. "We went out dancing. Afterwards out walking. Robin wanted to go into that alley, we were both drunk. I saw someone out of the corner of my eye, and then I heard the blast. I thought I'd been hit, but then she crumpled in my arms. I panicked and left her there. I knew she was dead and there was nothing I could do, but it wasn't that. I just ran. Fear, guilt, all of it. It was like a Chappaquiddick thing, I guess. I drove up into the mountains, burned my clothes, and then buried them. Had a change of clothes in the back seat."

"Why didn't you just tell the police someone shot at you?"

"Simple," he said. "I didn't want Mirina to know I was with her."

"But what about the great open marriage? I thought she didn't care who you slept with."

"She didn't mind if it was you, for some reason. But if it was anyone else, she was horribly jealous. I could never figure it out. I believed the police report that it was a mugging or some local pissed off at the gringo movie people. It wasn't until later that I began to suspect it was Mirina who'd shot at us."

"But that doesn't make sense," Nyia interrupted. "If it was okay with Mirina that we were together, why would she hire someone to break into my house or shoot at my car?"

"I don't have any answers," he said, his voice almost pleading. "I'm only guessing. Look, I've got enough money to just go away for a while. We could take off right after the filming. Just be together without Mirina, outside all that our lives have been up to this point.

When the divorce is final we could go to Europe. Rome, maybe. Paris. We were at our best in Paris, that year Mirina lived in New York. We could forget California. Just go on making films together. We have each other, Nyia. We always did, but I was so stuck. And I really hurt you. You're just thirty. God, you're beautiful. I never had children. We could have a baby. We could marry. Please. Will you? Marry me?"

Her skin felt icy. She watched the aqua radiance of the water wave across his face. Thought back to Spain three years ago, the night he sat naked by the window drunk on wine. How she would have loved to have heard that speech back then. But what she heard in the back of her mind now was this: *You have your own story going. Don't step into his.*

And why the shift now, this last desperate attempt of his? she thought.

Leonard grabbed her wrist and for the first time with him she felt truly afraid. "Carole was right," he said. "She called the ranch. Told me, 'Nyia's here and you get yourself on a goddamned plane and get your ass out here and ask her to marry you or you're an idiot. Anyone can see that plain as day.'"

He laughed, but it was cold. "Come with me now back to Santa Fe to finish the film, Nyia. As soon as it's over and the investigation is complete, we'll go."

"What about editing?"

"I can fly back in to do that."

"What about the investigation? Are you going to tell Quintana what you think about Mirina?"

He paused. "You're right." He put his hands over his face, then looked up. "It's a nightmare," he whispered. "Will you stay with me through it?"

He's acting, she thought. *Just continue. Continue with your plan.*

More than anything she just wanted to talk to Harm. With Mirina and Leonard there was no reality anymore. They had so fully become their own characters now that there was no way out for either of them. Sure, it could be Mirina doing these things, but she found it hard to believe Mirina would write her a bunch of love letters all those years.

"I'm freezing," Nyia said. "I need to change into dry clothes." Leonard followed her up the stairs. On the balcony he brushed against her, old and familiar. And over, she thought.

The door to the apartment was ajar and Nyia pushed in. "Thanks for keeping my whereabouts a secret, Mother."

Carole Wyatt emerged from the kitchen. "Did you propose?" she asked Leonard.

"Yes, ma'am."

"What did I tell you, Nyia? All this man has ever needed was a good attorney and a brand-new wife. And Leonard, I'm telling you, if you marry my daughter and ever so much as look at another woman, I will personally wring your neck with my bare hands. God as my witness."

"Mother," said Nyia. "You're crazy. You're both crazy."

But in her room she felt crazy. She couldn't stop shivering. She could hear her mother and Leonard laughing, her mother's man-voice. That laugh. That's where I learned it, she thought. To be someone else completely.

Looking in the mirror, she palmed her hair back, shivering in the damp towel. She tried Harm's number again, praying he'd be in. *Crazy, crazy,* she thought. *The whole web.* Harm's answering machine clicked on and she left her third message of the night, finally risking leaving the number. "Please call, Harm. Please."

Nyia felt the anxiety flutter and spread in her chest, something electric and hot just under her heart and she sat almost dizzy at the edge of the bed. Something about the two of them out there on the flowered divan with the TV on in the background and the strong smell of Chanel No. 5. She was right back in Paris. Sixteen, seventeen years old. Leonard would come for dinner and Nyia would sit silent, taking it all in while her mother drank, played Ellington on the hi-fi, charming the young director. Who, of course, must not have been charmed at all. He must only have tolerated her endless talk and brittle laugh, and charmed her back as a way to Nyia. Fifteen, her long hair silken over her naked shoulders. He'd fucked her at fifteen, he'd been thirty. And they'd both known it was wrong. Her mother's implicit, *Take her. Take her, but pay attention to me.*

But it is a vicarious pleasure, dolly, she once said. Carole's horrid mix of pride and hatred toward Nyia for her beauty, for her relationship with Leonard, for her talent, her success. Yes, she's always hated me, Nyia thought. Somewhere under all the need and dependence and control, actually hated me, her little more-perfect clone. I lived your dream, she thought. My nightmare.

A knock at the bedroom door. "Dolly?" Carole wedged her head in the door, her lips outlined in coral.

"Can you believe he actually came?" she breathed. "Nyia, love like that doesn't happen but once in a lifetime. It's a lifelong love. That's rare."

Nyia looked past her mother, down the lit hallway where Leonard stood, looking in the mirror above the couch. He caught her eye in the reflection. No smile. Just desire. And panic, that edge of things about to fly off into nothing. He could not, would not leave Mirina unless he thought Nyia would be there for him. She knew that. And she couldn't do it, couldn't even give him the illusion of it.

"Well, sweetheart, I'm going out. Don't wait up for me." She brushed past some papers on the bureau, knocking them to the floor. A blue envelope fluttered down. She bent and picked up the papers. "Oh, I'm sorry," said her mother. "I'm just so clumsy sometimes. Fan mail?" she asked, regarding the blue letter. "Well,

I'm off now." Then she closed the bedroom door.

Nyia picked up the letter, the last one from the ranch she hadn't given Harm.

When she glanced up, Leonard was leaning against the door. She noticed he was trembling. Inside, in the light, his eyes looked tired. She handed the letter to him.

"Did you write that?" she asked.

He turned the letter over to examine the address, as if unsure whether he had written it or not. The thin tissue shook in his hand.

"What is it?" he asked.

"It's from someone who loves me. Someone who is trying to kill me."

"This is trash, Nyia. You don't actually have to read the shit people send you."

"Are you trying to kill me?"

He tore the note in half, stepped toward her.

"I've been getting these letters for three years, ever since we broke up. At first they were love letters. Now they're just nuts. Like that one."

"If I want to tell you I love you, don't I just come right out and say it? I love you."

"You don't get it, do you?" She started to shout. "You don't even believe me. You discount me. I'm not real to you."

"I don't know what you're talking about. I came here to ask you to marry me. You think I'd kill you? You're the center of my whole life."

"Me and Mirina. And Robin. And Tess."

"I'm done with all that. I told you. I see where it leads now. Your heart becomes divided. Your whole life is divided. I came out here to mend this broken thing between us, which neither of us can stand."

She was crying. She hated him. She was through with him years ago. But he just went right on in his own mind as if nothing had ever happened.

"I can't marry you, Leonard. We broke up three

years ago. It's over between us."

"That's not true. I'm filing for divorce."

"Things change, Leonard. You broke me, so there's nothing good left. No trust."

He looked at her blankly. "I haven't been well," he said. "I went off my medication."

"What medication?"

"Prozac. I can't work. I've lost my creativity. It's a fog, it's all just fog."

"Leonard, I can't save you. I'm not your muse."

He stood. "Will you at least keep open to the possibility? I'm going through with the divorce with or without you, Nyia. And I do love you. I would never do anything to hurt you. We're all under a terrible strain just now. Just let things settle. But you will think about it?"

"Go, Leonard. Just go."

He stood, turned back toward her. "Whatever happened to the robe I bought you in France? The yellow one."

"Champagne?"

"Yes, champagne."

"Why do you ask?"

He paused. "What difference does it make?"

She watched him leave the room and walk down the hallway, close the door behind him. How many times had they played that one out? she wondered.

The hot water from the shower sprayed her neck and scalp. As she stood under it, she knew with certainty it was time to go to the police. She toweled off and dressed quickly in jeans and black sweater. And heard the sirens. Synchronicity, she thought. I don't even have to call the police, they will come to me.

They did. She listened as the sirens grew louder, wailing in that rise and fall scream across the darkness, stopping with a howl and sudden drop of sound down the street from her mother's building.

Another siren came in close behind it. Barefoot, she ran out, down the cement steps and across the courtyard. As she pushed through the glass security door, she remembered she had no key with her.

Halfway up the block two squad cars spun light across the front of a town house, the red shadows of palms swooping and swaying. Nyia walked toward the car in a dream, a rag of fear stuffed in her throat.

A neighbor was shouting at her, but the words went up in balloons out of the woman's mouth. Lifted into the air where Nyia couldn't hear them.

"Shots," the woman was saying. "I heard some shots."

A man yanked open the door of the white Mercedes. The car was running, jazz on the stereo, Thelonius Monk frenetic in his haphazard perfection. Leonard was in the car, the driver's seat.

A police officer pulled a gun. "Clear the area. Go back to your homes, please. There has been a shooting. Please clear the area."

No one moved.

Nyia stepped forward. "Leonard?" she said. "It's all right. I was just with him."

"Lady." The cop pushed her back.

"I said I know him," she shouted.

"You got to keep back, lady. You don't want to . . ."

As a police officer turned the engine off, the music cut to silence in the small circle of air around the car. Nyia pressed against the passenger side of the car and stared through the glass, the scream caught down in her chest.

The officer held two fingers to Leonard's neck. She could not look and could not turn her eyes away. The man shook his head.

"Is there a pulse?" asked another cop.

"No way."

The man looked up at Nyia through the glass. The

other cop picked up a gun from the floor of the car, and the cellular car phone, which had dropped to the pavement. Leonard lurched forward, slumping over the steering wheel.

Then Nyia spoke in a childlike voice no one but she could hear. "But where is the back of his head?" she moaned.

"Miss?" said the cop, taking her arm as she stumbled back.

TWENTY-FOUR —

HARM PULLED UP AT A STOPLIGHT NEXT TO A park in Santa Monica and glanced again at the address Dierdre had given him. In the zinc streetlights, the palms glowed with an eerie green. They looked fake and rubbery, in the dusk, dangling over the tennis courts and the giant bougainvillea. He heard sirens close by, more than one blasting through the quiet residential streets. As the light changed he noticed a homeless woman asleep beside the sidewalk. She must have heard the sirens too. She sat up suddenly, clutching her blanket. Her dog, a fat beagle leashed to a shopping cart, barked. The woman seemed to sniff the wind. She adjusted a clear plastic shower cap down over her matted hair, then lay back on the grass, yanking the blanket up over her head.

The sirens were loud now, he knew they were close. As he came around the corner he saw the squad cars and a rescue vehicle parked at angles halfway up the street, strobing over the neat bushes and tidy gardens. He pulled up too close to the end of the street, but there was nowhere else to park; slammed out of the car and ran up the sidewalk to where neighbors stood back from a white Mercedes.

Harm shouldered through them, "Excuse me," he said. He fumbled in his pocket for his identification, swimming through the red lights that striped the darkness. He grabbed an officer's arm and extended his badge, then saw the body in the front seat, the unmistakable red bleeding through the gap in the skull.

The cop pushed him back, the crime scene was being secured. "You'll have to back off now, buddy."

Then Harm spotted Nyia leaning against the opposite side of the car. She saw him, too, reached out toward him. "Private investigator," he told the cop. "Formerly with the FBI. Call Bud Hirsch in Homicide to check me out if you want. That's my client over there."

The cop looked down at the ID, waved his superior over and let Harm through to Nyia. He knocked his knee on the chrome of the Mercedes as he hurried to her side. She fell toward him, clutching at his shirt with her fists. Her body felt hard as stone and she rocked against him in a rigid, rhythmic way.

"It's Leonard," she managed to get out. "Leonard's been shot." She pushed herself hard against Harm's chest and held on like a kid. She wasn't crying. She was hardly breathing.

He stroked her hair, which was gone. Where was her hair? The back of her neck was shaved and her hair was dark.

"You can identify this man?" an officer asked her.

She nodded. "I was just with him. At my mother's apartment. He was just there. He just walked out the door. I was showering."

"Slow down," he said. "Slow it down. What's his name?"

"Leonard Jacobs." She said it slowly as if the cop were spelling it out. "He came to see me. I'm staying with my mother. She was the one who called him. I took a shower. I heard the sirens and I came out on the street. I came out and saw everyone running."

"Is he any relation to you?" asked the officer.

"He's—" Again Nyia stopped, looked at Harm. "He's my employer. I work for him."

Harm edged behind the car and faced the two cops. "This is Nyia Wyatt, the actress. Leonard Jacobs is her director, they've just been filming out in New Mexico." Harm began to explain, but an officer interrupted.

"Lookit, here," he said, reaching in across the steering wheel of the Mercedes to shine a flashlight on the floor of the passenger side. They both saw it at once in the disc of light, the thin, blue folded paper.

"Looks like he might have left a note," he called to the officer in charge. Nyia let go of Harm's arm and crossed in front of the Mercedes. "Can I see that?" she asked.

The cop held it away from her, turned it over in his hands, carefully avoiding touching it, protecting the paper with a white handkerchief.

"We ought to wait for a detective," he said.

On the other side of the car, a cop waved the medics from the rescue vehicle away, told them to forget it, the guy was gone.

"It says 'Nina' on it," said the cop.

"Nyia," she said. "That's me. Give it to me."

He considered for a moment, then handed it to her. "Try not to touch it with your fingers," he warned.

Harm watched over her arm as she opened it. It had not been sealed, merely folded. The words were typed and Harm noticed that the typing did not match that used on the other letters. Nyia mouthed the words to herself then read it out loud: "I just can't take it anymore."

She handed it to Harm, covering her face, turning away.

"Suicide. That's what it looks like," one of the cops said to Harm. "That's what I thought right off. Guy bit the gun. Skin's all gray around the mouth. Metal burns. Fuck. It makes you sick. You really got to hate yourself. You really got to hate everybody that loves you. So she worked with him?"

Harm glared at the cop.

Nyia turned back to Harm, shaking her head. "He wouldn't kill himself," she whispered. "Not in the middle of a film." She faced the cops. "He'd never do this. He just wouldn't. I've known him all my life." She looked bewildered. Harm guessed she was going into shock. Her voice was thin, with no affect. "I can't believe this," said Nyia. "It's not happening. He wouldn't do this to me."

"We'll get a positive ID from fingerprints and dental records," a cop said to Harm. "Depending on what's left of—" He didn't finish. "And we're going to want a couple statements. Hill, can you take care of that?"

"What kind of weapon was used?" Harm asked.

"A thirty-eight," said the cop.

Same type of gun used in that break-in last year, thought Harm. "Let's go back to your mother's place," he said. "Where is she, anyway?"

"She went out. She just left. She just left and Leonard and I talked. Then I took a shower and heard the sirens."

Harm spoke to one of the officers, gave him the address down the street. She walked like a sleepwalker, she was not awake. He put his arm around her.

"We argued, Harm." Nyia stopped, put her hand against the shredded bark of a palm. "He said he was going to file for divorce. He was just with his lawyer, discussing it. He wanted to marry me. That's what he said. I told him no." She looked up at the moon, tilted over the top of the apartment building. "Harm, if he's dead—"

He felt he had to cut her off. "He *is* dead, Nyia. You know that, don't you?"

She looked down at her hand resting on the side of the tree. "This is all real, isn't it?"

He nodded.

"I know that, Harm," she said quietly.

They walked up the street to the entrance to the building, Mar Vista in green letters across the pink stucco. If he'd come ten minutes earlier, Jacobs would have been there, would have been alive. Suicide. Jacobs and the blue note. *I just can't take it anymore.* Was that a confession, then? Too many holes, thought Harm. But what else? The obvious explanation. That Jacobs himself, as Nyia had suspected all along, had written the letters. Obsessed with her after she broke off with him. Their game together, their way of staying connected. Then the attempts to kill her, to get rid of her, thinking that with her gone he'd have some peace of mind. Mistakenly killed Robin. Fumbling the attempts during the break-in and the shooting on the Turquoise Trail. But why Tess on the tampered bike? Because he couldn't pull it off? Because he always sabotaged himself at the last minute? Empty bullets from a gun, leave them in the driveway, then go in to terrorize her. Tamper with the bike then put someone else in the part. Unconsciously unable to go through with it.

Possible. Still, Harm couldn't buy it. Why not? It was so obvious, that's why. Too easy. But sometimes solutions were that way. You pounded your head against a wall or chased down leads on some wild tangent that led nowhere and back again.

As they approached the glass double-doors to the

courtyard, a bald man in a plaid bathrobe came up behind them. "Here, I got a key," he offered. "I seen you here at your mom's, coming and going. She's so proud of you. Well, who wouldn't be? Did you know that guy? What, he did it himself?" The man peered at her through plastic-frame glasses, as if not believing either that it was she. He pushed the door open and they walked across a small courtyard around a pool. The man came over to them as they reached the stairs. "Say, I know this is a bad time, but would you mind?" He held out a scrap of paper he'd fished from his robe pocket, and a pen.

Nyia looked at him as if he was air, painful air, then turned and walked up the stairs.

The door to the apartment was open and the TV had been left on inside. Nyia sat at the end of the pink sofa and Harm sat down next to her.

"He was just here," she said. "He was just standing right here." She reached for the remote control and flicked the TV off. "How did you find me?" she asked.

"Luck. And Dierdre Fine. I talked with her earlier and she gave me your mother's address. I didn't know you'd be here, though."

"How does Dierdre know where my mother lives?"

"Dierdre tracked her down and interviewed her a week or so ago for the piece she's doing on you for *Vanity Fair*."

Nyia nodded. She stared at the blank TV and then doubled over, head on her knees. She started to cry, a long, high wail, her back shuddering in small, violent spasms. Harm put his hand on her back and let her sob.

There was a knock at the door and Harm stood to answer it. Several officers filed in and the pink room suddenly seemed cluttered with men in black. The detective had arrived to take the statements. James Johnson, one of Bud Hirsch's colleagues. Harm had met Johnson during a homicide investigation when he was still with the FBI. Harm fetched a paper towel from the kitchen and handed it to Nyia.

They sat at the glass table near the kitchen and Nyia repeated the events of the evening; returning from shopping and errands, finding Leonard by the pool, his explanation that her mother had called him, told him to come. She hesitated before explaining that they had been lovers, that he had asked her to marry him, that she had refused.

Then she told them Leonard Jacobs had admitted to being with Robin Reese down in Mexico the night she was killed and that he suspected that his wife had something to do with it.

Johnson was taking notes and another stood behind him shaking his head. Finally, she finished, her face very pale against the dyed black hair.

Then she added, "He said something about going off his medication. Prozac, he said. I didn't even know he was taking anything. Oh, I guess I knew he took various things. Sleeping pills."

"Where is his wife?" asked the detective.

"Santa Fe." Nyia turned to Harm. "Oh God, I have to call her."

"We can do that for you," the detective offered.

"No. I should tell her."

The detective reviewed his notes, then pulled the blue airmail letter out of a stack of papers. It was encased in a Ziploc bag now, at a slant against the clear plastic rectangle.

"And this—it's in keeping with all these other fan letters you've received over the years?"

"Same paper—same folding envelopes," she said.

"But it's been typed on something other than what he was using recently. All the recent letters were printed out on an Epson. This looks like a regular office typewriter."

The detective carefully removed the letter from the bag and opened it on the table. He pushed the letter over to her and Harm saw her close her eyes, as if she'd read it one too many times. She dropped her eyes to the blue paper.

"Don't you think it's kind of strange, that it's typed?" asked Johnson. "People usually write suicide notes in their own hand. Unless he had it all planned out."

She shivered involuntarily. "Let's just call Mirina and get it over with."

The detective ran his thumb along the top of the Ziploc bag.

Nyia stood and walked to the kitchen, direct-dialing the number, leaning on the white counter. "Oh. Manuel," Harm heard her say. "This is Nyia. I didn't know you were there. Let me talk to Mirina. It's urgent." But as she waited for Mirina to come to the phone she handed the receiver to the detective. "I just can't talk to her," she muttered and walked out of the apartment. She bent over the railing, looking down over the court-yard below.

Harm stepped out beside her and she clutched at his arm, drew him into an embrace. Her whisper was gruff. "I've got a whole box full of those airmail envelopes in the bedroom, *Par Avion.*"

Harm stepped back, held her arms tightly at the elbows, scanning her face for deceit.

"Why?" he asked.

"I had this idea," she said. "A plan . . ."

"To do what?"

But just then a frantic woman in a silver raincoat ran across the courtyard below them, tripping on a gar-den hose, catching herself and crying out, "Oh, dolly. Oh, my dolly . . ."

TWENTY-FIVE ─ ☆

CAROLE WYATT RUSHED UP THE STAIRS TO THE balcony, threw her arms around Nyia, smothering her in an embrace. Nyia couldn't breathe, pushed her back.

"What in God's name is going on?" Carole cried. "What did you do to the poor man?"

Nyia stepped back, incredulous, looking to Harm for help.

"Mother, he's dead, he's been shot. I didn't have anything to do with it. I can't believe you would even say that to me, blame me."

"I know he's been shot, for chrissake!" Carole was shouting. "You don't think I know that? I come home from a date and the entire police force of the city of Los Angeles is parked on my street and my neighbors are standing around gawking, telling me the famous director killed himself right in front of my house and you think I'm not going to blame you? Why would the man come all this way to shoot himself if not to blame you in some way?"

"I don't have to listen to this," Nyia spat. She stalked back into the apartment, back to the bedroom and threw her things into a satchel. She shoved the half-box of envelopes into a drawer. Please don't search in here, she thought. Oh God, that looks even worse. Finally Nyia took the stationery out and set it on the bureau.

There was a knock at the door and Harm leaned in. "They seem to have calmed your mother down, they're taking a statement. Are you okay?"

He saw the envelopes, the whole stack of them. "Nyia, what is this?"

"That was my plan," she said. "Look, I'm not writing myself those letters, Harm. I can explain. Please. I decided to write *him* some letters. The fan. I wrote to him in care of all the places that forward his letters to me. I had this idea."

"That was stupid!" Harm rubbed his face for a moment. Then he lowered his voice. "What idea, Nyia?"

"Miss Wyatt?" Johnson, the detective, was at the door now. "Your mother would like to see you."

Carole sat in a corner of the pink couch, shrunken against the floral pillows. She held a magazine in her lap, unopened, and motioned for Nyia to come sit beside her. Nyia sat in the wingback chair instead.

"I'm sorry," Carole whispered. "I shouldn't have said that. It was mean, I'm so upset. How could anyone have known he was so unstable? Oh, dolly, I'm sorry. I'm the one at fault, I'm the one who called him to come. Oh, he was probably going to do it anyway, here or the next place. What could anyone do? We didn't know. Oh . . . ." She trailed off into crying, her face shaking into a wad of Kleenex.

Johnson sat next to her on the couch.

"This is such a tragedy." She sniffled. "Finally, my only child was going to marry a wonderful man. I don't know why I even wanted her to marry. It's a stupid institution. Maybe people like hanging other people's towels up straight and rinsing out their milk glasses. I just wanted her to be happy. She was so unhappy without him, though she always pretended she was better off."

The detective looked at a pad of paper and read from his chicken-scratch handwriting. "So, your daughter shows up at your home here last night, you call Mr. Jacobs in New Mexico and tell him to come out here to get her and marry her?"

Carole Wyatt shrugged. "I know it was pushy of me. Who was I to meddle in their affairs? It was almost tongue-in-cheek. I always talked to him that way. I just knew he'd want to know where she was. It was in the papers, they were looking for her."

"And Mr. Jacobs arrived around six this evening? Miss Wyatt wasn't home, she was out shopping and getting her hair done."

"Destroyed. Getting her hair destroyed, just look at her."

Nyia put her head in her hands.

"What did you talk about?"

"Old times, mostly. Paris. New York. I hadn't seen him since Nyia broke off with him three years ago. We talked about my work in television. The possibility of a small role in some future film of his. He was terribly upset about this accident in New Mexico, Tess Juran. He kept going back to that. He was taking it all very personally. I fixed him a couple drinks."

"How many?"

She thought for a moment. "Two. Martinis. He always liked those when he wasn't trying to be so European. Campari and soda wasn't really his style. He was an American." She looked up for a moment, as if Leonard's spirit were ascending through the brass and cut-glass light fixture. "He was a great American director."

The police officer examined his notes again. "So you left here around seven-fifteen?"

"That's right."

"And Miss Wyatt," the detective turned to Nyia. "You spoke with Mr. Jacobs briefly and then proceeded to take a shower."

Nyia nodded.

"The first nine-one-one call about the shooting was logged in at seven twenty-seven. Now Mrs. Wyatt, exactly where were you at that time?"

Her mother put her finger to her cheek. "Seven twenty-seven."

"That's correct, ma'am."

"I was in my car on the freeway on my way to meet Mr. Harvey Stern."

The detective stared again at his notes. "So, basically," he said, "you were alone at the time of the shooting."

Nyia looked at her mother, who looked at her watch as if calculating again. She even placed her finger on the face of her watch, making a small circle.

"Basically," her mother said, looking at Nyia. "And so was she."

The phone in Carole's kitchen rang and a uniformed cop picked it up, spoke into the receiver, and nodded toward Nyia. "I'll take it in the bedroom," Nyia said.

Closing the door, she sat on the edge of the bed, picked up the princess phone. "Got it," she indicated to the cop on the line. Blessed quiet. It felt claustrophobic out there in that fluffy room.

"Nyia?" came Mirina's voice. "I want you to come home. I can't bear this."

Home, thought Nyia. The ranch was not home. Her mother's house was not. She even felt disconnected from her own house in Laurel Canyon.

"Mirina, is anyone there with you?"

"Manuel is here, of course. Jack and Dan and

Gino are all over at Bishop's Lodge. It's not that I'm alone. I want you. You're like family, you're all the family I—" Her voice broke then, but she didn't cry. Nyia heard Mirina light a cigarette, suck in hard. "They'll do the autopsy in the morning. I'll have him cremated and his ashes flown back here. Will you just come?"

Mirina in Tesuque at the ranch, Manuel Moravio there with her. Perfect alibi. Nyia thought about what Leonard had told her. Mirina could have hired someone. Nyia just could not accept that this was a suicide. She would be afraid to see Mirina now. Then she remembered her plan, and that Harm was with her.

"I'll let you know as soon as I can get a flight," she said.

"I need you, Nyia."

It was near midnight when Harm finished talking to the detective, Johnson, in the blue suit. The detective smoked a cigarette out on the balcony, tossing it down into the bougainvillea. Harm put his hand on Nyia's shoulder. "Do you want to get out of here?" he asked.

She nodded.

"Let's go."

He carried her satchel and suitcase down the stairs and waited by the pool.

Her mother was fixing another drink in the kitchen and the TV was on. Carole did not look up when Nyia said she was going to stay with Harm. "Go, go, get out," she slurred. "Send me a postcard from the funeral."

Nyia was silent on the short drive down to Venice. Harm parked the car in the garage of the hotel and they took the elevator up to a hallway that smelled vaguely of mildew and cleaning fluid.

"You travel in luxury, Harm."

"I didn't know you'd be with me. Do you want to get another place?"

She shook her head, too tired to go any further, yet almost vibrating from the adrenaline crash of the night, like having too much coffee before sleep, when the body goes down but the mind keeps whizzing, inventing itself obsessively.

Nyia stretched out on the bed, staring at the empty mirror. Harm sat across from her on the other double bed with the green plaid bedspread. Gold drapes hung across the far wall, some of the pleats fallen off the rod.

"Let's hear your idea," he said.

"I thought you said it was stupid."

"Convince me otherwise. Please."

She folded her arms under her head, still surprised that her long hair was gone. But it felt clean, cut away. She liked the way her neck felt on her palm.

"I want to trap him." She cleared her throat. "Him, her. Whoever. I can't take being stalked like this. Everyone close to me dying. This isn't just letters and videos, it isn't just somebody spying on me at a café in Cannes or a restaurant in Santa Fe. If I don't do something, take some action, I'm just waiting for him to kill me."

"The police haven't ruled out suicide. The note would seem to indicate Leonard wrote those letters just as you thought. It could be all over, Nyia."

"We both know it isn't." She shifted on the hard bed and said it again, "I want to set a trap."

"Tell me about it."

"Okay. The letters are usually sent to me in care of someone else. So let's assume the letter writer is someone I know, someone close to me, someone who at least has access to me through mail sent in care of people I know. Today I mailed letters to myself in care of everyone I can think of. People who know where I am and where I can be reached.

"Each letter is coded. If a person receives one of these, if they're straight ahead, they'll forward me the letter, right? If not, they see the letter written on *Par Avion* blues and they know it's not one of theirs. Plus, there's something else on the envelope to pique their curiosity, it's like they have to read the letter. This person is obsessed, right? So he's thinking, *What? What does this mean? Someone else is writing to her?* So on each envelope in the bottom lefthand corner it says, 'Ready.'

"So they open the letter. And this is what it says."

She handed him a folded blue envelope from her pocket.

Harm read it and refolded it. "Then what did you plan on doing?" he asked. "I mean, what exactly was your idea, Nyia? Ambush him somewhere and gun him down?"

She looked over at him, wide-eyed. "Yeah, maybe." The toughness in her voice did not surprise her. "Why not? It'd be self-defense, wouldn't it? He's killed two of my friends, assaulted me, now he's killed Leonard. Yeah, that's exactly what I thought I'd do, Harm. I even thought maybe you'd help me.

"My idea was to wait for him somewhere, maybe up at the cabin in Taos. I could wear a wire, or the place could be bugged. I'd at least say his name—or hers. Even if I died, at least you'd know who it was. I can't live like this, Harm, year after year, scared everywhere I go, waiting for blue letters. So, yeah, my idea was to blow the fucker away and testify in court that he tried to kill me but I killed him first."

Harm held up the letter. "What do you think a jury would make of this—in multiple copies, yet? This is commonly referred to as premeditation, Nyia. You could be doing time at New Mexico State Penitentiary out on your beloved Turquoise Trail."

"But I'd be safe," she whispered.

"Oh, yeah?"

Harm leaned back against the wall.

"So it was stupid, then?" she asked.

"No. Flawed. But imaginative. Original, Nyia."

"That's me," she said.

"But let's get Quintana in on it. And the L.A.P.D. may want a piece of it too. Let's be intelligent.

"I've got some things to tell you too," continued Harm. "I did some homework today. Saw the Reeses, a graphologist, even talked to John Sand, Leonard's former partner."

Nyia sat up and came over to him on the green plaid bed.

"Do you mind?" she asked. He moved over and she lay down next to him.

He told her about finding the postcard hand-addressed in her briefcase of junk, how the graphologist analyzed the writing and said it was Mirina's. That there was an actual screenplay being written by someone—by two people, according to a letter Robin had sent home. The screenplay was about fan letters, and it paralleled this whole situation exactly.

"Somebody's doing live research," said Harm. "Real life as a storyboard."

"That really fits," she whispered. "The videos, the way he films things, like he thinks this whole thing is a movie."

"Starring you," said Harm.

"Yeah." She felt cold then, burrowed close to him, her chest felt physically sore from the events of the night.

"Couple more things," Harm said. He told her about Dan Howe being involved with Robin, according to Sand.

"I didn't know," said Nyia. "I knew Leonard was hitting on her."

"But get this," said Harm. "Howe studied screenwriting at UCLA."

"Dan?" she asked. "I wonder when that was. He's such an administrator. I didn't know he did creative work." She let that sink in, putting it together into a picture of fragments, broken mirror. Nonsense collage.

"Do you want to see some of the screenplay? Robin's mother had some of it, pages found in Robin's things."

Harm went to his briefcase and pulled out several pages. "The graphologist says it's the same typing as the letters."

Nyia skimmed the screenplay, lines of dialogue, then cut to a new scene: *He lures her into the car. She hesitates, then goes with him, caught on the hook of his kiss.*

Harm continued. "Sand also told me some interesting things about the financial setup at Visionfilm." Nyia listened, eyes still on the screenplay, as Harm relayed what Sand had said about Mirina's ultimate control.

"None of this surprises me," Nyia said when he'd finished. Harm slipped his hand under her shirt, rubbed her back. "Everything points to Mirina then," she mused. "In collaboration with Dan Howe? In on it together? That would explain why Mirina has such good alibis. Where was Dan Howe tonight, for example, at precisely seven twenty-seven?"

"We'll find out tomorrow," he said. He slid his hand around her waist, but she caught it in hers. "I can't," she whispered. "Make love. Not tonight."

"I understand." He stood and stretched. While he showered, she curled in the other bed, eyes closed, feeling the roughness of the sheets. The night kept playing out in the vision behind her eyes, repetitively. She couldn't seem to stop it.

Naked, she crouched by her purse and took out her wallet. Hidden behind her library card was an old photo of Leonard. She slipped it out, staring at it. He was windblown, grinning. Majorca? No, Italy. Lirici. They'd gone away for a few days, left Mirina behind in Rome, working on her screenplay. Snapped this on the turret of a medieval castle turned into a youth hostel, the Mediterranean gleaming behind him. Nyia focused hard on the wrinkled snapshot and tried to bring his features back: nose, cheeks, jaw, forehead, eyes. Reconstruct him from the hole that was gaping at her in her mind, the gray, burned face, the face that now would always be missing.

When Harm came out of the bathroom, wrapped in a hotel towel, she went to him, her skin cold against his warmth. Smell of soap, his hair wet in her hands. She kissed him. Forget, forget. His mouth against her neck. She'd really missed him. More than protection, more than all this horror.

"Why did you cut your hair?" he whispered. He bent down, pushing his mouth against her thigh. She touched his shoulder below her. Breathed in quickly.

"I just wanted to be someone else."

Harm slept after making love, but Nyia lay awake in the utter blackness of the room, thoughts spinning. She kept focusing on the note, the supposed suicide note. What if he really had killed himself? Would a man, despondent, crashing off antidepressants and God knows what else, carefully type up a suicide note?

And yet, the note seemed a deliberate sign. The choice of stationery showed that. If it was a suicide note, it was also a confession. It said, *I am the one who has been doing this. I cannot stop.* Did he commit suicide to prevent himself from killing her? In some terrible way that did fit.

Perhaps Mirina, all along, had been aware of Leonard's obsession and his letter-writing. Perhaps all along she had been protecting Leonard. If Leonard had killed Robin, Mirina was Leonard's alibi. He could have been the one at her house in the mask—the one unable to go through with it. He might have tried again, followed her home from Albuquerque on the Turquoise Trail, seeing she was alone.

And what if Mirina had known all this and tried both to protect him and to get him under control? Therapy, antidepressants, alternatively encouraging him not to see Nyia, then indulging him. *See her, it's all right with me. Stop obsessing.* And what if now, after his obsession had resulted in another death—what if Mirina just felt now that she'd had it with Leonard. It was all just too much.

Picture, thought Nyia: Mirina confronts Leonard, says she will go to the police with what she knows. They argue. She says she's leaving him, perhaps turning him in. Say that, just then, Nyia's mother calls him, insists that he come rescue Nyia. The stage is set for his completion. He leaves Mirina, fantasizing that at last Nyia will reunite with him. If she will not, he knows he has lost everyone: Mirina, Robin, Tess, Nyia. He has utterly failed. He prepares for this ultimate failure by typing up a suicide note. Nyia alone will understand the significance of the paper it is typed on.

But Nyia refuses his proposal of marriage. He goes out to the car and shoots himself. The gun in Leonard's hand was the same kind that was used in the break-in and assault. Same kind of bullets found a year ago outside her Laurel Canyon home.

Stop. Nyia's mind wheeled, toxic in the chilled hotel room. She touched Harm's back as he slept soundly beside her. She sat up at the edge of the bed and felt her short, brushy hair, realized she must have slept, a scrap of a dream tugging at her. What was it? The plane she was in had blown apart, one wing falling away, tearing the side of the plane open. She was strapped in, hurtling down. Feeling under the seat in front of her, she found a black box, the pilot's black box, with some final words recorded inside. She opened the box and birds flew out, large, mottled crows. They leapt out, dangling their long claws, and swooped out the hole in the side of the plane.

NOW YOU'LL GO BACK TO SANTA FE, WALK THE
Plaza again, carry your grief around you like a shawl,
wrapped like the Pueblo women in star blankets in the shade,
ancient as bowls. Now I won't have to find you. You'll come to
me as I always dreamed you would.

There is an emptiness now that the story has been erased
and all that is left is my life again. You'll be back and I won't
have many chances. Maybe only one. One pure chance to take
you.

I have packed up nearly everything and the car is
ready. I checked the mileage up to Vegas. From there a quick
flight to L.A. From there to Bali. Now, how could you refuse
me? Passports, yes, they could track us, but we'll just keep
moving. A sailboat, maybe. Just open sea. Erase it all in
blue.

There isn't much time. I have reason to believe that the
person who put me up to all this in the first place, who

started it all, who destroyed my work, wants to destroy me too. She knows too much, she may turn me in to protect herself if she has to. And the irony is that it was her idea to begin with. I guess that is why she feels the story is as much hers.

So I wait for your return. And when you arrive I will be watching for my one pure chance.

TWENTY-SIX

HARM KNEW IT WAS A DREAM, BUT THAT DIDN'T
help. He sat before the computer screen, staring at a
blinking time bomb and the font-words, "There has
been a computer error. Select Restart or Resume."

He knew that it was no use, that either choice
would dump the entire contents of the document into
oblivion. He had just completed the most intelligent,
creative analysis and resolution of a case that he'd ever
done in his life. Its logic was not only rational and
exhaustively documented, but it turned on itself like
some incredible Möbius strip. Einstein must have felt
like this, he thought in the dream.

But now he had no choice. The answer was in the
computer, but any action he took would destroy all
that he had worked so hard for. He selected "Resume,"
and as he knew it would, the screen blanked out. When
the program came up on the screen again it was a per-

fectly empty document waiting for his perfectly empty
mind.

Just then the printer snapped on. My God, he
thought in the dream, the answer is not lost! He
watched as the computer printed out, one by one, each
of the letters that had been sent to Nyia, along with a
complete copy of the screenplay.

Ripping the pages from the printer wheel sprock-
ets, Harm began to read as the paper burned in his
hands. The smoke set off the fire alarm above his head.
Where was Nyia? The hotel room was in flames, the
sirens near.

Nyia jabbed him with an elbow. "The phone's ringing, Harm." He jolted awake and grabbed the receiver
next to the bed.

"Mr. B, this is your friendly neighborhood cop with
your Sunday wake-up call, and I can tell by your voice
that you have not seen a copy of this morning's *Times*.
Am I right? Bo? Bo? Are you human?"

"Hirsch. How did you know I was in town?"

"James Johnson told me. So here's the headline:
'DOUBLE MURDER MARKS DEMISE OF FILM; DIRECTOR
LEONARD JACOBS'S DEATH RULED HOMICIDE.' Thought
you'd want to know. Just ran into Johnson downtown
and he told me you were at the crime scene last night,
and staying at the Pacifica. A trace metal test on Jacobs's
palm indicated there was no gunpowder residue. Test
was negative. Somebody else fired the piece. They're
just getting the autopsy results now."

"Meet me for coffee?"

"You bet. How about that sidewalk place on the
boardwalk?"

"I might have someone with me."

"Wyatt?" rasped Hirsch. "You dog."

"And Hirsch? Don't gush, will you? Compose
yourself."

"I'll meet you in an hour."

Harm grabbed his watch from beside the phone. After ten. They'd slept late in the womblike quiet of the hotel, the darkness provided by those thick drapes. Nyia rolled over on her back. He was still surprised by her hair. She looked different, more chiseled. Sharper edged. She touched his forearm.

"I've got to make a few calls," he said. "Then a friend of mine from Homicide is meeting us for coffee."

"Homicide?"

He looked down at her. "They classified it a homicide."

"I know this sounds horrible, but I'm relieved," she said. "It means it's not my fault."

"It wouldn't have been anyway. Don't listen to your mother."

She rose and walked naked to the bathroom, her body muscular and sleek. He admired her, just took her in like he would any great, natural act of God. There was a slight ache in his gut this morning, and he needed coffee. The ache wasn't physical, he knew that. It was something totally selfish and melancholy: he could fall in love with her. It wasn't her looks and it wasn't apart from that either. But he couldn't let himself fall, and he half-knew she was using him, and he didn't care. Being with him made her feel safe. Being with her made him feel. And that hadn't happened in a long while.

Don't think about it, Mr. B, he told himself. Nothing lasts anyway. Even the ones that do make some kind of sense.

He flipped open the yellow pages, got the number for Southwest Airlines, and made reservations for them to fly back to Albuquerque tomorrow morning.

Then he took out a scrap of paper from his briefcase and dialed Quintana's number. "I'm sorry, Lieutenant Quintana is not in at the moment," said the dispatcher. "Can he return your call?"

When Harm gave his name, the dispatcher put him on hold for a moment, then came back on the line. "Lieutenant Quintana asked me to get hold of him on the radio if you called. He'll call you right back. Your number, please?"

Harm slipped on jeans, waiting for the phone to jangle as he yanked the drapes apart and the brilliant morning sun blasted in. He slid the glass door open and was about to step out onto the balcony when the phone rang.

"Quintana here. Been on the phone all morning with L.A. Nobody seems to know much of a goddamn thing. Only prints on the weapon are Jacobs's, mostly his prints on the car. No witnesses. So I gave up and went to mass with my wife. You got anything?"

Harm ran it down for him, everything, even Nyia's plan, the sending of the letters.

"That sounds tricky. Risky. Did you talk to the L.A.P.D. about it yet?" asked Quintana.

Harm said no, he'd wanted to run it by him first. "But the letters," Harm added, "she already sent them out."

Quintana was silent. Finally he said, "Let's wait until you get back here to set something up. I want to talk it over with Nyia in person."

Quintana was all right. Harm had always worked well with cops. He wasn't a renegade detective. Had been too long in those black shoes. The more they all knew, the better; that was how he saw it. Quintana didn't have anything new for him, except that Mirina Jacobs was determined to go on with the film. Even today she was directing reshoots of scenes with a new actress brought in to replace Tess Juran. She seemed relentless, Quintana said, unable to stop.

"So you'll be back here tomorrow?" asked Quintana.

"Mid-afternoon," said Harm. "And I've got a favor to ask. Those fan letters, I had some of them sent down to a crime lab in Albuquerque. Before I was in much contact with you. Could you get in touch with them and see what came out of that, if anything?" Harm gave him the name and number of the lab and Nyia came out of the bathroom. She fumbled in the suitcase for clothes. Harm said good-bye to Quintana and hung up.

"Hungry?" he asked. Nyia seemed clear-headed but quiet. He knew that in spite of leaving Leonard years ago, she'd never really resolved things with the man. His death would be rolling into her like fog now, along with her fears about her own safety. He saw that her plan about the letters was some kind of an emblem of salvation for her. Taking some kind of action was the light in the darkness of all this.

Just as they were about to leave the room, Nyia said she had to make a call. She dialed a number, examining a fingernail as she waited for an answer. She pressed the button down and dialed a second number.

"Nyia Wyatt for Suzanne," she said. "I'm in L.A. Is Suzanne still in Santa Fe?" Service, thought Harm. Nyia paused, listening. "I understand. No, she hasn't had any way to reach me here. She did speak with my mother this morning? No, I'm not staying there. Listen. Here's the number where I can be reached until tomorrow morning. But will you tell Suzanne that I'll be returning to New Mexico tomorrow? That's right. Thanks."

They walked out into the dark hallway, down the elevator, and out through the lobby into the sweet June morning. There should be nothing wrong on a day like this, Harm thought.

She took his arm as they walked the two blocks to the beach, the ocean dazzling and the boardwalk already crowded with runners, skaters, skateboarders, rollerbladers, walkers, gawkers, and weirdos. They got a table outside, ordered blessed coffee and then Harm spotted Hirsch in silver glasses at the entry. He always looked like such a cop, button-down white shirt, sleeves rolled up, navy slacks, and the tough-guy silver sunglasses. Hirsch was big, six-five, an overweight former college linebacker who enjoyed food. As he came over to the table, he took his glasses off. Harm introduced him to Nyia and he acted like it was nothing, she could be anyone.

"Here's what we got," said Hirsch. "Some of it's rough. Are you sure you want to listen to this?" he asked Nyia.

"Go on ahead," she said. "I've got to know sometime."

"First, the weapon was a .38—same as what was used during that break-in at your house, but not the type of gun used to kill Robin Reese. That was a rifle. The only prints on the .38 were Jacobs's. But they were in an odd configuration."

"What do you mean?"

"His prints were those of a man holding a gun in a conventional stance, pointing the gun away from himself at a target."

"So what?" Nyia asked.

"When a person shoots himself . . ." Hirsch paused.

"Go on," she urged.

Harm slipped his arm across the back of Nyia's chair. "A person will usually hold the weapon backwards, aimed at the mouth, and pull the trigger with his thumb, unless he was firing into the side of his head. But Jacobs's was a mouth wound. Are you sure you can hear this stuff?"

Nyia drank her coffee, just looked at Hirsch directly, nodding once.

"The car had prints—mostly Jacobs's. Apparently the car was cleaned weekly by Jacobs's housekeeper, even if Jacobs wasn't in town.

"The autopsy revealed that the point of entry of the bullets—two of them—was odd. His head was tilted back, chin up, with the angle of firing being slightly down toward the base of the throat. This is not indicative of a usual suicide. Most people look down at the weapon, and fire the weapon upward.

"It is very conceivable," said Hirsch, "that someone held his head back, fired, and pressed the gun into his hand, where it then fell to the floor of the car.

"There were traces of alcohol and Prozac in the body. This would concur with both Mrs. Jacobs's reports and his own—according to your statement, Nyia—that he had gone off medication several days ago.

"Another interesting thing is that Jacobs was in town to file for Chapter Eleven bankruptcy for Visionfilm Productions. Johnson got hold of the lawyer this morning. Apparently there were a lot of papers in the backseat of the Mercedes."

"I tried getting hold of the guy this morning," said Harm.

"He was having breakfast with us," said Hirsch. "Could have been a motivation for suicide. But since the death's been ruled a homicide, you got to look at it this way: somebody benefits more from Jacobs's death than from his filing for bankruptcy."

Harm told Hirsch about John Sand, about the alleged prenuptial contract.

"That's good, Mr. B, you're saving me time. I knew there was some good reason to buy you coffee. In addition to the lovely and beautiful present company, of course." Hirsch smiled. Harm knew he'd fawn sooner or later.

"What about filing for divorce?" asked Nyia. "He told me that was why he was in town. I had no idea Visionfilm was in trouble financially."

Hirsch consulted his notes. "Lawyer said Jacobs had papers drawn up for divorce proceedings a year ago."

"A year?" Nyia leaned forward against the white tablecloth.

"But he never did actually file. He had papers drawn up, but didn't act on them."

"He was lying, then?" Nyia looked out toward the

ocean, shaking her head. "God, that was convincing."
She started to laugh, but it was a bitter laugh. She
stopped short.

Hirsch glanced at his watch. "I've got to head back
downtown. How long you in town for, Bo?"

"Back to the land of enchantment tomorrow."

"I might come out fishing sometime. Got any
good trout spots? I could bring Seth. He misses Nickie
anyway." Then he stood, shook both their hands and
left.

"So do I," said Harm. That was who he really needed
to call this morning.

"You know, I used to live around here," said Harm.
"Up the hill there in a little bungalow. I'd ride Nickie
down the boardwalk on the back of my bike. I like living
in an orchard by a dried-up ditch a lot better."

Harm turned over the napkin and jotted down: *Call
Dierdre Fine, Nickie.* "You want to go for a walk?" he
asked. Nyia seemed contemplative, eyes on the water
and the loud gulls.

Hirsch had picked up the tab and they headed
south walking quietly, stopping to look at T-shirts,
Zoobaz, Spandex miniskirts, baseball hats. He bought a
couple things for Nickie and Nyia bought Nickie a pair
of purple sunglasses.

Walking on, she told him a dream she'd had, a
secret message in a black box turning into birds. It
made Harm recall his own dream, which he told to her.
"It's like some part of my dream mind thinks it has this
whole thing figured out, but poof—it's gone."

She stopped walking and turned to him. "But
maybe you do. Your dream ties in with the computer,
Harm. Those diskettes found in that truck, Nims's. And
the dot-matrix printing on the letters and the screenplay Robin's mom gave you. In a way, we had the same
dream," she went on. "A similar image. The information,
the answer, is recorded inside a computer, like the
black box in the cabin of a plane they find after a crash.

Your dream is saying the letters and the screenplay are connected. But how?"

"That's it," he said. "I've been thinking that the person writing the letters to you is the same one writing this screenplay. But Robin's letter said there were two people working on it. Maybe one of them is writing letters, and the other is making the letters into a screenplay. One person is this obsessive, demented fan of yours, and the other is someone documenting that person's sickness in the form of a story."

"And the screenplay wouldn't even have to exist as printed material. It could all be on computer disks," said Nyia.

"It could all be erased too." Harm turned and headed back in the direction of the hotel, Nyia running to catch up to him. "I'm going to call Quintana and see if he can get a warrant to search the offices and computer files of both Mirina Jacobs and Dan Howe."

TWENTY-SEVEN —⭐

HARM HAD PUT HIS GUN INTO HIS SUITCASE AND checked it on the Southwest flight to Albuquerque Monday morning. He wouldn't need it on the plane, he thought. Ever since yesterday, he'd been wishing he had more experience in field investigation, enough to have some sixth sense about being followed. He kept scanning three hundred and sixty degrees, trying not to be obvious. This wasn't his favorite position to be in. He liked to be the follower, the observer, the one with the hidden camera. He tried to open his peripheral vision, like he did in a duck blind as a kid with his grandfather. Dawn. Wet. Cold. You knew where you were and you knew they were coming. All you had to do was wait.

So he was relieved to be back in the middle seat of row seventeen, glad that for close to an hour he could stop that field-vision. Rest, think. Before touching down in New Mexico again.

Nyia turned the page of her magazine, then gazed out the window. Western California, the Mojave, below, red dust in the cracks of the earth.

He was glad to be moving again. The rest of Sunday had been long. Calls to Quintana, putting off Dierdre Fine, explaining why he'd stood her up at the Rose Café. Telling her just enough, but protecting Nyia's privacy and the integrity of the case. She said she was coming back to Santa Fe, too, that it was the biggest story of her life and she was staying with Nyia until they found out who it was. Nyia hadn't wanted to say good-bye to her mother. Enough, she'd said. I can't be around her unless she goes through treatment. Extremely unlikely, she'd added.

They'd made love again, the gold drapes pulled shut, and Nyia napped in the hum of the hotel air-conditioning while he went over and over his index cards, shuffling them and reshuffling them into a hundred patterns. He knew in his gut they were close and closing in. What they needed was evidence, something hard and clean.

The plane tipped sharply, banking down toward the mountains, and Harm remembered two years ago, flying into Arizona for that meeting in Tempe. That caffeine-edge of adrenaline in his belly. But he'd felt calm the morning of the meeting with his briefcase full of figures and money. He'd walked calmly in the hot sunshine into that trap. He had a bad taste for traps.

Nyia slept in the car on the drive from Albuquerque, waking as they exited into Santa Fe. Quintana was waiting at his house when they arrived, sitting in an unmarked car, reading the paper. They shook hands and Quintana told Nyia, "I understand that you got scared. But don't take off like that again. If things get real bad, we'll make some kind of arrangement."

"Like hide me?" she asked. "That's what I was trying to do."

"Didn't do much good, did it?" Quintana said. "Funny. People try to hide and they're easy to find. Other people disappear and you never can trace them. Usually it's kids. Custody battles and kidnappings. But, Miss Wyatt, if you feel like that again, what I'm saying is this—let me or Mr. Bohland know what's going on. We need your help too."

Harm opened the door and smiled at Quintana. The place was spotless, all evidence of the trashing cleaned up. "Thanks," he said.

"No problem," said Quintana. He sat in a hard-backed wooden chair. "I don't know if we're going to need that plan of yours, Miss Wyatt. I'm not dismissing it, but we're getting some things to go on now."

Harm stood, listening. Nyia put down her satchel and sat on the couch.

"I had somebody pick up those letters and the report from that crime lab this morning like you asked me to. There were hair samples in several of the letters and we did a DNA analysis. Warrants are being drawn up now to search not only the Jacobses' premises and Howe's rooms at the hotel where he's staying, but we're also getting personal search warrants. That means you search a person's body. We've got to get hair samples to see if the hair in the letters matches any suspect, as well as fingerprints. It's taking a little while to get all ready; we don't want to go into it unprepared, and we've got to get permission from a judge and prove we've got probable cause. It's very important how you gather this type of information. You can get just what you need to nail somebody, only to have it thrown out in court."

Quintana stood, looking around. "I wouldn't stay here. Been broken into once before, you know? You need a place to stay, you let me know. I've got a lot of cousins. Might not be a four-star hotel, Miss Wyatt, but they cook the best southwestern cuisine you can imagine and most of them are damn good shots, even the women. Especially the women." He headed toward the door, then turned back. "One more thing. I don't know why this caught my eye. When we were cleaning up the place, we found this."

He took from his pocket a small black feather. "It was the only thing we found that stood out," said Quintana. "You got a feathered dress, Nyia? Or a hat?"

Nyia glanced at Harm. "The hat from the film, from the New York sequence, Manuel Moravio had it with him the other night at dinner. He asked me to wear it."

"Excellent," said Quintana. "Now we're getting somewhere. I can include the costume department and Mr. Moravio's quarters in the warrant. I'll be heading out to Tesuque a bit later when the warrants are all ready."

"That's where we're going too," said Harm. "There's a meeting for the entire Visionfilm crew about continuing on with the film."

"Be careful out there," said Quintana. "Keep your eyes open."

Harm pulled up in front of the ranch, parking near the wagon wheel that leaned against the giant cottonwood. Jack Drieser came to the open door, stepped out onto the gravel drive. As Nyia got out of the Jeep, Jack went to her, embracing her. Harm pressed his arm unconsciously to his side, the gun there in the holster. He wished they were back in the plane, circling open space.

Drieser held Nyia's face in his hands, looking into her eyes. Harm could tell she was shaky, being back here. Drieser quietly said, "I'm really sorry the way it all happened. I don't think any of us realized, you know, how things were with Leonard. How bad things really were."

"Do you really want to finish the film, Jack? Do you think you can?"

Good, thought Harm. He'd felt her shift into acting.

"Yeah, I do," said Jack. "And I'll be honest with you. Not for Leonard or Tess or even Mirina. I'm selfish. I want to do it because it's my first real lead. And because I'm in it with you. And because I think it's going to be a damn good movie."

Nyia stepped into the house with him. "I'm so glad you're here," she said.

Drieser said, "What did you do to your fucking hair?"

Just inside the door on a long table there was a display of clay bowls, baskets, an arrangement of dried flowers. In a square basket next to a wood sculpture of a howling coyote, there was a stack of mail. Harm watched as Nyia reached for it, flipping through it quickly.

"Everybody's out back by the pool," said Jack.

"We'll be there in a minute," said Nyia.

Harm followed Nyia through the living room out onto the patio, went ahead through the open French doors, pausing briefly. *What?* he thought. *Go back a minute. What did I miss?* He turned around. *Strange sensation of going back for something you forgot, then forgetting what it was.* There, in the foyer, under the far end of the long table, fallen on the terra-cotta tiles, lay a single leather glove. He picked it up and stuffed it into his pocket.

No prints. Not on Jacobs's car, not in the cabin, not on the buck knife. Gloves, he thought. A man's brown leather glove.

Stepping out into the shade of the portico, he paused as Mirina stood. "Harm, thank you. Thank you for bringing Nyia home." She motioned for him to sit down.

Many of the people from the dinner party were gathered again, sitting in chairs in the lengthening shade beside the pool. He nodded at Dierdre—she'd gotten an early flight first thing this morning. She was in some new costume, black leather pants and chain mail, like some outgrown blond Cher. But she leaned back in her chair and put her red hightops on the table in front of her. She had a tape recorder going. Mirina must have given her full access to write about the film. If Visionfilm were losing money, they needed all the free publicity they could get for the film. Well, that wouldn't be a problem now.

He looked for Howe. He sat upright in front, near Mirina, in that fishing vest with the pockets, a visor.

There was Paulette, the producer he'd spoken with at the dinner party, standing next to Suzanne Scolfield in the late shade of afternoon. Gino and Connie, chewing gum. Jack and Nyia sat down and Mirina continued. Where was Moravio? wondered Harm.

"We figure on three days," Mirina said. "Three long days. All we really have left are a few sequences in the motel—that can be done in one day if we stay focused. And then the train scene. All of you know Katharine Palmer. She's come in to do Tess Juran's scenes and complete the film with us.

"Katharine, we're indebted to you. You're saving us."

Everyone applauded. Mirina went on. "Jack Drieser and Dan Howe will be assisting me in directing, and Manuel Moravio is going to take over script development and changes, although, from here on out, we will go with what is written. This should ease things and help us to finish on time. No more one-hundred-eighty-degree turns."

She fielded questions for a half-hour and then the group dispersed. Mirina put her arm around Nyia and they walked together back toward Leonard's office. Nyia glanced back once at Harm and he followed.

Mirina motioned for them both to sit. She stood for a moment behind Leonard's desk, a file before her, paging through notes and papers before sitting down. She let out a deep sigh then and put her head down on the desk. Nyia hesitated, then went to her. Mirina put an arm around her, shoulders shaking, a sob without sound, something never let out. Mirina sat up, held Nyia's hand a moment, her eyes dry. She wore her black hair loose on her shoulders. She'd aged, thought Harm, in the five days since he'd met her. She looked her age. Frozen, he thought. Then saw he was wrong. She swallowed hard, twice.

"I can't seem to cry." Mirina touched her throat. "It's all stuck right here. I suppose I'll break down a year from now. It just doesn't feel right to do it now. My family was like that back in Prague. Stoic. Survivors."

Nyia sat down in a leather chair.

"Everyone is so kind to do this. Without all of your generosity . . ." Mirina held out open palms. "Thank you, Nyia. I know how hard this is for you."

"Like you said, Mirina. It's for Leonard."

"I've been on the phone to lawyers all day." Mirina sighed. "I need to tell you why Leonard flew to L.A. in the first place. It's the money, it's Visionfilm. Things have been terribly mismanaged, I'm afraid. Leonard was getting ready to file for bankruptcy.

"That's why I'm pressing on with the film. Not just for Leonard. It's to save Visionfilm. Maybe it's to save me too. I don't understand why anyone would want to hurt us. Did you find out anything in Los Angeles, Harm, that would help me to understand what is happening? My actresses . . . my husband. Don't you see? I can't lose the film too. I can't lose Visionfilm now. So please don't judge me, as some of the crew have, for trying to finish the film. I really don't have a choice. And, anyway, I always believed in

Leonard's genius. You know what he'd tell us, don't you, Nyia? Put all the emotion right back into the film."

Mirina sorted through the papers on the desk. "Here's your mail, Nyia." Mirina extended a pile of envelopes and magazines to Nyia. Harm watched as Nyia spotted the blue letters.

Mirina glanced at Harm. "A number of those letters have come to the house today."

Nyia looked up, surprised. Harm closed his eyes. He'd forgotten to tell Nyia that he'd mentioned the letters to Mirina, as a way of getting her to open up. He remembered her telling about the envelopes spilling out onto her bed. *Hair follicles,* he thought. Quintana had found that hair sample. There could easily have been hairs in Mirina's bed, on her pillows.

Mirina repeated to Nyia what she had told Harm about misplacing the box of stationery. "Are you going to open them?" Mirina asked.

"Not just now," said Nyia. "I think I'll wait."

Mirina stood. "I'm going to finish packing up some things. I'm not going to be staying at the ranch. It's too haunted. Here is the number where I can be reached, a bed and breakfast in town."

Nyia looked down at the mail as the click of Mirina's shoes faded down the hall. She took out three or four letters, turning them over.

"I coded them," she reminded Harm. "Leonard. Mirina. Manuel Moravio, all sent here in care of the ranch. Mirina never opened any of them. And she's intercepted the one for Moravio. I bet he never saw it."

Then Nyia took one more letter from the stack and held it up for Harm to see. The address was typed in the familiar computer dot matrix. "There's no postmark on it. It was just left here." Nyia handed the letter to him.

"You open it," she said. "What does it say?"

He tore the envelope open. "It says, 'I'm ready too.'"

THERE'S NO TIME LEFT.

My entire life these past years has been one long hallway to a particular door. I've entered other rooms along the way, this door and that one, but always heading toward this final point of exit. And I'm here. I know where you have gone, I know where you are exactly at this moment. I have this evening to create the final scene. There will be no edit. This is live theater, total improvisation, and the outcome is unknown.

Seeing you again, with that halo of fear around you just shining, I understood: I have to get to you before she does. She is coming for you, I am coming for you, and it is only a question of which of us has your best interest at heart. I know you'll see the wisdom in choosing to come with me. You'll see that according to her plot treatment you have no such choice. No choice at all.

And having received your letter, I know we're both ready to make the right choice.

After the crew meeting, I went out to her car parked along the dirt road to the ranch. She asked me to go out there with her, talk in private. Everything is okay now, she said, now that all the evidence has been destroyed, now that the script has been trashed. No one will ever know anything. There's no way anyone can trace who wrote those letters, she said. She handed me the cash in a white envelope. This is for all you put into the project, she said. I'm sorry we can't take it into production, it's too risky now. You know that, don't you? she asked. I said I understood. I understood my life's work had just been invalidated by this stack of bills. A simple exchange. I didn't tell her that. I kept it to myself.

She got out and slammed the door. I don't know why I picked it up off the floor, wadded down between the bucket seats. She was rummaging in the trunk for something and I unfolded the tissue scrap, a receipt for gas at a service station in Las Vegas and the date, July 1, yesterday. It even showed the time—8:23 A.M.

I stuffed it into my pocket and got out of the car, walked back to the house. Las Vegas—July 1. And that is when I knew exactly what had happened. Five-hour drive to Las Vegas from Santa Fe. Catch a flight to L.A. . . .

That was when I understood with absolute certainty who killed Leonard Jacobs.

That was when I understood with absolute certainty that you and I, darling, will be her next logical choice.

But that option will never be made available to her.

So I've come back to my room, finished packing. There's one final scene to be shot. I sit down at the computer and write this, the screen glowing in the dark room. Look at my watch. You'll be there now. I know what I have to do.

TWENTY-EIGHT ☆

"THE TRAIN SCENE," SAID NYIA. "I KNOW THEY'RE bringing in a double for the scene when the car is on the tracks. But I don't even want to get in that car. Not after what happened with the Harley."

The French doors of the Pink Adobe were open to the courtyard, dusk light against the reddish walls, the lantern lit already. Nyia turned the glass jar with the flickering candle, staring at the pulsing flame.

"We can have Quintana's people look the car over, test-drive it," said Harm.

She sipped her margarita, looking around now at the Indonesian masks on the wall, on the trunk of the tree that went up through the mahogany bar, up through the roof by the skylight. Harm continued, "But what I want to know is this: how can you be scared to do the train scene and willing to participate in a sting to pull this guy in?"

"Control," said Nyia. "Because it's my scene. I'm directing. A car could explode, a train could derail. But waiting in a room somewhere with you and Quintana ready and I'm wired and I have a gun—"

"They might not want you armed."

"But I am armed. I'm armed now."

"Where?"

She glanced down at the pocket of her jacket. "I got it from the back room when we stopped at your house."

"That's concealment, Nyia."

"You're concealing," she said.

"I'm licensed to conceal."

Suddenly she reached across the table and took his hand.

"You're hyper," said Harm. "You're shaking, aren't you?"

"It's called fear," Nyia said quietly. "Leonard used to love it when I got like this. He thought I gave my best performance when I was afraid."

"If we go through with this sting, then I hope that's true."

"So do I," she said. "You know, I thought of something really strange today. Remember I told you that after my house was burglarized, I knew something was missing, I just knew it, but I couldn't figure out what it was?"

Harm nodded.

"I figured it out. I thought of it this morning at the hotel in Venice as I was packing, just putting my things in the bag, rolling up my sweatshirt and thinking about how my robe was missing from the cabin.

"That is the second time that's happened. I'm missing another robe, one that Leonard bought for me in Italy. It was one I only wore when we traveled and I only wore it with him. I haven't been able to find it in a year or so. It was silk, a peachy sort of champagne color. Harm, I think it was stolen by whoever broke into my house in Laurel Canyon."

"What made you think of it?"

"That's what's so weird. Leonard asked me about it. It was the last thing he ever said to me, in fact. He came back into the room as he was leaving my mother's and asked me about that robe, whatever became of it. That's what was missing from my house. That was the one thing. But because I only wore it when I was with him and because we'd broken up, I didn't miss it. I just knew something was gone from the closet."

The waitress leaned over the table. "Excuse me," she said. "Are you Miss Wyatt?"

Nyia nodded.

"There's a phone call for you at the bar—down at the end there."

Nyia looked over at Harm.

"Did you tell anyone we were coming here?" he asked.

"No, you did. You told Dierdre," she whispered. "Just as we were going out to the car."

Nyia pushed her chair back, but Harm motioned for her to wait.

"Wait a minute. I don't like this. I just don't like it. You're too visible. You go to the phone, it's like you're on stage."

Nyia glanced at the small windows that faced the street, the wide-open area of French doors open to the courtyard. "You mean, you think somebody with a telescopic range on a gun is sitting out there on that stone wall in front of that church?"

"He watched you here once before, remember? He got you on video—and we didn't even notice him doing it."

"Why don't you just come with me?" she said.

"I accept your invitation," the voice on the phone said.

She didn't recognize him. A man's voice, almost a

whisper. Trace of a foreign accent. Long vowels, Soviet, hard consonants. Eastern European, but not like Mirina. And definitely male.

Harm pressed close to her, listening.

"But of course your selection of a meeting place won't do at all. Wherever it might be, it's obviously a trap. How do you say it—a setup?"

"That's not true," she said. "I want to live. I see that I can only live by being with you, not apart. I need to surrender to that, and I have. I'm only waiting for your directions. Just tell me what you want, I told you I'm ready. You've captivated me. I can't believe I'm actually hearing your voice."

"I can't believe I'm hearing yours."

"I told you I want to be with you. I want to go away. I want you to take me away. Just tell me what to do."

"I'm sorry about Leonard, Nyia. I know how much you cared about him. I just want to assure you that I had nothing to do with that at all. But I know who did. And that's why we have to leave tonight. Because we're next. Both of us. There's no time left now."

Nyia raised her eyes to meet Harm's and leaned back into the corner behind the bar, scanning the room, the small windows. Her temple throbbed against the receiver.

"I want you to go to El Nido," said the voice, "tonight around ten. Wait at the bar. If I believe you came alone, you'll receive a call. And I'll tell you what to do from there. We meet on my terms or not at all. It has to be exactly right. Do you have that?"

"El Nido, the restaurant out in Tesuque," she repeated. "Ten. Alone. Fine."

"Nyia?" he asked.

"Yes?"

"Are you afraid?"

She said nothing.

Then his voice sounded different. The accent gone. She still couldn't place it. "It's just that I love you so much. And you have always been so far out of reach. I don't want you to be afraid of me. I don't know how else I could have been sure, made sure that you would want to be with me, that you would actually choose to be with me of your own free will."

"But, darling, I have no will anymore. You are my will."

The voice laughed. "God," he said. "You are good."

The voice paused and Harm bent closer to the phone to hear over the music in the bar. "There's one scene that will have to be done over," said the voice.

"What?" said Nyia.

Dial tone. Nyia set the receiver down on the phone, and turned back to Harm.

"Look," Harm said. "I'm going to call Quintana. We don't have to create some big setup. He's setting himself up. All we have to do is play into it." He took out Quintana's card from his wallet and dialed his number. The bartender turned up the music on the stereo and Harm faced the wall, covering one ear.

He spoke to Nyia over the blaring music. "I'm going to have Quintana meet us back at my house," he said loudly.

Nyia touched his arm to tell him she was going to go to the bathroom, would be right back, but he held up one hand, motioning *just a minute*. She walked toward the French doors. The restrooms were just across the small courtyard in the restaurant.

Later she would think, *That is how simple death is. It just waits for the right moment and no amount of protection or planning can save you.* She would run it through in her mind, the stupidity of it. But her mind had been full of what was coming: El Nido, cops outside in the parking lot. Ten o'clock, the bar. Action. Begin. She had stopped paying attention to the present moment.

And besides, there was some dumb, imagined safety in the fact that the man had just called her. Unconsciously she'd assumed: *Because he has called me here, he is some-*

where else. Whoever he is, he's not here. So her guard was down as she crossed the courtyard, glancing up at the cobalt light of the evening and the first stars. He was just walking into the courtyard from the street. When she saw him, he looked so relieved to see her.

"Nyia! Thank God you're still here," he called. "It's Mirina. You've got to come. She's having a complete breakdown."

Nyia stepped toward him, of course she did. She did not turn and run away. He took her arm, his car was parked on the street just outside the courtyard, the engine running.

It was an instant before the thought registered: *No.* Or: *Wait.* In that instant he shoved her down into the car, her forehead slamming against the steel edge of the upper door, the butt of the gun sharp against her temple, the noticing of it before actually feeling any pain and that odd sensation of the world disintegrating into tiny dots, coming apart, falling. Falling a long distance into black.

TWENTY-NINE ─ ☆

SHE WAS THERE. AND THEN SHE WAS GONE.

Harm hung up the phone. The call had taken, what, a minute? Two minutes. Quintana had agreed to meet them at his house immediately. He glanced back at the table, the small candle still burning, looking first one way, then the other. It was dark now and the courtyard was empty, a couple turning the corner into the restaurant. That was it. She'd just gone to the restroom. He waited nervously for a moment, then asked the head waiter to have someone check the ladies room. "It's an emergency," he told him.

A waitress checked and came out shaking her head. "I'm sorry, sir. There is no one at all in there."

The street in front of the Pink Adobe was not crowded. Strolling couples. Empty cars. Harm ran around back to the parking lot behind the restaurant, through the lines of cars toward the capitol building.

His car was parked up against a crumbling adobe wall. Over the wall, a yard. Swingset, apple trees.

"Nyia!" he shouted. Again.

Returning to the Pink Adobe bar, he grabbed her purse from the chair, threw down a ten for the drinks, then hurried out, frantic now. She wouldn't leave, he knew she wouldn't just leave like that. He had looked away for one minute, turned to face the goddamn wall, the loud music. He couldn't hear Quintana.

Then back inside. There was the waitress who'd been serving them.

"The woman I was with. Did you see her go?"

She thought for a minute. "Yeah. Someone picked her up, a car was waiting for her. I thought you went with her. I thought maybe there was some kind of emergency with the phone call and all. I thought you were going to run out on me."

"A car. What kind of car?" He was yelling.

"Hey, look, I didn't really see the car, all right? Let me see. It was dark. Blue, maybe. Black. A sports car. Kind of a fancy black sports car, I think."

"Did you see who was with her, who was driving?"

She thought for a moment. "No, just her. 'Cause just then I realized who Miss Wyatt was and I was, like, impressed and then worrying about your tab getting paid."

"But nothing else about the guy?"

"What is it? Is everything okay?"

He just looked at her helplessly. "Old, young, tall, bald, black, white?"

She shrugged. "Honestly. I never really saw the guy."

"But it was a guy?"

"I don't know about that either."

He grabbed the phone on the wall and dialed the ranch. No answer. He tried Suzanne's room at the hotel and she picked it up on the first ring. "Oh, God," she breathed when he told her what had happened.

"What kind of car does Dan Howe drive?" He was shouting.

"I'm not sure. It's a rental. Mirina might know. I just spoke with her. She was heading out to the ranch later tonight to pick up some things she left behind. Have you called that Quintana?" Suzanne demanded.

Harm backed the Jeep out of the parking place. Jolting forward, the Jeep screeched out onto Old Santa Fe Trail. Back toward Acequia Madre, back home. Quintana would be there in minutes.

She got in a car with someone. It had to have been someone she knew. But even so, why did she? She didn't trust anyone right now. She'd lapsed into trust. One false second of trust. Why?

He braked into the parking spot beside the house. *Quintana not here yet. Think. Think: Someone who knew where they were.* Dierdre knew. Why did he tell anyone where they were going? Why Dierdre? Because she could play a fucking game of pool? Who did she tell? Who overheard them?

Then he realized, Nyia had that gun. Said she knew how to use one. Played a cop's wife in that movie. But he didn't really know if she did. And like the mace she'd tried to use against the assailant during the break-in, a gun could be used against her. But at least she had it. It was someone at that crew meeting, definitely. Not some random person. Knew they were at the Pink Adobe. Had seen her, recognized her.

He unlocked the door of the house and pushed it open.

Where was Quintana? Why didn't they know more? Only fragments, claws and hair follicles, types of bullets. He needed something conclusive. He hated this. He wished he were back in numbers, tax returns, audits. It was so clear there. Things added up, goddamn it.

Suddenly he thought of her briefcase, her treasures

and trinkets. He'd found things there before, the post-card. Photos. He raced down the hallway, slipping on the rug. He'd shoved it back in that closet. He took it now and dumped it out, scrambling through the junk, looking for something, anything that would speak to him, tell him where she had gone. Who she was with.

What was all this shit? Earrings, buttons, wind-up toys, bits of lace all tangled in a fishing fly. Feather. Fishing.

That little feather found right here in his house. Photos scattered throughout the mess of objects on the bed. He began picking them up, frantically. Slow down, man. Slow. Think.

There it was, the group shot down in Manzanillo, taken out on the boat the night before Robin was killed. Nyia, Robin, Dan Howe, people he didn't recognize, Mirina, Leonard, Jack, Dierdre.

Wait a minute, he thought. The other day, the day he'd first met Dierdre. She'd been wearing a straw-colored hat over her white-blond hair. He pressed his eyes shut, trying to picture the hat, the brim. Wasn't there a tiny fan of feathers stuck in the cloth strap around the brim? *There was,* he thought. *Yes.*

The next snapshot in his hands, fish spread out on a rock. Ferns. Lure, bait. He picked up the fishing fly, lace all wound in its tiny brass hook. The screenplay fragments had spoken of luring the actress, using bait. What else had it said? *The hook of a kiss.*

Next to the display of freshly caught fish, a hand, a man's hand, and next to that, there it was, in the corner of the photograph: the buck knife. To clean the fish. Black buck knife, the one he'd found behind the bed in the cabin. The one that had sliced that quilt open.

Dan Howe wore that vest, that sportsman's vest with all the pockets. Fly fishing, Mr. Outdoorsman. Take Nyia fishing, calm her down. The fishing trip in this photograph took place the summer after she'd broken off with Leonard.

Then it clicked in him. Alignment. And, yes. Because the straw cowboy hat did not belong to Dierdre. It belonged to Jack Drieser. She had given it back to him that morning on the set. *You left this in my room.*

His throat ached tight as he threw the photo down. The image of Jack and Nyia that day in filming, making love for the camera, how he wondered if they really did it. The insistence in those letters. *I can only love you in the story. If I can get you into the story, you are mine. Unzip the wedding dress, over and over. Until death do us part. . . .*

Jack had been that close to loving her. But only in his imagination. Where he had now come to reside. Where was he staying? Out at the ranch? No, that Inn at Bishop's Lodge. Where would he take her? Synchronicity, thought Harm. What would he do? Leave her in a car on a goddamn train track?

No, he'd play it out. Voice on the phone as he'd bent close to Nyia. He'd said one scene had to be done over. Drieser wanted her. Was consumed with her. Consummation.

That was it. He'd do the honeymoon scene again with her, only this time really make love to her, consummate the marriage if only in his sick mind. Where would he take her? That motel up near Española. Half-hour drive up there.

Just then Quintana pulled up outside next to the Jeep, headlights glaring against the house like spotlights.

THIRTY

THE CAR HIT GRAVEL, BUMPED OVER RUTS AND pulled up near the far side of the house. Nyia put her hand to the side of her head, then sat up too quickly, a knife-sharp throb as she jerked toward the door, reaching for the handle. Jack snapped the emergency brake up, grabbed the gun that rested between his legs and lifted the gun to her head. She couldn't help it, she turned away. Near the dashboard at the front of the car, she glimpsed the cellular car phone. "You called me from your car," she whispered. "Don't do this, Jack. Why are you doing this?" Again she touched the side of her head, bleeding. The backs of her eyes felt scalded.

"What I want you to do is get out of the car and head over to the cabin as if nothing at all is wrong," he said. "Kind of lighthearted, you're glad to be back here, glad to be home. Do that thing with your hair, you know?" For the first time, he looked at her, looked her in the eyes. "Oh, I forgot. Your hair. I liked it better before." He waited. "Go ahead now." He gestured with the gun. "And don't look back at the camera."

She glanced toward the main house, all dark now.

"No one's here," he said, answering her unasked question.

"All that's left is just you and me. Finally. Go ahead now. I don't want you to have to do it twice."

"Do what twice, Jack?"

"The scene, Nyia. The scene."

As she opened the car door, her hand brushed against her jacket pocket, Harm's gun there, hard against her thigh. *Not Jack,* she thought. *Sweet, tender Jack.* Then stopped herself. *Right. Just go ahead and care about the man who's trying to kill you.*

For a moment, she considered bolting for the main house—but it would probably be locked. What's my best shot? she thought. Get him out of the car, shoot. Even if you only injure him. Then call on the car phone, 911.

"Go on," he said. "We don't have much time."

She stepped slowly from the car, feeling faint as she stood. He'd hit her hard; metallic taste in her mouth. One foot in front of the other. She heard him get out of the car, slam both doors.

"Keep walking," he said. The hills behind the house were black against the blue night. The horses raised their heads as she neared the corral. She heard the crows overhead in the cottonwoods. Was this it then? Pure resonant simplicity of image—that was all there was to it, wasn't it? No story at all, just moments you pass through and don't see, until you think: *This is the end of everything.*

"Right," he called. "Now turn and look at the horses for a second."

Then it struck her; *he was directing.* The way he was talking to her, instructing her. Just like Leonard would do before a scene.

But directing wasn't absolute control, Leonard had

taught her that. *Improvise,* she thought. She turned to face him.

Jack had the video camera on, resting on his shoulder. She couldn't see his gun, but as he came toward her, he took it from his pocket, nudged it up. "Continue," he ordered.

Play into it, she thought. Hand against her pocket, the gun. *Just feel it there. Save it. Right moment. Just the right moment. No other.*

"I'm only going in with you, Jack." Disarm him. Casual. "Come on. Why don't you carry me in? Over the threshold. It would be fitting. You still love me, don't you?" she asked. "This is what you've wanted all along. What we've both wanted."

She burned her eyes into the video camera, his face hidden behind the viewfinder. She gave him the finest, most demure sexual-longing gaze she could muster. Seconds. It was cold now. Early dusk over the foothills. What to do? I can't kill him, she thought. I can't. Shoot him in the shoulder. Or stomach, low down.

Then her own voice, silent but screaming, within. *You have to kill him.*

"Are you coming, then?" she asked.

Nyia turned and entered the cabin, sat on the wooden chair by the table. Where the kerosene lamp had been. How many days ago? Four? Five?

He walked in past her, then turned back, panning the room with the camera.

"Come here," she said.

He came toward her, still holding the gun. She unbuttoned the top two buttons on her shirt, arched her neck back. "I'd like to kiss you. I can't if you've got that thing in front of your face." She was silent. The camera buzzed as he pulled in for a closeup.

Kiss your death, she thought. *Whatever you have to do. Just let him know you're in his scene, but it's not totally his. Improvisation is two ways and it's alive. As soon as you stop acting, you're dead.*

Jack backed up and reached to turn on the lamp beside the bed. "I want you to take off your clothes, Nyia."

She shook her head. "First, I want you to tell me what's going on, Jack."

"You know."

"Tell me anyway. You've got to fill me in. On the story. Especially the back-story, Jack. I mean, if you want me in this scene, what's my motivation? What's gone before? And where are the other principals?"

Without warning he reached into his coat pocket, raised his gun to the side of his head and pulled the trigger. A muffled click. He grinned. Set the gun down on the bedside table. Jack turned off the camera and set it on the chair next to the bed. Then he picked up the gun again, opened the chamber, twirling it with one finger. Empty. No cartridges.

"Pretend," he sang out in a singsong voice.

He fumbled in the nightstand drawer, took out a small cardboard box full of brass cartridges, slid them into the chamber one by one.

"Would you like to lie down here with me?" he asked.

She shook her head. "Not until you tell me some things. Everything. Why should we have any secrets, Jack? Tell me now. A good director knows his story, even if the players don't. He always knows more. Leonard always did. He'd tell me the story, he'd draw me into it. Make it so real for me."

"You really want to know the story?" he asked.

"I have a pretty big part in it," she said. "I should know my part."

For a moment she felt beyond fear, pure in the burning moment, the small yellow disc of light on the wall over the bed where she had slept. He fingered the gun on his thigh. She reminded herself to keep breathing. It would be hard to shoot him facing sideways like that. *In the shoulder. Go for his hand. Too small, what if I missed? Maybe just stand, pull the gun out and fire. Don't think about it, you're still alive, you're still here. Don't think,* she told herself.

His eyes were still on her. "You know I love you, Nyia. I always have."

"Why didn't you just tell me?" she asked.

He shifted on the bed and she tensed. "Do you remember when we first met? Years ago, back in Paris? At the party at Suzanne's? My first part."

"I know."

"No, you don't. You really don't understand at all. I mean, at the party where we met. *That* was my first part. I was acting *then*. I was hired to play a part, not in a film, but in your life."

"What are you talking about?" Nyia asked.

"I was hired to play your lover," he said. "Paid very well, in fact. That summer we spent together after you and Leonard split up. My job was to get you out of Paris for a few weeks, make love to you, provide an interim affair so you would forget all about him."

"But we were never lovers, Jack."

"Only because you didn't fall in love with me," he said. He laughed to himself. "I failed at my part. 'Just friends, Jack. I only want to be just friends. I'm still so unresolved about Leonard. I just don't know.'" He imitated her voice.

Nyia felt sick suddenly, remembering back. "Mirina put you up to this, didn't she?"

He continued without answering her. "I was told by the person who hired me that when things happened twice—repetitions, patterns—it was God's sign to you that love was real. And it was, it was, Nyia. It was real for me. I fell in love with you. But you didn't love me.

"My payment, aside from money, was my first part in a film. A huge break for me. I never intended to fall in love with you. I just got so far into the role, I guess. Maybe it was because you were so out of reach. I saw that you'd never really love me until I was as powerful and as well respected, as successful as Leonard Jacobs. Why would you love some unknown actor?

"So I decided to wait. And instead, I began writing to you. I thought you'd know it was me, the French airmail paper and everything. I liked sending the letters in care of someone you knew, or even bringing them right to where you were staying. Delivering them myself. That's when I started keeping my notes too. I saw the beauty in the story as it was happening."

"Your notes?" said Nyia. Keep him talking, watch, wait.

"You know," he said. "For the story. The story I've been writing to you about. I don't know how I got going on it, but I thought, this would make a good story. The whole thing I was doing with you. Unknown actor becomes obsessed with beautiful actress, writes to her, figures out a way to get her to love him. . . . So I started making notes, a lot of journal entries. Well, not in a journal. In my computer.

"Finally, I showed it to someone. And she started to help me with it, thought it was damn good. She really encouraged me, but now I see it for what it was."

He stopped there, opened the chamber on the gun again, twirled it slowly, checking to make sure each slot had a bullet in it. This was good, thought Nyia. Talk him down. He seemed calmer. Distracted into his own voice. Let him run it out. Who was *she*?

"What was it, Jack?"

"Just her plan to exploit me. To rip off my story and make it her own. Right down to the letters. It even got so I would show them to her. She would make revision suggestions. I let her way, way too far into it. But she'd gotten me my first part and she was making fabulous promises about what she could do with the screenplay if I finished it. So I trusted her. Mistake.

"But then, I don't know what happened. You know, it really started to get to me how you wouldn't let go of Jacobs. How you were still so in love with him when he treated you like that. I hated him, I really started to hate him. I got the idea that he had to go. I saw it in my mind as part of the screenplay. Like, you know—the actress is still in love with her director, but he is murdered right in her presence. And she's released, then, you know? She's released to fall in love with the person who has been writing to her all these years."

Jack stood and walked to the window. He looked out through the white curtains. "I really should be getting all of this down," he said quietly.

"Why don't you, Jack? You could set up the camera."

He leaned against the wall, fingering the gun, but did not move toward the camera over on the chair next to the bed.

"So that's what happened down in Mexico," he explained. "You kept having all those little meetings with Leonard, secret rendezvous. I saw how he looked at you, I knew how much there was still between the two of you."

"Those were script meetings, Jack. I wasn't involved with him then."

He went on as if he didn't hear her. "So I followed you with him that night. Wearing your black dress. I waited for you in a car, out by the bar, I was drunk too. I fell asleep. When I woke up, there you were, on the street, kissing Jacobs, all over him. I hated you just then. For one split second, I hated you. You wouldn't have anything to do with me. It was Leonard, Leonard, always Leonard.

"Then I knew I hated him more. I got him in my sight, but it was too goddamned dark. I fired. But I shot you instead."

"Robin," Nyia whispered. "You thought Robin was me, she was wearing my dress."

"But I never meant to kill you. Or Robin. It was supposed to have been Jacobs."

"But you weren't even in Manzanillo that night,

Jack. I thought you'd gone into the mountains to see those ruins. You didn't come back until two days after Robin was killed. You had an alibi, the man at the hotel where you were staying."

"Yeah, I was careful. I drove over, checked into the motel, came back that night into Manzanillo. After I killed Robin, I drove back over the mountain and was there by sunrise. No one at the hotel knew I'd been gone during the night. I was clean. But it didn't matter. The cops down there thought it was some drug deal anyway.

"Everything changed after that. I guess it was the idea that I had killed you. I know it was Robin, but somehow the idea entered the screenplay that the lover might kill the woman he was so obsessed with. That's what would free him, to destroy her. And she thought that was fantastic. My mentor. A really good twist, you know? Of course, she didn't know the truth of it. About Robin and all.

"So I wrote draft after draft of the screenplay. She thought it was brilliant, going to make millions. Even said she would produce it, that she'd always wanted to do that. Then somewhere along the way I knew the lover would definitely kill the actress. I decided that it would eventually play out that way.

"I kept on with the letters. It was the only tie I had to you after Mexico. I felt the connection growing between us. I knew your life depended on me and I could feel the intimacy of that and the power. Your life became my dream, because you were only alive due to my mistake, don't you see?

"After Mexico we were so out of touch. But then there was the grand jury investigation, the depositions, all of us down at the lawyer's office together. It all came up for me again, I could see right away what any idiot could see, that you were in love with Leonard again. Again, again, like a crazy Ferris wheel, off again, on again, tickets please, how many tickets do you have?

"So when I read in the paper about a new script you were considering, I got the idea. Came to your house in the ski mask, that green coat. And Lord, I really did come to do it, baby. I did. But it was like I just couldn't go through with it. I took the bullets out and I pretended to kill you. Acted the scene, you know? Thinking maybe that was enough, because I knew I could never have you, but I couldn't kill you either.

"After that, I saw a shrink for a while. I didn't tell her everything, of course. Told her I couldn't seem to leave you alone, followed you around, went past your house all the time. And the letters, the screenplay.

"Everything that was really happening started going into the screenplay, even killing Robin by mistake, even going to your house and the empty gun. All of it became scenes in what I was writing.

"Then we started having the meetings for this film, *Trial and Error,* and I see there's no fucking chance again you're going to give me the time of day. I had mixed feelings by then. Like I said in the letters, I almost wanted you dead so that I could get you out of my mind; I couldn't stop thinking about you. Then having to play your lover in the New York sequences and your husband in the sequences we shot up by Canada. It was just too much. By the time I got to New Mexico I had to go through with it. I came into New Mexico a couple days early and worked on my screenplay around the clock and then showed it to the woman who was promising to produce the thing. Maybe it was like some kind of cry for help, you know? Because once she read it, she'd know the truth, that I really wanted to kill you. So that night, that night you drove to Albuquerque, I followed you. I hired a guy I met in a bar, some half-crocked guy with a pickup, paid him a couple hundred bucks to follow that pretty Mercedes and don't say a word about what happens to anyone. But I couldn't do it on the way. I just couldn't, I was afraid. I didn't know you were going to the airport to get Tess. On the way back I finally managed it. Your car drove off into that arroyo, and I thought, that's that.

"Then I found out I blew it again. You come out without a scratch. All you got was a sore neck. But now you're scared, you demand to hire a detective. And that's when she started to threaten me. Said I was nuts and she was going to turn me in to the cops if I didn't stop harassing you. I don't know what happened exactly. I went out to see the old guy, give him some more money so he'd shut up about my following your car and shooting at you. But instead I killed him."

Jack looked dazed, far off into the dream of what he was saying. He's in the story, Nyia thought. Far in. "But who is the woman, this mentor, Jack? Who is she? Are you talking about Mirina?"

"Don't rush me," he spat. "This is *my* story." He cleared his throat and went on. "I just started following you all the time after that. I knew what you did, I knew you were falling in love. Not only Leonard, wearing the wedding veil in this very cabin that afternoon. Yeah, I was watching over there from the pasture. Right over there just behind you. But then Bohland too. Anyone but me, Nyia. I wasn't good enough for you, was I?"

"Is that why you cut the brake lines on the bike, Jack? So I'd go flying off into the canyon and break my neck? But instead it was Tess," said Nyia. "Is that what happened?"

"Come over here," he said. Without warning he stepped toward her, grabbed her arm, and threw her on the bed. "I want you to put this on." He opened the closet door and took out the champagne-colored robe and the other one, the green one she'd been missing from that very closet. He laid them both down on the bed, the green one sliced down the middle. "Go on," he said.

When she didn't move, he tore at her jacket and pulled it off her shoulders and the gun fell from her pocket onto the bed. He pushed it out of reach with the barrel of the gun he was holding. Then took her gun, put it over on the table by the window, and turned around. "Put on the robe," he said slowly.

She started to undress. "How did Leonard know you had this?" she asked, slipping her arm into cool satin.

Jack hesitated. "He saw it in my hotel room a few days ago, he dropped in unexpectedly, it was draped over a chair. Why?"

"Because he gave it to me years ago."

"Perfect," said Jack. "Perfect for you to wear in my film."

"So Mirina is going to produce your screenplay, Jack? Or are you going to get Paulette to back you?"

"But here's the thing," he said, not answering her question. "I didn't fuck up that bike, Nyia. See, that's the whole irony of the situation." She slipped her boots and jeans off, put the robe on as he waited. "That was supposed to be my scene. Leonard had the big script meeting while you headed up to Taos with Bohland, announced I was going to be on the bike. No, the brakes were fucked up for me, Nyia. And why? I'll tell you why. Because my so-called producer, mentor, collaborator, decided it was time to give old Jack the heave-ho. Guess she thought I'd gone just a little bit too far and was really going to kill you.

"Because by then she'd read the whole draft of the screenplay. She knew about Robin, the break-in, everything. But guess what? She knew it was goddamned good too. And she wanted it for herself. She was the one who fixed the bike so I'd go off the fucking hill and break my neck. It really took me a while to figure it out.

"And she makes me trash all copies of the screenplay and the computer diskettes and says she's going to destroy the copies she has too. Fat chance. She was going to play off this whole thing and say she based the idea for the screenplay on what actually happened to the fabulous Nyia Wyatt. Her plan was to get rid of me, then produce my screenplay, my words, and claim she wrote the whole thing too. And no one would ever know."

Jack came over and sat next to her on the bed. He put the gun next to the bed and Nyia glanced over his shoulder at the .38 on the table across the room. She had made a terrible mistake, she realized. She should have killed him while she had the chance. But she'd gotten caught up in the story. She wanted to know all the details, how it had all turned out. The story would kill her, after all. . . .

"And Leonard," she whispered. "How did you know I was at my mother's? I suppose you followed him to L.A."

"I didn't kill Leonard," Jack said. "She did."

"*Who?* Who is she, Jack?"

He stood then and went to the window, pulled the curtains further open and looked out. He didn't answer.

"Where are you going to take it now, Jack? How does it go now, the story? Do we run away now into the sunset?"

"I shouldn't have told you all this, should I have?"

"Why not?"

"You're afraid of me now, aren't you?"

"Yes. Isn't that what you want, that power over me?"

Jack stood very still at the window. Suddenly Nyia realized he could not do it. *He can't kill me. He can't.* Slowly Nyia rose from the bed and walked over to Jack. She put her arm around his waist and with the other hand reached past him for the gun.

Jack tried to shove her away and she stumbled back against the wall. He came across the room toward her. *Now,* she thought, and fired, the gun kicking up as she squeezed the trigger back. Jack slumped to the side, grabbing his arm. His gun skidded across the floor. She fired again, the bullet missing entirely, gun jolting her arm up.

Jack drove toward her, threw her down to the floor. He knocked the gun out of her hand, slapped it across the wooden planks, under the bed. She struggled out from under him, reaching across the floor for his gun. His long arm reached past hers, his fingers closing around the weapon.

A gunshot blasted through the silence and she felt the numb heat of it needle into her.

THIRTY-ONE

"GET AWAY FROM HER, JACK."

He pulled his weight off Nyia. Suzanne stood at the door to the cabin. "Over there on the bed, get over there. Nyia, are you okay? Go over to the house and call the police. If the house is locked, break a window. Don't move, Drieser. Nyia!" she shouted. "Get moving!"

Nyia staggered from the cabin out into the darkness. She could hear footsteps approaching the path by the corral. She ran several steps, then collapsed, her thigh searing. I'm shot, she thought, reaching down to feel the blood on her leg.

Mirina bent down over her in the grass.

"Suzanne!" screamed Nyia. "Mirina's out here! She's in this with him!"

Mirina rose slowly and approached the cabin. Nyia tried to stand, but could not. She felt sick, stars waving over her as if she were on a rocking boat.

A shot cracked the black air, followed quickly by a second. An instant passed. A third shot blasted the darkness. Nyia raised herself up on her arms. She had fallen several yards away from the cabin door, but from where she lay she could see in the door, the lit room, the curtains pulled slightly open. Suzanne tossed Mirina the gun and ran to Jack's side.

"No, Suzanne!" Nyia cried. "Don't give her the gun!" Her own voice sounded grainy and faraway. She pulled herself across the dirt toward the cabin, her leg numb now. Had she been shot somewhere else too? Half-crawling, she neared the open door.

From down Bishop's Lodge Road, Nyia could hear the sirens' high wailing.

She wanted to scream into the cabin, there's a gun on the floor somewhere. Don't let Mirina have a gun, for God's sake. . . .

Nyia felt around on her body, the strange sensation she had been shot somewhere else. Not just her leg. No, she thought. The foothills were rounded humps of black, domes with stars above. *It was so beautiful here.* The peacock screeched from over by the house. *Everything was slowing down, slowing.*

Inside, she heard the women's voices. As she peered over the window ledge, she saw Suzanne take off a man's brown leather glove and stuff it into Jack's pocket.

Mirina's voice was trembling. "Why, Suzanne?"

"My God," said Suzanne, "can't you see what's happening here, Mirina? He was a maniac, he was going to kill Nyia. I think I shot her by accident. We've got to call an ambulance."

"The police are on their way, I can hear them," said Mirina.

"Well, he's dead now. It's over."

Mirina walked over to Jack, sprawled on the bed. She felt his neck for a pulse, then turned to face Suzanne.

"You could have waited for the police, Suzanne. You

killed him. You shot him three times, you could have just held the gun on him."

"He was coming at me, wasn't he? You saw it."

"Bullshit, Suzanne."

There was a silence, then Suzanne's voice, Southern-sweet and musical. "Mirina, you saved Nyia. You were so brave to have killed Jack. I never could have done it."

"You are crazy," rasped Mirina. "I don't know why you killed Jack, but I do know that you killed my husband."

"Don't be ridiculous, Mirina."

Nyia listened to their voices inside as the sirens approached. She slumped down next to the cabin, the grass wet around her. The cool air pressed down on her; it was hard to breathe.

"Why don't you have a little seat, Suzanne, and we'll just wait for the police to arrive? And while we're waiting, let me tell you a true story." Mirina cleared her throat. "Leonard called me the night he was killed. Called me from his car phone. So happens we were speaking—he tells me he's sitting in front of Carole Wyatt's apartment building and he's just proposed to Nyia and she's refused. I predicted she would. We've been through all this before. I told him I was the only one who could put up with him and he should get his ass back home where he belonged.

"Then he says, you're not going to believe who's coming down the sidewalk! Suzanne Scolfield. He calls out to you, Suzanne! I hear your voice and then I hear him cry out, What are you doing? and then I hear that shot, Suzanne. The shot that killed my husband. The shot you fired."

Suzanne laughed. "What a story!" she drawled. "Oh, Mirina, your ideas are so intricate."

"I'll tell you another thing," said Mirina. "I became very paranoid these last days and had a tape-recording device installed on my telephone answering machine. I taped all incoming and outgoing calls. Because I felt certain all this violence was being done by someone very near to us. I also had a strong suspicion that Leonard and I were being set up in some way. That is how I taped Leonard's call to me that night, Suzanne. That is why I have a recording of the final moments of my husband's life."

"That's preposterous," Suzanne cried. "Why, I was with Dierdre Fine in an exclusive interview at the time."

"I'm sure Dierdre will be more than happy to substantiate that you had left by the time those shots were fired. But why, Suzanne? That is my question. As strange as it sounds, I always knew everything Leonard was up to. He told me that he confided in you that he was going to go through with the divorce, that he was going to ask Nyia to marry him. And you knew that would be the end of your precious client. You knew that anytime Leonard and Nyia were together, you lost control of her. Leonard would run the show again like he had for all those years before you stole her away from Visionfilm. You wanted to make sure that they would never end up together, didn't you? But it was so stupid. Nyia didn't even want to be with him. She'd outgrown him. He was mine, flawed as he was. He was mine and you killed him."

"Mirina, there are no witnesses here. Nyia is outside, she couldn't really have seen who shot Jack, now could she? I say you're the one overcome with grief; you're the one who rushed out here to save our Nyia; I was several steps behind you and when I came in, here you stood and Jack was dead."

Nyia stared back into the darkness as the police sirens screamed into the yard, red lights whirling dizzily through the black trees. She pulled herself to the open door of the cabin. Perhaps she could get to the gun she'd dropped. . . .

"No one will ever believe that I shot Jack," protested Mirina. "Not in a million years."

"Why not, honey? You're the one holding the gun that shot him, and your prints are the only ones on it."

Mirina looked down at the gun in her hand. "How convenient," said Mirina.

Nyia watched as Mirina raised the gun and aimed it at Suzanne. Suzanne lunged toward her, screaming, "Give that to me! I'll kill you and your precious Nyia, I've got nothing to lose anymore."

Mirina held the gun straight, two-fisted, as Suzanne bolted toward her. Quintana slammed the door all the way open, and thrust Mirina up against the wall, jamming her arm up and taking the gun from her thin hand.

"Freeze," he barked at Suzanne.

Harm bent over Nyia just outside the door, helped her to a sitting position, and pulled a handkerchief from his pocket. He pressed it to the wound on her thigh, took Nyia's face in his hands.

Several squad cars scraped to a halt on the road outside.

"Turn to the wall," Quintana ordered Mirina.

Nyia was at the door now, leaning against Harm. Suzanne folded her arms. Her face eased into a grim, self-satisfied smile.

"You have it all wrong," Nyia told Quintana. "You've got the wrong person." The red powerlight across the room caught her eye.

"I saved your life, Nyia, God as my witness . . ." Suzanne started toward her, but Quintana nudged the gun toward her and she stopped.

Nyia motioned over to the video camera on the chair beside the bed. They all turned to see the camera running, silently documenting the true moment.

Finally Nyia said, "I think that camera over there is going to be a more accurate witness, Suzanne, than your idea of God."

HARM STOOD NEXT TO NYIA IN THE CURIO SHOP
out in front of the *Santuario de Chimayo*. She looked
exhausted, thought Harm. In the two nights since Jack
was killed she hadn't slept well, limping around the
house in her white T-shirt and bare feet. The gunshot
wound to her thigh still throbbed, she'd said. Last night
he'd found her in the back room, the darkness illuminated by the greenish hue of the VCR. She was watching the video he'd shot up at the creek the other day,
the closeup of Nyia and Nickie on that boulder.
"Tomorrow," she'd said, "after Mirina and I scatter
Leonard's ashes, I'd like to go out to the *santuario*."

Now she stared at the ceramic figurines of Jesus
and Mary, the selection of rosaries, books on miracles,
and medals of the saints, while Nickie perched out on
the cement front step, playing with gravel, sifting it
through his fingers. Yes, she looked tired but relieved,

he thought, in that flowered dress, some kind of chintz, dark roses on black shiny cloth. He stood close behind her as she bought five white votive candles. Then he watched her head slowly for the tiny, adobe church set back in the sand-rose hills.

"Can't I just stay out here?" Nickie squinted when Harm asked if he wanted to go inside with him. "Can I go down by that little creek behind the church and throw stones, Dad?"

Harm said sure, watching as the kid bolted toward the back of the church, scrambling over a stone wall. Outside the sanctuary, Harm waited in the small courtyard, giving her some time alone inside. She and Mirina had gone out to the shallow canyon behind the ranch that morning, throwing the last dust around the sage and rocks. Nyia had said she'd taken her time, used a cedar walking stick that had belonged to Leonard. It was a quiet affair, a big memorial service to follow in a few weeks in Los Angeles. Moravio had been at the ranch, his black hat pulled down over his wild hair, huddled in subdued conversation with Dan Howe by the pool.

And Quintana had stopped out to check on Mirina just as Harm and Nyia were getting ready to leave. Nickie waited in the Jeep as the three of them had stood under the cottonwoods, talking briefly.

"Velvet Cushion Billiards?" asked Quintana.

Harm had nodded. "Yeah. What do you do to think things out?"

"Eat," he'd said. Then added, "Thanks, man. We would have wasted a lot of time chasing up to that motel in Española looking for Miss Wyatt. You've got a good mind, Harm Bohland."

"It's funny," Harm said. "It wasn't Drieser's car that stuck out in my mind. I couldn't exactly remember what he drove, but I remembered that California license: MOVIE. I asked Howe whose car that was, my first day on the set."

"And if you hadn't put all that together from a bunch of junk in a briefcase, we never could have radioed the State Patrol, and they never would have tracked him speeding to the Tesuque turnoff and let him go by. I don't know if it was wise we told them to wait until we got there. We almost blew it."

Harm shook Quintana's hand. "Yeah. Well. If you ever want to shoot a few games."

Quintana smiled. "Next time I need to think, I'll give it a try."

Harm had opened the door for Nyia and she'd climbed into the Jeep. "What did Quintana say about the handwriting on that postcard being Mirina's?" Nyia asked.

Harm started up the engine and the Jeep rattled out the driveway onto Bishop's Lodge Road. He took a left, winding slowly through the peaceful foothills.

"Mirina said she remembered addressing the postcard," said Harm. "Jack came into the Visionfilm office one day and asked Mirina for your address. Mirina said, 'I'll mail it for you,' addressed it herself and sent it out. That's why her handwriting was on the postcard.

"Quintana told me a few other things this morning too. While you and Mirina were up in the foothills scattering the ashes. Apparently some old guy reported a stolen car a few days ago and when all this came out in the papers he called Quintana. Said he gave someone a ride from the movie set out to the highway and the guy stole his car at gunpoint. He identified Jack in a photograph. Jack's prints were all over the car.

"In Jack's pocket they found a receipt from a service station in Las Vegas on Suzanne's credit card. When they searched Suzanne's hotel room, they recovered an airline ticket stub that indicated she flew in and out of L.A. from Vegas on June thirtieth. She must have driven up to Las Vegas the day Tess died, sometime after

Leonard told her he was going to L.A. to get you at your mother's. Then she took a flight to L.A. and waited at your mom's for Leonard to show up. When the street was empty and he was out in the car making that phone call, she shot him. Mirina's tape of that conversation was pretty gruesome. I thought it was odd that she didn't call Quintana about that right away. But then he pointed out that there's a woman's voice on the tape, but you couldn't really tell if it was Suzanne."

"But in that final conversation between them, Mirina said that Leonard uttered Suzanne's name," said Nyia.

Harm turned north out of Tesuque and headed up toward the Chimayo turnoff. "Mirina was bluffing. One very smart woman. The thing that really got me was that when Mirina went over to check if Jack was dead, she pressed the power button on that video camera sitting on that chair next to the bed. All you can see of the video is a blanket, but it recorded their entire conversation. And Suzanne's confession."

"How did Suzanne ever know that Jack would take me to the ranch?" Nyia wondered aloud.

"Remember I told you that I called her from the Pink Adobe right after you disappeared? That's what signalled her that Jack had grabbed you. And in the screenplay notes that he'd given her was the draft for a last scene, a denouement, that was to take place at that little cabin. So she knew just where he was planning to take you."

"And they found all that when they searched her hotel room?"

"In a sheaf of papers locked in her briefcase."

After that Nyia had been quiet all the way to Chimayo.

Harm checked his watch, then went to find Nyia in the dark *santuario*. She wasn't sitting down in a wooden pew, but had taken her bag of candles up to the front. He stood in the back and watched her. She dropped each candle into a red glass and lit them one by one, then stepped back and turned away, surveying the front of the church, crowded with Christ figures. Maybe it was good there were so many of them, thought Harm.

She motioned for Harm to come forward and he walked up the center aisle and through the tiny door to their left. The walls of the small room were covered with abandoned crutches, neck braces, and Ace bandages, and shelves were crowded with more statues of Jesus and Mary, wooden, plastic, glass, ceramic, clay. Hundreds of snapshots and handwritten letters were slipped in glass frames of saints and tacked to the walls. Grandmothers, cousins, children, fathers, and mothers, grief to be let go of, pain to be miraculously removed. Harm leaned close to a Polaroid of a small child in a coffin. "Lord Please Take Into Heavin My Beloved Grandbaby Jerry Victim of Child Abuse, Better Off in Yor Care."

Harm watched as Nyia took a gold coin from her purse and set it on a windowsill.

Then she disappeared through an even tinier door and Harm stooped in behind her. Here was the small hole in the clay floor where the sacred dirt had been dug out. He wondered, with all the people coming here for the dirt, why was the hole so small? He supposed they brought in fresh dirt, maybe from the creek bed that ran behind the *santuario*. Had a priest bless it and call it sacred.

Nyia stood over the hole for a moment, not sure what to do. She had told Harm she'd always been afraid to touch the dirt for some reason. Like she didn't really deserve it, not being religious. At least in the conventional way, she'd said.

A thin, bony Hispanic man in a weathered straw hat and a blue plaid flannel shirt bent down through the door and dropped his hat to the floor. He followed the hat to a kneeling position before the hole, crossed himself, then reached in, scooping a handful of dirt and smearing it across his face and hair as if it were water. Looking refreshed, the man stood, crossed himself again, replaced the hat and quickly left the room.

"He made it look so easy," said Nyia.

Hesitating, she bent down, grimacing slightly, her palm to her injured thigh. Then she took a pinch of dirt and just held it in her palm, circling it around.

"Okay," she said. "Let's go now."

They stood outside, behind the *santuario,* looking at the cottonwoods along the river. Nickie crouched at the edge of the creek, laughing with a black-haired kid and reaching out into the water with a long stick.

Nyia turned to Harm. "I can't get over the notes Jack kept about that screenplay. Copies of every letter he sent, detailed journal entries about all his ideas for scenes. All the drafts. Page after page: *idea for scene.* And records of his activities, right down to killing Howard Nims. And those videos. I mean, it was all some totally documented confession, written and filmed as he went along. I can't understand why it didn't occur to him that it could be used as evidence against him at some point."

"Because he thought of it as fiction," said Harm. "I don't think it occurred to him that he was writing about his life. It was classic dissociation. It was almost as if he had a split personality, but instead of two completely separate selves, he saw some part of himself as story, as not real, as invented. Where his real life and his story bled into each other was all in that computer."

Nyia perched on a stone wall, leaning back to catch the sun in her face. "So Suzanne had taken all his ideas and was siphoning them off into her own screenplay?"

"Just like he told you. Oh, she revised. But Quintana found a copy in her hotel, copyrighted in her own name with no record of Drieser's contribution. It differs in places, but it's all Drieser's work. She wanted him dead, to protect you, all right. I don't think she probably had any idea how far gone he was. But more than that it was simple greed. She wanted to own all rights to that screenplay and she wanted to own you. So she murdered both men who threatened to take you away from her in one way or another."

"The parts that were the hardest for me to read were his early notes, when Suzanne first hired him to be my lover, to distract me from Leonard. It was so duplicitous and I was so naive. Bonus if he could get me out of town for the summer, bonus if he slept with me, big bonus if he could get me to leave the country."

"But the bonus he wanted most was a part in a film," said Harm.

"Well, she did get him that. What's so sad is that Jack was a fine actor on his own. He could have made it without doing all that."

Harm glanced up at a crow on a sagging branch nearby. "It was more than all that, though," he said. "It must have been the challenge, the intrigue. And he did fall in love with you."

"Yeah," said Nyia. "If you can call that love."

Nyia brushed some dirt from the stone wall, and looked back at the river. "I think all this dirt is sacred," she said. She was silent a while then said to Harm, "I still don't get how you figured out that all of Jack's notes and drafts would be on the hard drive of his computer. He told me that Suzanne made him destroy everything and that's how he knew what she was up to."

"It was that damn dream," said Harm. "That printer running amok, printing everything out even after it had supposedly been erased. When Quintana let me into

Jack's room and they hadn't found any papers or computer diskettes during the search, I thought of that dream. The image of all the information just being stored inside the computer even though the diskettes had been wiped out. I checked the hard drive and it was all there."

Nyia shivered in a gust of wind. "Synchronicity," she said.

"What?" said Harm.

"Nothing."

"Another thing Quintana told me while you were out with Mirina this morning. The note found in Leonard's car, the one Suzanne planted there—she typed it on a typewriter in the hotel office. A clerk Quintana interviewed gave a statement that Suzanne asked to use the typewriter and said she didn't need hotel stationery. She had her own. The clerk even identified the blue letters as the paper Suzanne typed on."

"What will happen to her, Harm?"

"Suzanne? She's got a damn good lawyer, I hear. She may get out on bail until her trial. But I don't think she's got a chance, with the voices that videocam recorded. Unless she can somehow get that thrown out as evidence. There will be a big trial. It'll go on for quite a while."

He watched as Nyia loosened her hair in the wind, looking down at where Nickie was now getting his sneakers soaked, walking on the rocks at the creek's edge.

"What will you do now?" asked Harm.

"You know what I'd really like to do?"

He shook his head, touched her cheek. He didn't want her to go. He knew she would. Back to her world, her films. Well, maybe that particular world was gone forever now. But she would go back, anyway, to what she knew. And he would never fit into it, though he'd had a fantasy or two of going to the Academy Awards, Nyia in that purple leather strapless dress, he in a tux and cowboy boots. Yeah. Maybe a signed glossy in his two-bit office would be all he'd have to show for his time with her.

No, more than that, he thought, much more.

"What would you really like to do?" Harm asked.

She lifted her arms. "Change into a bird again, like I did in *Wings*. I mean, just transform, fly away, disappear into the horizon. Be some other kind of thing, dark and primitive, but strong. Really strong."

"You are that."

She smiled. "What about you, Harm? What are you going to do?"

He shrugged. "I have my own idea for a screenplay now."

She looked pained, then rolled her eyes. "Please, Harm."

"Want to hear it? Okay. Here you go. A detective, hired to protect a beautiful actress, inadvertently falls in love with her. He knows there might not be a big chance for a long-term relationship, but what does he have to lose? So he asks her if she wants to go up to the Sangre de Cristo Mountains next week and go fly-fishing with him and his boy. He wants her to reclaim fishing as a positive activity in her life. She says yes and catches the most beautiful rainbow trout the man has ever seen in his life. They clean it and fry it up in a black pan on a wood stove along with some corn on the cob and some sourdough bread. Lasting happiness eludes them but momentary joy suffices, and once in a while in years to come she sends him a postcard from somewhere like Tangiers."

Nyia smiled and leaned over to kiss him. She looked down at the river, waved to Nickie. A crow lit down next to where she stood. It clutched at the stones with its small talons, and lifted its black wings, but stayed on the ground.

THERESA WAS PREPARING TO MEET HER
first client when the phone rang. She almost answered
it, then decided to let the answering machine screen
the call. But she listened as she stepped out onto the
patio, the woman's voice saying, "You don't know me,
but I got your number from ChildSearch America."
Theresa stopped. The phone was next to the open
window in the kitchen. "My name is Ellen Carlin, and
my child is missing. I've been dealing with the police
so far and it's been very frustrating. Nothing much has
turned up. The people at ChildSearch recommended I
call you. If you could return my call at . . ."

Theresa ran back into the house. "Hello? This is
Theresa Fortunato."

"I can't believe I'm getting through to you," said the
woman. "This is the first good thing that's happened.
Maybe it's a sign. They said it would take ages to get
in to see you, that you're backed up in appointments
for months, but if there's any chance that—"

Theresa interrupted the woman again. "I can see you this afternoon. Can you come at five? I'm over in Venice, just a few miles south of the ChildSearch office."

"Oh, thank you so much for fitting me in like this. I can't tell you what this means."

Theresa gave the woman the address and directions to her house. "And please bring something that belongs to your daughter, something metal if possible, some article of clothing, her blue dress or the shoes she left behind, the blue ones. Her coin purse, if you've got that. A wallet, someplace she might have kept money. A photograph would help. Jewelry is especially good, too."

Ellen Carlin cleared her throat. There was a silence. "Excuse me," she said. "I don't think I mentioned it was a daughter."

Theresa sat down on the stool next to the phone. She shouldn't have jumped in so quickly. *Don't get ahead of yourself,* she thought. But knew she was right anyway.

Ellen Carlin continued. "But she is. My daughter. And the dress she was wearing *was* blue. That was the one in the closet in her room, the one she must have been wearing. I took all her other clothes home to wash, so that's all she had left. And she left her shoes behind, the blue ones, just like you said. There they were sitting right in the closet. I have no idea why she didn't wear her shoes. She just loves those stupid shoes. That's why I'm just certain she didn't run off. If she'd run off she would have taken those goddamn shoes."

"Yes," said Theresa. "She wasn't wearing shoes because she was carried out." Theresa remembered the bed in the drawing, the bed in the car and the wheels, round and round. "Wheeled out," she went on, feeling it strongly. "I'm getting 'wheeled.' Where was she when you last saw her that someone might have wheeled or taken her out covered in some way, maybe with a blanket?"

Ellen Carlin hesitated. "That's just exactly what the security guard said. That she may have been taken out in a wheelchair or on a gurney. That someone might have made it look as though she was being transferred to a different hospital or even being prepared for surgery."

"Oh." Theresa breathed. "A hospital." She pictured the railings on the side of the bed in the first drawing. Not a crib, a hospital bed. A rolling hospital bed. Of course. *Shots, medicine. Better now that I'm taking care of you.*

"So someone has already talked to you about Tory?" asked Ellen Carlin. "Someone from ChildSearch or the police? Do they fill you in on missing persons?"

It was Theresa's turn to hesitate. The woman sounded scared, as if her privacy had been violated. Theresa had pushed in too quickly, too hard. Knowing things psychically could seem invasive, even if that's what people wanted.

"I did speak with Leslie Simon a few days ago. Did she tell you about the conversation I had with her?" Theresa asked.

"No. Just that she felt certain I should talk with you."

So Leslie had not told Ellen about the drawings. Leslie respected Theresa's work but the woman had a healthy dose of skepticism regarding psychics. Theresa noticed Leslie had difficulty discussing psychic work. She didn't trust the language and Theresa actually respected that. Leslie Simon would never have said to Ellen Carlin, "Please call this psychic I know who had a vision of your kid's blue shoes in a trance the other night." Theresa would tell Ellen about the drawings when she came.

Ellen Carlin appeared at Theresa's door at exactly five and rang the bell. Theresa came around the brick walk at the side of the house and opened the high wooden gate shaped in an Oriental form like the top of a pagoda.

Her first impression of Ellen was of softness, roundness. She was of medium height, her face large and handsome, a strong straight nose, wide mouth and large blue eyes. She was moonlike and full of space. You could fall into that face and keep going. Her brown hair was shoulder-length, shiny, and cut precisely in a chin-length pageboy like the girl's hair in the drawing. She wore dark berry-colored lip gloss but no eye makeup, her beauty understated and natural. Her gaze was direct, filled with grief and exhaustion, the delicate skin around her eyes slightly bruised from crying and lack of sleep.

Theresa judged her to be around thirty-seven or thirty-eight, shapely and slightly overweight in black bermuda shorts. Though her waist was narrow, her hips were large like paintings of Renaissance women. Her white blouse made her pale skin look even more washed-out. The hand she extended to Theresa was graceful, long-fingered, good working hands, a mothering, womanly presence, used to appearing competent, organized, loving, now fragmented in agony. Ellen's hand trembled as Theresa grasped it. Her palm was cold. She wore a gold wedding band on her right ring finger, changed over from the left hand. *Could be her mother's?* thought Theresa. But no. Divorced, she intuited. But why still wear it? She'd moved it to the right hand because she couldn't bear to part, entirely, from the identity the ring brought her.

All this came to Theresa in a witnessing presence as if someone just off to her right were taking notes. Theresa stepped back and took in the second look at her, through the other eyes. Just briefly, keeping her eyes slightly out of focus. Ellen was black-yellow at the center, in her chest area. At the heart, black, yellow, held in and contained. The woman was holding in tremendous grief, coping in a rigid and methodical way. For just a moment a flash of animal face pushed out of the woman's features, then receded back into her softness. *Cat. Mothercat. Undomesticated, fanged. The ragged fur.*

"Thank you so much for seeing me today," said Ellen. "I need to say I've never done anything remotely like this before and I'm very nervous. Especially after you knew so much when we spoke earlier."

"It's okay to be nervous your first time. I'm just glad you came." Theresa wanted to add, *I've been waiting for you,* but held her tongue.

Theresa led Ellen Carlin through the front gate, locked it, then continued down the sidewalk in the shade of a row of cypress trees alongside the fence. She had bought this house a year ago and it was good to have a place to conduct her readings that was separate from where she lived. Out in back of the small white clapboard house, a carpenter friend of hers had converted a tilting shed into a studio the size of a small two-story garage. Ellen followed her through the lavender and herb garden across the little patio where the wrought-iron table and chairs were shaded by a trellis of ivy, through the double row of white roses Theresa meticulously attended, and up the narrow wooden stairs to the studio.

The room where Theresa did her readings was walled in on three sides by large floor-to-ceiling windows. A white ceiling fan circled slowly overhead. A small white couch faced the back windows and unmatched wicker chairs were gathered around a rough wood table. On the table were objects that Theresa considered, now, more conversation starters than tools of her trade: a crystal ball; a leathery, worn deck of Tarot cards placed on a purple silk bag; a glass dish of *I Ching* coins; a dog-eared copy of the *Book of Changes;* a shallow box of white sand, a tiny rake, and seven smooth black stones set on the sand: a miniature Japanese rock garden. Clients could rake the sand into patterns if they felt agitated or peer into the glass, not to glimpse the future, but to see the blurred and upside-down image of the present. Three white candles, unlit, in a silver candelabra, a present from Theresa's grandmother, though she hadn't inherited it until her own mother had died a few years ago. The room smelled of jasmine, the day-old blossoms wilting in a glass vase by the window.

Ellen walked to the back, west-facing windows and gazed out over the jungle of odd terraces and second-story porches, telephone pole wires crosshatching the view, and one perfect, glittering strip of ocean visible between the Venice rooftops. Then she returned to the center of the room and settled onto the couch.

"Well, I'll go over the whole thing again." Ellen swallowed hard. "I've been over this with the nurses, the doctors, the hospital security, the police and—"

Theresa held up her hand as Ellen leaned back against the pillows. She felt it again, the cat body, furrish, warm, pressing forward up and out of the woman, the energy large and wild, but not in a hurry. Hungry. Theresa felt engulfed by it. She pushed her hand at the energy, palm up. *Back up,* she thought. *Back.*

The woman receded into herself.

"Let's just wait with what happened, the events and so forth," Theresa suggested. "It actually works better for me to just get some initial images. The police, the detectives will work the logical end of things, proceeding from clues and evidence, all of that. Where I can help is in the nonlogical realm. I'll just see what images I pick up from your being here. Did you happen to bring any of your daughter's things or a picture? And also what did you say her name was—Cory?"

"Tory. Short for Victoria. Victoria Margaret DeLisi. That's her father's last name. We're divorced." As she spoke, Ellen reached into a canvas bag and pulled out the blue sneakers decorated with silver and pink swirls of glitter. She also gave Theresa a school photo of the girl. She had dreamy pale eyes, not looking directly at the camera, and a lopsided smile as if she'd been caught by surprise. Her teeth were too large for her rosebud mouth, *new front teeth,* Theresa thought, *just grown in.* Her bangs were cut straight above her eyebrows and she appeared to be peeking out from under them. Tory looked shy, funny, unformed.

Theresa sat in a wicker chair across from Ellen and reached for one of the shoes. "We can just be quiet now," she instructed. "A reading is basically a kind of listening. It's a way of hearing outside the bounds of what we think of as normal conversation."

Closing her eyes, Theresa saw the shoe in her hands change into a small square box tied with a gold ribbon. In her imagination she let it transform: white tissue wrapping paper. Gift. The box became heavy and condensed. It quickly grew hot in her palms. She set the shoe back on the wooden table in front of the couch, her eyes still closed.

THIS WOMAN BRINGS A GIFT TO YOUR LIFE, said the Voice. THE GIFT HAS A TERRIBLE COST. THE COST IS WORTH IT. AS ALWAYS YOU HAVE A CHOICE WHETHER YOU WANT TO RECEIVE IT OR NOT.

The Voice came over her right shoulder, and from within. It had been with her a long time, soothing, low, sometimes quiet for months, then coming with very clear words as if spelled out in capital letters in the interior air of her thinking, right next to her thick black hair.

Nothing else came.

"Were these shoes a gift?" Theresa opened her eyes, looking at Ellen.

"Yes," said Ellen. "From Tory's father."

For a second, Theresa had the strange sensation that Ellen was reading her. A reciprocity, a kind of reaching into her, not the usual passivity of a querent.

"Have we met before?" Theresa asked.

Ellen was silent for a moment. "Well, I did hear you

on the radio once. A few months ago. That's why it felt all right to call you. It was some psychic call-in show a friend of mine was listening to in the car."

"That was 'Life Lines,' Camille Taylor's show on KPSI. Now and then I'm her guest since she's a friend of mine. She mostly does past-lives."

Ellen smiled. "Isn't that just L.A. for you?" Then she looked away. "I mean . . . well. I don't remember much from the show. Just that you sounded smart and like you had some common sense. And even though I don't believe in any of this, I suppose you made a strong impression, whatever you said."

"And you were surprised."

Ellen nodded. "I'm educated as a scientist," she said. "We're an awfully left-brained bunch of people, I'm afraid. We're always looking for proof."

"So are we," said Theresa. "We just have different methods. Let's go on."

Again, Theresa closed her eyes. She knew the gift image was more than just the fact that the shoes had been a gift to Tory. *What's in the box?* she asked internally.

Baby. Baby girl.

"Are you pregnant?" asked Theresa, eyes still closed.

"I certainly hope not."

"Does Tory have a baby sister?"

"No."

Weird, weird, thought Theresa. The baby shriveled up down to the bones, transformed into a small skeleton. A tiny white coffin collapsed to white dust blowing away. She didn't like this and did not want to tell Ellen what she was seeing. *Don't block,* she told herself. *Don't judge, just stay open.*

Then she saw an image of herself in church, St. Mary's, North End, Boston. *I am two or three. White lace dress, white shoes. Mother holding me by the votive candles. I burn my hand. Mom lost that baby.*

Miscarriage. Didn't hear about it until years later when Aunt Rose told me at Mom's wake. "Your mother was depressed after she lost that second baby, right after you." I never knew. Why didn't anyone ever say?

Stop. Clear your mind, Theresa told herself. *Erase and clear.* She didn't like this, reading for a client and having her own thoughts coming back to her like this. She'd been trained to separate the edges between the self and the other. Keep the channels open for the querent's pictures to come in. Not her own.

Theresa imagined a light surrounding her own body, emanating from her heart as if a wand were drawing a protective boundary around her. She continued drawing the line across the room to where Ellen Carlin sat, searching for the woman's heart. The light-line moved through the black-yellow but kept on going.

Here Theresa stopped. Her light had moved through the woman instead of connecting with her heart. She pulled her light back, her eyes still closed, Ellen quiet on the couch. It was like backing up a car.

Again she moved through the area of yellow-black. What did the colors mean? Sulphur. Charcoal, dust, fog. Smoke. Colors like a cloud but thinner. More like a fume, but no substance to it. She tried to remain there, *hold, hold, let the picture blink on. What do you see?*

But nothing. Theresa put her hand—this, too, in her imagination, her imaginal unconscious—into the area of yellow-black. Her arm disappeared. *Nothing past here,* she thought. Her heart leapt up, wings off a still branch. *Breathe, hush.*

Ellen was blocking her very strongly. Theresa didn't know if it was coming from Ellen, exactly, from her fear or from the intensity of her concern for her daughter. Or maybe Theresa herself was overinvested in the images she'd gotten in the drawings. Maybe it was the fact that she hadn't told Ellen about the drawings, it occurred to her now. Things withheld between them.

Theresa opened her eyes, shocked that Ellen was

not seated on the couch at all. She was gone. Startled, Theresa turned to look behind her. Ellen stood in the corner of the room pressed into the glass-walled corner framed by the view of the rooftops and the thin glimpse of the Pacific.

"Are you all right? What's going on?" asked Theresa.

"You tell me," said Ellen. "I guess I'm uncomfortable. I call you up and you seem to know things about Tory that I've never mentioned. I come ready to tell you everything I know about her disappearance and you don't even want to hear about it. Then you drift off into a trance and ask me totally unrelated questions about babies. I just feel . . . invaded. Look, I told you I've never been to a psychic before and if it weren't for Tory I never would. Maybe I'd just better stick with the police."

Theresa pushed her chair back and motioned for Ellen to come back to the couch. "I apologize," Theresa said. "Let's talk first. Of course this is uncomfortable for you. Look, I'm used to reading for people who are prepared mentally. I mean, they've chosen to see a psychic, they've chosen me, and usually had to wait quite a while for an appointment. They're chomping at the bit for me to do this. Forgive me. I don't mean to be insensitive. I need to slow down, this is all new for you.

"I should mention that when I do a reading, I almost prefer to know nothing at all about the situation I'm reading. Then whatever comes to me—pictures, words, images, voices—it's pure. It's not clouded by the intellect. But I can completely understand why you'd rather review everything first. Let's do that. And to tell you the truth, I have something I need to disclose. The reason I knew about the blue dress, about Tory being barefoot was that I had a very strong vision—or dream, if you will—two days ago. And out of that I drew these pictures."

Theresa showed Ellen the drawings and told her in more detail about the child's voice commanding her to draw. How she'd called ChildSearch to contact a few of the people she'd consulted with to see if the information fit, and that she had discussed the images with Leslie Simon. And then, this morning, Ellen had called.

Ellen was nodding and Theresa felt the trust level between them building. "These look just like Tory's drawings," said Ellen quietly. "They could be hers. It's uncanny. She's very artistic, always has been. Even at a very early age she could draw in perspective. She learned how to sketch like this, these wispy lines. But why would she come to you like this? Is that what you think she's doing?"

"I don't know," said Theresa. "Its rare these days for me to receive images out of nowhere like this. That's why I wanted to see you right away. I don't question a lot of it. I just follow the images and see what that opens up in people's lives."

Ellen leaned back against the couch pillows. She bit her lower lip as she studied the drawings. "Can I tell you about what happened now?"

"Absolutely," Theresa said.

"Tory was in the hospital for some tests—General Children's over in Westwood near the university complex. She's not been well for quite some time, there's been a history of medical complications, and I like General because it's small and there are so many specialists there. My mother always described Tory as a delicate child. There have been different things—kidney failure, digestive problems, blurred vision, fatigue, but they've never been able to diagnose the underlying cause. They've just never been able to get to the bottom of it all, which has been so agonizing.

"So last week she spiked a high fever, 104 degrees over an eight-hour period. At one point it reached 106 degrees so I brought her into emergency. On Monday she had tests and I was with her all day. She was in good spirits, did some crossword puzzles and wanted her hair done in a French braid. And she ate well at dinner. Jello. Cherry Jello. She loves that hospital food, can you believe it? I don't know why. She's been in hospitals so much. She likes the tray that swings over the bed and the way the beds go up and down with the push of a button."

Ellen stopped as if caught in her last memory of her daughter, a spoonful of Jello held to her small mouth.

"She even likes the hospital gowns," Ellen nearly whispered. She gazed out over the houses, then came to focus again on Theresa.

"I was with Tory on Monday evening until eight-thirty or nine, just sitting with her until I was sure she was resting quietly. Just sitting there knitting in the dark. Then I went home. Just after six a.m. the next morning—God, it seems like weeks ago now—" Ellen stopped, swallowing hard, hesitating. "The head nurse called me," she went on, "and asked if I had come back in the night and taken Tory home. That she was gone. Of course, I said no. They called the police immediately. Hospital security was alerted and they began a floor-to-floor search. Grounds and parking area, too, but . . ." Ellen lifted her empty hands. "Apparently she was abducted sometime during the night, probably between three and four a.m. I called Tory's father right away—he lives in Cambridge. Our divorce was not what you'd call amicable, but we communicate well about Tory and I knew he'd want to know right away. She spends some of the holidays and part of each summer with him. The police talked to him, trying to see if there had been any violation of our visitation agreement because Tory had just been out there with him. She got back about two weeks ago."

Ellen stopped her rush of words and seemed to hold her breath for a moment before going on. "I need to say that coming to you is just something I'm doing by myself. I'm not telling him about it. I feel that I need to have one outlet, one source of information that is outside his control. Can you understand that? I'd like my seeing you to be absolutely confidential."

Theresa nodded. "That's fine. And, by the way, I do have a contact with the L.A.P.D., and I might be able to get a handle on how the search for Tory is going if you'd like me to check into that for you."

"I would. I'd really appreciate that."

"What do the police think at this point?"

"As I said, they have very little. They're interviewing hospital personnel, parking lot personnel. They found nothing in the room itself, no fingerprints or anything like that. No one noticed anything out of the ordinary. There's just nothing. Poof. Thin air. Gone. My little girl is gone."

"All right," said Theresa. "Let's try the reading again. Now just relax, close your eyes if you want to, picture Tory the last time you saw her or just let your mind wander. All I'm going to do is notice what images come up in my mind and then I'll write them down on this pad. Then we'll start with those images and see where it takes us.

"Psychics read in many different ways. They use different methods—cards, tea leaves, smoke, dreams, tossing of sticks, coins, you name it. My preference is for my client to sit quietly in an open state, in a kind of listening or receptivity that we share between us. We make the opening together and in that opening I hear things, I see things. It is actually a lot like daydreaming."

Ellen seemed to relax. She uncrossed her legs and twisted the wedding band around.

Again, Theresa imagined drawing a line of light between the two of them, connecting them at the heart. Again she felt the yellow-black, a sort of amorphous color field, but no heart, no light. She kept moving through the center where she thought Ellen's energy should be. It wasn't there.

How else should I proceed? she asked inside. Just dark, dark behind the eyes. No image, no voice. Blank. Far under the quiet she felt her own anxiety rattling like a slow engine. Theresa shook her head.

LATER, she heard. She turned her head to the side, listening. Saw Ellen look at her oddly. Voices in her head. Theresa had been hospitalized years ago for the voices. It didn't fit into the realm of the logical world, she knew that. Fortunately, it no longer mattered to her if she fit into that world or not.

So it might be better to read from Tory's belongings later, after the mother leaves? she thought.

YES.

"OK," said Theresa, mostly to the Voice, but also to Ellen. "I'm sorry. I'm sorry the way this whole meeting has gone. What I'm getting is that I am to read later from Tory's things, whatever you've brought with you. For some reason I can't read with you here. Sometimes the heaviness of emotion that a person brings with them blocks a reading. It interferes. Why don't you leave me your number and I'll contact you when I've been able to do this more successfully. I'll try again later tonight and then I'll call you to let you know how it goes."

Ellen looked pained, then laughed, a dry, bitter spurt of a laugh. "All of a sudden I realized that I was hoping you'd actually contact Tory. Like you could just call her up on some kind of psychic telephone. Isn't that crazy? For all my scientific education, I had this wild hope that you'd just know where she was. Grasping at straws. Less than straws. Wind."

"If my previous contact with her was any indication, I'm sure there will be more information coming. It was a very strong connection," said Theresa.

Ellen picked up the drawings, but Theresa held her hand out for them.

"I'll need to keep these," said Theresa, "but I'll be happy to make copies for you."

Ellen nodded. She looked very tired. Whatever color she'd had in her pale skin was gone now. She jotted her address and phone number on the pad of paper that Theresa had set on the table, then stood and reached into her canvas bag. She pushed the shoes across the table as well as a small brass pillbox with the letter "T" inscribed on the lid. "I got this for her in Aspen last summer," said Ellen. "She loved it. She kept it with her all the time after that."

She stood, picked up the bag, and walked toward the open door of the studio. Theresa followed her down the stairs, across the patio and alongside the house in the shade of the cypresses. Then she unlatched the gate and held it open for Ellen.

Ellen turned as she left. "There's something else," she said. "As long as we're putting all our cards on the table. After you agreed to see me this morning, I did some research, checked out your references on file at ChildSearch. And Leslie Simon gave me some newspaper clippings about a missing person case you helped with—what was it, five or six years ago? You did a reading for a family whose daughter was missing and then you found her body. After that you worked with the police on what turned out to be a series of related murders."

"Yes," said Theresa. "That was me. I had never done that kind of work before. I still feel that my strongest work is in the area of personal guidance, clearing out the past, opening the heart, spiritual direction, relationships, career, money. Your basic fortune-telling."

"You don't seem like your basic fortune-teller."

Both Ellen and Theresa smiled.

"Missing person work—yes, I've had some success with that. But sometimes I've gotten a series of images that don't lead to anything. I'll be honest with you about that. I don't claim some kind of fabulous success rate. Sometimes I think the success comes when the images I receive stir up something in the clients themselves. Spur them to make their own intuitive connections. If that makes any sense."

"But when you read from Tory's pill box, for

instance, you could know if she was still alive or not?"

"I could," said Theresa. "Yes. I might get a strong feeling one way or another." She stared past Ellen at the green water of the canal. "She's . . . I already feel that she's alive, Ellen. Because of the way the drawings came, the strength and vibrancy of the images. It's not a guarantee."

"It's something. Well, thanks," said Ellen, extending her hand. It was the second time that Theresa had touched her and when she did, she felt an odd faintness come over her, a lack of air. Ellen put on her dark glasses. "I'll wait for your call," Ellen said. Her sandals clicked down the sidewalk toward Washington Avenue. As she passed, sleeping ducks rose up and slid off the hot grass into the water.

As she watched her go, Theresa experienced a dizziness. She leaned against the gate, closed her eyes and took several deep breaths. It was not as if she were tipping or the world was spinning around her. It was the sensation of no gravity, of flying down feet first through the air at a cold speed. Like a bullet flying through air. She opened her eyes as Ellen reached a large bougainvillea that dangled over the sidewalk. Ellen ducked under it.

Then the scene in front of Theresa disintegrated into tiny dots of color that coalesced into a cat, then a multitude of cats, extending back from where Ellen had just been, like repeated images in a dressing-room mirror. Just as quickly, the scene resumed its bright normality: Southern California, perfect late afternoon, rush hour on a weekday in L.A., the ground fairly vibrating from the traffic going home. Six o'clock.

Theresa shut the gate. As the latch clicked, she knew why she had not been able to read for Ellen Carlin, why she could not find her center, her heart-light during the reading. She was sure there were many things that Ellen had not told her and she was flooded with a certainty that Ellen had a very short time to live.

How long? she asked.

The cypresses moved overhead. Theresa stood locked in their shadows. Was there more?

Nothing. Wind in the flowers. *Grasping wind.*

She turned and walked back toward the patio. As she approached the end of the brick walk, she heard the voice inside.

Spoken, quiet as a whisper in a library:

THREE DAYS.

ORDER NOW!

SIX GREAT NOVELS FROM THESE BESTSELLING AUTHORS

TONY HILLERMAN
Coyote Waits   0-06-109932-5 $5.99/$7.99 Canada

SUSAN ISAACS
Magic Hour   0-06-109948-1 $5.99/$7.99 Canada

E.L. DOCTOROW
Billy Bathgate   0-06-100007-8 $5.95/$7.95 Canada

LEN DEIGHTON
Spy Sinker   0-06-109928-7 $5.99

STUART WOODS
Palindrome   0-06-109936-8 $5.99/$7.99 Canada

LOUISE ERDRICH
MICHAEL DORRIS
The Crown of Columbus 0-06-109957-0 $5.99/$7.99 Canada

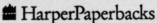